THE BIG HOUSE

Story of a Southern Family

ALSO BY J. KECK

In Paperback and eBook formats:

> The Big House – Story of a Southern Family
> > Book One
> > Book Two

> Homeless: The Dollmaker's Web *(Novella)*
> > The Dark Forest *(Excerpt)*

In Audio format:

> The Big House – Story of a Southern Family
> > Book One

> Homeless: The Dollmaker's Web

Readers respond to The Big House – Story of a Southern Family Series:

The vivid images of a time past, the rich layers of characters, and the complex family dynamics fashioned by the author of *The Big House* have inspired a compelling sequel. The thrill of first love, the danger of guarded secrets and the literal survival of The Big House are at stake. Minnie's very spirit and mettle are tested as J. Keck advances his epic, Southern novel.

Mark Sudock, Eight-time Emmy Award Winner

Author J. Keck's The Big House is a timeless story that reflects the very best of the American character when confronting adversity.

Darlene Quinn, Author, Webs Book Series – National Indie Excellence, Beverly Hills, and Readers Favorite Award Winner

A darned good read . . . Seems like a very real and true to life account of a young girl growing up in the South and the problems and realities of life. I highly recommend to anyone wanting to know about life in the South during that period. Very well written. For me, a truly great read.

B. Stapp

The Big House is beautifully crafted and touched throughout with lyrical grace. As a southerner who spent much of his childhood on a tobacco farm, I found the book very authentic in its depiction of the culture. I look forward to Mr. Keck's next writing.

Dr. R.H. Parker

This story evokes a time and place in our history—a time before WWII when the "old South" still existed. Its larger-than-life characters and picaresque situations remind me of Faulkner. One must know this milieu very well to write so convincingly.

This story did an excellent job setting up the places and characters. It was as if one was enfolded lovingly in another place and time. I found myself very much drawn into the story, I did not want to stop reading it. Minnie as a young girl in a trying family situation, then later having to make her own way through life, was interesting and moving.

C. Harrison

I thoroughly enjoyed reading *The Big House*. My roots are Southern and I can recall many stories of the same being told by my Grandmother and other family members regarding the war, the Depression and the different classes of "folks." I adore the character Minnie and love how she is so observant and learns so quietly from everyone around her. She's an old soul in a little girl's body. Such a little lady! I can't wait to read more.

Kim S.

This book captured my attention right at the start and held it throughout. The story was powerful and sensitive. It was amazing how Mr. Keck was able to describe Minnie's thoughts and feelings. I felt I really got to know her. I also liked that it was historically accurate even in small details. I hope there is a sequel as I want to hear more about Minnie.

N. Ruesch

My entire office read the book and each one of us enjoyed it immensely. We highly recommend picking up this book.

K. Thomas

"*The Big House* transports the reader into the heart and soul of a bygone era . . . a must read!"

Kathy Porter, Author, Indie Award Winner

The BIG HOUSE

STORY OF A SOUTHERN FAMILY

BOOK THREE

J. KECK

STONEHAVEN

Ordering information: orders by U.S. trade bookstores and wholesalers, please visit: www.CreateSpace.com or www.Amazon.com

Cover Illustration by Riley Dickens

Printed in the United States of America

The Big House – Story of a Southern Family (Book Three) / J. Keck.
p. cm.
ISBN-13: 978-0985032371 (Softcover)
ISBN-10: 0985032375 (Softcover)
        1. Literature & Fiction 2. Genre Fiction 3. Historical
        I. Keck, J. II. The Big House – Story of a Southern Family
        (Book Three)

First Edition: October 2016

10 9 8 7 6 5 4 3 2 1

To My Family and Friends

CONTENTS

ACKNOWLEDGEMENTS

This sequel to Book II of the series to *The Big House - Story of a Southern Family,* is the culmination of many years of thought and planning, though it follows Book II in less than a year. I am grateful to many individuals and the institutions that have made this book possible. Family and friends come to mind foremost for their unflagging support and belief in the book.

Next are the persons whose technical skill and breadth of information brought the novel to fruition. My editors deserve special mention: Nancy Rueschenberg, Linda LeMonchek, and, posthumously, Carolyn Bixby. As well, there are the individuals who read and contributed both their editorial skills and ideas to the development of material: Francesca Romero, and Tammy Mulvaney. Additionally, I thank Riley Dickens, artist and graphic designer, who brought his artistic sensitivity and skill to the cover. Additional thanks go to Sonia Fiore, the formatter, for her excellent layout and design. Many thanks to Katya Richter, who designed and built my web page, and maintained it with such professionalism and talent. Many of the same people I noted in Book II are important to the creation and development of Book III. My heartfelt appreciation extends to them as well.

Other important sources I would like to acknowledge are:

~ Dr. Ruth Hawkins at Arkansas State University, and Director of the Arkansas State Heritage sites, who gave generously of her expertise, direction and knowledge of the various heritage sites.
www.ArkansasHeritageSites.astate.edu

~ The Southern Tenant Farmers Museum, where I researched various resources of books, displays and newsreels of the land and people of the Delta. Many thanks to Linda Hinton, Director, and Bryan Pierce, Interpreter/ Media Consultant, whose video logs serve to capture individual legacy stories of real people who lived the history of the land, who remember their stories and the stories of their forebears who did so. www.stfm.astate.edu

~ Hemingway Pfeiffer Museum and Educational Center, which preserves the historical record of writer Ernest Hemingway during part of his career and marriage to Pauline Pfeiffer of the Pfeiffer Plantation. My sincere appreciation goes to Director Adam Long, Ph.D. of the museum and his generous and comprehensive knowledge of the relevant subject matter at the museum. www.hemingway.astate.edu

~ Historic Dyess Colony: boyhood home of Johnny Cash. Thanks to Larry Sims, Jamie Bass, facilitators, and Chelsey McFerris for providing the information of the unique founding of Dyess Colony, as a Federally-funded project in 1934 to provide 500 homes and land to families who were on relief at the time. It continues to be a thriving community to this day. www.dyesscash.a.state.edu

~ The Lakeport Plantation, and Blake Wintory, Director of Lakeport Plantation, the last remaining Arkansas plantation that remains on the Mississippi River. www.lakeport.a.state.edu

~ The Catholic Diocese of Little Rock, Arkansas, whose spokeswoman provided valuable information about setting up of a mission church, *i.e.*, what the Church would provide in the way of supplies and funding. www.dolr.org

~ Various individuals at local parishes in the state who gave of their time and historical knowledge of their various parishes.

~ The Internet, with all of its invaluable resources. Considerable information was available on the Free Black population of the pre-Civil War South, its population in the City of New Orleans, and its circumstances after the war during the Jim Crow era in the South. Also, the technical information was invaluable regarding farming, implements, and the prices of all commodities and hourly pay at that time; Wikipedia for information about the organization of Arkansas state government.

~ Various persons at the Chambers of Commerce of Memphis, and many small towns in the Arkansas Delta.

~ www.Arkansas.com, for its historical, social and geographic information, including the states flora and fauna.

~ www.Arkansas.gov

~ Harold C. Valery, M.D. for his generous time and medical knowledge of surgical procedures.

~ Howard Collection at Assistance League of Long Beach. www.info@ALLB.org.

~ The Terminal Islanders Club members and other ex-residents and their children who provided personal recollections and stories of life as young adults in the fishing village. www.terminalisland.org.

INTRODUCTION

The Big House is rooted in each generation's memories—
some memories blaze with life and vigor, others flicker
delicately, while others glow and fade away.   This is the
story of one plantation family and their heritage.

Part One

CHAPTER 1

THE NIGHTMARE

SATURDAY, 2:15 A. M.
JUNE 18, 1932
MEMPHIS, TENNESSEE

I awoke in a cold sweat. My heart was pounding. I felt tears flowing down my cheeks. I was having a nightmare—another one since Grandpa and Marie's funerals. Tonight's was particularly awful: the perpetrators were grinning as they poured gasoline around the Big House. Their faces became even more distorted by hate and glee as they did their dirty work, whooping it up once the fire was raging. Marie was screaming for help, begging, begging to get out of the burning house. I tried to do something, but I was powerless.

Now, lying in bed, my fear was replaced by boiling hatred of the men. I imagined them roasting in Hell. My heart, I knew, was hard as steel toward those men. "Yes," I murmured, "yes, yes, I want revenge."

I tried to will myself back to sleep, but I couldn't. Finally I stopped trying, got out of bed and went to the kitchen, where I made a pot of coffee. Once the coffee was made, I poured myself a cup, went to the dining room table and took a sip. I was still obsessed with thoughts of revenge. I sat there brooding, feeling the growing intensity of my emotions, when I decided to go to an old friend—my journal.

. . . . .

Dear Journal,

    I miss Grandpa and Marie with all my heart. It's only been less than two weeks since Grandpa died, and one week since Marie was murdered. Maybe—somehow— the perpetrators of the crime justified what they did because Marie was colored, and actually lived in the Big House. To them she was uppity. They didn't know her true worth, nor did they care. I did, though.

    Marie's value to Grandpa and the Big House could never be put into words. Yet I knew she did all of Grandpa's reading and writing, ran the Big House, ordered and paid for the supplies at the house, including the gin. Not only did she collect the rents from the colored folk, but also most importantly, she was their healer and protector. Of course, she wanted something in return. She gathered information from them that helped Grandpa know if the whites were planning something. It hurts me that she knew once Grandpa was buried, some of those *hateful people would come for her. I still feel sick inside that we didn't bring her back with us to Memphis when she pleaded with Mother to give her refuge. I'm sure Mother feels guilty about it, though she hasn't expressed any emotions other than anger.*

I've come to you because I had another terrible nightmare. In it I felt helpless and powerless, yet now all I feel is rage. I wonder if there is something I can do? I don't even know for sure who any of them are. I suspect Frank at the firehouse—and maybe some of the other firemen—may be responsible, because they were so contemptuous of Mother and me when we went to the station after the fire. I will just have to wait and see if Mother's plan works—"to even the score."

. . . . .

I tried to go back to bed and sleep, but I couldn't. The heat and humidity were oppressive. I got out of bed, slipped out of my gown and wiped off. I put on a cotton slip, thinking that if I write down what's on my mind I can calm down. Going back to the kitchen, I poured a cup of coffee from the still warm brew. My journal was waiting for me with an empty page.

. . . . .

5

Earlier this week, I was really nervous when I told the company I couldn't work weekends. Luckily, my supervisor told me not to worry that there were always others to fill in. That's a relief!

Mother submitted her resignation to Goldsmith's Cafeteria, where she had been working the past few years. We were all warned about her giving up her job, which meant less income, even though logically we knew there was plenty of money in the bank.

Of all the things, which put me on edge, Mother told me she'd deposited the bulk of her money in the same Memphis bank where I had my accounts. I was just relieved our last names were different. Even so, there is always the chance of an accidental meeting and the questions that would follow an encounter.

Yesterday, my worries about the bank happened, but not the way I had anticipated. When I was depositing my paycheck, I was mortified to see Beauregard walk over to a teller's station. Even though he hadn't seen me—or God forbid, acknowledged me—I felt the revulsion of those earlier years when everything came crashing down around me because of him: a forced marriage, then the legal separation. After my initial shock, I felt a momentary dull ache when I thought of Norton who was my fiancé, the man I loved—and still do. My heart still sinks, remembering the disastrous end for us. God, I hate Beauregard to the core of my being!

Well, I'm exhausted. I'm going back to bed.

CHAPTER 2
THE THREE T'S OF THE PLAN

Today was special. There, on our dining room table, was a real country breakfast. Mother must have thrown caution to the wind, and bought everything she wanted—slabs of ham on a platter, fresh hot biscuits, butter, preserves, scrambled eggs, and grits. It looked like a breakfast right off of the table at the Big House.

As soon as I opened my bedroom door, I pointed myself toward the dining room, where I smelled the freshly brewed coffee and the ham. As I entered the room, I heard Mother in the kitchen breaking the eggs and beating them with a fork in the frying pan. As I pulled my chair away from the table, there, covered with a red-and-white checkered cloth, was the basket of hot biscuits next to a stick of yellow butter that had already been cut on one end. It lay there so serenely that the butter all but said, *go on, cut a piece and slather one of those warm biscuits with my yellow, creamy goodness.*

"Minnie, go on, sit down. What are you waiting for?" urged Mother, now coming into the room with scrambled eggs on the plate.

"I—"

"Sit down," said Mother, slightly grinning.

"Mother, I didn't expect this—"

"Minnie, we're not going to go hog-wild spending money, but one thing we are going to do is eat well again." With that, Mother sat my plate down in front of me at the table.

"Well, get started before everything gets cold."

"How about Dad?"

"Oh, he's already eaten, but he should be back shortly."

I didn't need any more encouragement from Mother. I promptly took a sip of coffee and began to eat—or, more accurately, began the process of eating. What an unexpected surprise! I had no idea last night that Mother had already collected all the fixin's for our Saturday morning feast. This past Monday—the day after that horrible week of Grandpa's death and the funeral, breakfast was the surest sign that things were moving in a positive direction.

I worked my way through half of my ham, the scrambled eggs, and two biscuits when all of a sudden there was the sound of "toot-a-toot-toot," not once, but three times.

"That's James. Let's see what he wants."

"Dad?"

Mother nodded her head, got up from the table, and I quickly followed her out the door and onto the porch. There, surprised now for a second time, I saw Dad sitting behind the wheel of a new truck.

"Well, I declare!" I ran down the stairs and out to the truck parked next to the curb of the street, while Mother walked slowly behind me.

"What do you think, Min?" chortled Dad, grinning from ear to ear, barely able to contain his excitement.

"I think it's wonderful, but why—why a truck, Dad?"

"Ahhh, right." Dad's eyes sparkled. "The *Plan*—it's all part of the plan." He looked more like a child with a new toy truck than a real grownup. To say the least, I was both genuinely surprised and elated, while my curiosity had been aroused about whatever was "the Plan."

. . . . .

"So that's it in a nutshell, Minnie," explained Mother. "We either keep up with the times or we go under. We mechanize."

Sitting around the table with Dad and Mother, having another cup of coffee, I listened as they went over the plan, astounded they would actually have included me in their discussion.

"Anyway Minnie, as you know, the books showed us the gin is operating at a loss. If we didn't know it before Daddy died, we certainly know now the plantation itself is running at a deficit, because of the drought and the Depression. Like so many other farmers and planters, we will be out of business soon unless we change our practices. Again, that's where the plan comes in. With good planning and a lot of gumption, we're going to turn things around."

I heard Mother suck in air between her teeth, making the sound of someone who was confronting not only difficult decisions, but equally difficult choices.

"First, what makes the plan viable is we've got money to invest (God bless Marie ! for hiding it from the robbers). That's our strong suit. How and when we do things will be hard, but dealing with folks will be just as hard—maybe even harder, but I'll *not* let sentiment get in the way."

I squinted, indicating to Mother I didn't understand what she was getting at—what her and Dad's decisions were.

"I don't expect you to understand from this little bit of talk, Minnie, what the overall plan is, but we'll know more as we go along. Things will begin to fall into place."

Dad volunteered at this moment, "Minnie, for the next few Saturdays, including today, we three are going and looking at trucks."

"Trucks, as in more than one, Dad?"

Dad grinned. "Yes, Min."

"That's right," continued Mother. "Also, we'll start to look at trailers for hauling the cotton to the gin. Even though we've got them, I suspect, we'll find we'd be better off with new ones. Lastly, we're going to need tractors.

"We're going to buy—eventually—the equipment and do what a few other folks—especially up North—are doing. The way things are going, we either change with the times or we could lose everything."

"But Mother—" Now I got a glimpse of what these changes could mean to the farmers on our land. My reaction brought out the fire in her immediately, once it sounded like I was challenging her. Fortunately, Dad stepped in and smoothed things over quickly.

"Minnie, there's no part of this plan your mother and I haven't thought about. From everything I've heard from your mother, she has not made her decisions lightly. The last thing she wants to do is cause pain to others. We've suffered enough of that in the last few weeks."

"Yes, sir. I'm sorry, Mother." Dad and my apology seemed to cool Mother off. She continued to discuss the business, knowing she would not be interrupted or derailed by me.

"Minnie," said Mother, making an attempt to explain to me, rather than dictate orders to me, "like I said to Brother, it's either us or them. We're in a fight for our own survival." Mother took a deep breath and said grimly, "We could sell the gin and . . . the land—"

Mother saw the horror at that idea on my face.

"Yes, I didn't think you'd want to do that, Minnie. Not after all the hard work by our people over the years. No," Mother shook her head adamantly, "we can't just give up without a fight."

Dad entered into the conversation, saying, "Even if we decided to quit, we'd get a pittance for the gin after we settled the debts. A lot of people owe us money they can't repay now. We'd never recover the money. Lastly, what we'd get for the price of land, we'd almost have to pay someone to take it off our hands. So many landholders are in foreclosure such that land can be had for a song. That's the reality."

I nodded my head. I understood their reasoning. I had been seeing enough newsreels at the movie houses, reading enough in the newspapers, and hearing enough from people at the plantation and in town to know what they were saying was true.

"Also," Mother retorted, her voice hardening, "almost as important to me, I have a score to settle with some folks."

"Yes, ma'am, I understand that!"

"James and I knew you would, too. To be honest, it won't be easy or safe. Some of those folks are going to be mighty angry and want to take the law into their own hands. But that doesn't scare me." Mother got up, walked into the living room and returned, holding her purse. Opening it, she pulled out a gun—a Derringer.

Staring at the gun, I said, "Those people don't frighten me either, Mother. Not at all."

"I didn't think they did," confirmed Dad, smiling wryly. He pulled out of his vest pocket a gun and handed it to me. It's the same one as your mother's—a 20 stock Derringer. You ever fired one before?"

"No, sir, but Grandpa taught me how to shoot."

"Handguns?"

"Yes, sir, a .32 revolver."

"Minnie," said Mother, admiringly, "I believe I've got a daughter who knows how to take care of herself." Mother looked at Dad proudly. "She'll be fine, James."

Dad nodded and smiled confidently. "I believe she will. Now, let's go out and look for trucks, trailers, and tractors."

. . . . .

Coming home from our search for the "three T's," as Mother called them, I inquired about the garden at what had been the Big House.

"Oh, you know how I love my garden," Mother mused, evidently thinking back on her flower garden on Home Street before Dad went bankrupt. "I've already talked to Delia about the garden and keeping things going. She'll get Lizzie and Eddie's nephew, Jeddediah, to help her tend to things."

"Even the greenhouse, Mother?"

"Why, of course. That's where Marie had those lemon trees and healing herbs. Of course, I want to save those."

Mother—until now—never acknowledged knowing anything about the healing herbs. I waited to see if she was going to say anything more about them—about Marie's spies.

"Those healing herbs are valuable to us. With your nursing background, maybe you can use them at home, and—" Mother didn't finish her sentence. Was she letting me know she had always known how they were used by Marie to get information in exchange for healing?

"Anyway, the roses, vegetables, and fruit trees will provide us with lots of good things. We just can't let them go to waste, can we, Minnie?"

"No, not at all, Mother." I was really happy to know Mother had already planned to save the garden. Just the very thought to see the ruins of the house made me both angry and nauseous.

"Also, as you know all too well, I don't like looking back. Occasionally, I make an exception."

At this moment, I thought of the headstone for Bonnie at the cemetery. This had been one of her exceptions.

"So James and I made plans for the wreckage to be cleared away. I don't want to be reminded continually of the Big House. Also I want to keep the lousy scavengers away. The hilltop will be cleared soon enough."

Mother must have known how this would have affected me; she abruptly stopped talking. Perhaps the thought of it sank in for her, too, because she took in a deep breath and sighed aloud. "Anyway, I can't—and don't want to—stay at Brother's forever. Eventually, I'll either offer to trade his half-interest in the hill for some acreage of ours that's close to his land, or something else of value. Then maybe I'll build a house up on the site."

"What kind of house?" I said dully, not really wanting to know but still curious.

"Oh, we haven't really thought that far ahead. I suspect it'll be simple—three bedrooms with a cottage in the rear for the help—probably Eddie and his nephew. Eddie's up in years; he's gotta have some place to stay, and he's got no wife and child alive. If we don't build the house, we will the cottage since I want a caretaker for the garden and all."

"It's always a pleasure to see Eddie. He's such a cheerful, sunny guy, and he's been with us—" I faltered, ". . . for so long."

"He has, for a fact," replied Mother, growing quiet and reflecting on, I assumed, his many years of service and her own personal experiences with him at the Big House.

I knew she had a sense of loyalty like Grandpa and, I daresay, like myself for the men and women of her past from the Big House. They—unlike myself—seemed to fall into another category for her. If I thought too long on this, I knew it wouldn't be long before I was resentful, so I changed the subject. "I hope things are good for cotton this year."

Mother hesitated and now looked over at Dad, who spoke up. "Min, from what I've read and deduced, the market's not going to pull out of its decline this year or, quite possibly, for the next couple of years." Pausing, Dad looked back at Mother while speaking. "But when it comes to cotton, your Mother has a hunch either that cotton's going up, if not this year, then it certainly will next year."

"It's my intuition that tells me prices are going up." Mother paused. "This leads us back to the plan—where things stand, and what we *must* do." At this point Mother smiled at

Dad who, in turn, smiled back and nodded his head, appreciating her recognition that they were a team. Mother continued, "That being said, I trust James. He's an educated man. He reads, analyzes and has common sense. He's a builder in more ways than one."

"But you, ol' gal, you've got the dough."

Mother thought that was really funny and we all started laughing. Laughing aside, Dad couldn't have been closer to the truth. Mother had the money and planned to use it, of course, with Dad's help. Possibly, since I'd been included in the discussion, I would wait to see what her plans were for me.

. . . . .

Saturday Evening
June 18,1932

Dear Journal,

Aunt Ethel called Dad and Mother, asking for Jeanette's company. Mother readily agreed, feeling they didn't have the time to devote to Jeanette. Jeanette was happy, and was put on the train this morning. Surprisingly, no tears were shed by anyone.

Today, Saturday, Mother, Dad and I went looking at the three T's. The thought of spending large sums of money made me anxious, let alone them. The tension increased even more when they realized modernizing was not going to be cheap, which already had led to some bickering earlier in the week after talking with Al and Ben about the cost of equipment. Though Al and Ben knew their jobs, they hadn't kept up on the latest innovations, so Mother and Dad became cautious about taking their advice. What they really needed is someone they can trust, who knows modern farming and who can guide them.

CHAPTER 3
BACK TO THE PLANTATION

W e spent the next two Saturday mornings, June 25th and July 2nd, continuing to look at Trucks, Trailers and Tractors. There was a lot to learn for Dad, less for me, and even less for Mother when it came to the farm equipment. Of course, Dad understood better than Mother and I the workings of the trucks and tractors. We all learned a lot in a short period of time. Though more expensive, the Chevrolet Confederate was the truck of choice.

Afternoons were spent at the gin and out in the fields of the plantation. On the afternoon of the 25th when the temperature and the humidity were almost equal, Mother and I, along with Ben Sanders, the plantation manager, stood on a section of land where the planted cotton was coming up strong. Looking toward the river over a mile away, and wiping the sweat away from her brow beneath her hat, Mother asked, "So, Ben, of the 4,800 acres, where do things stand?"

A short, stocky man in his mid-fifties, Ben Sanders was a genial but hard-driving boss, no more so than now with the worry and troubles of the drought and the Depression. As far as we knew, he was the one person who could tell us the most about the land and how it was being farmed.

"Ma'am," said Ben, sweating profusely, his hands and neck creased from years of exposure to the sun and earth, "I'll break it down as best as I can for you. Reason I say that is, as you know, ma'am, thangs change over time—sometimes from one season to the next."

Mother, taking charge, directed the talk in the way she wanted, since she already had a basic plan and would decide when and where changes would occur. "The acreage, how's it allocated?"

"Ma'am?" said Ben, confused by the word "allocated."

I watched as Mother changed her stance and started over, trying to make Ben more comfortable. "Ben, I can see runnin' things smoothly keeps you mighty busy. Looks to me like you've done a fine job."

Ben, who had tensed up momentarily, relaxed. Then he began to speak in his Arkansas Delta drawl. "Well, ma'am, thar's more 'n 4,000 acres under cultivation, including the land around the sloughs, which are farmed mostly by the croppers, since it's first to flood."

I interjected, since I felt it was relevant. "It's got the most mosquitoes and snakes, but the best bottom land as well. So it's hardest to farm with tractors."

"That purty much sums it up, Miss Minnie."

Mother nodded, understanding my point—harder to farm with tractors. Having noted that, Mother responded to something more important to her now.

"You say, 4,000 acres, Ben?"

"Actually, 4,010—the extra 10 being down on the bend at what had been the Jones' property.

"Is that so?"

"Exactly, ma'am."

I could see that Mother was impressed with Ben's accuracy.

"Yes, ma'am, it is. But the rest is river land, sloughs, and woods. About 210 acres of river land on the slope and sloughs, but that dudn't cover woodland."

"How much is that?"

"Thar's over 200 acres of second growth, and 400 acres of old growth hardwoods. That works out to 4,810 acres total, less 500 acres for your nephew, Milton. That's 4,310, ma'am."

"Hardwoods, too?"

"Yep, ma'am. That's valuable wood."

"Guess we need to get in there and see what we got, don't you think so?"

"It'll be hard to git in thar to see the old growth since it's so thick with trees 'n stuff, ma'am."

Mother nodded, thinking about the value of the wood.

Before Mother could say anything else, Ben went on. "Gits a little more compli . . . cated, ma'am. As I was 'bout to say of those 400 acres of hardwoods, well they're a different story, ma'am. Mr. Charlie bought 'em, along with the cultivated land, from ol' farmer Jones, who was ailin' and couldn't pay his taxes and . . . and was 'bout to lose his land. Anyway, Mr. Charlie promised Jones to save his birds—the wild ones. That man was plumb crazy for birds."

"Yeesss," said Mother noncommittally.

"At least, most of that acreage is hardwood. The guy. . . never cleared it. That's why thar's the old growth wood. Mr. Charlie did right good by him. Lot of other folks would've scalped the poor guy when they bought 'im out."

Mother knew about that purchase, but was playing dumb.

I saw Mother's eyes widen when Ben said there was 2,155 acres—her half of her inheritance; the plantation having included twice that amount of land. My sense was he noticed it, too, which, I could see pleased him to give her good news.

Seeing that my earlier comment didn't upset Mother, I said, "Grandpa showed me a while back that those extra ten acres are real important to us, because it was there at the bend on our side where we were losing land to the river."

"Yep, that's why we been tryin' to do somethang. Always seemed purty much a losin' battle 'til we got hold of those ten acres across from that spot. Now we can actually do somethang real good, and keep the land from washing away. Ma'am, you got that 10 acres."

I had taken a chance speaking up twice in Mother's conversation with Al, but still it didn't seem to rankle her. Instead, she said, "How much did Daddy show you, Minnie?"

"Pretty much the whole plantation—one little part at a time."

"Really?"

"Yes, ma'am. Your Daddy had her all over the place," added Al.

"He did, for a fact," I said, smiling at those times together with Grandpa. "He even took me to the gin and explained the workings of the machines, too."

"I'm—I'm glad," responded Mother, her voice toneless and her face now expressionless, "that Daddy took such an interest in botherin' with you."

I nodded. I wasn't quite sure how to interpret her reaction, especially the words: "in botherin' with you."

"Almost forgot, Mr. Charlie picked up another hunderd acres of fine, cultivated land, 'cause of the same kind of situation with Jones."

"So that's what Daddy meant when he thought there was something else," Mother said under her breath.

But I heard her.

"He did tell me he was leavin' that land and their house to you."

"Yes, to you, only," affirmed Ben. "He was real clear 'bout that thar. Ma'am that also includes their house in town."

"All told, I think, you're lookin' at least around 2,155 acres, but Mr. Charlie might've put the deed of sale at the gin and not recorded it. He was doin' his best just to—"

"I know," said Mother in a caring voice. The excitement came to her voice when she mentioned, "I'll have to check the records at the gin for that paperwork."

"You'll want to look for the name William Parker Barnes. He and the wife already left. Not quite sure whar they were headed—maybe to California. Seems like a lot of folks goin' thar, ma'am."

"I'll want to see that land next week sometime."

"As you wish, ma'am."

"Kinda odd, ma'am. Their house—they built themselves a nice house in town for only havin' a hunderd acres."

"How far's it from the gin?"

"Couple blocks, ma'am."

"Good."

"I knew at that moment Mother would eventually move into that house.

"Shouldn't be hard to rent, ma'am."

"Interestin', Ben, thank you."

"You're welcome, ma'am. Also, I'm glad you're going to be around here. Too many shenanigans goin' on if you ask me."

"You might be right, Benjamin. We'll just have to see. It's like runnin' a rabbit down a hole; gittin' him out's the tough part."

Ben looked at Mother, appearing to me to be making a quick assessment of his new boss. My sense was he liked what he saw and what he heard from Mother. She definitely was in charge—and he knew it! She was Mr. Charlie's daughter. Though she kept her thoughts to herself, he knew she was making an evaluation.

If he truly knew the scope of Mother's thinking, he'd realize she definitely had a plan. She was definitely going to make money.

"Oh, by the way, Ben, do you own a revolver?"

"Yes, ma'am, of course."

"I want you to start wearin' it. You understand me?"

Mother looked at him hard. Ben stared back and did not blink.

"Yes, ma'am, I understand."

"Good!" Directing her gaze at me, Mother said briskly, "Minnie, we've got a meeting with Brother before ten."

As we were walking away, Mother called back to Ben, "Keep a rifle in your truck, too, hear?"

"Yes, ma'am, in the truck."

. . . . .

As we started back toward the truck, Ben called out, "Sorry ma'am, but there's somethin' else."

Ben walked over slowly, as if a heavy burden was weighing him down. "Could you come down with me to the river? I'll drive you back."

Mother caught his meaning. "Minnie'll come along."

Ben's body stiffened. "It's kinda shockin', ma'am. I don't think Minnie ought to see it."

"No, on the contrary, Ben. Minnie and I will follow behind you."

"Well, okay ma'am, but I wanted to warn you." He turned around, went back, got into his truck and starting driving toward the river.

I followed at a distance to avoid the dust being kicked up. By the time we reached the pecan grove at the far end, he pulled over. I angled the truck not far from his. Once we had gone down the slope to the river, Ben pointed to some bushes. "Over thar, ma'am, behind the brush." He went over and pulled the bushes back so Mother and I could reach the water.

Floating face down was a woman with something tied around her. The closer we came, we saw it was a toddler, evidently bound to her mother.

"Look over thar, ma'am," Ben pointed about twenty feet away at what appeared to be a man, with two boys tethered to him tightly. None of the bodies moved, given where they had washed ashore.

"What the—" Mother exclaimed.

"Yep, ma'am. It's sad, but it's happenin' more and more. No food, nowhere to go, this is what they do."

"Throw themselves into the river," Mother sighed. "It's only goin' to get worse."

"Uh huh, 'fraid so."

"Well, what do you do with 'em, Ben?"

"Bury them, ma'am."

Mother kicked off her shoes, waded into the water, and tried to drag the woman onto the bank, when Ben and I stepped in and helped her pull out the bodies of the woman and the child.

"Ben, give me your knife," I said, holding out my hand.

He pulled it out of its sheath and handed it to me. Mother yanked on the rope. "Minnie?"

Ben must have thought I was squeamish and reached out. That's when Mother blurted out, "Minnie, do it!"

Sawing through the wet rope, it snapped loose and the bodies fell back to the ground. I stared, partly numb, yet I began to feel the deep sense of tragedy and loss. Suddenly, I saw Mother pry the baby from its Mother's arms and lay it face up on the ground. Even though the faces had only begun to bloat, it was apparent by the prominent cheekbones and the sunken eyes, they had starved.

"Damn her—the stupid woman! If the mother really loved this girl, she'd have taken her to an orphanage. Let her live and grow up. At least she could have tried to . . . Oh, hell, what's the use of cryin' over spilt milk? What's done is done."

Mother's words sliced right through my heart, especially when she mentioned the orphanage. Was that Mother's idea of love? Had she wrestled with the idea of suicide when my father abandoned her with Bonnie and me? I would never know the answer to those questions since Mother made it clear she didn't like to look back at the past, let alone discuss it.

I handed back the knife to Ben, whose face was filled with pain.

"Ben, how've you—you—" asked Mother.

"We got a real nice spot near the woods where we bury them—in unmarked graves, ma'am."

Mother walked over, picked up her shoes, and slid her wet feet into them. Looking down on the bodies, she took a deep breath and closed her eyes for a few moments. "May God have mercy on their souls." Mother made the sign of the cross and turned around. "Let's go, Minnie. There's work we need to take care of at the gin."

Without losing stride or turning her head, Mother called back, "When you're through with this, Ben, we need to talk. There'll be more of this in the future, so I want to talk with you."

"Yes, ma'am. I gotta git hold of Tom. Usually the two of us take care of things—quiet like."

"Good. Then, you come to the gin."

"Yes, ma'am. Of course, ma'am."

We trudged up the slope, got into the truck and drove back to the gin without a word being said, other than one moment when Mother grumbled to herself, "The damned woman."

CHAPTER 4
THE GIN

The following humid Saturday after our talk with Ben and Uncle Bob, I drove the truck to town to meet with Mother and Al at the gin in the office. It was hot! Surprisingly, no one was cranky—not even Mother.

"What's the date again, Minnie?"

"July 2nd, Mother."

"Well, that gives us a little over six weeks before the harvest."

A man in his early sixties, Al had a long history with the family and knew Mother when she was in her teens and he was a cutter, clearing the land. After Grandpa built the gin, he hired him to work there. Slowly he worked himself into becoming the first—and only—manager.

Mother said he was a straight shooter and was glad he was in charge. She knew she could work with him—even more, that she could trust him.

Mother seemed to ask all the right questions, which pleased him. The questions she didn't know to ask, Al volunteered the information when he saw Mother was ready to hear it. He wasn't pushy with Mother. He knew her well. He seemed to know how to talk to her, which made for a good working relationship.

Mother spent the workdays both on the land and at the gin. At the gin, she wanted to know about the equipment, the transportation, and the workers. She got acquainted with the men inside the gin and the suppliers. She asked Al what he needed: what was urgent and what could wait. Mother wanted to know what equipment was worn out and needed to be replaced (that also included workers). She was having him spend a lot of time with her so she understood the operation from top to bottom. Mother wanted to know not just what the machinery was for, but how it operated. She made a detailed inquiry into all of the supplies in the two buildings: the ginning equipment in the big one, especially the compressors; storage of cotton seed, bale bagging, and ties in the smaller, narrower one.

Even though we had been prepared by the chaos of the office that first day of our visit, we made an attempt to bring some order to all of the paperwork. As Mother began to review the finances carefully, she came to an early conclusion: Something would have to be done about the outstanding I.O.U.s from farmers. However, Al counseled that money couldn't be squeezed out of a stone. She'd have to wait until after the picking and baling of this year's cotton. The price of cotton would tell them what they could reasonably expect to do about the debts.

While I was filing papers, I wiped sweat from my brow as the fan whirred away in the office. Above the sound of the motor and rustling papers, I could hear Mother talking loudly to Al and the men on the floor.

"Y'all don't have to worry, except you gotta be ready for the harvest. So tell me now if anybody's having trouble with somethin'."

There were a few complaints, but Al assured Mother he'd handle everything. I think there was still some anxiety on Al's part until Mother said, "Oh, by the way, I'm getting a new Chevrolet pickup for the gin's business."

Now there was a rumble, but it was one of excitement that came with change. Mother certainly knew how to improve morale. They sensed Mother was not going to sell out, but she was there to make things better for everyone. Only later would they learn Mother was far harder an employer than Grandpa had been in his later years.

It soon became apparent to me—by the number of calls that either Mother made to Dad or Dad to Mother—they were in daily contact, discussing business. I learned they initially had made a decision to keep Dad out of sight as much as possible since he'd be viewed as a Yankee. That decision, however, did create problems of a different kind, most particularly for a woman and her daughter doing business and giving men orders.

Mother, having declared her intention to her brother that she would be the "bad guy," now would start to draw up a list. People had to be notified their labor would not be needed this season. Tenant farmers would be notified over the next few years they were being evicted for no reason other than they occupied our land. Of the one hundred thirty-five families—one thousand persons, more or less—many would have to go eventually. Some would be allowed to stay. "Business is business," is what Mother called it. The underlying text to that was simple: *Don't waste my time. Get out of my way.*

After speaking with Al, it was still relatively early in the afternoon. The men worked steadily in the gin. With the hum of activity outside the office door, Mother and I compiled slowly and carefully another list on a small, new pad Mother kept in her purse.

"Okay, Minnie, let's go."

The first thing Mother and I did was to pay a social visit to none other than Mrs. Katie Johnson.

CHAPTER 5
A HUG AND A KISS

"Oh, my! What an unexpected—and pleasant—surprise. Nora, child, you just come right on in and I'll make us some sweet tea."

I had been standing to the side of Mother, so Mrs. Katie Johnson must not have seen me.

"Let me just give you a big hug, honey." She stepped forward—just far enough to see me. "And, dear, dear, sweet Minnie." After hugging Mother, whom I knew did not like to be touched, let alone hugged, she put her outstretched arms toward me. "Now, sugar, let me just love you up, too. You wouldn't want me to play favorites." She lightly grasped my arms and bent over in a make-believe hug.

Thank God the woman didn't get any closer, let alone do one of those cheek-to-cheek kisses. I guess—not to be flippant—this was my lucky day. In that first glimpse, I noticed the last few years had not been too kind to Mrs. Johnson. I surmised her drinking had caught up with her: She had more weight around her waist but her arms were still thin, her hands now sort of splotchy while her face looked puffy. Somewhere in her late fifties, her hair was now completely gray. One thing had not changed—her beady little eyes. I wondered whether she could control that waspish tongue of hers.

Given the purpose of our visit, it wouldn't be hard to keep my head low. Mother was in charge and knew exactly what she wanted—part of which was for me to observe and listen. I didn't have a doubt once Mother was on the move, Katie Johnson would forget about me altogether.

"Why," Katie chirped giddily, "no more dilly-dallying. Y'all jus' git right in hyere."

Mother was working her plan. After sipping tea and pleasantries, she said, "Katie," (oddly, she did not say "ma'am," I guess for whatever her reasons), "I've been thinking about you—how loyal you were to Daddy."

"Oh, honey, how could I've ever been anythang less? Charles," Mrs. Johnson reached up with her handkerchief and appeared to dab at her tearless eyes, "was such a gentleman and soooo kind. I jus' can't express the depth of my feelings for your Daddy."

"Katie, I can see that. I know Daddy felt you were one of—no, you *were*—his best friend."

"Well . . . well, I declare! I'm at a loss for words—"

I sat there, staring and thinking to myself, *'At a loss for words?' That'll be the day!*

"You honor me, Nora Belle. I could never imagine a higher tribute. No, I just cain't."

"There's got to be something more, Katie."

"I beg your pardon, honey?"

"I mean, I've been thinking, what on earth could I do for y'all? I mean something that'd reward you and your boy for all the years of loyalty and hard work."

"Oh, Nora, we don't want anythang but your friendship."

I felt like I did years ago, when she paid Grandpa a visit. I thought to myself, *Liar, liar, pants on fire.*

Now I could see Mother had Katie's full attention with that fine-sounding word—*reward*. Katie could barely contain herself, the hint of greed narrowing her eyes. If I were a mind reader, I'd swear her words would be: "Just tell me—tell me

29

now, girl!" Instead, it looked like she was painfully holding her breath—waiting.

"I've given this some mighty hard thinking, Katie—"

"Yessss—"

"And, I realized that you rent this house."

"Yes, honey, we do." Katie looked down at her lap, where her hands were folded in a tight grip.

"It's not right, I said to myself. They deserve more."

Now I saw Katie hold her breath for certain.

"I want you to own this house, and I've got a plan."

"You do?"

I didn't know whether to call Mother the black widow or the Venus flytrap at this moment. I must admit I was almost breathless at this moment, too, but for a different reason than Katie, as I watched and listened to Mother draw Katie into the trap.

"Oh, most certainly I do, Katie. I want to give y'all a mortgage on the house."

"But—"

"No 'buts', and I know just how to do it. We'll give your boy a raise at the gin. Promote him—so there's not too much jealousy—and make sure he can afford the payments which, incidentally, will be affordable—much lower than any bank. To show y'all my deepest appreciation, I want to make sure there's enough of a raise so there's money left over."

"Nora, never in my wildest could I—I ever have imagined such generosity and kindness. I just don't know what to say."

"So, if you think your boy would be in favor of this arrangement—"

"Oh, I know he would! I do, indeed!"

My interpretation: *If he didn't, I'd wring his neck!*

"Well, Katie, let's make it happen."

"Of course . . . of course, we will."

"I was wondering if I might ask one little favor of you."

"Dare you ask, Nora? Whatever I can do, just ask me and I'll bring the mountain to Mohammed. I think that's the expression." Katie furrowed her brow in a moment of doubt about her allusion.

Mother nodded her head. "Well then, since you simply know everyone in this town . . ."

"I most certainly do. I do, indeed."

"I need a little information."

"Anythang, anythang at all, Nora."

"It pains me to have to ask you this, Katie, but I know there are some folks—menfolk—who didn't take kindly to the Big House."

Now Katie was visibly shaken, her eyes widening.

"It would be ever so helpful to know the names of the perpetrators—the perpetrators of the fire that destroyed everything I held dear."

"But Nora, how could I—"

"Katie, I'm *asking* you for help."

Mother had closed the loop. She wasn't asking; she was demanding. Mrs. Katie Johnson knew she was between the proverbial rock and a hard place. She was also frightened.

"Nora, you must know that some of the folks are really mean. They'd hurt us—kills us if they even thought I had—I had said somethang."

Mother stood up, taking one step away from the sofa.

Almost jumping up, Mrs. Johnson went to reach out, her nervous hand grasping for Mother's arm. "Please, Nora, please stay," Katie said in her panicky voice. "Please, honey, you haven't finished your tea. Oh yes, indeed, finish your sweet tea."

Instinctively, I had risen from my place. Now I watched Mother slowly lower herself, her eyes and her body's posture revealing nothing.

"Katie," confided Mother, directly. "If there's one thing I'm noted for—and Minnie—" Mother glanced in my direction, then brought her gaze back to Katie. "*I can keep a secret.* And that includes Minnie." Now speaking slowly and deliberately,

THE BIG HOUSE III

she went on, "Not a single other person will ever know. You have my absolute guarantee."

"Your absolute garantee?"

"My absolute garantee!"

Mother had switched to country dialect. She was one with the town and one with all the folks who live here. That was the final drive of the hammer onto the nail, and the expression on Katie Johnson's face loosened and became less tense. Mother had fattened her up, now came the squeal and the slaughter.

The names of the perpetrators didn't surprise either of us, except for one—Hank Higgins, Grandpa's best friend, confidant—and—head of the Klan.

CHAPTER 6
MR. HIGGINS

Mother asked me to park the truck a few blocks from the gin. She said she wanted to walk off some of the tension and to think. Admittedly, there was a lot to think about.

Once we were walking down the sidewalk on our way back to the gin, a deepening silence descended. The birds may have been chirping and flitting between the overhanging trees, the cicadas rasping in the bushes, the heat waves shimmering off the street on this seemingly lazy summer day, but there was nothing peacefully lazy or comfortably familiar about the sounds and sights around Mother or me. Both of us were still wrestling with the unforeseen betrayal by Grandpa's best friend, Mr. Higgins. With the shocking information of this particular betrayal, Mother, I sensed, not only was coming to terms with Mr. Higgins, but was planning her strategy toward the other criminals who had been responsible for destruction and murder.

"Minnie," said Mother suddenly, "I want you to stay overnight, and go back to Memphis tomorrow."

Jolted by Mother's voice and unexpected request, I responded earnestly, "Of course."

"You and I will take the morning train, and be home soon enough for me to have a good talk with James."

Though I had been looking at Mother, she stared straight ahead, and had slowed from what had been a moderately brisk pace to one slower and more deliberate.

"I accepted—without my brother—an invitation to Hank's place tonight—for dinner."

"An . . . invitation . . .to *that* man's house?"

Mother snorted, "He's still a man—a man with all of his weaknesses, even if he'd been smart enough to fool your grandpa and cover his tracks. Now that we can see his tracks—*where* he's been, I have a sneaky suspicion where he's headed."

I looked over at Mother and nodded my head. Below the surface, my emotions were intense. There was a strange incongruity about them, seething hot and surprisingly cold as ice. I made a point to keep the desire to strike back tightly controlled.

"Obviously, I'm not going to let my hair down the way I might have. Instead, I'll let him and Milly to do most of the talking. I'm sure they'll get around to letting me know what's on their minds. That's why I want you there. You know how to keep your mouth shut and listen."

I wasn't quite sure if Mother had given me a rare compliment. Had she? Or was it a backhanded compliment? Before I could say, "thank you," Mother spoke. "So tonight— tonight, you watch and listen carefully, Minnie." Mother paused. "You might say you're sort of in training."

. . . . .

Having been told by Grandpa that Mr. Higgins was a prosperous farmer who owned around 900 acres, I expected more inside the house. From the day we stopped in the car outside of his house a few years ago, I assumed because of the size of the house and its fresh paint that it would have better furniture. Yet what we saw was sparse and simple. Other than the sofa, nothing was covered with fabric, including the chairs around the dining room table. A couple of lamps shed light over the living room but the wattage of bulbs, which was not adequate, created a dim, slightly depressing atmosphere. Only the hanging light over the table was bright, casting shadows at odd angles on our faces, making everyone look as severe and harsh, as unforgiving and Spartan as our surroundings.

It was a simple country meal—fried chicken, yams and biscuits. I thought there would have been more on the table since we were guests—and more importantly—given Mother's suspicions for our visit. Their tableware could have been found in any tenant farmer's home. Simple utilitarian plates, glasses, and flatware (not silverplate) were laid out on a plain, somewhat stained but clean oilcloth, which substituted for a proper tablecloth of fabric or crochet.

After we'd gotten through polite condolences and reminiscences about Grandpa, there was the usual small talk about weather, crops, boll weevils, and the tough time making a living from farming these days. Still, the conversation was polite and cordial, but there was a discernible underlying tension I detected in Milly and Hank beneath the strained expressions of their faces.

Hank looked particularly miserly and unforgiving, given his features. A tall, gaunt man, the weather had turned his skin to what looked like leather, stretched tightly over the bony structure of his face. The wide, lipless mouth was more of a slit for an opening that allowed sound to come out of him. What had been the whites of his eyes were yellowed and bloodshot from working out in the glare of the sun for years.

Milly, on the other hand, was both different and yet similar to her husband. Of different stock than Hank, Milly was short, plump, with wide-set eyes. Strangely, I felt more uncomfortable with her than with her husband. The expression in her eyes was vacant and devoid of feeling that gave me an eerie impression of being viewed more like an insect under a microscope, which wasn't my experience with her husband.

Hank was fully engaged when he looked at me. Yet again, rather like his wife there was something impersonal to his gaze, but it wasn't detached. Instead, Hank was scrutinizing and evaluating—no, calculating—my very worth as a person. I knew I had come up short in his appraisal of me. Then it dawned upon me—he was questioning my bloodline. Why my chestnut colored hair, when the rest of my family is blonde? Knowing I was sitting with someone in the KKK, let alone the head of it in this part of the Delta, I realized what those men had said about our family—and must have said about me in particular. I was sure none of this was lost on Mother, either.

He had, I noticed, the nervous habit of flicking the end of his hooked nose with the tip of his finger, which emphasized its beak-like appearance. At any moment, I imagined he'd sprout wings and fly around the room, screeching and plunging down on us, talons outstretched.

It was only near the end of the meal when the underlying tension I detected began to surface. Hank's talk grew morose, sinking downward as he talked of the Depression and the grueling years they had had to endure. The more personal his hardship, the more intensely Mother listened, her eyebrows now arched while an almost invisible smile turned up at the corner of her lips. All the while she nodded and said the appropriate things to assuage his woes, which seemed to encourage him to talk more. I could see now Mother was drawing him out.

"So Nora, that's our situation. We're desperate."

Mother's expression hadn't changed all evening. She arrived looking pleasant and she remained so. That is, she was unruffled. The muscles in her face and body showed she was completely relaxed, which suggested to me she knew she was in control. Whatever her feelings, they were known only to her, though I had a pretty good idea they were as hostile and unyielding as when we first arrived at the house.

"Well, I can see you are in a difficult situation." Now the tone of her voice changed to one that was businesslike and matter-of-fact. "Everyone's in the same boat these days, including us. Money is scarce, Mr. Higgins." The words were those of a banker. They lacked compassion and kindness.

I saw Hank's eyes blink, then squint as if he were trying to look directly at the sun.

"I *cannot* provide you with a mortgage, especially with the loss of Daddy's house and all his possessions. (Mother's voice had lost any hint of country speech.) Like you, we are *land rich, but cash poor.*"

His reaction was predictable. I watched his face become a frozen mask while he tried to adjust himself in his chair, seemingly trying to find a comfortable spot where none existed on the wood surface.

"But, Mr. Higgins," Mother continued in a monotone, "my husband, James, has a small savings. I think I might be able to persuade him to buy your land."

"Buy my land! My Gawd, Nora, that's all I got."

"That and the house," said Mother.

"My house—!?"

I thought I'd cringe, but all I had to do is remember who Mother was talking to—a snake. No, she showed him no mercy, nor would I if I had been in her place.

"Mr. Higgins, you bought those extra 800 acres of land— nearly doubling your holdings—off of those two farmers at the wrong time—unfortunately, just before the market crashed. From what you have told me, you paid cash for that land. Then you've taken out two mortgages to survive; and . . . there are the back-taxes you failed to pay (and we know how the government feels about that)."

Mother folded her napkin and placed it on top of the table. Milly fidgeted. Hank took a deep breath and groaned audibly.

"It sure sounds like to me—and I do not make light of your dilemma—you are—to use a common expression—up the creek without a paddle, sir." Mother lifted her eyebrows and shook her head, telling him somberly, "It's a difficult choice you face. You're gonna lose your land—and house—mighty soon, whether you *sell it* to us, or . . . let the bank take it, or . . . the government, whichever comes first."

To actually hear those words spoken by someone shook him and his nervous wife to their core. I watched him go from anger to despair in seconds. He obviously had nowhere and no one else to turn to, and had assumed Mother would be both sympathetic because of his "friendship" with her father, and able, because of her inheritance, to help him. He sat there, rigid, clenching his jaw, and stared across the table. Finally, he lowered his eyes.

Not lifting his unwavering gaze, he asked, "What—what would you pay for it?"

"$2,500 dollars, Mr. Higgins."

"Two thousand and five hundred dollars? My God, that's highway robbery! That's not much above $1.50 per acre. I got some of the best farmland around," he implored. "And then my house; it's gotta be worth . . . no. No! I just won't—"

"Okay, I understand." Mother sat there and waited. And she waited. And I waited with her, listening to the clock ticking on the mantle.

Taking a deep breath, he said, "I got no choice."

Milly shook her head, reached out timidly and put her hand over his two hands, clenched together on top of the table. He turned to her and gave her a withering look of utter contempt, which made her jerk back her hand as if she'd been burned by fire.

"How much do your mortgages total, Hank?"

"A thousand dollars."

"Well, I cannot afford to pay you this price for the land and pay off the mortgages, too," responded Mother, shaking her head and wearing a mask of mock sympathy.

"What are you sayin', Nora?"

Looking directly at him, unflinching, Mother replied, "$1,500. We can pay you $1,500."

"And your back-taxes, Mr. Higgins, how much are they?"

He glared at Mother and chose not to speak.

"Well, Mr. Higgins, your taxes are a matter of record."

"Five hundred . . . dollars," he hissed.

"Is that all of them—drainage, road, and school taxes?"

"Yeah—"

"Thank you. One thousand dollars, that's after we've deducted the taxes you owe."

"No! You won't get it! I refuse to—" He stood up, looking like he would either strike Mother or flee the room. "That's little more than $1.00 per acre, woman. Even now with the value per acre, you should be able to get more, but . . ."

Mother shook her head. "The banks—what few there are—aren't lending. Private money has all but dried up and, sadly, you've run out of time to try to find someone who's willing to give you another mortgage 'cause it's too risky."

"This is robbery, woman."

"I'm sorry you feel that way."

"And you," Mr. Higgins stuttered "you ain't countin' the value of my house. I—I—"

"Mr. Higgins, I'm sorry, but I cannot pay any more." Mother clicked her tongue, looking impatiently at him. "I'm not even sure James will go along with it."

"Huh? James," he said incredulously, "*he* won't . . . do that?"

"Times are hard, Mr. Higgins. It's his money. I will not be able to convince him, unless . . . unless I can tell him it includes the house."

"The house, too," he moaned pathetically.

"I'm afraid so."

He sat down and looked at Milly, whose eyes were closed.

"But we ain't got no place to go."

Mother said nothing. She just sat there.

"All right, Nora," he said, totally defeated. "We'll take it. But the cotton, soon we'll be picking it. I've got 1,600 acres ready for the market."

Mother shook her head. "You said and we all know, it costs more to raise and bale cotton than what you can sell it for. So all we will do is plow it under. There's no money in that cotton. It's just going to cost us to get rid of it." Mother was relentless.

Hank hung his head. There was no more fight, no more hope in him.

"Mr. Higgins, let me give you a good piece of advice. The best thing for y'all is to go to California."

"California?!" He looked like he'd been stabbed through the heart.

"Everybody's going there. I've heard Bakersfield is where a lot of Southerners are going to work in the oil fields. You'll be around your own people. You and your boys can get jobs."

"You think so, Nora?"

"Of course. I heard they're hiring now." Mother paused to let what she said sink in. "If we take care of business this coming week, you and your boys can load up your trucks and be out of here and in Bakersfield the following week. With a thousand dollars—maybe I can squeeze $100 more for gas out of James—you've got a future, sir. You'll have jobs in no time at all," Mother said confidently.

"You think so, Nora?"

"Of course I do, Mr. Higgins."

"Okay," Hank said, bringing his hand up to wipe his brow, resigning himself to his circumstances. "I know there're others who went, and they were dirt poor. At least we'll have some money. We won't be like the rest of those poor fools," snarled Mr. Higgins disdainfully, contempt lacing his every word.

Those fools, I thought, *were exactly what he thought of us.*

. . . . .

Once we were in the truck, Mother said dryly, but with a hint of satisfaction, "You reap what you sow." She paused, then said decisively and coldly, "Now for the rest of those lowdown bastards."

"Who's next on your list?"

"Frank! Frank, we'll take care of him next."

To put the conversation on a more positive note, I mentioned, "That's one thousand, six hundred acres, Mother. Mr. Higgins has some good farmland."

"A thousand, six hundred acres for the Big House and for a life—Marie's," Mother said bitterly. She stared out the window of the truck. A summer shower started and blurred our vision until I turned on the wipers.

As soon as we reached the train station, I would park the truck and Uncle Bob would come in tomorrow and pick it up. But now, on this moonless night, everything was dark around us except for the lamps from the truck lighting our way along the road to town. I slowed down, but there were no lights, either from cars behind us or in front of us. We were alone on the road.

We listened to the rain, the drops falling harder, striking the roof, as well as the windshield. Soon it was pouring rain. The heavens were opening up, as if it were one great outpouring of sorrow and grief for us and everyone else—maybe even Mr. Hank Higgins.

The sound of the rain grew louder, providing a poignant backdrop for the sadness in Mother's voice.

"What small compensation for all we've lost, Minnie."

A full minute must have passed when Mother said, affirmatively as much to herself as to me, "Don't look back."

Mother asked me to pull off the side of the road because of the heavy rain. Exhausted, she fell asleep. I had my journal under the seat, but listened to the rain, feeling comforted until I was aware the sound of rain had been replaced by a profound silence

. . . . .

Saturday night
July 2, 1932

Dear Journal,

I can't believe all that's happened, and I'm determined to write you. Things are moving so fast—some of them good, some of them not so good.

When Mother and I were surveying the plantation with Ben last week, he took us down to the river to show us the bodies of a family that had committed suicide. It was gruesome and sad for me at the same time. However, Mother was angry, which only made me angry with her because of the same way she reacted to Bonnie's suicide. Something strange did occur for me when she said that this Mother could have put those children in an orphanage and given them a chance to live. I thought about those years Bonnie and I spent in the orphanage; she wouldn't give us up. She could have killed us, but she didn't. I never looked at it like that. All these years I've held a grudge against Mother about it. Still, I can't forgive her for getting angry at Bonnie's suicide.

Today at noon, Mother paid a visit to Mrs. Katie Johnson. It took my breath *away, watching how she got Katie to give us the names of the perpetrators. Mother is the true Steel Magnolia. I took a certain pleasure in watching Katie squirm, especially since she'd been mean to Marie. Later that evening, Higgins was all but forced to sell his land to her— 1,600 acres, which means she has nearly doubled her holdings to close to over 4,000 acres. I can only suspect there is more reckoning to come. I felt—and feel—no remorse whatsoever for Higgins and his wife. Rot in hell! My anger toward those people has not diminished one iota.*

CHAPTER 7
EVICTED!

Once we had left the gin Sunday morning, Mother had me drive us out to Frank's place. She was packing Dad's Derringer and checked my purse to make sure I had mine with me. Her unspoken message: *Do not trust anyone now.* As we both walked to the door, me standing slightly behind Mother, my purse was open.

Knocking—more like pounding—on the front door, Mother dropped her hand and rubbed it across her purse.

Suddenly, the door opened wide. Frank stood there with only his pants on. Matted and wet, thick black hair covered his barreled chest. He looked unsteady on his feet. He crooked his elbow, leaning it against the doorframe. The rank, foul smell of liquor mixed with sweat from his unwashed body hung heavily in the humid air, forcing us to step back.

"Frank, this is for you."

"What 'cha got?"

"Here!" Once he had it in hand, Mother said, "It's an eviction notice. You're leavin' the land and the house."

"Why?"

"'Because I want my land back. It's just . . . business."

He looked at the notice, then looked up at Mother, then me. Not blinking, Frank dropped his arm, swayed back and forth, swiveled and slammed the door in our faces. We heard him crash into what must have been a table and chair.

Mother and I walked back to the truck, taking the chance we wouldn't be shot in the back.

"Thank you, Minnie, for backing me up."

"I'm glad that's done." I meant it, too!

"We'll see."

As we were driving, we felt the truck bouncing along the unpaved road on our way back to the gin. I rolled down the window and there was the smell of the freshly soaked earth—our land, the land we loved and would fight for, and—if necessary—die for.

CHAPTER 8
"TOM, IS THAT REALLY YOU?"

"**M**a'am, I got wind Franks's gunnin' for you. So—"
"That's not supposed to scare me, is it? You know me better than that, Al."

"Reckon so, ma'am."

"You've been with Daddy and me too long to think I'll back down," Mother sniffed. "I'm surprised it's taken the man so long to get around to doin' somethin'. 'Guess I overestimated him."

"Minnie, you always keep track of the date. Just what is it?"

"Saturday, July 9th, nineteen hundred and thirty-two."

"I know it's Saturday, young lady. So don't get smart with me," Mother said, only half-jesting.

I sat there looking at Mother, knowing the lioness reared back the day she came home after the fire. She was determined to take charge and to make her Daddy proud. The only way in her eyes to do that was to survive, face danger head-on, and get more land. Damn anyone who got in her way.

"Al, would you go check out the compressor and tell me what you think? I'll come out later and we'll decide whether it needs replacing."

"Yes, ma'am." He started to turn when Mother said to me, "Minnie, go over to the post office and see if I've got any personal mail there. They're still slow to send it over here." Al and I both left her office together. I went down the block, checked, and found no mail waiting for Mother; so, I went back to her office.

I had just taken hold of the doorknob, turned it, and stepped forward when suddenly the door opened, which caught me off-balance. Seconds later I stood there, looking up into a stranger's face whom I quickly recognized.

"Tom—Tom, is that really you?"

Somewhat shyly, as I remembered him, Tom said slowly, "Yes." Hesitating momentarily, he looked at me, too, then said, "Minnie?"

I nodded my head and held out my hand. "Nice to see you again."

"Me, too."

We shook hands now, as adults. I noticed Tom looked ten years older than his 23 years, but then, that's farming. The land and weather took a steady toll on the people. What I remembered from that summer week of fishing with Tom, a lean, blue-eyed youth with sandy-colored hair and half a head taller than me (who looked so much like I imagined Grandpa had in his youth), was still the same, yet with a deeply-lined face and the dry, calloused hands that showed his continual struggle to wrest a living from the land. Year by year, season by season, the earth, the broiling sun of summer, the cold harsh wind, the driving rain and sleet of winter had sculpted Tom, the man.

"What're you doin' here, Tom? Gosh, it must be every bit of eight years since—"

"Yup, 'guess so."

"Well—"

Now I prepared myself for a slightly sarcastic but good-natured retort when instead, quite seriously, Tom said, "I was in to see your mother, Mrs. Gibson."

I took a breath. He knew who my mother was. Before he could speak, I cringed, suspecting the nature of his visit with Mother.

"She was nice, but I understood her position—times are tough for everyone. So I didn't take it personally when she told me she didn't have a job for me, which meant we'd have to give up the house and the land, since I can't afford the mortgage."

I didn't know what to say, but fumbled, "I'm . . . I'm sorry, Tom."

"It's okay. We'll get by." He hesitated, uncertain about the future. "I was able to save a little bit. She's a wonderful lady. She gave me a check for $100, which should help us 'til I find work someplace else."

Not knowing what to say, I heard Tom say, "Well, nice seeing you, Minnie." He walked away and out of the gin. Turning back to see Mother looking up at me from behind her desk, she shook her head. "I didn't want to do that. He seems like a good boy—someone with a family."

I was frantic. I had to do something. I had to save Tom and his family, but before I spoke, I closed the door slowly, trying to gather my thoughts. I knew if I pleaded for Tom, Mother would probably turn angry and reprimand me for making things more difficult for her. She made her decision, and once she decided on a course of action, best get out of her way.

"You know that man, Minnie? Seems nice. Apologized for not coming to the funeral, but said his wife lost her mother that same week and they were out of town."

"Sorry to hear about the funeral, but I just know him casual-like. We fished together as kids one summer. Other than that, I heard from Marie that he used to help Grandpa a lot."

Reaching across her desk and picking up a sheaf of papers to tend to some other business, I realized I had to give Mother more details to get her interested.

"When I was sick at Grandpa's, Tom would come by and Grandpa would give him all sorts of jobs—like drive him out to the fields or to town."

"Uh huh."

Growing more desperate in my attempt to keep Mother engaged—yet not arouse her suspicions about my intentions— I tried making a subtle personal plea. "I believe Marie said he was real helpful to y'all at the Big House during the Great Flood."

Startled, Mother looked up. "Oh, yes. He was very helpful. That was a terrible time." Mother took a deep breath and shook her head all but saying *I don't like looking back.* She now started to gaze at the papers.

I knew I had to try to keep her attention, so I said what I thought might catch her interest and reconsider her initial decision. "Marie told me how valuable Tom had been, starting off with small jobs for Grandpa, then finally ending up being Grandpa's right-hand man—like an assistant manager, since Ben is getting up in years."

"A manager—a manager's assistant?" Now Mother looked back up at me.

"Yes. Over the years, he learned so much from Grandpa, Grandpa began to turn over a lot of responsibility to him. Tom, according to Marie, ended up giving orders to the field hands, and sort of coordinated things between Al, Ben and Grandpa. He also drove out and helped bring in supplies during the planting season."

"Uh huh—" Mother set the papers down and continued to listen.

So I gave her the last bit of information that might change her mind. "He even learned to drive a tractor over at this one owner's land at the far end of the county."

"He did?" Mother asked, impressed.

"From what I heard, he could repair just about anything— Uncle Bob's old truck, equipment, just about anything. Marie said she didn't know if he ever slept, working his own land, taking care of Grandpa's jobs, and even filling in for Ben. Said, too, he was probably the only person—other than family—Grandpa ever really trusted."

Mother volunteered, "Daddy played his cards close to his chest, even with family."

I didn't say a word, waiting to see if I'd "played my cards" right.

"Minnie, you go catch up with that boy. Tell him to come back to the gin and see me by eleven this morning."

"Yes, ma'am, but I don't know where he lives."

"At the end of the road where the old house burned down. You know, John Henry's place."

I knew all too well, but I didn't want to let Mother know how I knew—knew about the fire when I sneaked out that night, or the house Grandpa built for Tom and his family right on the same spot.

"Oh yes, now I know where. I'll drive over and tell him."

Mother bent back to the paperwork.

I closed the door to her office with a real sense of personal satisfaction. It was the first time in my life I'd been able to change Mother's mind. Secondly, and if truth be told, I was thankful to have saved Tom and his family.

· · · · ·

Toot! Toot!

I'd gotten Tom's attention just as he turned onto the old country road. Stepping aside to let the truck pass, he was surprised to see me driving and stood there, unflinching, as I drove up and stopped in front of him.

"Tom, get in. I'll carry you to your house."

"Oh Minnie, you don't have to go out of your way."

"But I do, Tom. Mother's orders."

Tom looked quizzically at me, saying laconically, "Orders?"

"Yes, get in. I'll tell you what she said."

Appearing somewhat dubious but now smiling slightly, Tom climbed in while I shifted gears and drove down the rutted road. "Mother told me to tell you to come back to the gin and see her this morning at eleven."

"Okay, I will."

Driving a little farther, I said, "I don't know for sure, but I think Mother may be reconsidering her decision. Of course, she wouldn't tell me."

"Why might she be reconsiderin', Minnie?" Tom said, not turning his eyes from the road.

"Well, maybe she needed to know a little more about you—what you did for Grandpa. Like knowing his land like the back of your hand, givin' orders to the field hands, workin' at the gin when necessary. Oh, yes, especially—especially—that you know how to drive a tractor, and you know how to repair trucks and things."

"I do?"

"Now, don't play with me, Tom. Both Grandpa and Marie told me about you, so don't pretend you don't know anything. I know how you fellas are out here. Not much gets by you," I joked, knowing he'd pick up on my humor.

"Well, if you say so, Minnie."

"That is what I'm saying, and—"

"Minnie," Tom said, quite seriously, "I tried to come visit you when you were so sick at your grandpa's, but I was told you were too sick to see anyone."

"I appreciate the thought. Thanks for telling me."

"It was more than a thought, Minnie."

At that moment, I saw the house ahead and I started to brake. Rather than see Beth, who worked with me at the burlap factory and to my painful disappointment—over five years ago—married Tom, my first puppy love, I stopped the truck abruptly but all too late. Beth was waiting on the porch.

"Well, Tom, I think I better get back to the office. I know Mother's got something for me to do."

"Minnie, you can't just leave without saying hello."

I heard the tone of his voice, and I couldn't refuse him. Relenting, I got out of the truck as he closed the door on the other side. Holding back, I watched as Tom walked a few steps ahead and waved at his wife and family.

I could see that Beth was standing there, anxious and expecting the worse. Beside her stood two little towheads, a boy and a girl. Another child was on the way. Beth was very pregnant.

Once we were at the foot of the stairs, I could see Beth trying to place me when Tom said, hopefully, "I'm supposed to go back at eleven this morning. Mrs. Gibson, Mr. Charlie's daughter, might—just might—offer me a job."

All that tension she'd been holding was visibly released. She reached over and steadied herself against the narrow post on the porch. I could see tears were running down her cheeks. Regaining some measure of control, she wiped her face dry.

"Aww, Beth, don't 'cha worry. I told you not to worry. Minnie here, Mr. Charlie's granddaughter—" He didn't get to finish his sentence when Beth looked at me directly, then came down the stairs and over to me.

"Minnie, is this really, really you—from the burlap factory?"

"The burlap factory?" Tom said, dumbfounded.

"Yes, it's me," I said, not smiling.

Beth understood my reaction. Not a word more was said about the factory. Instead, Beth became country—congenial and hospitable, saying, "Come right on in, and have a piece of cornbread. I'll make us a pot of coffee."

I begged off the invitation, knowing cornbread was probably all they had to eat. I wouldn't take the last piece of food off of their table.

"I wish I could, but I have to get back."

Beth seemed to understand, offering another invitation, "Don't be a stranger, hyear? You come back any time it suits you; we'll always be glad to see you, Minnie."

"Thank you, much appreciative. Well, see y'all."

I drove off, knowing something more would be discussed between them, but I felt confident nothing would ever be said openly to me—or anyone else—by Beth or Tom about the factory.

. . . . .

When Tom came out of Mother's office at 11:30 a.m., he was beaming. Mother walked him to the door and said, "Like I said, you start today. I'll have Brother and his boys drive over. They'll leave you with the truck, the Ford. Also, I'll call in on the telephone during the week—every night, mind you, around six—to talk with you and Al. Then, next weekend, we'll go looking for another company truck—one for you to use, and my brother can have his back."

"Yes, ma'am. I'll get on the jobs you told me about right away. Thank you, ma'am, for everything. Really appreciate it."

Mother's eyes gleamed when she said, "Just don't disappoint me, Tom."

Tom, not catching Mother's humor, turned deadly serious, saying, "Mrs. Gibson, there's nothin' I wouldn't do for you and your family. Nothin' at all, ma'am."

"Thank you, Tom." Mother turned, and I saw her smiling as she walked toward her office.

Looking around at me, she said, "Minnie, give Tom a ride home. Brother will bring over the Ford and leave it with him. He'll come back here once that's done."

Getting up from my makeshift desk, I walked over to Tom. We left the gin and got into the truck.

My hands were on the steering wheel when I heard Tom say, "I see you got married."

"What?"

"Your wedding ring."

"Oh, that," I said. I pushed down on the accelerator, driving down the road without another word said between us. Neither of us broke the silence.

As I turned from the tarmac onto the country road, Tom shouted, "Minnie, stop!"

Thinking there was an emergency, I applied the brakes instantly; then looked over at him. "What?" I watched him open the door, walk off the road, bend over, and come back into the truck.

"Here, Minnie. Remember this little fella? First one of the season."

"Oh, I remember, it's a lovely little flower. You found and picked one of them for me, the day we finished fishing and you started to walk me back to the Big House. That's when you . . . you asked me if you could hold my hand."

Somewhat embarrassed by putting that experience into words, the truck idling still, I groped for the shift to put it into gear, when Tom asked, "Minnie?"

I paused and looked over at Tom, who was chewing his lower lip, like he did that day when he asked to hold my hand. I knew now he'd been dwelling on how to ask me something.

"Minnie, are you happy?"

Totally unprepared for that question, I stared directly at him. A few seconds later, I replied honestly if not a bit too bluntly, "Tom, I work every day to keep my mood up. I stopped thinking about whether I'm happy or not. Makes things easier that way."

Tom did not drop his eyes from mine. He waited seconds more. Ruminating, he nodded, "Minnie, that's the most intelligent thing I've heard anybody say in a mighty long time." Smiling, he said from the heart, "I always knew you were smart—and deep."

"Thank you, Tom." I re-engaged the gears and drove toward his house and his family.

"I like Beth. She's a good woman."

"Yes, she is, Minnie."

We were silent as the car rumbled along. I knew then that Tom and I could be friends.

I was pleased. Things went better than I could have hoped for. Mother not only kept Tom on, but also gave him a real job. I could see he was already thinking about not just Grandpa's Ford but the truck to come. Such are men, I thought: cars, work, food, and a pretty face is all they need. That is, unless they're a family man like Tom. He cares and cares deeply.

I smiled to myself. Mother was already implementing her plan—she had a good, solid team, especially since 'she' had decided to keep him on.

CHAPTER 9
TOM AND THE PLAN

Sunday morning at Mother's insistence, I drove to Tom and Beth's house and told Tom Mother wanted to talk with him at 10:00. Tom seemed quite happy and I carried him over there. Mother was waiting outside the gin as I steered the truck onto the lot, motioning for us to come inside. She turned and walked briskly back to her office. I was almost shocked by her behavior. It seemed almost unladylike and Northern for its lack of civility. Not Tom; he didn't seem to take notice of it at all.

Once we were in the office, Mother got to the point. "Tom, I got to thinking about our conversation."

"Yes, ma'am?"

"I want to start to modernize farming and the gin. But the gin's for another talk. To begin with, there's the harvest season. I figure I'll need new equipment. What I'm talking about are trucks, trailers, and tractors, along with some other things."

"Yes, ma'am, those are the right things. We could get more done quickly."

"That's what I thought. Right now I reckon three trucks— one for the gin, and the others for you and Ben, the manager."

Mother looked over at me and began to talk to me. "Minnie," then turning back to Tom, she went on, "my husband and I went looking for trucks last Saturday. We got an idea of what truck's the best, but you tell me what you like."

"Personally, I think the Chevrolet 400 six-cylinder Confederate is the best for a lot of reasons, but it does cost more. The Ford's okay," said Tom, while shaking his head, "but I still think the Chevrolet's gonna work out best here, especially when it comes to haulin' the trailers."

"That was our thinking, too."

"Also, you'd probably get a better deal on two at the same time."

"Why's that?"

"Since it's already goin' on July and the new models will be out in the fall, you might be able to do a little more horse-tradin' over the price."

"Thank you, Tom. Now we want to get some tractors."

"Again, ma'am, you might consider the price'll be better now because of the year's half gone—plowing's done."

"Makes sense, Tom."

"Yeah, we can store 'em in one of the barns, 'til we need 'em."

"Hmmm—"

Tom, following up on what Mother said, mentioned, "Tractors, huh? You mean the Fordson?"

Mother nodded her head. "Yes, five of 'em."

"Whooee!" Tom exclaimed. It was apparent Tom knew the price of the Fordson—$750—almost twice the price of a Ford car. He also knew very few farmers could afford the cost of one tractor, let alone five.

"How many acres will they cover?"

Chewing his lip, considering her question carefully, Tom replied. Pausing, he tried to put the best face on the news, "Six to seven hundred acres, weather permittin' and having the men who know how to handle them. By the way," Tom grinned and spoke with confidence, "there're three men who know how to drive a tractor—sort of."

"What'd you mean, sort of?"

"Well, I took the men up with me last year—I'd already been up there the year before—in the early spring and late summer to a big place south of Blythe—I'd done some work for 'em the year before—and the men started to get a feel for driving the tractor and pulling the equipment behind. But they're what you need. We don't wanna waste time on 'em. They come kinda ready-made."

Mother smiled for the first time.

"We oughta, with a little work, be able to get a couple of other fellas taught enough to drive the other tractors."

"Very well. Now, to get back to the equipment—"

Tom's eyes brightened, warming to the subject. "Well, ma'am, we can use some of the equipment we got, but it's taken a beatin'. Eventually you're gonna need to replace things like the breaking plow, disc, hippers, a planter, and cultivator. Maybe some extra farm supplies for the field hands."

"A breaking plow for tearing up and breaking the soil into slabs?"

"That's right, ma'am."

"We used 'em behind mules."

"Still do, ma'am. Your daddy didn't want to bring in tractors."

Ignoring his comment, Mother added, "And disc for grindin' the clods up. Is that right?"

"Yes, ma'am, it is."

Mother was building up steam, falling back into country speech and showing Tom she knew what she was talking about. "Hippers are for makin' furrows; the planter is for seedin'; the cultivator's for . . . for keepin' the rows clean of weeds. We're still gonna need field hands for hoeing to keep the weeds from around the cotton until pickin' season."

I could tell by the expression on Tom's face, he realized Mother was no city girl; though she'd been away from the land for over twenty years, she knew the old ways were still used by most people—mules, plows, and such—but she was aware of some of the newer equipment, too.

"I think you've 'bout covered it, ma'am."

I noticed something in Tom's eyes—maybe an unspoken sadness. Like myself, now he realized the scope of the changes—changes that would ultimately come at the cost to the tenant farmers' and field hands' chances to make a living from the land. Most of these people he knew by name.

Mother, however, didn't notice his reaction and went on to say, "Well, that was a good talk, Tom. We'll see what we can do to get you a temporary truck—Daddy's Ford. You be back at 2:00."

Tom's eyes brightened. "Thank you, ma'am."

"Minnie, tonight leave our truck here for the gin. Later, Tom can have it. Brother will get his Ford back, and we'll get new trucks for the gin and Ben.

What that meant for us: Trolleys and taxis—taxis now that we could afford the luxury. For Mother, a car was one luxury too many, where in Memphis it would be sitting on the street most of the day. Vehicles were for work.

CHAPTER 10
DERRINGERS

That afternoon after having picked Tom up, I went into the office to tell Mother he was waiting outside, when Frank burst through the door, slamming it behind him.

Gun drawn, he snarled, "I'm gonna shoot you, you uppity bitch! I'm glad the house burned! The goddamned thing was downright obscene. You folks rubbing our noses into the dirt!"

As soon as he got the last word out of his mouth, Tom came through the door, knocking Frank off balance just before Frank pulled the trigger. BANG!!! The shot reverberated in the small room. The angle of the gun, having jerked upward, sent the bullet off its intended mark, blowing out the window over Mother's head.

BANG! I shot my gun and fired, hitting Frank in his firing arm as he was stumbling to the side. He dropped his gun in pain, just as Mother grabbed her gun and purposely shot at the ceiling. I stood there, my gun pointed at Frank, as Tom rushed around the door. Instantly, he dove onto Frank, then the manager close behind him rushed in, and both men pinned Frank to the floor.

"Get some rope!" yelled Al, hearing the stampede of men coming toward them. Moments later, Pete rushed in and tied Frank's hands behind him, then started on his feet.

That's when Mother bellowed, "Don't hog-tie him, just get him up."

Tom and Al hauled Frank to his feet.

Mother walked around the desk, bent down, not taking her eyes off Frank, and picked up his gun with her left hand. "You won't be needin' this."

By now a crowd of men were gathered at the door when Mother, standing up and holding a gun in each hand, called out loudly, "I wanna thank y'all."

Coming back behind her desk, she put Frank's gun in her desk drawer, sat down, and placed her own gun in front of her. Nodding at me to put away my gun, she watched as I slipped it back into my purse.

Now glancing up at the men, Mother nodded, "Y'all can get back to work. Everything's under control." Looking back at the manager, "Al, call the sheriff," commanded Mother, "but leave Frank here. Tom, you hold onto him."

As soon as the door closed, Mother grumbled, "Gonna have a little talk with you, Frank."

"Tom, Minnie, what's said here, stays here."

"Yes, ma'am," said Tom respectfully.

"Of course, Mother."

"This includes you, too, Frank, if you know what's good for you."

"Yes ma'am, I understand," Frank sputtered, now humbled, bowing his head.

"Now listen to me and listen to me carefully, Frank. When the sheriff gets here, you're goin' to jail! Then, it's off to a chain gang. You know what that means?"

"Yes, ma'am, I do," he groaned.

"*Or* . . . I don't bring charges."

Frank now looked up at Mother, not really comprehending what he heard her say.

"That's what I said; or, I don't bring charges. Frank, what's the value of your cotton?"

Looking confused, he thought a moment. "About 8 cents a bale, and—"

"Yeah, I know what it's really worth. Remember, you rent those eighty acres from me. I know how much you can get off the land, and . . . that is, if the weather holds."

"Looks like, ma'am, it'll—"

"There's no 'looks like' with the weather and we both know it. We don't know anything until we get the last of the cotton picked," Mother said sarcastically. "As far as the price, last year cotton sold at 6-1/2 cents a bale. Nothin' tells me it's gonna be higher. We both know that, too."

Her voice now dropped to a matter-of-fact, business-like tone. "Also, Frank, I know you ran your cotton through our gin. We baled it, meaning the books show you came up short, owing us money. Am I right?"

"Yes, ma'am. You are."

Staring at Mother, I could see she had already cooled off a lot, because her eyes were now appraising the man before her, as well as calculating what she was about to say. "The sheriff's gonna be here any moment. So let me get to the point. I'll buy the crop in the ground for 6 cents a bale, put the money in your pocket, get you patched up. By Friday, you and your family better be out of town. Go west, 'cause the house'll be comin' down the next day, which doesn't concern you since you rent from us."

Frank's eyes flitted nervously between Tom and me, then settled back on Mother.

"I don't care where you go, but get out of Arkansas 'cause if you're still here, sure as the sun rises in the east, I'll have the sheriff on you like ducks on a junebug. He'll cart you off to a chain gang, boy. You hearin' me?"

"Yes—"

"Yes, what!?" Mother's eyes flashed.

"Yes, ma'am. I hyear you."

"Good. Just so we understand each other, I'm gonna have the sheriff check in on you every day—to make sure you're keepin' your end of the bargain. At the first sign you're doin' me wrong, he'll take you in.

"Make mischief before you leave, and I'll get wind of it. As God is my witness, you'll be dragging a ball and chain around your feet while your wife and kids go the poorhouse. Well?"

"Yes, ma'am. That's mighty fair of you."

"Good, 'cause I hear a siren comin' this way; and, Frank, you know who that is—the sheriff."

Standing up, Mother directed, "Minnie, Tom, you wait here and keep Frank company. I'll have a talk with the sheriff." Mother put her gun in her purse, then left the office, closing the door behind her.

Looking at Frank, a broken man, did I feel sorry for him? No! I still remembered the fire as if it were yesterday and the Big House in ruins. More importantly, Marie was murdered like a trapped animal. No, I didn't feel sorry for this man—no matter what part he played in the fire. His treatment and the laughter of me by him and the other men in the fire station left me with an enduring hatred of him and his cohorts.

Mother took care of business while Tom and I were in the office. Watching Frank, not that he was a danger, Tom and I were still on edge. Watching Mother to see how she handled things not only brought back a certain normalcy for us, but also gave us an added respect for her.

We heard the sheriff's car drive off, but Mother didn't reappear immediately.

Within fifteen minutes, she came through the door. "All right, Tom, you and Al, take Frank over to the doctor's. He's expecting y'all. Once he's patched up Frank, then the three of you come back here."

"Yes, ma'am," said Tom, with increased admiration for Mother showing on his face.

"Right away, ma'am," repeated Al.

Once the door closed behind them, Mother snorted, "As far as anyone's concerned, I shot Frank. We don't need any legal problems around you. Everyone knows the louse was gunning for me. Understood?"

"Understood, Mother."

Putting her gun back in the drawer, still leaving it open, she thought aloud, "I have a feeling cotton's going to sell for 8, maybe 8-½ cents a bale this year." Taking a deep breath, she patted her perm down, making sure the hairs were in place.

"Minnie, looks like Tom's earned his first day's wages already."

That was Mother's way of saying not only was Tom hired, but also he was now important to her. Maybe, even more, she liked him.

. . . . .

Tom was definitely impressed and, I suspect, he saw a lot of Grandpa in Mother. She wasn't frightened, nervous, or trying to be nice and avoid trouble with Frank. Instead, the man was in her way and she wanted him out and gone. She might as well have knocked out his teeth. Toothless and shamed by a woman, given enough money to get his family and him far away and time to find a job, he escaped the chain gang. He might not feel grateful, but he knew he'd been lucky.

Yes, Mother knew men, especially men like him, who lived hard, drank hard, and swaggered around 'til someone tougher beat the hell out of them.

CHAPTER 11
THE INCIDENT

Following the Sunday when Frank tried to shoot Mother, word had gotten out and around town about the "incident," as polite Southerners are wont to do when they refer to something unpleasant, controversial, or awful. In this case, the incident was the shooting. The way things were handled in our social encounters varied by class, even by the time of day.

This happened to Mother—and to a lesser extent—to me. Whether they were townsfolk, independent farmers, or sharecroppers, whites or coloreds, we realized we were recognized and treated somewhat differently than we had been before the incident.

Though we were the largest private landowners in the county and owned the gin, the great majority of people didn't openly challenge us, which could be interpreted as respect. Still, I realized that I have really learned there are different levels to respect. Simply put, there is the grudging or clever respect for someone who has more power than you do, which so often has to do with money. Only by association did I have that kind of respect. There was moral power, which I didn't presume to discuss in our situation. Possibly, in our case, I felt the respect that was shown us had to do with courage—two women who knew how to use a gun and who were prepared to defend themselves against a bully, marauder or potential murderer—

sort of like Great-Grandmother Keghel, who stood on her porch with her gun when the Union soldiers had come down her drive to pillage her home.

Yes, I determined respect was what this change was all about—the respect people have for someone with courage. Grandpa had it. Mother showed it clearly and decisively. Perhaps I had it, since I hadn't flinched or cowered. Yes, there was a change in people's attitude toward us when they passed us on the walk, or spoke to us during the course of daily work at the gin, paid us our rent, or planted our fields.

. . . . .

"Minnie, how do you do?" asked Mr. Smith at the general store, rather than his customary question, "What can I do you for?"

"I'm just fine. And you, sir?"

"As good as it gits, ma'am."

Ma'am. It felt strange hearing that from an elder, who called me all these years by the names, "Tootsie," "honey," or "Minnie."

As soon as I walked indoors, one old farmer sitting with his cronies and drinking coffee against the sidewall, nodded and tipped his hat at me. Whether by his actions or something he mumbled, the other men looked over or actually turned their heads around, some tipping their hats, others simply nodding, one of them doing nothing at all.

I smiled, nodded, and turned back to Mr. Johnson.

"I just came in for a soda pop, sir. This morning's hot!"

He went over to the cooler, picked out a bottle, came back and asked, "Do you want to drink it now or later?"

"Now, please."

"Jus' like you always did, except now—now you're a young lady, and don't have a mess of fish with you."

"I guess you're right. I haven't had any time for that. Maybe someday." I thought about what I was going to say, and changed the topic. "I think I'll get one for Mother." As soon as I mentioned Mother, I was sorry to draw attention to her.

Mr. Smith looked over his wire-rimmed glasses. "How is Nora these days?"

At the mention of Mother's name, I noticed the conversation going on against the wall must have stopped and some of the men's eyes were now on me.

"She's fine." I realized I had to give them something to hang onto. This was a small town. Whatever I did or didn't do and say would be noted—for good or ill. Those who were predisposed to like us would continue to view us favorably. Those who did not like us would have more reason to view us unfavorably. Most crucially, those whose minds were not made up could be swayed in either direction.

"Mother sends her regards and regrets she's been too busy to get away." I had to think fast. "She told me to thank you and all the other good people who came to her daddy's burial'."

"Well, you tell Nora I understand. I know how hard it's been on y'all. I hope things are improvin'."

I knew he was creating an opening for me to talk more, the details of which would then be shared with others. For now, I figured, this was enough. I needed time to think about what I wanted him to know or think he knows about us, more particularly about our plans. It was guaranteed Mr. Smith was the best way of spreading news. Nearly everyone came into his store.

"You'll excuse me, sir. I think I recognize a few gentlemen over there, and I want to thank them personally."

"Of course, Minnie."

As I walked over to the men, I remembered Mother telling me not to be surprised if nearly everyone had heard about us buying Higgin's land, which meant Hank wasn't going down without poisoning the well for us in town. So Mother cautioned, "Be prepared for anything. That is, any kind of question, even an offhand remark that sounds like a slur."

"I recognize some of you gentleman from Grandpa's burial. Mother and I sure were comforted seeing you there, so I want to say thank you again."

All but one stood up, not taking off his hat. Each man introduced himself and acknowledged me. A couple of them glared at the lone holdout, sitting there glumly.

"Please, gentleman, take your seats. Like I said, I just came over to thank you." Looking down at that one farmer, a surly and unhandsome man of forty or fifty, I said, "I don't believe I have *your* name."

"Small," he said. "Jeb Small." It was impossible not to see his teeth, or what were left of them. Broken and yellowed, when he breathed out the words, the air smelled of rotting gums.

I reflexively stepped back and watched as he spat into the tin can, already filled with nasty dark fluids of chewing tobacco and snuff. Some of my true feelings must have come out by the way I spoke his name, "Yes—yes, Mr. . . . Small." He was small-minded, ill-mannered, with a chaw ring around his lips.

"I hear your mother bought—more like stole—Hank's place!"

The faces on the other men ran the gamut of emotion from fear to outrage, from approval to disapproval, from disgust to sly satisfaction.

By the expression on the face of one farmer and his body leaning forward toward Small, I could tell a rebuke was coming, but I didn't want to be in the midst of dissension in the group, so I said quickly, "I don't really understand business, but what grieved me was to have him call everybody around here, 'fools in a hick town'."

Anger flashed across most of the men's faces. A couple looked dumbfounded. Mr. Small winced.

"Well, gentlemen, thank you again for your kindness." As I turned to go, even Mr. Small partially stood up as I turned and walked away. Nodding at Mr. Smith, I saw him smile widely and wink at me.

"Higgins was the 'fool'," rasped one man's voice, which was quickly followed by another, who sneered, "He was a damn fool. Got himself over a barrel, trying to take on too much."

"Oh, Minnie, don't forget your mother's soda pop," said Mr. Smith, just as I was passing him.

"Thank you, sir."

Under his breath, Mr. Smith, chuckled, whispering to me, "This oughta keep things goin.' Think I'll be selling 'em some more snuff and cigarettes. Excuse me, Minnie." Picking up the coffee pot, he called out, "Anyone want more coffee?"

"As I went to push the screen door open, I heard someone else say heatedly, "Higgins was tryin' to be another Charlie Coymen. That ol' fool didn't know he was outclassed." Now other voices joined in, but the door closed behind me.

I knew who were our friends. Importantly, I knew who were not. Most importantly, I knew who could be influenced by a kind word and a civil gesture. Did I have to make the effort? Probably not, since we owned the gin and most of them were dependent on our services—and credit—but it was still better to make the effort. As Marie had said to me, "You catch more bees with honey than vinegar."

I left for the gin.

CHAPTER 12
THE LIST

B y the time I got to the gin, I saw Uncle Bob's car—
Grandpa's Franklin—pulling away, headed in the direction
of his house, five miles away. At the same time when I glanced
around, Mother was just going through the door.

As I went into the gin, the manager looked over at me.
"Hi, ma'am, your mama's just gone into her office," said Al
who, evidently, had been explaining to a couple of fellows how
he wanted them to do a proper cleaning of the equipment.

"As I was sayin' to y'all, everythang's gotta be up and
runnin' before the cotton starts rolling in. Might seem like it's
early, but before you boys know it you'll be up to your necks in
cotton and lint."

As I went into Mother's office, I said, "I just got back
from Mr. Smith's. He sent over a soda pop—free."

Mother nodded her head, opened the bottle and took a
swig. "I'll have to thank him. It's refreshing in this heat."

"I saw a group of men there, sitting and chewing the fat.
When one of them looked up and saw me, he tipped his hat,
along with most of the other men."

Mother nodded her head. "Is that right?"

"After I got my drink, I went over and introduced myself."

Mother looked a little surprised, knowing I wasn't
normally so forward.

I gave her the names of the men, lastly coming to Mr. Small, mentioning his trashy behavior, including his attack on her personally.

To my surprise, Mother didn't seem either shocked or angry. Her only response was, "So, what did you do?" she said, tilting her head to the side.

"Not much at all—just said I didn't really understand business, and I was disappointed in Mr. Higgins' comments."

"Interesting," said Mother, running her thumbnail across the nail of her forefinger, back and forth, obviously taking in what I'd said. "What do you make of it?"

I didn't expect Mother to ask me what my thoughts were, which surprised me. "I figured in a small town news travels fast, and everyone's got an opinion."

"And?"

"Seems like people either like you, don't like you, and some are just neutral—they can go either way. So that's why I said I was surprised and disappointed that Mr. Higgins thought everyone was a 'fool in this hick town'."

Mother laughed! "I didn't know he called it a hick town."

"Maybe he didn't, but that's one of the things he might have meant."

"Uh huh. Anyway," Mother looked amused, "what you said had them at Small's throat. That's all that's important. You turned most of them against him. Clever."

"It seemed like the important thing to do. Get those who hadn't made up their minds on our side."

I noticed Mother looking at me in what seemed an odd sort of way. She seemed to be seeing another side of me, finally saying, "You got the majority of them *tanning his hide* for you, so to speak. The troublemaker had no allies, at least none who would defend him openly." Pausing to consider what she was going to say, Mother closed the ledger and leaned back against her chair. She rubbed her thumbnail across the nail of her forefinger, which seemed to be akin to Grandpa, who tugged at his moustache before he said something important.

"This reminds me of something important that I heard from Katie, which I planned to mention to you. Seems she was all a-fluster when I saw her this morning. In this case, she had every right to be. Katie told me there was a problem—some folks have been saying two Klansmen had been forced out of town by me."

"What are you going to do?"

Mother smiled, opened her purse, pulled out a pad and shoved it toward me. There was a list of twelve names—the same names Katie Johnson had given us, plus one."

"I should've known."

"It's not so surprising, is it?"

"Nooo, I guess it isn't now."

"Jeb . . . Small," Mother drew out the sound of his name, the last syllable dripping with resentment. "Jeb Small. What a despicable—" Mother paused momentarily.

"Bastard," I said curtly.

Mother smiled wryly, looked up at the ceiling for a moment, then brought her gaze down until it was level with mine, and nodded slowly.

"First off, the sheriff warned me that Jeb wasn't much better than Frank. That's when I paid another *friendly* visit to Mrs. Katie Johnson. After a good grilling by me, she admitted Jeb was not only a cousin of hers, but also he'd been involved with the others that night." Mother was apparently offended by Katie, who thought she could slip this one by her. "Obviously, Katie didn't want to implicate her own people—partly out of loyalty, I suppose, if you want to give her credit for being loyal to anyone but herself. But more than likely," Mother sniffed, leaning back in her chair, "she wanted to keep any suspicion of mine off of her own son—her meal ticket."

I had been standing all the while, when Mother motioned for me to take the chair closest to her. We both knew Katie's son worked here at the gin. As Great-Grandma Keghel said on more than occasion to me about those times after the war, especially when the subject of Jesse James came up, "speak softly, the walls have ears."

Mother rubbed the back of her neck and took a deep breath. "Given the choice between having a house of her own or sacrificing a family member, I wasn't at all surprised she talked." Mother sat there, satisfied she not only had known she would get Katie Johnson to squeal, but also she squeezed the last bit of information out of her—she'd even given up the names of all the perpetrators for her own self-advantage.

"That explains, Mother, why she knew all of the names of the men in the Klan."

Mother just looked at me for a long time and lowered her chin, never taking her eyes off mine. Then she held out her hand. I gave the pad back to her. "Let me see. I think I'm gonna haf (Mother was slipping into country speech, unknowingly) to make some alterations to the plan."

Mother must have already given the matter serious consideration because she spoke deliberately and with conviction. "I'm going to go slow—maybe slower than I had anticipated, but I will go smart," she reflected, holding the list in her hand. "People like Small, we won't touch for some time. Gotta handle him carefully. He's got no real power, except his mouth. In the end he would, however, cut off his nose to spite his face."

I obviously didn't quite understand Mother's last remark about spite, and she turned to see if I had. Seeing I didn't get the point, Mother went on. "The man's dependent on us to gin his cotton. He doesn't own much land and just gets by, but from what Katie's told me he's vindictive. So even though his words will come back to bite him, he'd still spout off and try to cause us trouble."

"Could he?"

"Let's just go back a few years. You told me Grandma Keghel told you about the bushwhackers who tried to kill your grandpa. Well, we certainly don't want to make ourselves a target for bushwhackers. Some of these men wouldn't think twice about killing our kind."

I nodded my head. I certainly knew what she meant by "our kind." Not only did we have land—lots of it, money and the gin, we, especially Grandpa, "sold out" by being fair and even helpful to the coloreds. Probably most galling to them of all, he actually had one of them—the "Negress," as Frank called Marie—living in the Big House. They waited to see where we stood: with them or against them. Now, with the "incident," Frank and Higgins gone, it was looking more and more like we were out to get them, which was true.

"So take a look at this list. You know any of 'em, other than Jeb Small?"

"Just two—the lawyer and one of the tenant farmers who rents from us."

"So what we've got here are two upstanding citizens in this town, and six poor cotton-pickers—two of them tenant farmers, two sharecroppers, *on . . . our . . . land.* Another one on this list, Katie tells me, is a sharecropper who lives on Jeff Jackson's land, the third largest landowner in the county, with two thousand acres next to Brother's land. Jackson," Mother hissed, "is—if you didn't notice—on that list, too. He's a Klansman and helped burn the house down. Another interesting point is I hear he's got money problems, which is good to know.

"Minnie, are you paying attention to me?" Mother said sharply.

"Yes, Mother, I am!" That sharp rebuke brought me back to the Mother I had always known as a child. This time, though, the resentment came out of me quickly and bluntly, which didn't go unnoticed by Mother.

"I'm a little short on the fuse, Minnie, so bear with me."

Not an apology, but an explanation and an indirect acknowledgement of my feelings and my age. I figured I could brood or I could move on and be useful since we both had the same goal—to get rid of the perpetrators.

"Anyway, now that Hank's in California, according to one of his kinfolk here, and Frank and his brood are in Louisiana with his wife's people, based on reports from the sheriff, who did you think is next on the list?"

There she goes now. She's actually asking for my opinion. So, some things are changing, even if others have remained the same. "The next to go, I assume, would be people who live on our land since we can get rid of them fast, except you said you have to move slowly."

"Exactly! Since we've got Klansmen who are suspicious of us, we'll have to make some adjustments, which brings me to a discussion I had with Tom this morning about this one on the list." Mother pointed to one name: John Beal, one of the sharecroppers. "According to Tom, 'The man is as 'dumb as dirt, with a bunch of brats who are as dumb as him and his wife.' Tom's face scrunched up when he told me, 'They all run around unwashed, without shoes and shirts.'

"They are," said Mother disdainfully, "one sorry lot. I know because I went over for a visit."

"A visit?" I said incredulously.

"Yes, a visit. At first Beal was suspicious, but I talked down to earth to him and his misses, and got 'em to laughing about some damn fool thing. That's when I handed her a bag of candy, telling them Daddy would've liked me doin' that and, incidentally, I'd be runnin' things from now on. That certainly warmed up his wife, who could see the value in being on speaking terms with us. I also could see she was tough as nails, a scrapper, and—"

"And," I said, venturing a guess, "could keep Beal in line."

"Precisely—"

"To get back to the plan, I thought you and I would both go out—separately—so it doesn't take as much time, and introduce ourselves to all our tenants. Engage them with a little country talk, then tell them to feel free to talk to the foreman." Mother's eyes almost glowed, saying, "We'll even send every single family one of them a Christmas card with one whole dollar bill in it."

"Mother!"

"That's before we start some of the evictions, which will not include any of them in the Klan. We'll stick solely to business. We'll stay away from the Klansmen for a few years on our land; let things settle. Dispel any thoughts that we're after them. Eventually, though, we'll whittle them away."

I could almost imagine Mother whittling a piece of wood, cutting away pieces until it took the form she wanted. In this case, though, they were people. Then I remembered we were talking about Klansmen—the perpetrators.

"First, though, I'm gonna get that lawyer!"

"The lawyer," I said in amazement, "he's probably the best educated in town."

"Yes, the dirtiest and sneakiest, and also in the Klan."

"I'm gonna start patronizing the new lawyer in town, Mr. Peterson, whose working out of his home. He's a young family man, and . . . he's ambitious. Right now he's struggling. So . . . I'll start by giving him some business that has to do with the bank here in town (I'll get into that in a moment). I'll make him our lawyer. We'll use him for the evictions."

"The evictions," I responded. Hearing that relieved me of one of the things I was dreading most—having to personally send innocent, helpless people off of our land with nowhere to go. Of course, that didn't include the Klansmen, but I did wonder about their wives and children.

"I don't think it looks right for a lady to be handling such crass things." Mother's voice had reverted to that of a genteel Southern woman, only to change again into the businesswoman. "We'll try to keep our distance from evictions as much as possible. As far as business goes, looks like we'll need most of the people we have for this year's season, and many of them for the planting season. If the price stays depressed this year, then we'll store the bales."

"But where?"

"To start with, in *Mister*—" Mother emphasized the word, derisively, ". . . Jenkin's house and barn. Most of them, in a warehouse."

"What warehouse?" I asked, not knowing of any but some small ones that were already used by the railroad or a few other companies.

"We've decided to build one. With James doing the drafting and overseeing some of the work, it should be ready by mid-fall. The space should take the bulk of the cotton if we need to store it and, if the following season is bad, be able to accommodate most of that, too. Hopefully it'll be a good year, but I don't take anything for granted anymore."

"Mother," I said, shaking my head, taking in a deep breath and exhaling, "you mentioned altering the time schedule, Mr. Small, Mr. Beal, Mr. Jackson (who has money problems), evictions, the lawyers, storage and building a warehouse. I—"

I was ready to suggest she might need some extra help but she cut me off, which would have annoyed me. I didn't want to find myself being one of her lackeys, but I realized she had not finished talking. It would be better for me not to take things personally until I heard her out, which would allow me either to comment on what I heard, or to wait and mull everything over. Also, I appreciated that she actually paid me a compliment for the way I handled the situation at the general store.

Mother stopped and waited a moment. Then she picked up the pen, slowly wrote down another name on the list, and handed it to me, maintaining eye contact.

Once I saw the name, I looked up and said, questioningly, "But that's the banker, Mother. I didn't know he was in the Klan."

"He isn't!" Mother said with emphasis, slowing her speech. "Though he wasn't a perpetrator, the banker ransacked Daddy's trunk. He stole things, and *I'm gonna make him pay*." Her jaw clenched so hard I could hear her teeth grinding together in frustration. "I can't get rid of him without—"

"Without shooting him," I said, half-seriously.

"Yes—yes, without . . . shooting him," said Mother, darkly.

We sat there with our own private thoughts, ruminating in silence the banker's fate, neither of us sharing the kind of pain he deserved—a pain that would be equivalent to what we feel.

"On a more realistic note, Minnie, regarding the banker, Norris, I've got to make it worth his while to see that it is in his own self-interest—'self-interest' is the key word here, to want to handle my business. It won't be just keeping our checking account full which means free money for him, but possibly taking out some short-term loans with him—as if we needed them," Mother joked. "He'll make money—easy money. That's the key.

"Then I'll have the lawyer, Poindexter, draw up and review the paperwork, just to add a few more nails into the coffin of that scoundrel lawyer. I'll keep him busy drawing up documents and such things. I'll become his mother's milk. It's only when he's dependent that I'll have him. If James comes up with some better ideas, then so be it."

Pausing, she pursed her lips and waved her forefinger back and forth. "I'm gonna bury those men."

Mother took a deep breath. "I still have to work out a few more details with your Uncle Bob. I've been keeping him on an allowance, but I'm gonna have to settle affairs with him."

"I thought everything was divided up already."

"No, not quite. I've had to work out the details of the plan."

I just stared at Mother and she back at me. "Uncle Bob is family," I stated.

"Right. All the more reason to be careful."

Careful. Careful was the operative word. I knew Mother could be careful, yet what came to mind wasn't meaning emotionally attentive, but as thrifty and cautious, not wanting to let go of the money.

"I'll arrange for him to come over to the office this afternoon, Minnie."

"He might have things planned," I objected.

"I know that! I'll have him come over after lunch—away from the family."

"Away from the family?" I was suspicious.

"Yes, away—away from . . . the family. And I want you to be here, Minnie. I'll also call the banker and tell him to expect us.

"On Saturday?"

"On Saturday."

CHAPTER 13
BROTHER

Mother called Uncle Bob and told him to come in after his lunch. Around two o'clock he came through the office door without knocking, which startled us. Bringing his warm, open country smile with him, I smiled back.

"Howdy, girls! What can I do for you, Nora?"

"Brother, you remember what you promised me—I would be in control."

"Yes, Nora, but some of the boys think—"

"I know what they think. That's why we call them boys, and why you are their father. It's as simple as that. Now, Brother, are you arguing with me? Because if you are, you know what I told you—I'll leave you—leave you on your own. Then where'll you be?" said Mother firmly, but darkly.

My heart went out to Uncle Bob when I heard Mother's words: *I'll leave you—leave you on your own.* I felt my stomach tighten, then came the anger, remembering that day in the dining room when she sent me away as a child.

I heard Uncle Bob begin to sniffle, his eyes tearing up.

"Bobbie, honey, talk to me. What's wrong?"

"My kids—no, just one of 'em—yells at me and tells me I'm funny in the head and that I don't know what I'm doin'."

"Aww, honey, I know you've got your woes. But I'll protect you—and I'll protect the rest of your family, too. Just trust me." Mother grasped his hand in hers. "Do you trust me, Brother?"

"Yes, ma'am. I mean, yes, Nora."

"All right. This is how it's goin' to be. Nice and simple," Mother whispered, as if she were comforting a child.

"We're goin' over to the bank and we're goin' to set up some accounts for you and the family. The boys will be fine. Don't you worry, Bobbie. They'll be just fine."

Mother would take care of him—and us—as best she could under the circumstances. Dad already warned Mother of the problem with the family and the boys wanting to get their hands on the money. He also got Mother to promise to wash her hands of her brother if things turned ugly. Eventually, she came around to Dad's reasoning.

I watched as Mother led Uncle Bob out of the gin and over to the bank.

Two hours later Mother walked back into the office, opened the desk drawer and placed a checkbook and a passbook inside.

"Well, let's see how this works out. I almost regret promising James not to get between Brother and his sons when it comes to the money, but I have and I'll hold to my word."

I was still upset with Mother when she threatened Uncle Bob with abandonment. I knew what she was doing was best for him, his family, and us as co-owners of the gin, but I hated the way she callously threatened him emotionally.

"I'll tell you, Minnie, so you know where things stand— just in case something comes up that you have to deal with. It wouldn't surprise me if you get an earful from one of your cousins. He may try to bully you."

"That won't work with me, Mother. Even though they're family, I'll not be pushed around."

"No, I don't think you will. I know that stubborn side of your nature."

That didn't sound like a compliment from Mother since she had a heavy hand with me for anything I might have said or done that seemed defiant or contrary in her eyes. "Stubborn," as far as I was concerned, was just another word for "contrary."

"Do you expect a problem?" I asked.

"Only when the money runs out. That's why I tied most of the money up."

"You mean at the bank?"

Mother explained. "I gave him nearly all of his share of the cash at once—thousands of dollars (four thousand dollars I held back for some other 'administrative' things). You should have seen Brother. He actually started shaking," said Mother, laughing.

I smiled, but I definitely didn't feel like laughing. There was nothing amusing to me about poor Uncle Bob, shaking because he actually realized the money he was holding was his own and he wouldn't lose his land.

When Mother stopped laughing, her eyes now stared at me in a cold yet thoughtful way. "I immediately asked for the money back, then took him across the street to the bank. To see the banker's expression was precious."

"Wasn't the banker one of the men who went through Grandpa's trunk?"

"He was. I haven't forgotten that. I'll take care of him later. But to get back to Brother, we opened two accounts—together.

"Since we own the gin together, we each deposited equal amounts of money in two separate accounts. One, the checking account, is for payroll and daily miscellaneous bills. The savings account is for equipment, which requires two signatures. This way, I can keep complete control over that one."

"How's he going to remember this, Mother?"

"It's simple, I wrote it down for him and for myself. We both signed the instructions and had them notarized. These instructions also include the amount for a third account—his personal checking account, which is for his payroll, supplies, or what-have-you. That one doesn't involve me. The fly in the ointment is the boys and his wife will be able to get at it."

"What a temptation," I said, thinking about all of the things they'll want, now that they know their daddy has more money than they could've imagined.

"I figure those boys are gonna want everybody to know that they are important now. That means cars, booze, and women. I'll just wait and see how Brother does with the money and all those itchy fingers at home. If he loses control, then it'll confirm my reasons for having a backup."

I guess I didn't really pay attention to Mother's comment about a "backup" because I was thinking about my cousins. "It won't take them long to go through that money, Mother, unless . . . unless it's because of cousin Will, who has been on his own since he was thirteen. Riding the rails and picking fruit all over the country, he's not like the others. He knows what it's like to have to feed himself."

"True," said Mother, contemplating that possibility.

What I didn't say was that Will—like myself—knew the value of a dollar. Maybe I didn't have to say that because I was aware of Mother looking at me in a knowing way, which suggested to me she understood my meaning.

"Also, Will's wife-to-be," I went on, pointing out another strength of Will's—his girlfriend, Ellen, "she's had it really rough. Being taken in young by her uncle and aunt, she—" I hesitated and decided it was best not to pursue the subject. Instead, I took a different tact. "She's got a high school education, and from what I've seen, she'll be after Will to save and plan for the future once they marry."

"I didn't know they were that serious."

"They've been going together since they were in grade school."

"Imagine that. Who knows, you might be right about Will and Ellen, but I'm not gonna speculate about them. What I do know is—as night follows day—there's gonna be a lot of wranglin' at Brother's house, now that his wife and kids know about the money. Especially once he tells them of the Memphis account."

"Memphis?"

"Oh, you don't think I'd let Brother get control of *all* that money, do you? That's what I meant when I said that I had a backup." Mother opened her purse, took out a bulging envelope and pulled out a stack of hundred dollar bills. "There's $10,000. This is going into a joint account at *our* bank in Memphis, which will put it out of reach of the boys. Two signatures, brother's and mine, will be needed for any withdrawals. That money will ensure he modernizes and has money for emergencies, especially if his money runs out of his personal account."

I saw Mother was really trying to protect Uncle Bob and the family, which, for some odd reason, reminded me of an old expression: *no good deed goes unpunished.* Fortunately, for Mother's sake, she promised Dad if things started to go bad, she'd not let herself get entangled in their affairs. I knew Dad was right. There was only so much she—or for that matter, we—could or should do.

When I thought about the "we," I reminded myself it wasn't my money or land, though I was expected to be involved with the plan—that is, the work on the weekends. All the while I'd be holding down a full-time job at the telephone company. No, I'd definitely not involve myself with whatever came of the "wrangling" at Uncle Bob's.

. . . . .

Just as we were leaving the office, Mother stopped. "Minnie, come back. There's something I want to show you."

As I took my chair, Mother, already seated at her desk, pulled out a lower drawer. To one side of the top of her desk she placed some papers. In front of her, she carefully placed what looked like a metal box, smudged with ash and grime.

Reaching over, she picked up the papers and said, "I found them, but it wasn't too hard. Marie must've been the one to place them in one of the ledgers—somewhere she knew I'd look." Mother handed them to me.

"From what I can tell, they're deeds to the Parker Barnes' properties. Just like Ben told you."

I looked them over.

"This means that the plantation had four thousand, nine hundred ten acres—less Milton's share—before Daddy's death. As Ben did say, though, the Parker Barnes' farm and the house belong to me."

Mother thought for a moment. "And that is that, Minnie. I'll trade Brother the Parker Barnes' farm, since the land's already close to his, for the hill, which is a little less than one hundred acres." Mother took a deep breath, sighing, "The hill . . . look at this, Minnie." Mother handed me the metal box.

I slowly went through the contents of the box. "They're all cards, Mother—birthday and Christmas cards from Grandpa to Marie." I had to stop and control my emotions. "Looks like she kept every one he ever gave her. How . . . how sweet." I went to replace the cards when my eye caught a little box. I opened it and out fell a thin gold ring, nothing more.

I looked up at Mother, who was peering at me.

"If you want the box, take it, Minnie."

I did.

. . . . .

Saturday
July 16, 1932

It is really sad for me to see how Mother treats Uncle Bob. He just seems so helpless. It's not that her intentions aren't basically good, but to see him browbeaten by Mother just hurt.

Another sad thing was to see Marie's cards from Grandpa that had escaped the fire in a metal box. Mother gave them to me yesterday. When I have time to myself at home I'll go through them or, wait, just wait until I know I'm ready.

Mother made plans to move into the Parker Barnes' house this next weekend, since it's 'hers'. Once she saw that it was furnished—and nicely, she was determined to get out of Uncle Bob's place as soon as possible. She also made arrangements for Delia, one of the servants at Grandpa's, to take care of the house and to prepare her meals. Lizzie, her niece, would—just like she did at the Big House—assist her aunt in the house and tend the garden. Mother not only likes fresh vegetables but fresh flowers on her table. Fruit would come from the trees on the hill.

CHAPTER 14
MISS VIRTUE

July through mid-to-late August oftentimes was a slow period. Admittedly the cotton needed to be tended, but the changes Mother was planning for this small town would be mind-boggling by the standards not only of the summer lull, but for the town itself.

Put quite simply, Mother stated the order of business in this period before the cotton was ready to be harvested. She planned out her agenda—two projects totally to be expected, and a host of other "secret" projects undreamed of by anyone—other than Dad.

Normally I would not have put all of these changes under the heading of "business," but Mother did. She did so with the speed and fury of a tornado, knowing it wouldn't be long before the harvest in late August.

. . . . .

"Again, I'm sorry to hear about your wife, Otis."

"Thank you, Miss Minnie. That's mighty comfortin' of you."

Otis's wife passed away in the late fall of 1929—a couple of months after Marie and I visited her with Marie's healing herbs. Otis told me he married a younger woman named Dede in the Spring of 1930, to make sure his children had a mother. Along with getting a mother, his children got two stepsisters. They were all crammed together in one of the small one-bedroom rental houses that now belonged to Mother and Uncle Bob.

"Now Dede, be sure to give the child a tablespoon of the syrup three times a day, or whenever the child starts coughing badly."

"Yes, ma'am."

"Just mix half of cup of honey with all the juice you can squeeze outta this lemon. It should be enough to get her by."

"Yes, ma'am."

Somehow there was one lemon left on one of the lemon trees in the greenhouse. I brought it, along with a small jar of honey, to the house. I now—officially—dispensed my first remedy in town. Now that Marie was gone, I'd taken her role, somewhat, of trying to help where and when I could the town's colored folk. As Marie had done and told me to do, I did the healing and spying under the pretense of collecting the rents.

Otis walked me out the door, having already told me what he knew or others had told him about the "white talk" in town. Probably the most important information came from a cousin of his in the next town over, who worked inside the Jackson household. Seemingly, Mrs. Jackson was worrying aloud to one of her people that though her husband hated Mother for how Mother treated Mr. Higgins, her own husband might have to come to the "witch"—evidently Mother's new name among some folks—for a loan, especially if cotton didn't sell high this year. They were, according to all reports, desperate.

Knowing this information confirmed Mother's suspicions, I observed her as she patiently waited for the noose to tighten around the neck of the man at the top of her list. The Jacksons were running out of time.

Being one of the perpetrators, Jeff Jackson was never far from Mother's thoughts. Always the pragmatist, Mother noted his land abutted Uncle Bob's land. Conveniently, it would be a matter of taking a carving knife, so to speak, to his land —in part or entirely—and his house, then adding it onto her own operation. While doodling on a piece of paper, Mother sardonically hissed, "Just to show my good faith, I'll buy him and his whole damned family bus tickets to California."

. . . . .

As I drove to what had been another rental—the colored schoolteacher's home, I replayed my earlier conversation with Mother and Dad this morning.

"Everything's in place."

"Everything?"

"James, you explain it to Minnie."

Dad, who had already read his paper and was sipping his coffee, dropped any hint of his Southern accent and became the Northerner he was bred to. "Minnie, your mother and I went to the president of the bank in Memphis, last Monday."

"James, excuse me for interrupting, but Minnie, I did say I'd get that crook who went through Daddy's trunk."

"You mean the banker, Mr. Norris."

"Exactly!"

"Your mother's got tens of thousands of dollars in that bank. The point is that your mother has lots of "leverage"—the power to influence others and to get what she wants. In this case, 'Cash is King' these days, which definitely doesn't escape the bank."

"Mother told Mr. Higgins everyone is land rich, but cash poor."

"Indeed! Your mother, however, is *not* cash poor. That money sitting in the Memphis bank is very much appreciated by the bankers. So when I told them we need a branch of the bank where we do business and the local bank might be shaky, I was fairly certain as to what they'd do, but your mother furnished the *coups de grace*."

"I mentioned to the president," said Mother, looking concerned, "I'd heard some depositors saying they'd been hearing rumors about the safety of their accounts, the bank may be overextended with loans, and possibly the government might be looking into the bank's practices. I told a few of the right people another bank may be coming to town real soon, which seemed to relieve them."

"Your mother told them," said Dad, winking at Mother, "she might have made a mistake by speaking too soon and telling someone who happens to be the town gossip she might be changing her account to a new bank that was coming to town."

"Mrs. Katie Johnson?"

"*The* Mrs. Katie Johnson," said Mother with a half-smile. "When she asked me if I was worried I just left it vague, saying I felt, as a good friend, that I should warn her. When Katie asked me if that meant she couldn't tell any of her family or friends, I just shrugged and said, 'I trust you'll do what's right by everyone, Katie'."

Dad cut in. "I'm sure no newspaper could have gotten the news out any sooner."

With that, I laughed. I liked Dad's humor. It was direct and to the point.

"Since James isn't familiar with Main Street, he didn't know what storefronts are vacant. I did. I already inquired about the rents. So I told James. He then was able to tell the bankers what is available, as well as the rents."

"That's the way," I said, "you got them to do your bidding?"

"Well," said Mother, arching her eyebrows, "they hemmed and hawed about setting up a small office over there, but when I told them we already talked to one of their competitors, the deal was made."

Mother smiled. "They'll be over there in a month, just before the cotton's harvested. If this doesn't put the nail in the banker's coffin, someone else will."

I must have looked at Mother oddly because she fleshed out her thoughts more clearly. "Minnie, he's gonna have to call in his credit. He won't be able to continue to extend some of those mortgage payments that either are due soon or, more importantly, the ones that are overdue. He won't be able to carry the borrowers along."

"I see what you mean now about the coffin—his coffin!" Mother, I realized, would have her pound of flesh one way or the other.

. . . . .

I drove down the block and parked. Standing on the corner among all the unpainted houses and shacks was one white house with a walkway and some rosebushes lining the way. This was Miss Virtue's house. She was the only credentialed colored teacher in town. Her house originally belonged to Grandpa, but Marie suggested he sell it to Miss Virtue years ago, and he did. She made her last mortgage payment in early 1929—just before the Crash.

Going up the well-swept walk, I climbed the steps and came up to the door and used the brass knocker. I waited, then, moments later, the door opened and standing there was an older, slightly plump colored woman, with her hair pulled back neatly into a bun on her neck. Greeting me were a pair of lively eyes that glittered like shooting stars and a broad smile that was both warm and welcoming.

"Miss Minnie, how nice to see you. It's been so long."

"It has. Nice to see you, too."

"I'm sorry I wasn't able to attend your grandfather's burial, but I was sick."

"I hope you're doing better now."

"Oh my, yes, much better. Thank you for asking. Please, accept my condolences and give them to your mother."

Unspoken was any mention of the Big House fire or of Marie.

"Won't you come in, Miss Minnie?"

"Thank you, I'd like that."

I followed her into a living room. Though small, it was nicely furnished. A red leather chair, a love sofa with a beautiful covering of green damask, and a rocking chair were placed around a medium-sized, lovely walnut coffee table. Along one wall was a hardwood bookshelf, which, I surmised, held her prized possessions. In a space between two bookends on the center shelf, stood a stand with frame of what appeared to be her college degree.

"May I make you a cup of coffee or a cup of tea?"

"Thank you, but no. Maybe some other time that would be nice, but right now there's something I need to discuss with you—at the school."

"At the school!?" Her surprise quickly faded away. "When—when would you like to go there and talk?"

"Now, if possible."

. . . . .

"So you can see, Miss Minnie, this is what we've got here."

I saw tables and benches, which substituted for desks. "How many students to a table?"

"Three—"

"With one book between three students?"

Miss Virtue nodded.

"Well, Mother asked me to contact you because there might be some things changing for you and your students."

"I don't believe I understand, Miss Minnie."

"Marie left you a $250 fund that you can use any way you want for the school. Mother is the executrix of the estate."

"My, my, just imagine $250! I just don't know what to say. I'll be able to do so much with that."

I could see Miss Virtue was almost overwhelmed by the information, imaging the things that could be bought for her students. She shook her head, stunned for a moment.

"Also, we'll try to get the school board to agree to change the name of the school to the G.W. Carver Public Negro School with a memorial bronze dedicated to Marie Duvall.

"Do you actually think you can get them to do that?"

I listened to Miss Virtue's English. Definitely Southern, she spoke slowly and carefully, enunciating her words, conveying an easy command of her grammar. She, I learned, received her degree, a scholarship, from a school for teachers in New York City. What baffled me was why she would have wanted to come to a small Southern town like this, with all of its limitations. Even more inconceivable to me was why she actually stayed here.

"Mother will break the ice with the school board by suggesting she'll make a donation to the local white school, paying for new books and other things. Once that's done, it opens the door for her to do more."

"My goodness, all of these changes make my head swim."

I was surprised at her remark. I had seen the differences between the two schools and how very poor this one-room schoolhouse was, yet Miss Virtue didn't seem to begrudge Mother's donation to the white school.

"Yes, but there's more. Part of your fund is going to be increased by a donation from Marie's nephew, who lives in Canada. Jacques Duvall has agreed to match Marie's donation. Mother also wants to donate $250.00, which will increase the school fund to $750.00."

"They would actually do this?"

"Actually, Mr. Duvall has already wired matching funds for Marie's portion. Here is his address in Canada."

"You don't say. I declare, I'm at a loss for words, Miss Minnie."

"Mother's donation will be made in the Memphis bank that holds Marie's funds. You'll need to open an account there.

Mother will transfer money to your account. This way everything is kept private. Mother wants to shield you—and your donors—from the townsfolk." I could see Miss Virtue was trying to put the pieces of the puzzle together, so I added, "It won't be long before you have direct access—through Mother, of course—to the funds in a Memphis bank."

"I'm grateful, no matter how much there is or how it's administered. This is a gift from the Almighty."

"Remember, on the way over here, you told me you taught grade school from 8:00 a.m. to 11:00 a.m., and high school from 1:00 p.m. to 4:00 p.m. I forgot the exact numbers of your students. You also said on the way over here you had a volunteer assistant—one of your high school graduates, who helps you with the students."

"Usually I have 30-40 students in grades 1 through 4; 10-15 in grades 5-8, and four or five in High School. Ella, who graduated from high school here, works along with me a couple of days a week. Miss Virtue inhaled deeply, her chest dropping slowly. "Not many can afford to spend the time to go to high school, let alone finish, so I graduate—maybe—one every two or three years."

I didn't quite know what to say at this point.

"But I did get two of them to college. One actually finished (the other died in the Great War). William, who lives in Memphis, is a good boy. He sends me a check every year— sometimes more, sometimes less, depending upon his situation." Miss Virtue smiled proudly and said, "It might have taken thirty years to get someone all the way through college, but it's been worth it."

I so admired her spirit at that moment. If anyone had gumption, it was Miss Virtue. I was bursting to tell her more. "Well, there's going to be enough money to paint the place, get proper desks, books and supplies for this room and . . . for the other room."

"What other room?"

"Another room will be added onto the school with a storeroom that runs along the back that connects the two rooms. This can be used for supplies and a small library for the students."

I saw Miss Virtue look a little perplexed about what I was saying, so I explained the plan in more detail. "The porch will be widened with two separate doors to each of the rooms. You can decide whether you want to teach in this room or the other one. Your volunteer assistant will be happy to know she'll get a small stipend for working."

"That'll help her and her family out a lot," said Miss Virtue appreciatively. "She'll be able to be here more, which will relieve me of so much of the work—not that I'm complaining. I love what I do and am thankful I get paid to do it."

"Oh, yes, the pay part. Mother said you'll be getting a small salary increase, too. She'll get the school board to give you a small raise. Then she and Mr. Duvall will contribute a small amount as 'gifts' at the end of the year."

Now Miss Virtue looked dumbfounded, her eyes growing moist with emotion. She sat there, not uttering a word, listening intently.

"Hopefully in another year or two, according to Mother, if things get better with the price of cotton, another part-time teacher will be hired to help you teach. That's another reason for the room. Also, if cotton prices do well, the dirt on the playground for basketball will be tarred with asphalt."

Miss Virtue sat down and put her head in her hands. There was only the silence—a very long and enduring silence. Finally, Miss Virtue said softly, "I knew someday something good would happen. I knew all I'd done wasn't going to be in vain. That is why it is so important to have faith. Thank you, Miss Minnie. Please, tell your mother—"

She couldn't finish her sentence. I reached down and put my hand on her shoulder. "I'll tell Mother, and Jacques Duvall. He'll be happy to know Marie's life—"

This time, I couldn't finish my sentence.

. . . . .

Saturday, 11:00 a.m.
July 23, 1932

Dear Journal,

I have a couple of minutes before I have to return to the gin. I figured I'd let you know just what happened.

I don't know what inspired Mother to do as much as she has done for the colored school in town. I have my own thoughts, but I don't want to be negative toward her motivations. I'm just glad she decided to do it. I'm also pleased Jacques decided to help. I feel really good, too, that I was able to do my part, knowing I helped Miss Virtue and her students. I just hope it all pans out. You never know in a small town like this who might take issue with it, then do something rash and mean—like burn the school down.

Before I left Miss Virtue at her doorstep, she told me Marie was her best friend. When Marie had time, she'd come over to her house and the two of them would drink tea and discuss literature, history and other subjects. She also said Marie would help her with French lessons which, she, in turn, would teach some of her brighter high school students. She even joked that her one college graduate, who stayed in touch these many years, still signed off his letters in French. I felt sorry for her. I wondered how she could stay so positive when only one of her students made it to college.

Unexpectedly, she presented me with a real gift. She offered to tutor me in French. Since I had continued sporadically my lessons from a first year French textbook Mrs. McDougall from the Catholic Girls Residence had given me six years ago, I was happy to get instruction from a teacher. All I need is time.

P.S. Otis tells me what's going on with the whites, which is invaluable information and intrigues me. For the time being, however, everything is pretty much quiet with not much to report. At times, I imagine myself rather like Mata

Hari, the famous woman spy in WWI. Knowing what happened to her, I do not want to get caught. So, I am cautious. As an old expression in the family goes: "Don't let your right hand know what your left hand is doing."

CHAPTER 15
BACK TO SCHOOL

A t the office during lunch, the phone rang. Mother picked it, and quickly said, "I'll be right there." As she was putting the receiver down, she announced, "Minnie, you'll have to go to the school board meeting without me."

"Me?"

"Yeah! Two new compressors are at the train station, and I gotta see that they get here safely."

I'd scheduled the meeting with the school board and had a general idea what her plan was. Even so, not having planned to be there, I was caught off balance.

"Minnie, time's short. If I'm going to get these things done before the harvest, I need to act now. In this case, you will! We need to be seen as caring about the community, and there's no time like the present."

"I—"

"I'll write down the basic things I want done and the amount of money I want to give." Mother scribbled down some notes, then picked up her checkbook. "Here's a signed, blank check."

I took the check, put it in my purse, and went to take a bite of my sandwich.

"You know I don't like to waste time or to be late, so eat up. I want to go over more details with you."

. . . . .

"Mrs. Beck," (I hate it when I'm called by my married name!), "here is the list your Mother asked for," said Miss Charlotte Brown, a bookkeeper at the school and keeper of the minutes of the meeting. A pretty, well-spoken young woman, she was the daughter of the local owner of farm equipment in town, who employed a part-time mechanic to help him out when necessary. "You'll find the books we need—the titles, their prices, and the number of copies we need."

The local school board had six members and was responsible for a host of decisions that ran from books and supplies, teachers' salaries, volunteer help, minor building construction and maintenance, along with a few other sub-categories, one of which had to do with appropriations for the colored school in town. Mother had purposely *not* mentioned anything about her plans for the colored school.

"What I did, Mrs. Beck, was to give you three categories. Category one includes the books we need urgently. Some students are actually sharing these books."

"Why is that, Charlotte?"

"Because they're older, ma'am."

"How old?"

"Fifteen years plus."

"My goodness." I looked at the list, remarking, "These are important—arithmetic."

"How many students—" I took a breath, and said to no one in particular, "Oh well." I asked clearly, "What's the total amount needed for new books?"

"One hundred and sixty-eight dollars and forty-six cents."

"Well, it's got to be done. Where's my pen?"

I opened my purse and began to write the check when Miss Baker, a retired teacher and spinster, said crisply, "Mrs. Beck, I really don't think you should be doing this."

"Doing what?"

"Buying the books."

The rest of the board was suddenly quiet—so quiet that you could have heard a pin drop. Looks of disapproval spread across their faces. Finally, Mr. Oliphant, a ruddy-faced man who taught at the school, retorted, obviously agitated, spoke for presumably everyone except Miss Baker, "If not now, then when, ma'am?"

"We need to do some community fundraising and do this ourselves."

"Fundraising? Everyone's broke, Miss Baker. What do you—?"

Petulantly, Mrs. Baker responded tartly, "I don't think it's good for our children."

"Not good, for the children?" asked Mr. Solomon, who was Jewish with a small store that included clothing, shoes, watches, watch repairs, and general knickknacks. He and his wife were active community members. They belonged to more than a few civic organizations (that would have them) and were contributors to the local newspaper.

Mother had me find out everything—everything I could about the board members before we went into this meeting: their names, occupations, standings in the community and, most importantly, their religion. There were two Methodists, two Baptists, a Catholic (whom Mother had already established contact), and a Jew, whom Mother bought supplies from. She knew she had these last two voting members as allies.

"Well, Nora has a past," smirked Miss Baker.

"Don't we all?" said Mrs. O'Connor, the Catholic.

Wasting no time, I said bluntly, "Exactly, Miss Baker, what is your problem?"

"Nora, if my memory serves me right, she's the first woman ever to get a divorce in these parts."

"My mother did," I said slowing down my speech.

"We have an obligation to protect the morals of our young people."

That shocked Mrs. O'Connor, but it didn't deter her from inquiring impartially. "Didn't our Lord say, '*Judge not, lest ye be judged*'?"

At this point, his face red, Mr. Oliphant interjected. "Miss Baker, let me say quite clearly, you've been downright insulting. I for one am sick and tired of your petty interference with this board!"

Annoyed but not dissuaded by his comment, Miss Baker persisted. "She's not a good example for the children."

"And," replied Mr. Oliphant, derisively, "I suppose you *are*, having never been married?"

"Well, I never!" Pursing her lips, she primly got up and left the room.

This must have happened before, because no one seemed to give the disturbance much attention. It appeared as if everyone was going on with business as if nothing had occurred, when Mr. Solomon said, "I, for one, offer you an apology, Mrs. Beck, for Miss Baker's downright uncivil behavior."

"You're damn right!" snapped Mr. Oliphant. "It was rude of the old busybody."

"Yes, yes," the chorus echoed around the room, except for an elderly woman, Mrs. Tucker, who looked as severe and uncompromising as Miss Baker.

"Rude! How dare you call her rude, Mr. Oliphant! Unlike the Jew, I think you owe Miss Baker the apology, not *this* woman," barked Mrs. Tucker. The tone of her voice was harsh and unyielding. It was obvious to me she was a fighter.

"Shut up!" snarled Mr. Oliphant.

Ready to attack, Mrs. Tucker was stopped suddenly by the intervention of the mayor, Tom Church, who stood up and waved his hands. "Enough, enough!" he commanded, getting everyone's attention. A somewhat tall man, handsome, and younger than I would have expected of a mayor, he definitely knew how to make his presence known and brought a quick end to the bickering.

The board realized both Baker and Tucker had most likely jeopardized the donation, when I suggested, maintaining my self-control, "These things happen. Shall we get back to business?"

Mother told me earlier she anticipated problems—one in particular, her divorce. "Best be prepared, Minnie, and know with whom you're dealing."

Still standing, Mr. Church spoke like a true politician. "Listen, ladies and gentlemen. We must work together to help our children. I suggest," he said firmly and in a no-nonsense tone of voice while still managing to smile, "we take care of business and leave anything personal to one's own conscience. Now as Mrs. Beck so appropriately said, 'Let's get back to business.' Miss Brown, please continue with what you have there."

Everyone noticed the mayor's eyes lingered a little too long on Miss Brown and her bosom, who was obviously a favorite of his. She blushed. As for myself, I was intrigued by the mayor's looks—a fine, if not handsome man in his early thirties. There was a nagging question for me. He reminded me of someone else, yet I couldn't recall who he was.

"There's also, Mrs. Beck, on my Category Two list, one particular book that should be looked at seriously. Though we have enough of them for the students, they're worn and outdated. I am speaking of the English books. Also, the new editions include a section on calligraphy, learning to write longhand."

"How much are those?"

"One hundred and seventy-two dollars and twenty cents for all the ones we need."

"All right." I checked those books. "That's a total of," I mentally added up the amount, "$340.66."

I saw everyone looked relieved at this first meeting. "Thank you, Mrs. Beck. I—I mean, we just can't tell you how much we appreciate your help," said Mayor Church. Everyone nodded and smiled. "It's more than we had hoped for."

I smiled, too, saying, "Now that the issue of the books is taken care of for this year, let's discuss paint."

"Paint?" asked Mrs. Bean, perplexed. Heretofore, she had remained silent and nearly invisible. A mousy sort of woman, she was plain to the extreme with stringy brown hair and no makeup. I couldn't even see what the color of her eyes were— possibly some combination of light brown or hazel.

"Of course, the children need nice clean classrooms. So Mother already had a painter tell her that it'd cost about $45.00 to paint them. He would use a couple of helpers and get started this coming week, since sooner is better than later."

The members were in a state of shock momentarily when they realized Mother was donating more money. They also understood the painter's urgency, since he and his help would be involved with the cotton harvest in August and September.

"Now everyone clapped loudly and enthusiastically—even Mrs. Bean, which somewhat embarrassed me. I looked down in a modest gesture to avoid being a grandstander. However, I knew I did feel a certain pride, having made this impact on some of the town's more public figures.

"Please, please, I know Mother would be so overwhelmed by your support," I said politely, waiting for the informal applause to subside. "There are two other things Mother wanted to tell you. The children need a new school bus. My step-dad has already found a Ford AA school bus that's built out of steel with safeguards for the children. With your permission, I'll tell him to buy it."

Mother was good. She had told me to say those exact words *'with your permission'* at this time. She knew what the reaction would be.

At first, everyone sat there dumbfounded, not quite sure they'd actually heard she was buying them a real school bus— just released this year by Ford—not a truck, covered with canvas, which was what they were using now. Suddenly, Mayor Church reacted, saying loudly, "Yes, MA'AM! We'd be most appreciative. Certainly! Certainly, we will." There wasn't a single nay from anyone else on the board. Only Mrs. Tucker scowled, yet she remained quiet.

Now was my cue. "Perhaps I might suggest that since you're using a truck—the truck with the canvas top—you might consider transferring" (I didn't say "giving"), "that to the colored school? This, I admit, is my idea."

Initially there was a stunned silence, partly since no one had heard me take credit for something and partly because this was the last thing anyone expected or wanted to hear. Mother, I drilled down, said to me that she hadn't thought to propose this, but she thought it was a good idea. "Don't y'all think so?" Before anyone could answer, I went on, "It'd prove to those folks up North we do take care of the colored children."

Once again, it was Mayor Church who took the initiative, saying soothingly and looking at me all the while, "Yes, of course. We kill two birds with one stone. We get a new school bus for ourselves, and provide the truck to the others, in case any Northern do-gooders come snooping around. We'll stand out from all of the other towns around here, which won't escape Little Rock and the governor's attention. When they want to show visitors a model school district, we'll be the one. They might even provide us with some extra support."

I saw the mayor was very persuasive, except for Mrs. Tucker, who now leaned forward, her lips parting, but she never got a word out.

"Lastly," just as Mother told me to do, I spoke up decisively at this moment, *"not* to overlook athletics, that school ground of yours needs some equipment and the basketball court needs asphalt. That'll cost $40.00. Mother would like to see the children have some fun. They study better that way."

At that time, Mother had taken my breath away, not because of what she had proposed, but her reasoning for doing it.

I'd like to see the children have some fun. They study better that way.

When I thought about my own childhood, fun was not one of those memories. Resentment had begun to fester below the surface when I had looked at Mother, wondering how she could have said that and made it sound so true.

I don't think she was actually lying. She might actually have believed what she was saying, but why couldn't she have felt that way earlier—earlier in my own life?

Again, the impact of my words pleased everyone on the school board immensely. They started clapping and came over.

I found myself now surrounded by these same people, telling me how much they appreciated "us" for all "we" were doing for the children and the town. That seemed to take the sting out of my earlier feelings toward mother. Instead, the sincere appreciation of the people and their happiness was infectious when they were so positive about the help from "us." Mother had accomplished one of the goals she set for herself— get the support of the school board, and what most likely would be the teachers, the students, and many of their parents. Total Cost: less than $450, not counting the bus, which Dad had already located and bought second-hand from the Memphis School District at $350. Even Memphis was having trouble operating a fleet of school buses.

I opened my purse, took out the check, and looked up. Smiling at everyone in the room, I asked, "Miss Brown, what is the exact cost of everything?"

"Miss Brown," said the mayor, "what figure do you have?

"Just somewhere less than $450, less the cost of the bus. I believe, just give me a moment." She was trying to add up the numbers to get an exact amount.

Dropping my eyes, I noted, "It's $445.60."

. . . . .

Saturday
July 30, 1932

I met with the school board the following Saturday, explaining that Mother had urgent business and couldn't attend.

Quite simply I was there to make sure the board honored its commitment to the colored school. I was assured Miss Virtue had been contacted and informed about her "new" school bus and the change of the name of the school to the G. W. Carver Public Negro School. Below, a bronze plaque would state: In Memory of Marie Duvall. Donated by Jacques Duvall.

I smiled to myself and thought such is compromise. I'm surprised I was actually able to get them to rename the colored school with only a phone call to the mayor earlier in the week.

. . . . .

Within two and a half weeks the books had been delivered, the bus delivered, the schoolrooms painted, and asphalt was being laid at the white school—just as Mother had promised. One week later Mother had the carpenters at work and the linoleum installed at the colored school. Moreover, Miss Virtue had already ordered new school texts and desks for her students when the truck was sent over to her school.

There was some grumbling in town about what the Negroes were getting but, by and large, the talk was about the white school—what it was getting and how the kids would benefit.

Mother's plan was laid out well, so almost nobody paid attention to two other projects. Two of our vacant houses in town had already been painted. For those who noticed, it was assumed Nora was going to a lot of extra expense just to please a tenant, or in this case, two tenants.

Though the townsfolk were mostly in awe of Mother's generosity, of course, there were a few critics, who were quickly marginalized by the city council and the newspaper.

Dad couldn't be happier. Mother had him working on multiple projects, including making shelves for the new—and only—town library. Not only had he lined up books that had been donated, bought cheaply at pawnshops and second-hand stores, and culled from the Memphis Library, but also he and some of his men were doing the carpentry for the bookshelves.

I dropped by to see his work in progress. Some of the men had already sawed a lot of shelves, which were neatly stacked to one side; most of them were already painted.

"When will you be done?"

"I'd say by next week—Wednesday."

"That soon, sir?"

"Min, that soon, if not a day earlier."

"Did you already get your mother's approval for Tom and his brother to drive the trucks over to Memphis and pick up the books?"

"Yes. Her only reservation is, of course, the timing—that nothing interfere with their responsibilities here."

Dad looked confident and said, "That won't be a problem. I've already got the books set aside. The people over there in Memphis are waiting for us to come and get them."

I could see Dad really felt good about being busy. He'd gotten the books for the library. He liked to work, using his hands, and having a crew. Between this smaller project and supervising the warehouse, which he'd begun weeks earlier, he saw progress. Dad was all about progress and getting things done. All that pent-up energy not only had an outlet for planning and buying equipment, but also for actual physical labor and supervising others in construction. Dad's engineering degree really paid off, whether building and running his own riverboats, or building and supervising these jobs in town.

"It really feels good, Min, to work and get results. I'd started to doubt if I'd ever have this kind of life again. Now, just look."

"Mother's real proud of you, Dad. You're a real team—you and Mother."

"Min," Dad said, looking me directly in the eyes, "You're part of the team. Never forget that!"

I nodded. I believed Dad. I still had my reservations about Mother. I'd been expendable once; I couldn't completely trust I wouldn't be again.

. . . . .

Dad was on schedule. He had everything in place, including the books on the shelves by Wednesday, which had allowed Mother to send out invitations for the opening.

"Not bad. Not bad at all," he said, his hands on his hips.

"Dad, it looks great! Has Mother seen it yet?"

"Nope. I thought I'd enjoy this moment before she does, since that critical eye of hers was always finding a flaw somewhere."

I didn't say a word, but I totally understood what Dad meant.

"Nora, as I understand it, said she'd tell the mayor late today."

"Really? Not even the town councilmen?"

"Nope. Your Mother wants him to put on a show."

"Won't the others' feathers get ruffled?"

"I'm sure he'll be made to understand it's just between her and him. So he'll keep his mouth shut. It's definitely in his own best interest to please your mother."

"I'm sure he will. I remember him from the school board meeting."

"Yeah, I heard about that from Nora. Seems there were a couple of feisty old hens there."

"Oh, there were, but they really didn't get me off course or, for that matter, even get my goat. I knew how to handle them and, I dare say, everyone else, including the mayor."

"Yeah. From what your mother said, 'He's a work in progress'."

"Mmm hmm."

"Tomorrow, she'll formally invite the mayor, town councilmen, clubs, school board members, the local and surrounding newspapers to the Saturday opening. Nora will formally deed the place over to the town the following Friday."

"Presto, the town's got a public library," I said.

"Presto, she's wrapping them right around her little finger."

I glanced at Dad and he winked back, holding up his little finger.

. . . . .

Saturday, the public library was christened and its doors opened. Of course, Mother made it an event to be remembered. There, inside the library, sat the dignitaries of the town—the mayor and city council, the sheriff, representatives of women's groups, ministers and a visiting priest. Everyone was there, including the editor and a writer from the local newspaper, along with newsmen from adjacent towns. A press release was sent to a Little Rock newspaper, which would be read by the governor and legislators.

Sitting there, I was amazed at the outpouring of sincere appreciation from the people. The mayor, God bless his soul, exceeded our expectation by his political performance. Nora Gibson, daughter of Charles Coymen, might as well have been eulogized as the Second Coming. Mother was satisfied; Dad pleased. I was impressed and glad so many had benefited from Mother's plan.

Even Miss Brown was there, who, I believe, both inspired and distracted the mayor from his official duties. His eyes glistened, his tongue waxed poetic, Southern oratory soared, his gaze flitted back and forth between the crowd and the slightly exposed cleavage of Miss Brown's ample bosom. This time, I knew she was very aware of what she was doing. She was fishing for a husband, and the fish was Mayor Church.

CHAPTER 16
THE CHURCH

Dad continued to work on multiple projects—the colored school, and now a church, all the while supervising the building of the warehouse which, hopefully, would be ready in late October or early November.

Having finished with the library, Dad worked on the second painted house. Mother's 'rental' showed bright and white. Dad had cut two new, smaller window openings at the end of what had been a living room and dining area. It wasn't until Thursday and Friday, two days before services, that he framed and installed the colored glass windows, then proudly attached the cross atop the pitched roof of the house. Just below the cross in an alcove, a carved, unpainted statue of the Virgin Mary was firmly attached, which would remain practically camouflaged until it was decorated.

Some of the townsfolk, if they'd noticed the work earlier, might have gotten suspicious when he brought in the pews and attached the folding kneels, but Dad, along with two local Catholic helpers, did the work. No one was the wiser that a Catholic church would soon be here.

With the installation of the new windows, seating, and an altar that had been erected on a raised platform, the local carver's wooden crucifix would be set in place. Small paintings of the Stations of the Cross were hung on the walls. Afterward the same carver's statue of Mary above the stairs was now carefully painted for all to see. The gold-plated chalice and other altar cups and pieces were to be kept at someone's home, since there was some apprehension about how some Protestants might react, especially Klansmen.

Early Saturday evening, the work was almost completed. Mother watched as the last of Station of the Cross was hung.

"No, no, no, it's crooked. Tilt it a little more to the right."

"Yes, ma'am."

"Didn't I tell you, Minnie? I'm just glad she was satisfied with all the other work we did. I did everything to make this place perfect."

"I can see that, Dad. And, it is perfect."

"That's just about . . . IT! Stop!" Now they're all hanging just right." Mother sighed, "Yes, just right."

A man had come in and cleared his voice, which got my attention. He was holding a package.

"Mr. Bordeaux, it's you," I almost whispered, already adjusting myself to the church setting. Please, come in." I motioned. "Mother, look who is here."

Turning around and grinning, Mother extended her hand, "Mr. Bordeaux, I think you've brought us a treasure."

The man smiled modestly and walked over to Mother, handing her the package.

Mother handed it to Dad and she unwrapped it, revealing a carved, wooden crucifix. Christ had been gilded with gold leaf, which mother had supplied to the carver.

"Ohhh, yes. What a beautiful work of art, sir. Please, you put it on the altar."

Once the cross was on the altar the building was now a church. Small statuary of Mary and Joseph were off to the side with *a prie-deux* set before each of them, where worshippers could kneel and say a special prayer. Ten votive candles inside red, glass cups waited to be lit at the feet of Mary and Joseph.

An hour later, many of the local Catholics began to trickle in, dip their fingers in the holy water and make the sign of the cross. A sense of awe radiated from their faces, as if their church were some great cathedral. We were, they knew, officially now a Mission Church, which would receive a visiting priest on Sundays. Tomorrow would be a big day: a beautifully robed priest and altar boys would come down the aisle behind another robed priest swinging smoking incense, the fragrance permeating the room. The mood would be set.

After the last person left that evening, Mother, Dad, and I sat in the first pew.

"Well, ol' gal, you got yourself a church," Dad said proudly.

"Indeed. It was about time."

"Huh?" reacted Dad.

"Oh, not you, James. I mean, it's about time the people in town had a church to worship in. You did a mighty fine and wonderful thing, James. Thank you, dear."

Dad and I were equally taken aback. Mother never addressed anyone but Jeanette by the term, "dear."

"So I'm now a 'dear'. Does that mean I need to start calling you 'sugar', 'honey', and 'dear'?"

"As you like, dear."

Mother was really showing her feelings, letting down her guard. I guess she didn't feel rushed, harried, or the need to be in charge. Maybe it had partly to do with the setting—being inside a church. Or, that she could take pride in doing something as special and meaningful as making a sanctuary available for the Catholics in town. Again, she'd been keenly perceptive—almost political—in making this a group project, so everyone could feel pride and accomplishment in the establishment of *their* church, St. Mary's.

Some parishioners contributed what little money they could; others labored to transform the dwelling into a church, which contributed to the morale of their Catholic neighbors. Mother admittedly bore the major expenses, deeding over the property, fixing it up, buying the colored glass for the windows, and the Stations of the Cross.

"We'll be coming to Mass tomorrow morning."

"Do I have to come, too?" questioned Dad, making a mock show of it for Mother.

"You, too, and don't be late," said Mother playfully.

As for me, while they talked and played around with each other, I sat there, soaking up the experience of being somewhere spiritual. I hadn't felt this way in ever so long. Maybe it had to do with being, in a sense, alone without all the other parishioners. Maybe it had to do with a sense of real accomplishment in a very special way. In any event, it really didn't matter. I was glad to be here and able to go within myself and feel something long absent.

. . . . .

After we left Mass, assembled on the street were two colored families, including Miss Virtue, waiting to attend their own separate service.

Mother explained to Dad she had had me contact the bishop in Little Rock. "Minnie, you tell James your own story."

"I called and spoke to the Bishop in Little Rock."

"And?" Mother urged.

"I told him we were building a church here, and asked him if the Church would provide the sacraments to coloreds. At first he seemed hesitant, then he told me it was all right with him. Ultimately, he said, it was the parishioners who were the real hurdle. Some churches allow it, while others refuse."

"How did you convince the parishioners, Minnie?"

"Oh, that was Mother's job."

"Nora, just how did you go about your magic?"

"Hmm, by a little of this and a little of that, and—if you must know—by mentioning the mission of the church."

"I didn't know that was part of the mission, Nora."

"Well it is, more or less," Mother equivocated. Shrugging her shoulders, she added, "At least as far as these people know."

"Nora," joshed Dad said in playful disapproval, "did you tell a fib?"

"Not really, James. The Bishop gave Minnie a pretty good idea what was what."

"Oh," said Dad, not completely satisfied by her explanation. The expression on his face said he remained somewhat unconvinced, knowing Mother as he did.

"The other part," lifting her eyebrows, "was getting the priest to do it. Actually, he was *a lot easier* than some of his flock."

"So much for the flock, my dear."

. . . . .

Sunday
August 14, 1932

Dear Journal,

Today was almost as special as yesterday evening in church. Or, it was just as special, yet in a different way. Every local Catholic in and around town must have shown up, along with some visitors from other towns, wanting to help celebrate the opening and consecration of the church.

Father Joseph, the priest, traveled from Wiener, which is located over an hour away. His enthusiasm inspired the parishioners. Everyone was happy yet solemn, as was befitting the Mass.

I took the sacrament, having confessed to Father Joseph earlier. This was the first time in years—since college—I had taken it. At some level I made my peace with the Church.

It was the first time I saw coloreds attend a Catholic church, that is, a church attended by whites. I really have to give Mother (and myself) credit for making that possible. I felt good that all Catholics now had a place to worship and to get the sacraments.

Mother had to do a little arm-twisting of parishioners, but it wasn't the threat of withholding money or her support that brought the holdouts over to her side. It was speaking to their pride as Southerners and Catholics. First, they would stand out favorably in the Bishop's eyes by joining other ministering parishes in the state to the coloreds. Secondly, and more significantly, she spoke to the strength of Holy Mother Church, and that they as Catholics were doing what Protestants failed to do in their mission to serve believers of all races. Mother could be brutal, but in this instance—for the most part, she was persuasive in getting what she wanted. Ultimately, I know no one wants to cross her.

By the time we had finished celebrating with food and drink at the nearest home, we were happy but exhausted. A sense of accomplishment filled all of us. Time to go home. Time to go home and sleep!

I almost forgot to mention, Mother moved into the William Parker Barnes' house in town. Once she saw the house, she decided it was a lot better than one of her rentals. With a high foundation, an enclosed, screened-in porch, it had been kept up immaculately. With hardwood floors, it had three bedrooms and a separate dining room with a fully equipped kitchen. We were all surprised at the house, since the Barnes's only had a hundred acres of farmland.

A couple of days later, a letter addressed to them arrived at the house. With no forwarding address, Mother opened it. The son, who was a doctor, wished them well on their vacation, and told them they'd have their own servant when they arrived at the family home in Atlanta. Life would be far better for them in Atlanta than it was here.

Dad got a good laugh out of that, saying that Mother wouldn't have to feel guilty putting out an old couple with nowhere to go. It was obvious they would be living better than we do. Mother smiled wanly, making me wonder if she'd felt any guilt whatsoever.

CHAPTER 17
COTTON, COTTON EVERYWHERE

The waves of heat rose from the ground, along with the humidity. Looking out over the fields before, behind and to my sides, the white cotton seemed to shimmer under the unrelenting rays of the noonday sun.

"My God, Ben, it's beautiful."

"It is, ma'am. Nothing like seeing it when it's spread out for miles."

He paused, seemingly trying to catch his breath in the scorching heat on a windless day that only made breathing more difficult. The stifling humidity had us both dripping sweat, our clothing clinging to us, much as if we'd climbed out of a warm bath. I felt like I was going to wilt.

"Well, your mama's got things goin' for sure. Look at the field hands coming from all directions, emptying their loads of cotton into the trailers. Everythang's goin' jus' fine."

I watched as the men—and boys—dragged their sacks behind them. A fit young man could pick a hundred pounds of cotton on a good day, working from first light until dusk.

"Yep, finally, I think we've got a good year. Now, if only the prices—"

"If only the prices are good," I continued.

I glanced over and watched some of the older boys tromping down a trailer full of picked cotton, making room for more after the sacks had been weighed and accounted for.

"Now that we've got them trucks—thar goes one, haulin' a loaded trailer off to the gin—everythang's movin' faster. It's kinda exciting, ma'am. This hyere mecha . . . ni . . . zation is puttin' this plantation ahead of all the rest. 'Course, it means . . . we won't need as much help later on."

I didn't say anything. I knew we needed fewer people this season—people who were out of work. Fortunately, Mother kept as many pickers in their homes as possible so we'd have enough of them, but also when the time came after the season for her to evict them, she would. At least they'd have money in their pockets.

"Look, Ben, over near the slough, there are the mules—just like in the old days; like it's always been."

"Yeah, they'll be the last to go—if ever. That's the richest land, but the worst 'cuz it usually floods. Living 'round it means snakes, mosquitoes, and all sorts of nasty critters everywhar. You might've noticed, ma'am, most of those sloughs have some water in 'em all year, even when it freezes."

"Just how many are on Mother's land?"

"Oh, it's kinda hard to tell at times, but at least six, I reckon."

"'Guess there'll be croppers or tenant farmers around for a long time, then."

"Yep, 'cuz a tractor don't work good the closer it gits to 'em. That's why we need the mules and all."

"What did Mother decide about these folks?"

"Well, looks like she'll keep a lot of the tenant farmers—at least, that's my understandin'."

"Why's that?"

"Oh, I guess, 'cuz they got their own mules and equipment. She don't have to bother with that stuff no more."

"That makes sense, but there's sure gonna be a lot of croppers evicted over the next few years," I said, with the slightest tinge of sadness to my words.

"Yep. Thar sure will be. Cain't be helped if you're gonna—as your mama says—'keep up with the times'."

"No, I guess, not."

"How many kids are there, Ben?"

"Hard to say. It varies, but with each family everyone works, 'cept the woman of the house, cooking and tending her vegetables, and her babies."

"And the babies?

"Ben got my meaning. "Oh, anywheres from five to ten, I reckon."

"Uh huh."

"Your mama's done a heap of good for those kids, though. As soon as the seasons over, they'll be in school, 'cuz of the new school bus and all."

What I didn't say, "the ones that are still here."

I looked out over the cotton, thinking how long this way of life's been going on and how much longer it would, even with the changes that would come. The land would stay the same. Just the people would change—in one way or another.

"You're right, Ben, Mother's done right by those children. A lot of 'em who never would see the inside of a schoolroom will now."

"That's right, ma'am. That's what I was tryin' to say. Progress, that's what it's called. Progress makes thangs better."

. . . . .

September 25, 1932

Dear Journal,

Mother and I fairly negotiated four hundred acres more of land from large landowners who needed cash. She had me negotiate them. With the first man, Mother was by my side. On the second occasion, I was on my own. By and large, she was satisfied with my performance. The third deal went well. Our new lawyer put the finishing touches to the Contracts of Sale. Afterward, I drove Mother to the County Courthouse to have the documents recorded. She wanted me to get the experience (for what that's worth!). As we walked away from the courthouse, Mother glowed. "That makes a total of 4,405 acres!" My own self-confidence has been increasing with every transaction and everything I've been doing to help run the plantation. I really feel good about this!

I only found out today that Mother had taken nearly half of Uncle Bob's money—what she had set aside for "administrative costs"—to fund her charitable projects for the town. However, she did make an exception to his "contributions." The exception was that he didn't have to pay for anything associated with the Catholic church in town, since he wasn't a Catholic. I felt her justification for the unknown use of his money very self-serving and unfair. Her reasoning was simple: "He benefits from them whether he knows it or not." What a stretch!

CHAPTER 18
BAD, BAD, BAD

"Yes, I understand," Mother said, hanging up the phone. I must have looked glum. I knew in my gut what the news was. By October 1ˢᵗ our cotton was baled, but it had nowhere to go.

"No matter where you turn, the brokers, the papers, all of them, the news is the same: cotton prices are down. We've got another bad . . . bad . . . bad year, Minnie."

Running her fingers through her hair, Mother said, gazing down at the books, "At least we know where we stand with our accounts here at the gin, and . . . it does help to have money in the bank; more than I can say for most of these people." Mother ran her hand over the ledger. "I can give them a little more credit, but eventually—"

Mother looked up and saw me staring at her. "You think I'm hard and unfeeling, don't you, Minnie?"

"I know we have to pay our bills or, ultimately, we don't eat."

Mother gazed at me, telling me she knew I had not answered her question directly. Instead, I'd given her the response that I understood her predicament. The issue of her feelings, well, they were *not* something I wanted to discuss. Instead, taking a deep breath I said, "At least the warehouse is finished."

"At least the warehouse is finished," Mother said, relieved. "We'll keep our own crop there—maybe Brother's, too. If I do, then I'm charging him half the cost of construction of the building and storage fees, which still leaves him with a $1000 in his account for "administrative fees". Though, there's no point in saying anything to him about that. He still benefits. Once we bring in Higgins', and Frank *the fireman's* crops, we'll store them in Higgin's barn—and the house if need be. I just wish he were here to see it," Mother said, laying her pen down on top of the desk and looking at me, the lids of her eyes slightly closing. Bringing her hands together, she folded them and laid them in front of herself. "So much for bad trash."

Mother pulled her hands apart and rubbed her thumbnail back and forth along the edge of her forefinger's nail, thinking. After a prolonged silence she said, almost cheerfully, "Let's talk about your little visit to the Jacksons."

CHAPTER 19
RETRIBUTION

A week later, I sat in the truck a little ways down the road and looked at the house. A wave of resentment and outright revulsion swept over me. The house was nice—very nice. A large two-storied house, it said money, success, and power in the Delta, where so many lived in downright poverty. Few of the towns boasted a home like this, let alone in the countryside. Only Grandpa's Big House surpassed it in beauty, grandeur and a true sense of Southern history, but the Big House had been destroyed, along with Marie, and one of the culprits lived in this house.

I got out of the truck—far enough away not to have drawn attention by the sound of my arrival, and gazed at this odious structure. The smell of wet leaves after last night's rain should have been clean and fresh, yet the smell that wafted over to me was one of decay and corruption. No one had bothered to sweep up the fallen leaves for some time. Even from this distance, I saw leaves on the porch were piling up into irregular bundles against the front wall of the house.

Walking toward the house, I could see it had not escaped the Great Flood. Unlike Grandpa's Big House on its hill, this had been built on flat land that stretched out as far as the eye could see, which meant the Flood of '27 had inundated this well-to-do home like it had the shacks of the poor. Even with effort, the high-water mark of the flood could not be concealed by the white paint. A dirty smudge of a line wrapped itself around the outside of the walls, indicating the water almost had reached the second story. The second floor survived, dry and out of reach of destruction. Unlike Uncle Bob's home, this house must have ceilings at least nine or ten feet high—just high enough to escape what had been the ten-foot deep water. Still it had, I figured, taken a lot of money for repairs. The Jacksons had to use a lot of money—more than likely cash—to repair the damage, along with the wreckage to the property generally, which would be one more reason for their lack of funds.

Then they resurrected themselves, as most moneyed persons can do, and the house stood there proud, powerful, and pleasing to the eye. It stood there to please the guest, to awe and dominate the poor by its very presence. Unlike the Big House that had been built in the antebellum style with columns that reached to the roof, this house had six modest-sized columns which supported the balcony above, overhanging a deep, shaded gallery—more in the Louisiana style—where the occupants and guests could lounge on hot summer days, sipping their drinks while watching the field hands at work, a blanket of white cotton spread out before them.

Rather than a once prosperous and imposing house, what I saw was the embodiment of evil and arrogance that lorded itself over the surrounding countryside with a group of people who'd known little want and much success and pleasure. That is, until the Great Depression engulfed them, too. That's why I was here. My job was to humble them; to send them fleeing like so many poor folks already on the roads headed North to the factories, or to California to pick crops. Yes, I was here to destroy them—their family—and bring justice for what they had done to everything and everyone I held dear. They had ruthlessly and callously robbed me.

. . . . .

"Minnie, where's your mother, Nora?"

"She sent me because she's busy."

"But there are important business matters I want to talk with her about."

"Oh, she knew that, but . . . but felt I could get the gist of things, and—if necessary—even make decisions for her."

"You!" said Mr. Jackson, a tall, fifty-something, heavyset man, whose vest was bulging from overeating or from too much drink. It wasn't hard for me to imagine him as a planter in the Old South with cane and whip, which he would use at the slightest provocation on *his* field hands and servants alike.

"You!" he said again, the volume of his voice increasing. I figured he was upset by my slow response.

Mother was right—not only was he insulted, but also he was furious—just the way she wanted him to be. He was definitely flabbergasted and off-balance. "Ready," as Mother said, "for the plucking." With her direction, I would not sign an agreement. I was to make preliminary notes and strike a tentative agreement, which she'd review. I was to find out what his situation was and test my negotiating skills, having had the benefit of watching her in action with Mr. Higgins and a few other farmers, not to mention the times when I was a child that I accompanied her to the pawnbroker. She would later confirm or deny the "agreement," based on her willingness to accept the terms. Sometimes she would back out, saying my daughter had no authority to negotiate on my behalf. Mother gave me specific instructions to show him the utmost respect.

"Sir, I think you'll find me most helpful. My mother can be a difficult person at times, not that I'm saying anything disrespectful toward my mother, since she knows— sometimes—she rubs people the wrong way."

"Sometimes—sometimes!" he fulminated, venting his spleen.

"Jefferson, I declare," said a soft but determined voice, "we have a guest here. What did you say your name is?"

"Minnie, ma'am." I did not tell her my last name, which would have required an explanation for Mother and me having different surnames, acknowledging that Mother had been divorced—if she didn't already know that.

"And you're Nora Belle's daughter, is that right, honey?"

"Yes, ma'am."

"Well, I'm Loretta Bingham Jackson. My people are South Carolinians."

I knew what that meant from what Great-Grandma Keghel had said about those Southerners before the war, who looked down on people not from the East.

"We're dyed-in-the-wool Charlestonians—for better or worse."

She definitely had put me on notice as to her pedigree. I believe Mother called that one-upmanship, titling the balance of power in her favor.

"Jefferson, I declare," and she all but shoved her husband to the side, taking me aback by her almost brutal display of power. "We have a guest, so mind your manners," she said, half—only half—joking. "Come right on in, honey," she cooed, taking me by the hand into the house. Her hands were smooth and soft—soft like a woman of leisure.

This was going to be a lot more difficult than either Mother or I realized. I felt the undercurrents and tension between them, as well as the hostility toward me that had been shown openly by the husband, yet covered up by the wife, whose genteel mannerism concealed a first-class manipulator and a woman of no uncertain power.

"Let's go into the parlor and get comfortable. Tilly!" she commanded, raising her voice loudly, "get on out here! You hear me, girl?" Seeing my reaction to her words and the tone of her voice, she changed ever so quickly once Tilly appeared. "Tilly, we have a guest. Would you bring sweet tea for all of us?" she said as the well-bred hostess, but with the firmness of the woman of the house with her servant, which obviously caught the cook by surprise. Tilly had been yelled at often.

"Yes, ma'am."

I saw Tilly glance at me. What I smelled was fear. I felt doubly on guard now and took a sidelong look at Mr. Jackson, whose eyes still blazed and whose mouth was turned down. He could barely stand to look at me, let alone have me in his house. His scowl was that of the main character right out of the book *Wuthering Heights*, which I had finished reading.

Once we entered the parlor and had taken seats, Mrs. Jackson continued to speak in the most general of terms. "Oh, I declare this heat is unseasonably warm, and here it is already the first of October. Don't you think so, dear?"

"Yes, Mrs. Jackson, I do." I would keep this as formal as possible, which would be a constant reminder to me that I was here on business.

"Oh, I do worry about our children."

"I beg your pardon, Mrs. Jackson?"

"Well, all three have decided to spend the holidays in Charleston with family, once they are out of school for the season. Jefferson Junior and Walt study at Duke University in North Carolina, while our dear, little Samantha (she's only 13) is enrolled in a girls' academy in Charleston."

They were all getting good, expensive educations—at least for the time being. I can't say I felt any compassion for the boys, but I felt something akin to sympathy for their daughter, who, when I heard her age, reminded me of my age when I was yanked out of boarding school and left to fend for myself. Somehow, I doubted she'd have to fend for herself, yet I knew her life was going to change. Suddenly I was brought back to the purpose of my visit.

"Mother told me once I got here to get to the point and find out the nature of our business, since she doesn't like wasting time."

I could see they were both absolutely stunned at first. Then they both flushed with anger.

"What—what did you say, young lady?"

"Oh, excuse me, these aren't my words, ma'am, but Mother's. She gets impatient with me if I take too long with anything—anything at all."

"I can sympathize for you, honey. You must be under a lot of pressure, having such a demanding mother," said Mrs. Jackson, with no hint of caring in her voice.

Suddenly, Mr. Jackson cut in and said brusquely, "Tell your mother—"

"Tell your mother," rushed in Mrs. Jackson, rescuing her husband from a likely obscenity, "we'd like to make a business arrangement."

I could see Mr. Jackson was stewing, which Mother hoped would happen once I was so direct. It was all he could do to restrain himself from exploding. Was I frightened? No—not in the least! I had been prepared ahead of time by Mother to expect this. My Derringer was in my purse.

"What kind of business arrangement?" I said politely. I took my pad and pen out of my purse.

"We," said Mrs. Jackson, "want to . . . to take a loan out with Nora."

"Oh," I said, "as Mother told Mr. Higgins and repeatedly told others looking for loan money, 'we're land rich, but cash poor.' However, possibly Dad might be able to help, since he has a small savings. How much do you want?"

"Around $5,000 dollars, dear."

"Why so much?"

"Well . . . well—"

They were both at a loss for words because of my bluntness. Now I did what Mother told me to do when negotiations got to this point. "Does it have to do with your mortgages?"

"Yes, dammit, it does, girl," growled Mr. Jackson.

"And the back taxes on your land? I've got the numbers from County Records. You have defaulted $700 on your drainage taxes," I paused for effect, "and on your road and school taxes."

"Why, you—"

"Jefferson, shut up!" Mrs. Jackson snapped.

"Mother said your mortgages are due shortly, but she can only pay off the $2,000 mortgage on your original holdings—the 2,000 acres and the house. In addition, she wants to give you a cash payment of $1,000, which includes the taxes."

They sat there, speechless.

I looked around the room—as Mother advised me to—at the décor, appraising their well-furnished and comfortable surroundings. Obviously, as one of the major landowners in the county, they spared no money in creating a home that would be the envy of most people in the Delta.

"Unfortunately," I said most respectfully, "she cannot afford to pay off the mortgage on the additional thousand acres you bought in early 1929 at the top of the market." I shook my head, saying forlornly, "No, that will have to go into foreclosure."

Now they looked at me in disbelief, as if a freight train were heading at them while they were stuck on the tracks in their car.

"Mother also wants to do as right by you as she can, and give you another choice. If you choose to keep your house, she'll deed it over, along with two acres for $200. This will include one of your barns and *most* of your vegetable garden. To make sure you have a source of income, she wants to provide you with 100 acres to sharecrop."

"Nora," stuttered Mr. Jackson, "is *offering* us to live in this house, and . . . and she wants us to be sharecroppers on a hundred acres of *her* land—the land that had been *ours?* Did I hear you right?" demanded Mr. Jackson, in a voice that dropped to a low, menacing quiver that barely constrained his outrage.

"Almost. Let me look at my notes." I turned back a couple of pages which I already knew by heart, then looked up and blinked, saying, "Mother also said since you already have a lot of equipment and people who live on this land, she could pay you to be some sort of helper—kinda like a riding boss."

Both of them glared at me with an intensity of unwavering hate.

"A . . . helper?" he shouted.

"Oh, she said, because of your age, you wouldn't have to ride a horse. You use one of our trucks?"

I looked up and saw his body was shaking, not from fear but with rage.

"Lastly," This was the *coup de grace*, as Mother called it, "by the way, how many trucks do you have?"

"Four," said Mrs. Jackson dully.

"Chevrolets or Fords?"

"Fords."

"Oh—"

Tom, who had worked for the Jacksons, had already given us all the facts days earlier. They spent thousands of their cash and mortgage money for new trucks and tractors, thinking they'd mechanize and the downturn in the market wouldn't last long. They got a deal on them in the first quarter of 1930. Then came the drought the next year. Of course, the Depression only got worse. Moreover, they had to take out another mortgage on their new property with a due date of January 1933—just like the first mortgage. They had taken that one out—like so many other farmers—just to cover living and operating expenses, and loan payments, having completely exhausted their capital.

"So what's wrong with Fords?" said Mr. Jackson defensively.

"They're cheap. Mother likes Chevrolets."

Both Mr. and Mrs. Jackson's mouths dropped open.

While they were still in shock, I asked, clipping my words, "And the tractors, that's right. I was told not to forget the tractors. How many do you have?"

"Seven," replied Mr. Jackson.

"Seven," parroted Mrs. Jackson, looking confused.

"Did you pay cash for these?"

"Yes. Same as on the trucks."

"I see, so *they are used*, but . . . they're still . . . relatively new, so they've got some value left in them. She'll give you $100.00 each."

At that, Mr. Jackson started to rise, but his wife said wearily yet still in a commanding voice, "Jefferson, *sit down!*"

"Mother said I could make a tentative offer to you, meaning, that is, *if* we can spare the cash."

"If you can? You—"

"Mr. Jackson," I said, interrupting him, "Mother talked to the cotton brokers this past week, as well as this morning. I was there only hours ago. You must know," I said with a furrowed brow to convey my distress at the news, and a sense of urgency in my voice to tell him how dire our situation was, "that the prices are stagnant. We'll have to plow our crop under. Everyone will. The market is dead." I let my voice trail off on an even more depressing note: Dead. "Dead as a doornail."

They knew I was right. Husband and wife looked at each other. There was no more fight left in them. It reminded me of the Higgins' that night when Mother finally cornered them and went in for the kill. There was no more room to maneuver.

Now I came in with the "irresistible offer." Peering down at my notes, I added up the numbers. "Based on her first offer, she'll pay off the mortgage of $2,000.00 and the various taxes on your original land holdings of 2,000 thousand acres which, like I said, will not include the mortgage on your newly acquired land. Additionally," I said, matter-of-factly, "Mother will pay you $1,000.00 cash for the land and house, and $100.00 each for your tractors and trucks and . . . let me see here . . . and $200.00 for the rest of the equipment."

They sat there like figurines on a shelf. I looked over at them, seeing they appeared unable to comprehend what was being said and what was happening to them.

"That comes to—" I said, figuring out the costs, ". . . to roughly $2,300.00. Of course, you already understand if you decide to stay and become a sharecropper, adjustments will be made to compensate for that. As a sharecropper, you know, this deal is dependent upon us taking the equipment. Therefore, less the house, and maybe one truck, you'll get about $1,900.00."

I didn't hear any dissent from them. Then came the words from Mrs. Jackson, "We'll not be sharecroppers. Nooo, Never."

"In that case, then, I'll tell Mother your decision. She knows how disappointed you must be, but under the circumstances since hardly anyone has money, it's all she can afford. She told me to tell you if you choose to go to California, she might—just might—be able to convince Dad to give you an extra $75.

Mr. and Mrs. Jackson's eyes met and they nodded a brief consent to one another. Turning their eyes on me, husband and wife nodded. The deal was done.

Again, I was reminded of the Higgins'. How similar the end was for both the Jacksons' and the Higgins'. It was just a matter of getting there.

. . . . .

When I returned to the gin and sat in Mother's office, she said, simply, "Well?"

I showed her my notes, and explained what happened. I told her in detail—every last fact about the Jacksons, their house, the equipment and the agreement. I left out nothing, including their final decision.

"You got the land, the house, and all of the equipment," Mother said, appraising the deal. "That means we will spend a lot less of our money for new tractors, trucks and equipment." Mother slightly smiled. "You saved us over $5,000." She paused. "That money includes the trucks and the tractors and the equipment."

"Except for two trucks, which they're keeping."

Mother looked at me, barely concealing her pleasure, saying, "Even so, you were less charitable than I would have been." Now rubbing her fingers together for some seconds, she finally shook her head, fully taking my measure, thinking aloud, *"a lot less charitable."*

I all but spit out the names, contemptuously, "Higgins and Jackson—those murdering thieves expected to steal all of Grandpa's cash and humiliate us."

"Don't forget the lawyer and the banker, Minnie."

"Yes, they were all in on it. They'd divide up the money among themselves and then pick us off, forcing us to sell the plantation."

"That's right, Daughter, that's right." Mother sat there, looking at me, and took a deep breath. "No, not a thimble full of charity in you for the Jacksons."

I shook my head slowly. "No, not a drop!"

. . . . .

Uncle Bob, Dora, and their sons didn't wait for Jefferson Jackson and his wife, Linda, to close his front door. Walking right past him, they rushed into *their* new home, while the rest of the Jackson family waited in a caravan—a car, and two trucks, pulling trailers behind them. Whatever they couldn't carry, they had burned.

"The key is in the door, along with the spares on a ring." Jackson held out his hand for the gas money."

Mother went to hand him the money when I nudged her. "I'll check to see if they work." I wanted to make sure the key hadn't been driven into the lock."

"After pulling it out and reinserting it, I said, "It's good."

Mother hadn't thought about that. When I caught her eye she smiled at me and her thoughts all but gushed: *"Clever Girl."*

"And your gas money, Mr. Jackson." Mother neither smiled nor frowned. She handed him the money, adding, "I got James to give you an extra $15 for your trucks."

"You damn—"

"Jefferson," Linda hissed, "just get in that car! As for you Nora, you ought to teach that daughter of yours some manners. She's severely lacking in a good upbringing."

"Minnie, remind me of that when we get back to the gin."

Linda, recognizing a first rate manipulator, pivoted and mustered every ounce of what it meant to be a dignified well-bred Southern lady. They walked off with her arm inside her husband's across the porch as if she were going to a coronation.

"Y'all have a safe trip," Mother called, adding insult to injury.

Mr. Jackson jerked as if he'd been slapped, and started to turn when his wife's stern voice, commanded, "Jefferson—Jefferson don't give her the satisfaction." And they went to their car and drove off.

Mother opened her purse, pulled out her pad. I watched her cross off the name Jefferson Jackson. Sliding it back into her purse, she said, "Let's go." And started to walk to the truck.

I called out, "No, Mother, we earned this in more ways than one. I want to see this place." And I went through the front door.

"Uncle Bob, how're y'all doin' in your New House!?"

. . . . .

Sunday Morning
October 15, 1932

Dear Journal,

I drove Mother out to the Jackson place. Unlike the Higgins', they set out for South Carolina, where his wife has family. All this happened while Uncle Bob and his family moved into the house that same day, Mother having traded him the *house, a small barn, five acres and $1,000 cash in exchange for the gin and the hill where the Big House had stood. You'd think they'd inherited a palace, they were so happy. Tom brought his brother, Timothy, to look over our land and assume the position of riding boss—even though he was only twenty years old. Tom would keep a close eye on the operation. All this caused a dust-up with Brother's sons, who expected to take over the entire operation. Again, Mother had a hand in convincing her brother to cooperate with Timothy. Against this backdrop, I watched as Mother's list gets smaller. She mused whether it would be the banker, Norris, or the lawyer, Poindexter, who'd be next to go. Finally, we agreed that most likely it'd be the banker, since the Memphis bank had opened its branch two doors down from him. Yesterday Mother closed her account at Bailey Norris' bank and opened another with his competitor. Mrs. Katie Johnson almost tripped over Mother as she rushed through the doors on the bank's opening. Others quickly followed. The stampede was on.*

Mother's plantation now includes more than 6,800 acres, 400 additional acres having been bought earlier from three small farmers. Only one man had been difficult. Mother watched me negotiate that sale, which assured her I could handle Jackson.

The plantation was now almost triple the size of Uncle Bob's. We heard through the grapevine that the size of Mother's holdings rankled some of his sons, especially the "fault-finder." Mother was unfazed, saying, "They had their chance. They chose cars, booze, and women—just like I told you they would." Only Will and Ellen were genuinely praising Mother's efforts and, from what I surmised, they'd make a concerted effort to influence Uncle Bob to conserve, to mechanize and to acquire more land.

CHAPTER 20
THE BANKER

The last week in November was cold, wet, then icy. Sleet sliced through the evergreens and bushes like sharp little razor blades. No one went out that Saturday unless they had to.

I had to. It was Saturday and a day of work at the gin. Mother and I were doing paperwork and answering the few calls that came through, when suddenly we heard noise outside the door to the office.

First came the sound of heavy footfalls, followed by Al's plaintive voice, "Nora." Next came the knock on her door.

"C'mon in, Al."

He rushed into the warm office. (Mother had a small electric heater, while the rest of the gin was unheated.) Al's cheeks were red from the cold and a long history of heavy drinking. His breathing was labored, making it hard for him to get his words out. "Norris . . . Norris the banker, he's dead."

"How?" asked Mother, slowly and dryly.

"Hung, ma'am. Hung!"

"You don't say."

"I do, ma'am. It's kinda crazy. Who'd 've thought?"

"Yes, who'd 've thought," parroted Mother.

"Thar he was in the back of his own house, hangin' from a tree."

"What kinda tree, Al?"

"What kinda tree, ma'am?" Al repeated, amazed Mother would ask him a detail like that. "I dunno. An elm tree, I reckon. I don't rightly recollect. But there he was, stiff as a board, ice hanging off him. Looked kinda gruesome, if you ask me."

"So you saw him."

"I sure 'nough did, ma'am."

"His wife let out a scream early this morning, and I jus' happened to be comin' outta my house. I, along with my neighbor, Jones, came runnin'. Got over thar, 'n she showed us. So Jones got on the phone and called the sheriff, who told 'im not to cut the rope or do anythang. Well, it war too late, 'cuz the only Christian thang to do was to cut 'im down."

"You did the right thing, Al. The right thing." Mother's voice was flat and without emotion.

"Thank you, ma'am, but the sheriff he don't agree with you. Said it was a crime scene 'til proved otherwise."

"Oh, I think he does go on. Don't you, Minnie?"

I nodded my head in agreement. "He does."

"Well, Al, it's decided. There're two of us who think jus' like you do."

"Awww shucks, ma'am. The sheriff seemed mighty mad at the time, but as soon as we were walkin' away, he put his arm 'round my shoulder and said, "Let's go get us a hot cup of coffee. I'm cold as hell.""

"So what'd y'all talk about?"

"Nothin' much. Mostly the weather. Then we skedaddled over to Smith's to drink some more coffee and jaw with the rest of the folks. Funny, nobody seemed much interested in the hangin'."

"'Except his wife, Al."

"Yeah, Miss Nora, 'cept the wife."

"Pity," said Mother.

"Huh?"

"I said it's a pity."

"I reckon so, ma'am. Well, I gotta tie up some of that burlap before my hands git any colder."

"Al, jus' go on home. It's too cold to do anything worthwhile. Jus' go."

"All right, Miss Nora, if you say so."

"I do say so."

"I appreciate that, ma'am."

Al walked out of the room.

"Minnie, go over and close that door tight. The cold air's getting in here."

Coming back to take my seat, I said, "The banker—"

"Minnie, nobody likes a banker."

. . . . .

November 26, 1932
Saturday

Dear Journal,

The banker, Bailey Norris, hanged himself. Surprisingly, he didn't die by gunshot. Mother did say once the new bank was in town and he lost her account, along with a lot of others, his time was limited. He'd have to call in some of his overdue loans and mortgages. I got the impression from her that somebody would shoot him. What seems strange to me is Norris didn't seem like the type who had the courage to commit suicide. I remember hearing that when some of the banks closed, Grandpa showed up and demanded his money. Norris didn't quibble and gave Grandpa his money. He knew Grandpa was ready to shoot him. I guess the banker had enough because he opened his doors a couple of weeks later.

Anyway, thinking back on Mother's response this morning, "Nobody likes a banker," something didn't seem right. Why would he go out in sleet and ice and hang himself in his backyard? If he actually got up the gumption to kill himself, he certainly wouldn't have done it like that.

Also, the sheriff's response to Al upsetting a crime scene was simply, "Let's go get a hot cup of coffee." It sure seems like this is over and done with, as far as the sheriff is concerned.

Mother got the banker. I wonder how long before she gets the lawyer?

CHAPTER 21

GIFT FROM A GOSSIP

Mother signed another check to creditors, shaking her head. I knew she was watching the money go out, with little— other than rents on houses—coming in. Oftentimes, even rent monies didn't always come when they were due, if they came in at all. I sat there, entering the amounts of bills on one ledger, then stood up and filed them in one of the drawers. Suddenly I heard Mother say, "Minnie, I want to talk to you—about something."

I stopped what I was doing and sat down next to her— where the heat was.

"You remember what I said?"

I gazed at Mother, who lifted her head and our eyes met.

"I said things are brewin'. James has been talking to me about things. As you know, Minnie, he reads newspapers—one all the way from New York City that comes to the house once a month, and magazines—business ones. My point is James, as I've always said, is an educated man and follows what's happening in the country."

"I know," I responded, "sometimes, after dinner or on Sundays, he'll ask me to read an article and want to discuss it with him. It's hard for me to understand a lot of it, but he'll explain it."

"That's good. I don't have the time for reading anything, but he does talk to me. Says things are getting really shaky all over the country, but he's warned me they're particularly bad in the Delta."

"That's what I've heard from Dad, too."

"Well, I don't much pay attention to politics other than in Arkansas, but I am a Democrat. I suppose you know James is a Republican—a dyed-in-the-wool Republican. Used to, when he wanted to get my goat, say he voted the party of Lincoln—the man who freed the slaves. Once I caught on, he couldn't get a rise out of me, so that was that. Of course, I knew slavery was wrong, but that Northern attitude of self-righteousness and superiority galled me and still does."

In a huff Mother stepped out of the office. Moments later, the telephone rang. Seemed strange to hear it ring this time of year in the office, but I picked it up.

"Speaking."

"Well, hello, Mrs. Johnson

"Well, Minnie, I didn't know if I'd be seein' you and your Mother, so I wanted to wish y'all a Merry Christmas and a Happy New Year, even if it's the first week in December."

"Oh, Mrs. Johnson, what a kindness. You're always so thoughtful," I said insincerely.

There was a moment of silence, I suspected, because what I'd said totally caught her off guard. I had never gushed at her like this before.

"Well," she stammered, "if it weren't for you and your mother, honey, me and my boy wouldn't be celebrating the holidays in *our own home!!* I—I mean we," now she was regaining her composure and—with it—her pomposity, "we just cain't thank y'all enough. You're jus' so generous to us."

"We try, Mrs. Johnson. It's the little things that count—standin' by your friends when they need you most."

"Oh, Minnie, you dear, sweet, sweet girl."

Mother came into the room. "It's for you, Mother Hold on, *Mrs. Johnson,* Mother just came in and I know she'll want to speak with you."

Making a face, Mother grimaced. Then, she motioned for me to get close. She wasn't letting me get off the hook, so to speak. She held the telephone receiver between us, so that I would hear the conversation. I had no idea Mother could be so catty. She also was being playful, enjoying getting even with me. *This was a first,* I thought.

"I called to wish you a Merry Christmas, and to thank you for all you've done for us, Nora."

Now, I was the one to make the face. The woman was being true to form: she'd called Mother, not me. At least, I had learned a thing or two from Mother about how to be insincere when it suited the occasion. In this case, it was one phony talking to another one. Somehow, I didn't like it and won't do it again.

"Well, do I have somethin' to *tell* you!! I just heard it from Dotty."

"I'm on pins and needles, honey."

"Well, you know that ol' lawyer—the one nobody likes no more."

"You mean—"

"I do indeed, Nora. Imagine this! According to Dotty, she just happened to be comin' down Main Street and there the man was, takin' down his sign. All his furniture had been moved outta his house. He managed to get his desk and other thangs onto the back of the trailer, and he put up a sign, "Closed.""

"Really?"

"Really, Nora. I declare! Well, it was 'bout time someone like 'im left our good town. He just wasn't fit to be around good Christian folk, especially when—"

Now Katie Johnson's venomous tongue had gotten ahead of common sense. When she sensed the empty silence on the other end of the line meant Nora wasn't particularly happy with where her gossip was going, she changed course, and abruptly said, "Well, honey, I jus' had to wish you and that darlin' daughter of yours all the good tidings for a Very, Very Happy New Year."

Mother looked at me; she was bored yet elated. Bored now with Katie, elated with the news. "Well, Katie, you and your son have a lovely Christmas and Happy New Year. You'll never be far from our thoughts."

I realized Mother had not said, "far from our *hearts*."

"Oh, thank you, Nora. What a joy you are to us all, dear."

"Bye-bye, Katie."

"Bye, sweets."

Mother put the receiver down and thought for a moment. Then Mother opened her purse. She pulled out a pencil and the familiar-looking pad. "If ever there was a better Christmas gift—"

I watched her as she slowly scratched the name of "Poindexter" from her list.

"Well! That does feel better. This holiday season is certainly headed in the right direction!"

I smiled. "It is for a fact!"

CHAPTER 22
SOMETHING THAT MATTERS

On December 10th, Saturday morning was absolutely frigid, but without the rain, sleet and ice of the preceding weeks. The robin's egg blue sky was crystal clear, though this beauty and windless day were lost to us in the office at the gin. Mother's heater was on and we were going over the expenses for the year, as well as the income. Everything was being cross-checked twice. Mother was satisfied the ledgers were correct.

Just as we were ready to leave, there was the sound of someone outside shuffling toward our door. Startled, Mother immediately pulled open the top drawer and grabbed her gun. Simultaneously, she motioned for me to take a defensive position behind the door. By the time the person reached the door, I watched as Mother held the gun in her hand, pointed directly ahead, waiting.

Then came the knock—short little raps, one after the other.

"Mrs. Gibson, it's Norma May Polk—one of your tenants."

Mother shook her head, indicating to me she was at a loss. She didn't know who this Polk woman was. With her gun she motioned to me to stay put, but she lowered her arm, still holding the gun beside her.

"C'mon in."

149

Slowly the door opened. A bedraggled woman in a man's patched and ragged coat that reached down almost to her ankles came into the room. Rubbing her reddened hands together, she said somewhat humbly, "Ma'am, you probably don't know me. My children and I are sharecroppers who work about forty acres of your land. It used to belong to the sheriff."

"I see—"

Mother and I both looked at each other, surprised by the state of this woman who didn't speak country. Instead, she appeared to be a well-educated lady, who had an accent from another state farther east.

"This is my daughter, Minnie," said Mother, motioning at me standing behind the opened door with my back against the wall. I still held a gun in my hand.

"Nice to meet you, Minnie."

I put the gun inside my purse and extended my hand. "I'm glad to meet you, too, ma'am."

I saw the shocked expression on her face when I called her "ma'am." Obviously, she hadn't expected to receive that kind of recognition.

"Come right over here and sit next to the heater."

"Oh, I couldn't do that. I'm sure your daughter—"

"No, no, sit right down," Mother said emphatically.

Cautiously, Mrs. Polk went over and looking at me for approval, she waited. When I smiled, she sat down and couldn't help herself, extending her red and roughened hands near the heater. Closing her eyes for a moment, she seemed to be soaking up the heat as one would in a hot bath.

"How can I help you?" said Mother solicitously. I could see Mother had taken an interest already in this woman, who would come out on such a cold day to the gin, hoping to talk with her.

"Well, Mrs. Gibson, I didn't come to ask you for anything, which must be a relief to you since you probably have so many who come to you asking for your help."

Mother and I were surprised. Mrs. Polk had more or less spoken to what our thoughts were about her visit. Uncharitably, we determined she needed something.

"I wanted to thank you, ma'am; truly thank you from the bottom of my heart."

"For . . . for what?"

"Well, now my children have a chance—a chance for an education."

"I don't believe I understand," said Mother, honestly confused at this moment.

Seeing Mother's confusion, she turned to me. "Ma'am, you must appreciate what I mean, since it is obvious just looking at you, that you've had a good education. You must know how important that is."

"Well, I do," I said hesitantly, realizing she'd misjudged me for having a better education than I did. "But my mother has a better education than I."

Surprisingly, Mother responded, "I've not been to college like you, Daughter."

I nodded, appreciating Mother's recognition.

Turning her gaze to Mother, she added, "So, Mrs. Gibson, you have no idea what it means now that there's a school bus. Now my children can get to school, and there are *new* books! True, the other children laugh at them because they're poor, but I tell them they won't always be if they study hard. They will make it and get ahead. That's why I work my fingers to the bone. Of course, they have to help out, or—"

No more needed to be said by her about that—Mother and I both understood her meaning. I, and I suspect Mother, felt sincerely for her plight, for her courage, gumption and maybe, more importantly, for her desire to tell us her appreciation for us.

"Mrs. Polk," Mother said, measuring her words, "where do you come from?"

"From Virginia, ma'am. Richmond, to be exact."

"From Virginia, you say. Who are your people?"

There was a slight smile that crossed her lips. She knew what Mother was getting at. "We're related to the Lees."

"Robert E. Lee?" said Mother.

"Yes, ma'am."

"I could see you are different."

"Yes, I did get a fine education. I married early and we came west, to another county here in the Delta. My husband quickly took sick. We had used up all of our savings when we heard the sheriff needed sharecroppers. He was kind enough to let us work a piece of his land. Unfortunately, my husband, who was a teacher, was already too sick to do much. After a year, he passed away. However, at least we have a home. I'm grateful for that."

"I can see you are." Mother rubbed her fingers together, thinking. "Your husband was a teacher, and you have a good education. Do I understand you correctly?"

"Yes—"

"I have a vacant house here in town and the school needs another teacher. Do you per chance speak French?"

"I do."

"And you know your history and such?"

"I do, ma'am." For the first time, Mrs. Polk's face brightened.

"Well, I'd like to propose you take that teaching position and move into town."

"But I don't have a teaching certificate."

"Oh hell," said Mother, "we'll get you in as a substitute teacher and find a way to get you your certificate. I'm sure that can be arranged."

I was shocked by Mother's honest generosity and caring for this, heretofore, unknown woman. Mrs. Polk was speechless. Finally, she uttered, "Do you think it's possible, ma'am?"

"I not only *know* it's possible, I *know* they'll hire you. Minnie, what do you think?"

"You're right, Mother." I thought for a second, weighing and balancing the pros and cons of saying anything more. Mother never liked someone who was wordy or took up unnecessary time. She did like, though, agreement—when she was told she was right. "As you said, Mother, Mrs. Polk has all the right qualifications. She'll be an asset."

"Yes, that's the right word—an asset. People understand assets and liabilities. Thank you, Minnie."

For the second time, I appreciated Mother's recognition and, now, her compliment. How truly, truly few of them had I ever received from her.

"Well, Mrs. Polk, now that it is settled, Minnie would you carry her home in the truck.?"

· · · · ·

"May I call you Minnie?"

"Yes, ma'am, I'd like that."

"I would like to invite you into the house, but we have no heat and—"

"I understand."

I really did. The house was a typical tenant farmer's dwelling, except it was even worse than most. The chimney had collapsed and, worse yet, no attempt had been made to repair it in a long time, leafless vegetation nearly covered the pile of bricks. What appeared to be the beginnings of a young sapling also had pushed up from the ground below the bricks.

I had no idea how they were able to stay warm, other than lighting the wood burning stove. The flue had an outlet where the kitchen should be, but no smoke trailed out from the opening. The penetrating cold brought my gaze to the long icicles hanging from the roof, the hand railings up the stairs, and the barren trees that sparkled in the light of the winter sun. Though nature might seem beautiful at first, the reality of frozen puddles of water around the dilapidated hovel cried out desperation and starvation within for a mother and her children.

I was angry. This kind of abuse and lack of caring by the sheriff was callous and scandalous. It was obvious that he wanted to punish her. Why? Possibly, since I observed Mrs. Polk was a relatively attractive woman in her late thirties the sheriff probably had been rebuffed by her once her husband died. His neglect of her and her family was his way of showing his superiority and power over this "uppity" woman from the east. All he had to do was wait. Eventually, she'd be forced to come around.

I gazed at the "house," and noticed the porch was sagging. On closer inspection, the unpainted structure was built in the typical fashion of three rooms, one right behind the other. At that, it was even smaller than most. The only ventilation came from the door and one small window in each room.

"If things were different, like I said, I'd invite you in, though what we have is meager. As my parents, God rest their souls, always said, 'share' and 'be grateful for what you have'. I've never forgotten that, even though today isn't the right day to ask you in."

"Believe me, I understand. My family and I have known hard times."

Mrs. Polk seemed stunned by the news. Then she nodded her head, suggesting she understood things deeper than mere words could convey. She had not turned her head away until now, and looked me directly in the eye. "Thank you, Minnie, for telling me that. I want you to know, whatever you or your mother say to me, stays with me." Mrs. Polk paused. More than likely sensing my feelings, she said earnestly, "Your mother and you will have a good ally in me. I will be forever in your debt."

I felt in the deepening silence of this short time, she was someone of substance and integrity—someone to be trusted. She was sincere.

"Thank you for carrying me home, Minnie. It's much appreciated."

"You're welcome, ma'am. See you soon."

And I meant that.

She opened the door to the truck, closed it tightly, and ran quickly to her house. I could only imagine what it was like for her children, waiting in the cold for their mother.

As I backed out along the dirt road that was more a path than a road, I came back to the one-lane asphalt. The drive back to the gin gave me time to think.

Mulling over the last couple of hours, suddenly the word "ally," said to me by Mrs. Polk, triggered something within me. One single word acted like a lightning bolt that illuminates a nighttime landscape, or a kaleidoscope where the pieces of colored glasses fall into a pattern.

Allies, yes. Mother was creating alliances. It was all a big puzzle where pieces—in this case, people—had to be placed and positioned in this small town for the maximum gain on her investment (money) and the security of her inheritance (the farmland and the gin). It most decidedly had to do with personal safety, too.

All the players—allies—were there. Each person in one way or another had been rewarded, whether individually or together, as members of the town. Mother used the schools, the school board, Mayor Church, the newspaper, the sheriff, and so many others in many different ways—from employment to largess. This even included my contacts with the colored people in town and all the information that came by way of me to her, for example, Mr. Jackson having been in need of money.

I wondered, since I was included in her dealings, was there a design for me to learn from her, or—more than likely since we were not close—was I simply useful and cheap? She didn't have to pay me a cent. I decided I would give Mother the benefit of the doubt, which meant, in my case, to realize Mother's intentions toward me largely depended on time and circumstances. It was as simple as that—I didn't know what Mother's true motivations were toward me.

. . . . .

After lunch, I drove over to the little general store. "Mr. Solomon, maybe you remember me from the school board meeting?"

"Oh yes, I do. Your mother was so generous."

"Well, you may not know it, but a Mrs. Polk is being considered for a teaching position as a substitute and as a part-time teacher."

"Yes, I had a call from the mayor at noon that we're to interview her tomorrow at your mother's request."

"Well, Mother asked me to bring you this check and to let her and her children draw upon it for clothing and shoes."

After discussing Mrs. Polk's situation with Mother, she had me take her wood for the stove and food for the family. I also was to pick her up late in the afternoon and bring her and the children to the store for clothing.

I gazed around the store and saw what he had—clothing, shoes, household items, school supplies, stationery, even vacuum cleaners. Hats were behind the counter—one shelf for men, the other for women.

"She did?" said Mr. Solomon incredulously.

"Uh huh." I handed him the check.

"This . . . this is for $125.00!"

I looked at him, not wanting to show my personal feelings or thoughts. Though he had demonstrated to me, he was a natural ally during the school board meeting, best to let him think this was a case of charity and goodwill, along with Mother's skill in recognizing the talent of this woman.

"Mother felt with your help, Mrs. Polk and her children could look nice."

"I'm glad. I'm glad, indeed, Mrs. Gibson has confidence in me."

"That's just the way Mother"—I almost slipped and said "planned it" when I caught myself—"is. She thinks about the people here."

"It's nice your mother has taken so much interest in this small town. It's really raised the morale of so many of us."

Mr. Solomon was nice—a really nice person. Of medium height, dark curly brown hair and pleasant features, his eyes set him apart from many people around here—full, dark brown eyes that were both soft, yet penetrating. Intelligence definitely showed in his eyes. His voice set him apart, too. Though he had a Southern accent, it was ever so slight with a slightly nasal sound to it, which intrigued me.

"She'll be glad to hear that. Mr. Solomon, if you don't mind me asking, where are you from—I mean your accent is different from the Delta folks."

"Oh, you picked up on it, did you? Suffice it to say, I'm not from here or parts around. I come from what used to be called a 'border state'."

"A border state?"

"Yes. Before the *war*, there were four Border States around the old Confederacy—Missouri, Kentucky, Maryland, and Delaware."

"I didn't know that."

"There were and, in a sense, still are four Border States. I happen to come from Maryland—near Washington, D.C., so my accent is different. My grandpa fought for the Confederate States, while his older brother fought for the Union. Because of my father's history, I was naturally drawn toward the South."

"But how'd you get down here if you don't mind me asking?"

"Not at all. When I was traveling, I happened to pass through Memphis, met a young lady, got married, then we moved over here to set up business since her father already had a store there."

"I see." Knowing he was Jewish and having heard what I thought was a slur against him I said, "Isn't it a little difficult over here without a . . . a—"

"A synagogue?" he answered, looking a trifle bemused.

"Yes, to be frank. I know it was for us, since Catholics didn't have a church until—"

"Until thanks to your mother."

"I guess so."

"Well, about once a month we go over to Memphis for *Shabbat*."

"What's that?"

"That's like Mass is for you. It's our religious service."

"How interesting."

"I can see you like to learn," he said kindly.

"I do, for a fact. Now I've learned things I never knew about before. When I stayed at the Big House, Marie would teach me all sorts of—" My voice began to fade away. I knew I was starting to feel emotional.

"I'm very sorry about the fire and, most particularly, Marie Duvall. She used to come in here and shop. She had a very good education. Many times . . . many times," Mr. Solomon looked down and waited, "we had some very good, intelligent conversations."

Slowly looking up at me, I could tell Mr. Solomon was emotional. I was aware he knew the Klan hated him only slightly less than they did coloreds, and somewhat more than they did Catholics.

"Sir, I think we have some things in common."

"I suppose we do. I hadn't really thought about it like that."

"Mr. Solomon, it has been a pleasure seeing you again. I'll let Mother know we had a nice conversation and understand each other," I said, smiling. "Did you know Mother knows how to make matzo ball soup?"

"No! Well, I declare."

"She does, sir, and it's delicious."

Part Two

CHAPTER 23
THE COMING STORM

Since the Great Depression only got worse, I watched as conditions deteriorated for nearly everyone. Few persons and families escaped. Plantation owners, small landholders, tenant farmers and sharecroppers were scraping by, but their plight only continued to get worse. More than a few planters and small farmers lost their land, and joined the swelling ranks of evicted tenant farmers and sharecroppers, all of whom became a swelling migration of the unemployed. For those who still clung to the land, their fear, the gnawing question, whether spoken aloud or not, became: Who would be next to suffer loss and how bad would it be?

"Minnie, what did you say the date was again?"

"Saturday, Christmas Eve, December 24, 1932, Mother."

"My how this year has passed by! Don't you think so, Daddy?"

Dad grunted with a mouthful of food.

Mother did not go to the gin today. Instead, she went shopping. Now we were enjoying our time together. Moreover, she had adjusted her weekly schedule, going to the gin on Tuesday morning and leaving Sunday afternoon to come home. This new schedule meant we had great cooking two nights a week. The rest of the week our evening meals were patched together, partly from leftovers.

"The year's almost gone, thank God," said Dad. "What an awful year. Yet . . . it's been good to us in unexpected ways."

"Hopefully, '33 will be better, Dad," I said hopefully.

Dad didn't say anything, brought his lips together, and exhaled through his nostrils, which always indicated he was biting his tongue, so to speak, not wanting to say what he really was thinking.

"Minnie, remember on the train home last Saturday, I said things are bad for everyone, especially since cotton went bust this year? Made nearly everyone's life even more miserable." Mother paused, looked down, took a deep breath and continued. "Things are a-brewin'."

"Things are what?"

"Things are a-brewin' in the Delta," said Mother ominously. "I'm only interested in the politicians over there and in Little Rock—the ones who affect the plantation. I don't keep up on the country's politics, but Daddy does."

"Nora?"

"Well, you're an educated man. You keep up on everything. I was never much interested in the news and now I don't have the time, even if I were. But what you said to me recently worries me, particularly now that you've worked and lived in the Delta. You got to know some of the folks, what they're thinking and what they're talking about. You know what I mean?" asked Mother, frustrated. "About the politics—the damned politics."

Dad came to Mother's rescue. "Minnie, there's a lot of social unrest in the country. Remember what I told you about foreign influences—like communism and fascism?"

"Sort of, Dad, but I have trouble understanding what they're about, and what they have to do with us."

Dad rolled his eyes. "Minnie, you've got the communists on one end, who want to take everybody's property and money. You've got the fascists on the other, who want to make war, hurt the Jews, and are socialists—socialists, who aren't much better about people's money and property. Unless you happen to have millions of dollars—or whatever their currency is—and you're willing to play ball with the secret police, you're just a pawn in their game."

I saw Mother nod her head, meaning she was trying to listen, but it was questionable how much she cared. Likewise, for me, I had a little better understanding than Mother, but I nodded, to show Dad I was paying attention.

"Then, you've got the American way. We're capitalists. We are independent, hardworking people who believe in people's right to have money and property without the government telling us what to do."

"Minnie," interjected Mother on a lighter note, "all of these 'isms' confuse me. All I know is I vote Democratic, and, James, forgive him Father for he knows not what he does, votes Republican."

Dad knew he was being made fun of now but he took it in good humor, and went on to try to explain what this was all about. "Minnie, I told your mother things aren't good in the country. People are starting to doubt the American way of solving problems, so some are going toward the extremes."

"You mean like communism and fascism?"

"Exactly! How this applies to us specifically is what's happening in the Delta. A lot of people are being evicted from the land and the only way of life they've ever known. Others are scared to death of what's going to happen to them and their families. You've got the planters and small farmers on one end, now the tenant farmers and sharecroppers on the other. It's a dangerous situation, and I'm afraid it's going to get much worse."

Mother, now taking a sober tone, said, "Isn't this talk of yours about the socialists coming down here and riling up the folks?"

"Well, yes, and yes again. All over the country people are being riled up, but not like they are in the Delta, or . . . they will be."

I must have looked dumbstruck because it hadn't dawned on me foreign ideas would catch on down here. I knew I'd been reading the world history book for the last four years, ever since Marie gave it to me. I had a grasp about the background of the American, French, and Russian revolutions. That's when I said, "Are you talking about a revolution, Dad?"

"Damned right, I am! Thank you, Minnie. What your mother said about things a-brewing in the Delta is true, except I'd say they are seething and explosive. There's so much pain for so many people."

"I know," I said, having seen so much misery around me, not only on my trips to the country, but also in Memphis itself—the lines of men waiting patiently for a bowl of soup and a slice of bread. It was pitiful.

"To make it worse, a damned socialist, Norman Thomas, who ran for mayor of New York City, says he wants to come to the Delta. Maybe he wants to help the tenant farmers and sharecroppers organize a union. Who knows what else he wants to encourage people to do?"

"Will that help those folks?" I might as well have thrown gasoline onto the fire. Dad looked like he was going to explode.

"Minnie," Dad said patiently, trying to control himself, "this is not whether these people will be helped temporarily. It's how it could affect you and this family."

"How?"

Again, Dad stayed patient, letting out his breath slowly. "Minnie, this is a union—a damned union. When someone's in a union they listen to their bosses, who tell them whether to work for someone or not. Nora might not get any of these people to work for her unless she agrees to pay them more."

"Minnie," interrupted Mother, "I recognize what these folks need is higher wages or a bigger percentage of their crops if they're going to feed their families and keep a roof over their heads. They—"

"Nora, that's not the way capitalism works. Capitalism—"

"James, people have got to eat. The ones who work for us do—and their families. They've got to have a roof over their heads. Also, they've got to have enough if they're going to pay the rent or mortgages on our houses."

"Nora—"

"Daddy," said Mother soothingly, "I'm not really disagreeing with you, because what I'm saying doesn't change the plan. I've already evicted some folks, and I will continue to evict more in order to mechanize (to use your word, honey). I'm just saying the tenant farmers and sharecroppers who are working for us need certain basic things."

Dad was about to say something when Mother went on. "We'll deal with this when we have to. The real problem as I see it—and I think Daddy will, too, once he hears me out—is we've got a real tightrope to walk. It's not just this union thing, which may or may not come to pass, but the other planters and their supporters we have to deal with. The planters—if they think this union thing catches on—won't hesitate to do whatever they can to hurt folks, which means if they think we aren't one of them, they'll make life hard for us. The workers we need, but we won't get them if they think we're trying to hurt them. So the way we thread the needle is with our "plan"— we mechanize. It's simple as that."

"You are right, Nora. That's what must be done and what we already are doing. Unlike the planters, the farmers and sharecroppers, we do have the money to do this. It's just going to take some time."

"James, you're right to be upset about this socialist . . . what's his name?"

"Norman Thomas."

"Yes, Norman Thomas. He might get his union. The folks will want to be paid more, but we can weather the storm. We just have to be certain we don't rile up too many people, or let ourselves get all riled up. Then the plan will work out just fine."

Dad shook his head, made a loving smile to Mother, walked over and gave her a kiss on her cheek. "You're not just purty, but you're smart too, ol' gal."

Mother said, "Let's go to the living room. I'll clear the table later."

Soon we were seated and comfortable.

Mother looked up, went to the radio and found a station playing dance music. It was upbeat and pleasant. She returned and picked up her sewing. I picked up my book and Dad, after a few moments, lifted his book off of his lap and started reading again.

After an hour or so, I got up and said, "I think I'll write in my journal." Dad was deep into his book and didn't hear me. Mother looked up, nodded and went back to her sewing.

. . . . .

December 24, 1932

Dear Journal,

This year is gone. It has been a very productive and exciting year, but it has also been one of the saddest in my life. Grandpa died. Marie was murdered. Both Mother and I vowed vengeance, and we've gotten a measure of it. More is to come.

Mother took over the plantation and began to modernize it. She then made it her mission to take control of the town by creating allies.

She bought the Jackson plantation, 2,000 acres including the house, and their farm equipment for a song. Not to toot my own horn, I negotiated the deal. Mother complimented me for being even more ruthless than she would have been with them. I have mixed emotions about being that kind of person.

Higgins, Grandpa's supposed friend and also a planter, was destroyed a month earlier by Mother. She bought 1,600 acres of his land and his house on the cheap. Good riddance to bad rubbish!

Even though I wrote I had mixed emotions about being ruthless, if I'm truly honest with myself, I was pleased about Higgins and Jackson. Those men were involved with burning down the Big House. Do I feel badly for their wives and family? Honestly, I choose—and "choose" is the word—not to think about them. I guess you can call them the casualties of war.

Since this past summer, Jeanette has been away at her Aunt Ethel's in California. Her Christmas package had cards for everyone, along with photos. She's happy, and that's that.

I am exhausted and saddened by this year. I'm going to bed.

A very Merry Christmas Eve to you, Journal!

CHAPTER 24
JANUARY 1933

"Nora, I don't trust Roosevelt."

"I know, James. It's a risk, but I think it's worth taking."

"You're right. People are always going to need power for their utilities, but we don't know if this new administration isn't going to nationalize everything."

"Nationalize, James?"

"Yeah, socialism, Nora, taking people's property; nationalize, socialize, it's one and the same thing."

"I see what you're saying. I just don't see Roosevelt wanting to do that."

"Nora, don't you understand that—"

"James, don't make fun of me or mock me."

"I'm not. All I'm saying is the man is untrustworthy and his policies could really hurt us."

I listened to the back and forth between Mother and Dad while we sat around the breakfast table.

"Okay, Nora, I'll give you there's an opportunity. Best to buy the company before the man's inauguration—before he starts coming out with his policies and laws. The Democrats totally control Congress, the Senate, as well as the White House. They can do whatever they want."

"Anything?"

"Well, not as long as the Supreme Court stands up to them."

"I see, but as far as I'm concerned, we've got an opportunity right now, Daddy. Let's take it. If we don't, someone else will and they'll have control over something we need at the gin: power."

"I can't argue with you there, Nora. Better we control the Utility Company than someone new. The price is right, that's for sure. But the company is in debt because a lot of customers can't pay their bills or have trouble paying them. Who knows how long that's going to last? We could be throwing the money down a rat hole."

From what I heard of the discussion, it seemed pretty plain to me. The company is bankrupt and would be up for sale. The price is a lot of money, especially given Mother's expenses the previous year. Who knows what might happen this year? Still, I decided to toss in my two cents' worth.

"Dad, I'm a simple thinker, but common sense tells me everybody either needs or will need utilities. Some tenant farmers and croppers don't use much (if any), but a lot of other folks at home, at the schools, and other businesses do."

"Thank you, Minnie. That's exactly the way I see it, too, James. Let's get it while we can. We'll control the utilities for our gin and other businesses in town. It's an opportunity."

"I've never been one to turn a blind eye to opportunity. I think the older I've gotten, though, I've become more cautious, Nora."

"No more so than I am, James. Now I'm not going to buy the company unless I have you tell me you're in agreement. I'd be a fool because I don't know anything about running a company; in this case, a utility company. I need you. I know I can't—and probably shouldn't even try—if you're not in charge of the company."

Mother must have said all the right things to Dad because he nodded, appreciating her confidence in his business acumen ("acumen," a new word I learned).

With Dad's help—and the dictionary—my vocabulary expanded, allowing me not to feel so self-conscious about my limited education. Dad could discuss almost anything I had read. Even if he hadn't read the novel, he would ask me questions about the plot and the characters, which gave me a greater appreciation of the writer. Dad became my private college professor. However, I always waited to ask him questions when Mother wasn't there in order to avoid any complications. Mother could get testy if she thought I was getting too much attention from Dad.

"So that means you agree, James?"

"I do. I'll go over on Tuesdays, and come home Thursday nights; unless, of course, there's an emergency."

"Then let's take care of business before the 'big day'."

Dad winced at the thought of Roosevelt taking over.

"Minnie, I want you there next Saturday when we discuss the details of the sale. It's better if you're there with Daddy and me. Understood?"

"Yes, Mother, I'll be there."

Mother could be confusing in this way. I hadn't expected she'd make that request—or demand. When it came to business, she wanted me involved—involved up to a point. Even after an event or some such thing, I could still end up pondering why and to what purpose Mother wanted my participation. Only recently has she been sharing more of her personal thoughts about people and situations in the Delta. Still, I was often left with more than a few unanswered questions regarding her many motivations.

. . . . .

Mother chose the timing of our visit to the mayor's office two days after the article in the local newspaper reported the town's utility company had been bought by Mrs. Nora Gibson, daughter of the late Charles Coymen, and one week before President Roosevelt's inauguration. Mother made sure she was mentioned in the article as the largest private landowner in the county, as well as owner of the gin. There was no doubt about who was in charge of the wealth in town and, for that matter, a growing force in the county.

"Mrs. Gibson, how nice to see you." Mr. Church was paying homage to Mother by waiting the appropriate amount of time before addressing me. "It's also a pleasure to see you again, Mrs. Beck."

Mother took the initiative immediately, before I could acknowledge the mayor's greeting. "It's always a pleasure to see you, Mayor Church. I like everything I see you doing on the job. This town wouldn't be what it is without you."

"Aw, ma'am—" He sounded country. "I'm just tryin' to do my best." And switched over to the better educated politician he was, saying, "I, like all of the folks in this town, owe you a massive debt of gratitude for what you've done for us, and continue to do. I can't imagine where we'd be without your support." He had to take a breath. "I think I can speak for all of the voters that you've given us hope for the future."

This time Mother waved off the compliment with false modesty. "Oh, Mr. Church, you are too kind. I'm just tryin' to do my civic duty." Mother beamed. She liked the recognition from the mayor. It didn't hurt, too, that he was young, vital, good-looking, and ambitious—"ambitious" being the operative word, since she knew she could control him.

"What do I owe the honor of your visit?" said Mr. Church, much like a *supplicant* (a new word) might do.

"Oh, I almost completely forgot. There's a tiny favor I have to ask of you, sir."

"Of me? What could I possibly do for you, ma'am?"

"Well, I would really appreciate it if you could suggest to the city council a somewhat insignificant—but, I think important—change."

"I'm sure they'd be most willing to help."

"That's so comforting to hear. I always knew you were a man who could get things done."

Mother paused and looked down at her nails, rubbing the nail of her thumb across the nail of her forefinger, which distracted the mayor momentarily.

"I hate to bother you with such a small detail, but it's time," Mother looked up at the mayor and said dryly, the smile now disappearing from her face, "that the school board be modernized."

"I'm sorry, ma'am. I don't quite understand what you mean."

"Like I said, it's really a small detail, but one that's important to *me* and, of course, to others in town. " Mother hesitated. She wanted to make sure she had the mayor's full attention. "My daughter and I discussed the issue for some time since our last meeting with the board. We feel y'all need a change."

The mayor seemed to hold his breath, remembering the acrimony of the first meeting that I had attended. He straightened up and appeared to prepare himself for possibly bad news.

I was surprised. She unexpectedly had brought me into the discussion by her mention of "our" discussion. I tried not to show my surprise by keeping my expression unchanged while appearing to be engaged in the conversation, which required the training of an actress. I was painfully aware Mother would want me to contribute something to this discussion.

"Ma'am?" asked the mayor, perplexed.

"I would like you to propose to the council a new rule: No one over sixty-five years old can serve on the school board or, if that's not possible, it be expanded by two or three new members. I believe board members are appointed by you and the city council."

Mr. Church's jaw dropped. Regaining his composure, he muttered, "Yes, we can make those changes, ma'am."

"Good! I think that's what you had in mind, Mother."

"I did." She nodded her head in approval.

"Yes, I added, "a rule that would get ride of dead wood and bring in new blood as soon as possible."

"I couldn't have said it any better, Minnie."

Mother had not wasted time. She told him exactly what she wanted and when—NOW! We all knew who the dead wood was—Miss Baker, the spinster, and Miss Tucker, her friend.

"Yes, I agree, he said, slapping his hand on the table top. By all means, we need the right people on the school board." He didn't miss a beat, and was there to do Mother's bidding.

Mother had briefed me before the meeting of this plan, but hadn't prepared me for what was to happen next. At that moment, there was a knock on the door. Mother looked across the room, saying, "I do believe Providence is at hand."

The mayor, looking confused, walked across the room and opened the door. Standing before him—at first I didn't recognize her—was Mrs. Polk, who said, "I hope I'm not late. Mrs. Gibson asked me to come and meet with y'all."

The mayor regained his composure quickly and ushered her into the room, saying, "By all means, come right in, ma'am."

The woman who walked across the room was not the same woman in rags I'd taken home nearly two months ago to that shack across the river on a cold winter's day. No, the Virginian aristocrat had emerged from her cocoon. Mrs. Polk wore a lovely blue dress that showed off her figure. Her nails were manicured, her makeup applied ever so deftly to accentuate her best features—especially her high cheekbones. The cut of her hair was perfect. She carried the slightest whiff of perfume.

The mayor pulled out a chair for her and she took a place next to Mother in front of his desk. I could tell the mayor's interest lingered. His nostrils flared ever so slightly to smell of the perfume, and his gaze fixed a tad bit longer on Mrs. Polk's ample bosom once he was behind his desk and in his seat of authority. He definitely was a bosom man.

With that thought, knowing that my bosom was larger than either Mrs. Polk's or Miss Brown's, I had a momentary surge of jealousy and desire to compete. Odd, I mused. He might be tall, affable, and handsome, but he wasn't my type. The politician—no depth—was of no interest to me. I could read him like a book; there was no mystery whatsoever.

Cursorily, Mother acknowledged Mrs. Polk, saying, "Nice to see you. Your timing is perfect. We were discussing the school board and the mayor was kind enough to hear me out."

"Oh, Mrs. Gibson, I was riveted on your every word."

I'll bet he was, I thought. He was aware that his future was slowly unfolding in front of him. The politician he was knew when to tread softly and when to strike out boldly. Now I could see he knew what must be done.

"Oh, of course," Mother said with conviction, "I'll do my part, though I might not be able to attend *every* meeting."

I suspected that was my cue. "I'll be happy to attend, as along as the meeting is on a Saturday or Friday evening."

"Thank you, Minnie." Without changing her gaze from the mayor, Mother noted, "I can always count on my daughter. She's a good team player. That's what I like—good team players."

The message certainly wasn't lost on Mr. Church, who piped up, "I'm in complete agreement, Mrs. Gibson."

Mother went on, "Mrs. Polk has graciously accepted my invitation to let you know she would be happy to do her part and also be a member on the school board, but first—"

"But first," picked up the mayor, "I—I mean—the council needs to take care of that little technicality. Then I know I can safely assure you that Mrs. Polk will be most welcome as a new member on the school board."

Again, as if on cue, Mrs. Polk leaned forward and said in her best Virginian accent, "How lovely. I would be honored, Mr. Mayor, to serve *our* community in my own, humble way."

"It is we who are honored by you, Mrs. Polk, and by Mrs. Gibson and her daughter for your commitment and farsightedness in serving our little town."

Now I knew where this was headed.

Mother spoke. "Knowing that Mrs. Polk is far too modest to sing her praises, I shall. You'll have not just a wonderful substitute teacher, but someone who—let us say—will bring youth, intelligence and vitality to the board. I'm sure you'll agree with me."

Slightly stuttering, he replied, "I . . . I completely agree with you, Mrs. Gibson."

"I'm so glad to hear that. I am always amazed at your abilities, Mayor Church. I can see a wonderful future ahead for you. Few men of your caliber exist. This town has so much to be thankful for in your leadership. I'm sure it won't escape Little Rock's notice."

"Little Rock, ma'am? You mean the state capitol?"

"But, of course! A man such as yourself will definitely be in state government in no time at all, especially with a few good words from the right people."

His full lips parting, he flashed his politician's smile that all but reached from ear-to-ear. His teeth were so perfectly straight and pearly looking that nearly any woman would be charmed and mesmerized by the handsome mayor, with his thick, dark brown hair. "Mrs. Gibson, I'm sure at the conclusion of the next council meeting, everything will be taken care of satisfactorily. Yes, indeed, new blood, that's what we need, and . . . that's what we'll have!"

Mother stood up, smiled, and held out her hand, which was the signal for all of us to take our leave.

Now I understood Mother's "plan." She had land—over 7,000 acres. She owned the utility company, the gin, and now was in control of the school board committee with her people on it. Mrs. Polk would, indeed, be a useful and formidable ally. Knowing Mother, I suspected there was more to this meeting than met the eye.

. . . . .

Saturday, two weeks before Easter, we were right in the midst of the planting season. Activity hummed all around us, both in Memphis, given all the calls coming from the Delta, let alone my work at the telephone company. It was my work, which temporarily looked like I would be going off the rails because two girls quit due to exhaustion. I was under enormous pressure to choose between my job at the company and my work in the Delta. Fortunately, on the day I was to give my decision to the company, three—not two—women with experience were hired and started the following day. Disaster had been averted.

The following day, Saturday, Mother notified me she had planned another meeting with Mayor Church. As she said before we left, "I'm counting on you, Minnie, if I need your support. I'm letting you know this will not be easy on anyone."

Once we were in the mayor's office, Mother waved away the formalities quickly and came to the point of her visit. "Mr. Church, I'd like you to run for office and represent our district in Little Rock as our assemblyman."

"Me, ma'am? I don't know quite what to say."

"As a candidate, you'll win with my support."

"I—I—"

Still standing, his long legs made him at least a half—if not a full—head taller than most men in the community. His height gave him a somewhat imposing quality that wasn't missed by either men or women.

Yes, I thought, with his looks and personality he was a shoe-in. I watched him as he tried to absorb the sudden news. His hazel-colored eyes with a faint yellow ring around the irises, stared directly at Mother, the keenness of both his instincts and common sense apparent to me, if not to Mother as well.

"Then, it's yes," said Mother abruptly.

"Of course, ma'am. It most *definitely* is!"

"Mr. Church, you're a young man with a future. However," she said ominously, "you have a cloud hanging over your future."

I was as confused as the mayor and felt a sense of foreboding, knowing how manipulative and ruthless she could be when she had an agenda.

I saw the mayor was completely caught off-balance by the sudden offer of Mother's support for his candidacy to replace the current office holder, who'd resigned for embezzlement of public funds. Initially elated, his expression changed. He looked genuinely mystified, then on guard, then concerned by Mother's comment about a "cloud hanging over" him as a candidate.

"Well, Mr. Church, I'm pressed for time because of the planting season. So I'll come to the point and not mince my words. You're not married! A good-looking young man like you needs a wife. People expect that."

I saw Mr. Church's expression. It must have looked like mine. I had no idea Mother was about to tell him he needed to get married. Her implication was clear—he needed to get married in order to get her support. Still, the abruptness of her comment had taken his breath away, as well as mine.

"Well, I believe I have—"

I smiled. I knew he had someone special in mind: Miss Brown, who worked for the school.

Suddenly and abruptly, Mother cut him off. "Yes, I think Mrs. Polk is the perfect woman."

"But Mrs. Gibson, I have—"

Again, Mother cut him off. "I'm sorry to spoil the surprise you had for us by naming Mrs. Polk outright. You've probably been waiting for the appropriate moment to tell us and everyone else. Such is love."

Mother smiled, but the smile did not travel up to her eyes.

I started to stand up and leave the room when Mother urged, "Minnie, please stay. It's important."

I lowered myself into my chair and glared at Mother. I felt the greatest compulsion to scream at her, but I didn't.

Something about the tone of her voice told me to wait. Perhaps it was the tone of her voice, which alternated between matter-of-factness and kindness.

"Mrs. Gibson, really, I want to say—"

"Of course you do, Mayor Church. But let me be blunt. Your career as mayor and from what I can see, your career in state government (this does not exclude even being a congressman from the State of Arkansas) is dependent on you marrying without scandal. There are just certain things—I think you know what I'm referring to—" I could see Mother was pausing, to let what she was saying sink in. "—things people will not accept here, not even up North."

Whether Mother physically grabbed him like she did me in the hall in the home of the Trudeaus, or grabbed him with the intent of her words, the man sat there, horrified—horrified by what Mother was saying. I felt a growing rage toward Mother, yet there was something about *what* she was saying that was different than what she said to me that cost me the man I loved, Norton. This was somehow different and, as Grandpa would say, *keep your powder dry*. So I remained seated.

"Do I really need to spell things out for you, sir?"

Mr. Church slowly shook his head. "No, ma'am."

"You may see this as an intrusion—just someone meddling in your personal affairs, but it is really more than that, young man. I want to invest in you, but I don't invest in losers. Probably more important, as a Mother, I know the consequences of interfering in a child's life, then having things turn out badly. When that happens it cannot be undone, no matter how much a mother or father would want to go back and change things."

I sat there, stunned. Mother was apologizing to me, off-handedly, for forcing me to marry Beauregard. I was so taken aback, I almost lost track of the purpose of her talk with the young mayor.

"I digress. To return to your situation—and mine, as one of your supporters—Mrs. Polk is a widow with three lovely children. A woman like her needs a good husband. Moreover,

I daresay I did notice on our last visit you found her attractive. She is, but she is more than a physically attractive woman. She has the background of a public figure's wife. You've probably already discovered how intelligent, mannered and gracious she is, just from your experience at the board meetings. Together, you two can go a long way."

"But—"

"Let me come back to the reality of your situation. You can't afford to have children—certainly not with an unsuspecting girl like Miss Brown. It'd ruin you and her. The opportunity you have is staring you right in the face. You, young man, have a ready-made family, and a wonderful career ahead of you. Do I make myself clear?"

The mayor nodded his head and took a deep breath.

I could see nothing more needed to be said on the subject by anyone.

. . . . .

"I truly don't like this kind of business, Minnie."

"Then why'd you do it?" I said curtly. Surprisingly, Mother did not react to the negative tone in my voice or the harshness of my question.

"Oh, for two principal reasons. One, I see potential in this young man. I want him to be an ally. He can go places, especially with some support from us. But, like I said, I don't back losers. Secondly, he'd be a loser as sure if he gets married to Miss Brown. On a more personal note, I was trying to protect him."

I had my suspicions about what she was getting at in the meeting, but they were still only suspicions. "Protect him?" I wanted to laugh at what Mother just said, but I caught myself. *Better to keep a cool head*, I counseled myself. *Instead, draw her out.*

"Yes, protect, him. I know it's hard for you to understand why I'd feel protective, but I do."

I said absolutely nothing. I still had strong feelings about Mother having interfered in my life—I might honestly have said *ruining* my life. Now I was watching her do the same thing to the young mayor. Had she absolutely no conscience? The man wasn't even related to us.

"I paid a visit to Miss Virtue."

"Miss Virtue?" I said incredulously.

"Oh, yes. Sometimes you have to talk to the right person to get accurate information. Miss Virtue has lived in this town for decades. There's not much she and Marie didn't know about everyone."

"So?"

"So, I reminded her of what I've done for her and her school, and what more can be done—or not."

I was angry and resentful Mother would use and bully Miss Virtue to get what she called "accurate information."

"Let me put this in the pleasantest way possible. I never talk this way, but right now I will. Once upon a time a mother gave birth to twins. She had taken the precaution not to have them around her husband, or any of her family or in her town. She chose a colored woman from another town miles away as her midwife. As she feared, one of the babies was born white, the other colored. She left the colored baby with the midwife, who had no children of her own. This young mother returned to her husband and to her town with a lovely newborn baby. Everybody was happy, and they have remained happy to this day. End of Story."

"End of Story?" I said, reluctantly.

"Minnie, did you even consider what it would be like for a mother at birth to have to give up one of her twins—never to see the one again; to have the baby snatched from your breast?"

I remained silent, partly trying to think this through. It was admittedly extremely difficult to give Mother the benefit of the doubt. She already had held hostage Miss Virtue to get what she wanted. I felt myself brooding. It was all I could do just to hear her out.

"Let me, as a pragmatist with an occasional soft spot, ask you: What would happen to a white couple in this town who had a colored baby?"

Since I didn't answer Mother, she continued. "At the very least, they'd have to leave. If they really loved each other, they would either go North or to another Southern state, but they'd give that baby up for adoption, and probably never have another child. Some marriage, huh?

"Or, Minnie, let's just say Mr. Church isn't the man I know him to be, that is, he's a politician. Let's say he actually admits to the truth about himself—he's been passing as white. If he doesn't get lynched then and there, his marriage and his career are finished in this town or anywhere around. At the very least, the people will tar and feather him, and run him out on a rail."

I grudgingly gave Mother my attention, actually beginning to listen rationally to what were not implausible outcomes to the situation, knowing how people thought and acted here.

"Or, let's say he's an opportunistic and ambitious man, the two not being mutually exclusive, and he blames his lovely wife if their child is born colored. She is either lynched or she blames some poor colored man, who gets lynched. Ultimately, he divorces her and she can never marry again, at least not in this town.

"Or, he can do the right thing."

I looked straight ahead. "Yes, the right thing," I responded bitterly. I didn't say anything more, other than nod my head.

· · · · ·

The week after Easter Sunday, on a beautiful April morning, Mrs. Polk, the widow, became Mrs. Church. Mr. Church became her husband and the "proud" father of three ready-made children. As Mother outlined for him, he was married with children and his future career appeared bright. Neither Mother nor I accepted the invitation to attend their wedding, expressing our disappointment by way of a previous engagement in Memphis.

Mother had, though, given the wedding gift to the 'lucky' couple a week before the wedding. On a day when the office was officially closed, Mrs. Polk met us in the small foyer and showed us into the office, where Mr. Church sat behind his desk, smiling his politician's smile. He rose and met Mother and me as we walked into the room. His measured stride across the room was slow and dignified.

"Welcome, y'all."

"Thank you. It's so nice to be here," said Mother, almost straining under the weight of her beautifully wrapped gift. "If I may," Mother brought the gift toward the mayor's desk, "I'll just unburden myself."

"Of course. Let me help," said the mayor. Mrs. Polk, her eyes wide with excitement, reached out and grasped the package. "Dear, I'll take this." The gleam in her eyes betrayed the realization of not only the weight, but also the value of the box as its end slightly dipped down under its own weight.

"Mrs. Gibson—Mrs. Polk switched to the formal title for Mother—you really shouldn't have, not after all you've done for all of us."

Mother waved away the compliment. "Please, you two lucky people—"

I looked over at the mayor, but like a true politician that ever-ready and ever-fixed smile was all gleaming white teeth, as Mother completed her thought. "You've got a lifetime of happiness before you. Now, to get things rolling, do open your gift from my family."

The mayor stepped to one side as Mrs. Polk reached over and slipped the envelope out from beneath the silk ribbon. Opening it, the lovely cream-colored card was admired by her for the weight and quality of the paper. Then with all due ceremony, she opened the card, and read the beautifully engraved message: *May you be forever happy, Captain and Mrs. James Gibson.* Mother insisted Dad use his title even now, when he no longer piloted his riverboats. The card did not go unnoticed, either by Mrs. Polk, and certainly the mayor.

With exquisite taste—it was her bearing and the way she used her hands—Mrs. Polk slowly and carefully opened the gift, obviously determined to save the paper and the silk ribbon. I could see Mother appreciated the widow's grace, as well as her desire not to waste the wrapping. Putting the wrapping aside, Mrs. Church looked down at a relatively large black velvet box.

"Oh my, I just can't imagine—"

Lifting the lid with a sense of drama and ceremony, she and the mayor gasped.

"Nora!" Mrs. Polk quickly caught herself, saying, "Mrs. Gibson, I don't know what to say."

The widow, soon-to-be wife, picked up first a knife, then the dinner fork and salad fork, and a spoon, and laid them out as if she would for a proper dinner. There was a momentary hush. Mrs. Polk picked up a soupspoon with an ornate engraving of the single letter "C" for "Church." She held it as if it were a sacred relic.

"I expect great things of y'all," crooned Mother. "Y'all will need the right silver for your guests. They'll be a lot of important people at your home for dinner."

"Well, to start with, when things settle down," said Mrs. Polk, "we'll want you and your family to dinner. Most certainly, won't we, dear?" and she looked over at her husband-to-be.

Mr. Church didn't miss the importance—nor the burden, that is, the indebtedness—of the moment, and reached out both of his hands toward Mother. "I think I can speak for both of us when we thank you for all you've done for us."

Mother smiled, but the tone of her voice was serious. "Now, young man, don't you disappoint us. I've got big plans for you and your lovely wife."

Trying to shift the tone away from the implied message from Mother, I said, "Looks like y'all will be having a lot of late night dinners—lots of fun."

Mrs. Polk laughed. "Indeed, Minnie. Indeed, we will."

Looking at the mayor, I jested, "You've officially entered the ranks of the aristocracy." Not quite understanding my meaning, I said explicitly, "You know you've got to live up to the standing of a Virginian gentleman."

Mrs. Polk laughed, along with Mr. Church now.

I looked over at Mother. She nodded once. She understood, and approved. Mr. Church would be—if he didn't screw up—raised higher than any of his previous imaginings.

CHAPTER 25
A CLOSE CALL

On my way over to Liza Green's place on the last Saturday in April, I had my healing herbs. I was content with my decision not to return to the hill, even though Mother had cleared away the wreckage of the Big House. Instead, I had Delia bring me all of the healing herbs I needed for a patient. Having met her in the garden, I had pointed out and labeled all of the herbs, both in the greenhouse and the garden, which I would need and that she was to tend for me. I drew a little diagram of each herb with their names, so she would have no trouble identifying them.

It was on that visit to Liza's that I received the kind of information that was always valued. Liza, a canny old colored woman, lived alone in a one-room house, which she rented from Mother. Her husband dead, her children long since moved away, she tended a small vegetable garden and worked at odd jobs. From what I knew and sensed of her, she was a woman in her late sixties, who was grave and secretive. Sometimes she had something to tell me, but not often. However, whatever she did reveal to me always carried an air of importance.

"Miz Minnie, as you know I'm not one to tell tales. I keep my mouth shut. I learned that early. There is some folks you can trust. Marie, bless her soul, done told me you're like that. I don't hold nothin' back from you, especially if I think it might be somethin' you need knowin'."

"Liza, what might that be?"

"Well," she dropped her eyes to the floor, "I does the cleaning up at that *special* house outside town where the men come for the girls."

"I see—"

"Not long ago, I done seen what look like the mayor's car parked there. The house was supposed to be closed, but I done heard music on the inside. 'Course, I didn't go in but come on home, and waited a few hours before I come back. By then, the car be long gone."

"I'm not quite sure what to say about that, Liza."

"I only tells you 'cuz I know your mama. She likes that boy and she tries to help 'im. Also, he been the best mayor to us folks ever. Seems like he got a special feelin'. He ain't hurtful or nothin' toward us colored folk, if you knows what I mean."

I felt my guard go up, not sure if Liza was probing me for information or only volunteering it. So I said nothing, on the offhand that she knew more about the mayor than she was saying outright. To let Liza know I was listening carefully, I nodded my head slowly.

"I figured I best tells you. I ain't given to idle gossip. Don't hold to spreadin' rumors neither, Miz Minnie."

"I know you don't, and I appreciate that. Thank you, Liza. Remember what I said about the herbs? Make a strong tea with these and drink it twice a day. Also, drink lots of water. Then I'll look back in on you next Saturday, when I come in."

"Thank you, Miz Minnie, you're a real comfort. Hyere, take a couple sugar cookies I done made."

"How'd you know I have a sweet tooth, Liza?"

"I try my best to know and to please."

. . . . .

"Where have you been, Minnie? I've got bills that need to be sent out."

I thought before I spoke, finally deciding it was in Mother's—and possibly the mayor's—best interests to tell her what happened over at Liza's.

"Liza cleans that 'house' outside of town, and said she saw the mayor's car parked in front," I said directly.

Mother's ears perked up. She went on full alert.

"It was a few days after he got married—when the place is normally closed! I said for emphasis."

Mother motioned for me to take the chair to the side of her desk. Once I sat down, she leaned forward and dropped her voice, though there was enough noise outside the door in the gin to keep the conversation private. "You might as well know what I later told Mr. Church after we met with him, the day he agreed to marry Mrs. Polk."

Our eyes met and held, which told Mother I was fully listening to her.

"The following week, I dropped by and asked him if he'd drive me over to the land across the river. Once he was out of the office and we crossed the river, I told him to stop his car."

"Why?"

"Because I had something serious to go over with that boy. He may be the mayor, but he's still kinda green behind the ears. I gave him a piece of 'fatherly' advice."

Mother saw me question her use of "fatherly" advice.

"That's right. Neither his father nor his mother are of much help to him now."

I prepared myself for what Mother might say.

"In short, I told him to tell Mrs. Polk he'd suffered some sort of injury and he's medically not able to be a full husband to her. I assured him she is not the type of person who would kiss and tell. So he doesn't have to worry about his reputation."

"Did he agree to that?" I said, wincing.

"Yes, but it was like pulling teeth. Any healthy—or not-so-healthy—young man would be aghast at anyone thinking that, let alone knowing it to be true. You understand what I'm getting at?"

I nodded. "In nursing school the condition's called 'impotency'."

"Minnie!" Mother said, shocked at my language.

"Well, it is, Mother."

"I know, but most polite people don't talk like that."

"Of course. I'm sorry."

Mother adjusted herself in her chair, trying to find a more comfortable position. "To my surprise, Mr. Church said he already had had that conversation with his wife-to-be, and she actually said she was relieved to hear it."

"How's that?" I said incredulously.

"The boy told me that Mrs. Polk doesn't want any more children. That part of married life was never really appealing to her. His take on her is she feels strongly about him moving farther along in politics, and providing a good home for her and her children. She'll do her part to make him a success."

I raised my eyebrows, indicating I was amazed at how much there is to know about people. They rarely are quite the way you imagine them, and many have their secrets.

"In this case, it worked out well for the mayor."

"*That part* did," said Mother with emphasis. "Now, there's this other problem you've brought me. I'm definitely going to have a talk with that boy. I'll let him know I understand that he's obliged to *take care* of himself. Just—"

Mother seemed at a loss for words, and uncharacteristically was fumbling her way through what she wanted to say.

"He can't do this sort of thing anywhere near here, and that includes the State of Arkansas. I've got plans for him. News will travel. His future is in Little Rock or in Congress. That's where he'll be most useful to us, but—"

I watched Mother wrestle with what or how she wanted to say something.

"Oh hell, Minnie, I'll tell him he can't make a mess in his own backyard and think it won't stink. People will talk. He's got to go and take care of his business in Memphis. I don't give a damn where he does it—or, for that matter, with whom—just . . . not . . . here!"

CHAPTER 26
A SHORT VISIT

I visited Miss Virtue. After a pleasant afternoon of drinking tea, she walked me to the porch where we carried on our conversation.

"I'm glad you came by, Miss Minnie."

"I am, too."

Though we hadn't spoken directly about the mayor, I felt Miss Virtue understood my mother and I were two very different people. It was important to me she know on an unspoken level that I didn't approve of the way Mother extorted the information from her.

"Oh, Miss Minnie, life is strange, indeed."

"Why do you say that?"

"Your family—your grandpa, you and your mother have done so much for this town. I know if it hadn't been for your mother and Marie, the children here at the school would still be getting an inferior education. Now they've got a chance."

"I'm glad to hear that. It means a lot to me to know things have improved."

"Indeed, they have! I don't think I could have kept up my spirits much longer. Hope only goes so far. I know that now. I didn't realize how little was left inside of me until y'all came along."

I looked into her eyes to see beyond the sparkle to something deeper within her. I suppose some people might have said her soul. At that moment, I caught the fragrance of the roses lining her walk. Taking a deep breath, I savored the fragrance. "Your roses are so lovely, so fragrant, but you don't have any red ones."

"No, I'll tell you a little story. I was once given the most beautiful red rose, but one day it died. It didn't just wilt. He, I mean, it died."

Moments filled the fragile silence, like droplets of dew falling to the ground and forming a puddle of water.

"From that time on, I decided I was happiest with yellow and white roses. Maybe they don't have the headiness and intensity of red, but they please me nonetheless. Don't you think they're pretty, Miss Minnie?"

"I love roses."

"Well then, follow me."

Miss Virtue picked a gorgeous yellow rose, and handed it to me.

"Thank you." I inhaled. "Mmmm, the scent." Pausing before I spoke to smell the rose again, I reflected, "You know, when I see these, I think of the garden behind the Big House, with all the roses and things Marie put in. Gosh, all those herbs and the healing she did. She always taught me something new."

"Yes. She was a healer and a good midwife, too."

As the old expression goes, *you could have knocked me over with a feather.* I had not expected to hear that. At a loss for words, all I could think to say was, "I truly miss Marie."

"I'm sure you do. Like I said before, she really loved you."

That touched me deeply to hear that from her.

"I miss her, too, Miss Minnie. She was really my only friend; someone I could talk to. We had so much in common. Things like our family history."

"Marie told me her family were *gens de couleur libre.*" I was probing.

Miss Virtue laughed. "Your French is good."

"*Un peau.*" I held up my fingers up the way Marie did when she said that.

"To let you in on a little secret, that was one of the things we had in common. Though my people were from Maryland and hers from New Orleans, they lived similar lives before the Civil War. It was only to be expected, though, Marie's family living in New Orleans would have things, including travel and education, that mine didn't have. We always enjoyed comparing our families. I guess you could say it gave us a perspective on ourselves we otherwise wouldn't have had."

"Pity, none of it is written down. There's so much to tell."

"Well, Miss Minnie, your assignment is to write it down."

"Maybe—maybe someday, but I think if I'm going to have 'perspective', I need to come back and we talk over tea."

"I'd like that, Miss Minnie. I really would like that."

. . . . .

July 10, 1933
Sunday

Dear Journal,

Well, the mayor has a wife. Mother has made her investment in him—and his wife—and we'll see if it pays off.

I have a lot of mixed feelings about the whole affair, but it'll take time for me to sort them out. I suppose this will happen over time, once I see how things work out between Mrs. Polk—or I should say Mrs. Church—and her husband. I'll try not to prejudge their situation. Interesting, within a month of their wedding, Miss Brown became Mrs. Williams, marrying Sheriff Williams' grandson, Hank, who is now the deputy sheriff and who lives next door to Mother in one of her rentals. His grandfather shows no inclination to retire, especially while we are all in the midst of the Great Depression.

I visited Miss Virtue today. What a lovely experience! What a lovely lady. Everything was flowing along fine until I was about to leave. Miss Virtue mentioned that Marie had been a midwife. I knew this was no idle comment. No, it opened up a whole can of worms.

Mother had the mayor's secret and she had used that information! Now I was asking myself if Marie had been the midwife for the twins. More importantly, since Mother said the midwife had kept one of the twins—the colored baby—it made me wonder about Annie, Marie's daughter. Annie had taken such good care of me in Memphis when I was a child, but Annie had not lived with Marie until she was fifteen when she was trained for the position at our house.

I sensed a secret. Annie and the mayor had the same birthday. I knew because I always gave Annie a birthday card. While I was in the mayor's office, Mother asked him casually about his birthday, which happened to fall on the same date as Annie's. It may only be a coincidence, but there is definitely something suspicious about this. It raises the very real possibility that Annie, who lives in Los Angeles, has a twin brother, the mayor, who lives in the Delta. I wonder if they ever met unknowingly, when Annie worked at Grandpa's or if they might meet accidentally in the future. When I ponder this, it does seem most unlikely. By this time, Annie must have children of her own and would be unlikely to travel.

Even though there is some sadness to think that Annie might not be Marie's daughter by birth, I'm confounded by the notion. Why would Marie leave Annie money and jewelry if she weren't related?

Still, that doesn't change the way I feel about Annie, who was so good to me. I miss her, even more now that Marie is gone. When I remember all those stormy nights that I got frightened as a child from the thunder and lightening, I would go and climb into her bed and feel so

*comforted. I know it's foolish, but I long
to feel—*

Sunday
October 22, 1933

Dear Journal,
 I don't know why I waited so long to write what the really big news is: The price of cotton is up! The soybean (not plowed under) and corn crops bought in money, too. Along with Roosevelt's farm policy, we not only covered our expenses easily, but also were able to buy more farm equipment, including ten more tractors and two trucks.
 For us it's been a hard year of work, and a good year financially. Dad took charge of the utility company and things improved, that is, profits. Will's fiancée, Ellen, was hired there as part secretary and part bookkeeper.
 Following the advice of a government agronomist (a new word I learned this year, meaning the economics and management of farmland), we planted what would have been unused land in

corn, soybeans and vetch—soybeans and vetch often being plowed under to renew the soil. The planters, including us, have made out well, which wasn't the case for many of the others. We were especially fortunate, since we had last year's cotton stored in the warehouse and inside Jenkin's house. Frank's little patch, and the crops from the Jackson' and Higgins' plantations all were sold.

Though Mother evicted many families, which was part of her plan to modernize the plantation, she didn't do it for the sake of government subsidies. Most importantly—unlike anyone else we knew—she gave every family some money to help them. That surprised me since she's always been telling me not to be sympathetic when it comes to business. Even with her charity, the evictions made me sad.

Mother was wise to have done so much for the town. The townsfolk and all those out on farms who have benefited, have mostly praised her as someone who cares. With these people, she is known by her deeds, not her words. Though

Mother is known to be a divorced woman, that hasn't affected the Catholics in the parish. They appreciate her for providing them with a church.

Many planters applaud her to her face, but we've heard from their help, she is either criticized for her waste of money, or giving common people ideas about questioning their betters, or trying to buy goodwill. "Sour grapes," Dad calls it. A few planters are truly friendly and genuinely praise her for what's she's done to help others.

Tom has been a godsend—just as Marie said he was for Grandpa. Loyal, trustworthy, he works like a dog. We are so lucky to have him.

CHAPTER 27
COTTON UP!

This was the first year we had the kind of Christmas we had as children, even if the country was in the depths of the Great Depression. Jeanette was home for the holidays. Besides the stockings filled with oranges and nuts, we had a tree, lights on the tree, and presents. Truth be told, I think this had to do with the first good year for cotton in a long time. The Depression might be at its worst, but cotton was up!

"Jeanette, slow down," Dad barked, trying to eat and listen to her.

"Okay, okay, Daddy. I know you've heard the story before when I first got back, but I got a card from Aunt Ethel. She mentioned they're still dealing with what happened because of the earthquake."

"What earthquake?" Dad said playfully, knowing full well about it.

"Oh, you know, the . . . You're just pulling my leg, Daddy! Anyway, there we were, sitting at the dinner table on Saturday, March 10th, at 6:00 p.m. in Long Beach, California."

"At 5:55 p.m. At least, that's what the newspaper said."

"Sir, please let me tell my own story."

Dad nodded his head and we all hunkered down for the onslaught. Thank goodness we had a great meal, so I could listen with one ear and concentrate on my food. It seemed a little rude to me that Jeanette wasn't paying more attention to Mother's cooking, but Mother didn't seem to mind. I think she was just happy to have Jeanette at home again.

"Goodness, there we were—Aunt Ethel, my friend Betty, and me—sitting at the dinner table, when at 6 p.m., things began to rumble and shake. Suddenly, right before our eyes, our dinner and everything else slid right down one end of the table and onto the floor! It was both truly amazing and scary at the same time!"

"So what did you do, honey?" asked Mother, as if she were hearing the story for the first time.

"Oh, that's when it really got even scarier! Things were falling off the walls, off the stove, and out of the cupboards. Glasses and plates were smashing. Even," Jeanette exclaimed, "some of Grandma's Asian art from the Oriental Palace was destroyed. Aunt Ethel called that a real tragedy."

"The Oriental Palace?" asked Dad.

"You know. A Mrs. Howard owned the shop, and it was on Magnolia Avenue and 3rd Street. Anyway, to get back to what I was trying to tell you. It was just awwwful." At first," Jeanette sounded winded, as if she were actually living through the experience, "we thought the whole house might come crashing down! We ran for our lives—Aunt Ethel, Betty, and me. So we were stumbling and trying to stay upright while the house swayed, and we ran into the streets. Lots of other people were already out of their houses, watching telephone poles going back and forth, along with the trees and houses. It was *really, really* scary."

"It was that bad, was it?" Dad chimed in.

"Oh, Daddy, you have no idea! Some people were crying and screaming that it was the end of the world. It seemed to last for an eternity, but finally it stopped. We all waited. Then there'd be what's called a tremor (that's like a small earthquake). Anyway, they just kept coming—you never knew when. Finally, around midnight, after it seemed safe enough to go into our houses, people started pulling out mattresses or just blankets to stay warm, and we all slept outside. All night!"

"Sounds terrifying!" Mother exclaimed.

"Oh, you have no idea. It really, really was! The next day—fortunately for us, the house was well-built—"

"Do you remember, I came out to put some of our houses back on their foundations, Jeanette?"

"Of course, I do, Daddy, but that's not the point. You didn't arrive for days later."

"That's true."

"Anyway, what a mess! Downtown was unbelievable. You had bricks everywhere. The entire fronts of some buildings had collapsed, leaving the insides of offices and rooms open. You could see some people's entire bathrooms—tubs and all. What a mess. Also—" Jeanette's expression changed to one of seriousness, "the radio said sixty-eight people were killed."

"Now, that's truly sad," I said, meaning every word of it.

Jeanette said solemnly, looking at me with a now pained expression, "It really, really was. Though I didn't personally know anyone who'd been killed, still—"

"Nora, would you pass down the scalloped potatoes, please? They're really good!"

Jeanette shot Dad a mournful look, her eyes all but tearing up and saying, *"How could you, Daddy, be thinking about potatoes at a time like this?"*

When I glanced at Dad, I noticed he wasn't aware of Jeanette's pained expression. If he did know, he knew she'd get over it. He was right.

This was a good opportunity for Mother to remind Jeanette to eat. After a couple of bites of her dinner, chewing and swallowing quickly, she was telling—no, retelling—her story of the Great Long Beach Earthquake of 1933.

"This wasn't all—no, not by any means! Our high school was totally and completely *demolished*—demolished to smithereens!"

"You don't say—to smithereens?!"

"Oh yes, sir, just destroyed!" said Jeanette, with an utter sense of finality.

"Sooo," Dad was finishing up his meal, "where'd you go to school?" he asked, trying to look interested by giving Jeanette his full attention now that his stomach was full.

"Oh, it was bad, sir." Jeanette glanced over at Mother and me to make sure we were listening, failing to catch Dad looking over at me and rolling his eyes. "We had to finish the semester going to school in tents. Would you believe that? Going to school in tents!"

"No, how awful," said Mother, diverting Jeanette's attention so that she wouldn't see her father was actually smiling, and close to laughing at the dramatic moment and picture Jeanette was reenacting for us again, after two previous performances.

"Yes, it was, ma'am. I can't tell you how cold those tents are in winter; and how hot they are in summer. It was almost unbearable, but I stuck it out. I knew it was important to Aunt Ethel that I get a good education."

I looked over at Dad, who lifted one eyebrow in a questioning expression while he stroked his chin. I knew he was thinking the same thing as Mother and me—Jeanette was sent back for the holidays by Aunt Ethel because she couldn't control her.

"Thank goodness City College wasn't hurt, because that's where I won my award from the fraternities for Best Impersonator."

"And what, pray tell, was that for, young lady?" asked Dad.

"I'll show you." Jeanette got up from the table and disappeared into the living room. Seconds later came her voice, as she came through the doorway, "I just sashayed across the stage in this fabulous long dress with a parasol. I stopped at the right moment, turned to the audience, and . . . I put my hand on my hip like this, held my parasol down, and . . . said in this really sultry voice: 'Come up and see me sometime'."

"You didn't!" I said in mock surprise.

"Oh, I certainly did! I looked and sounded just like Mae West from the movies. The guys went wild. That's how I won the award."

"Was there anything else that happened?" inquired Dad, encouraging Jeanette to finish the story.

"Yes," Jeanette responded, sounding annoyed. "They took the award back when they found out I wasn't in college."

"Aww," I said.

"Yes, they did! But the story has a happy ending. The fraternities felt really bad about it, and they got me a little inscribed statue, letting me know I was still their favorite. Also, I got more than a few offers for dates."

"How did Ethel feel about that?"

"Oh, not so good."

"I'm sure she didn't," said Dad, shaking his head.

Jeanette smiled weakly.

Mother tried to come to Jeanette's rescue when Dad cut her off. "Young lady, was there anything else that came out of this?"

Jeanette didn't say anything, but looked straight ahead and over my shoulder.

"Do you think Ethel should have approved of your behavior?" said Dad, now clearly irritated.

"No, sir," Jeanette said timidly. "Actually, I was embarrassed when I was up on the stage, but—"

"Jeanette," said Mother quickly, "you're the only one here who hasn't finished eating. I'm gonna serve dessert if you don't hurry."

"Yes, ma'am." Jeanette ate quickly, not looking up.

I looked at Dad. He stroked his chin. Mother smiled awkwardly, and at a loss for words. I could see, and I suspected

Dad and Mother could see, that Jeanette felt ashamed about the whole situation, but she couldn't or wouldn't admit to it.

Seconds later, Jeanette placed her knife and fork down. "Ma'am, I'm done."

. . . . .

Once we went to the living room, Dad and I picked up books while Jeanette disappeared upstairs. Mother pulled out a box of cloth remnants, and threaded her needle. It wasn't long before Dad broke the silence. "Well, I hope you are satisfied now that you've elected that Democrat."

"I am. I am, indeed," Mother said, now having picked up her sewing, which looked like a series of miniature stained glass windows made of various colors and fabrics in a pattern of squares within squares within squares, along with cross stitching here and there. Louise, who has some art books, showed Mother that this looked like the artist Paul Klee.

"You mean, Franklin D. Roosevelt, Dad?"

"One and the same."

"I voted for him, too."

"Minnie, didn't I explain to you all about capitalism and the American way?"

"Yes, sir."

"Well?"

"Dad, things are bad all around, but you've got to see how bad they are in the Delta. People are starving."

"Minnie, it's only temporary. Things will automatically get better. Once people get a little more confidence about the economy, they'll start spending again. That's the way it works."

Mother jumped in and said matter-of-factly, "You can't tell a starving mother with children to hold on for another year or two." Mother paused, deciding how she was going to phrase something. "Daddy, you've explained to us all about the "isms" which, incidentally, I only got a gist of." Mother shook her head. "Something had to be done 'cause President Hoover didn't know what to do."

"I was thinking, Dad, about what you said. I've read this world history book four times since Marie gave it to me. I'm not saying I understand a lot of it, but when I read about the revolutions—"

"Which ones?"

"Not ours, but the French and Russian revolutions, what I could make out of them was people were starving. They were sick and tired of wars and depressions."

"Minnie, there were a lot of reasons for those revolutions. Look at England and us. There haven't been any revolutions."

I had nothing to say to that and was going to keep my mouth shut, when I thought about what I was reading and hearing in the news, listening to folks and seeing things all around me—my personal experiences, which made me feel bad and worried me. "Dad, in the Delta, people are starving. And even when I'm in Memphis, I see the men—healthy, working men—standing in a long line just to get a bowl of soup and a slice of bread. It just makes me think, things can't continue like this much longer without trouble breaking out. Also, it's pitiful. Didn't you say, 'Always give a baloney sandwich to anyone if he comes to the door and tells you he's hungry'?"

Dad nodded his head, his expression changing to something that looked kind of depressed. Maybe he was thinking about himself, not having been able to get a job on his own because of his age.

. . . . .

December 25, 1933

Dear Journal,
Sorry, the year has all but passed before I could get back to you.

Well, the world didn't end. Norman Thomas, the socialist, didn't arrive this past February. Boy, did Dad go on and on about that! That's why I didn't tell Dad a couple of members of the Socialist Party have been active this past year in the Delta. What I heard from Tom was they were assuring new members Mr. Thomas has accepted an invitation to speak this coming February.

For us it's been a hard year of work, and a very good year financially. Will's fiancée, Ellen, was hired there as part secretary and part bookkeeper.

We were right; there would be intense turmoil this year in the Delta. Planters, along with small landholders (not all of them, of course), have pitted themselves against tenant farmers and sharecroppers. Merchants and townsfolk have been caught in the middle in terms of their earnings and their sympathies. By far, however, the worst has been for the coloreds: evictions, intimidation and cheating—cheating these people out of their wages or crops. Most sickening are the killings—lynchings to be exact.

The suffering of the landless is hard to imagine. Dad says that Roosevelt's farm plan is well meaning, but he predicts none of the money will get to any of the sharecroppers and tenant farmers, because it relies on planters and the others to share their increased income, which has come from not planting a third of the land in cotton.

I continued to study French with Miss Virtue every other Sunday. We began to get to know one another to the extent we can joke and laugh together. I'd say we have a genuine liking for each other. Miss Virtue shared more of the town's secrets and intrigues, being close to her students and their parents. She complimented me on my ability to pick up French, and she inquired—politely—if I'd mind if she could review English grammar. I was quite pleased by the idea because it definitely could be improved upon.

The phone company is the phone company. Doing my job there is good for me. Not only am I independent, but also I have a chance to socialize—at work— with some of the girls, and I can get to the movies at least once a month. I LOVE the talkies. Movies are so much better now. I still see a lot of actors from the silent films acting with their eyes. One real advantage to the movies and to the telephone company for me is that, whether Mother knows it or not, it gives us time apart with less chance of conflict.

The fun part is having Jeanette back with us—if only for a short while.

Jeanette was living with Aunt Ethel during the Long Beach earthquake. Her letters were vivid. Dad went out to put the rental houses and apartments back on their foundation. He had to repair a lot of cracked walls and ceilings in the rentals. Fortunately, nothing happened to the oil wells. She's spending the holidays with us now and talks non-stop.

She caught all of us by surprise when she said that she'd gone to a Japanese village. She pulled out some pictures of what she called an *Obon* festival, but it was Dad's sharp eyes that noticed a sign in English that said: Hashimoto Company. Jeanette admitted it was a Japanese fishing village between

Long Beach and San Pedro on an island—Terminal Island. A high school friend, Tommie Ito, took her to visit his young cousins: Harry Baba, and Kazuko and Tomiko Shibata, whose names were written on the back of the photos. She had us fooled, because everyone was dressed up in what she said are traditional Japanese costumes.

The house will be a lot quieter without her once she leaves for California in little more than a week. Sorry to see her go.

I realize, on a more serious note, my hate toward the perpetrators is changing a bit into a greater sadness and longing for Grandpa and Marie. Still, I would not show any of them mercy.

CHAPTER 28

MORE OF EVERYTHING

February 1934 was particularly cold. Sunday we were huddled around the fire after a good Sunday dinner when Mother said, bored with the music coming over the radio, "I'll go to my room." Translation: "I'll go and look at some magazines."

In a deeply serious tone of voice, Dad said, "Nora, stick around; I need to talk with you. I told you things are bad in the country. These union people are busy trying to undermine us."

Mother and I both looked up at Dad, waiting for him to continue. "I read this morning that Norman Thomas, the socialist, came to the Delta. I knew he'd come calling. He's out to make trouble."

"What kind, Daddy?" asked Mother, deciding to sew.

"Other than the visit, the newspaper didn't have much else to report on. So I can't tell you anything more. I just know that man means trouble for everyone—particularly for us."

Mother and I already heard about his appearance in the Delta a few days after his arrival. Other than visiting a couple of fellows who were socialists, there really wasn't much to know about his his stay. At this point, we couldn't discuss anything specific.

"Socialism" has been around in the Delta for quite some time. It's not totally foreign to folks there, but I don't have an opinion about it other than it's one of the 'isms' you talk about." Mother went back to sewing together the braids of a rag rug of various colors.

I partly listened to a program of light classical music on the radio, when I glanced up at Mother. I knew she had to always be busy with something, and the bad weather provided a creative outlet for her. Yet while she worked, I suspected her mind was largely on the business of the plantation. Because the planting season was months away—and a bone-chilling wind blew down from the north—she was basically housebound. Other than a day trip this past week and a cursory meeting at the gin with the managers and riding bosses, she huddled—like the rest of us—around the hearth. The blazing fire with the faint smell of smoke and the sound of popping, crackling logs gave off both a comfortable and comforting warmth that filled the room while the wind knocked and rattled the house outside.

Dad, since he wasn't going to get a rise from either Mother or me, settled back and stopped fretting. Reaching over, he picked up a book he'd been reading, and was quickly absorbed in it.

"What 'cha reading, James?"

"Oh, just one of my old books in German—when I was at the university."

"You don't say," Mother commented, surprised by the news.

Dad smiled and went back to his reading.

"What's it about, Dad?"

"It's a collection of German poets—men like Schiller, Von Rilke, even Heine."

"I had no idea you liked such stuff," Mother said, half-listening.

"There was a time ol' gal, when—"

"What made you pick it up now, Dad?"

"Oh, there's one poet, Heine, I like. If the Nazis get their way, nobody will be reading any of his poetry."

"Why?" I asked, interested in Dad's response.

"He's Jewish. They've already proscribed—banished—writers like him."

"You don't say," responded Mother, looking up. "What a silly reason for not letting people read him. The next thing you know, those crazy people will tell folks not to eat matzo ball soup."

"That's an interesting observation, Nora," Dad said, obviously intrigued by Mother's allusion to soup.

"Just imagine if Mr. Solomon, who runs the general store in town, wasn't there. Where'd people go to get the things they need?" Mother paused, thinking. "By the way, why'd you learn German?"

"It was simple. The Germans were leaders in industry and science at the time. I was getting a degree in engineering, hence it was helpful to read—and write—the language."

I heard Dad say "read and write," which made me wonder if he could speak German. "Can you speak it, sir?"

"No, not very well. I don't have any reason to use it."

Since I was learning French from Miss Virtue, I decided, then and there, that as well as learn the grammar and such, I wanted to learn to speak it. What good is it if you can't communicate with a person?

I nodded, then picked up my book, hearing Dad ask me, "And what are you reading, Min?"

"Oh, something by a lady, *Pride and Prejudice.*"

"Not an easy read, I've been told."

"Nope, it isn't. I can't get over just how polite they are to each other—more than Southerners, and I thought we were the ones with manners. They do go on sometimes," I said, somewhat annoyed with the book.

"Then why read it?"

"Oh, the librarian said it would be good for me."

"When was torture ever good for someone?" Dad replied.

Mother for once didn't say anything, but she did smirk as she continued with her work.

"I started it and I'm almost finished, so there's no point in stopping now."

"Determination will get you a long way."

This time Mother looked up, but neither did she smile nor smirk. Her expression was indecipherable. Then, whatever her thoughts, she looked back down, her jaw muscles tightening and relaxing as she continued to sew. Moments later, she jerked and cursed, "Damn, I broke the needle."

. . . . .

In July, we were already sweltering and trying to get comfortable after breakfast.

"My Gawd, they went and did it. They went and formed a Union."

Mother and I both heard about it Monday after the Sunday meeting occurred between Norman Thomas, the socialist from New York City, and two Delta men who were socialists. We discussed it briefly and decided not to tell Dad. We knew he'd find out about it soon enough. Now was that time.

"Damn, this happened almost a week ago. Of all the times," Dad said, frustrated, "for the paperboy to get sick. They didn't have a replacement. Let me," Dad thumbed through another paper, speaking more to himself, "let me see if it's in the New York newspaper."

We waited. I pretended to read my book. Mother was crocheting, and pretended not to be listening. We knew that soon enough we'd hear him fuming, letting off steam. Afterward he'd have something intelligent to say, once he calmed down.

"Well, I'll be! Nora, just where is this place?" He showed Mother the article.

"Oh, west of Memphis."

Dad nodded his head, but I could see he couldn't place it.

The paper says it was held in a place called the Sunnyside Schoolhouse. Would you believe a school board would allow people like that to use their facilities?"

"I declare," Mother said, looking up briefly and trying to look interested.

"Yes, someone should have a good talking to them about that."

"I daresay someone will, James."

"Goes on to say that two Delta men, Ward A. Rodgers and," Dad adjusted his reading glasses, "H.L. Mitchell, were part of this scheme with Thomas." Dad read on quickly, hurriedly saying, "Seems this came out of a meeting back in February, when Thomas met with them and a man named Edward Boston, who'd been evicted with his family. That's when they got the bright idea for the union—the STFU—Southern Tenant Farmers' Union."

"You don't say?" said Mother patronizingly, since we heard about this meeting from one of our sources months ago. Word does get around.

I saw Dad had caught onto Mother. Looking back at the newspaper, he said, "'Guess this is the first time ever that a union has been formed with both white and colored members."

I suspected Dad was baiting Mother because he said, nonchalantly, "Well, it's 'bout time something got integrated in Dixie."

Mother probably didn't know this was the first union in the country that had a mixed membership of whites and coloreds, so she visibly reacted to Dad, not because of the mixed race union, but because of the attack on the South. Dad lifted his eyebrows and said, looking all so innocently, "I'm a Republican, the party of Lincoln. He freed the slaves."

"There you go, James, getting all uppity. Y'all think you're so high and mighty, let me tell you—"

Dad started belly laughing. At first Mother was offended because she thought he was laughing at her ignorant Southern ways, when she realized what he'd done. Then she started to chuckle. Finally, we were all having a good laugh together.

"Nora, I couldn't resist it. I take this union stuff seriously. I know I get worked up about it. When I saw nobody else seeing how this could affect us, I—"

"You decided how to get my attention. Well, you got it!" They both smiled at each other.

"James, like you, I have no problem with whites and coloreds cooperating and finding ways to make things better for everyone. That's not an issue for me—not like it is for many of these folks. However, history tells me people have gotten hurt in the past. I'm afraid more will again. I remember—"

Dad knew and I knew what Mother was referring to—Marie and the fire.

Mother took a breath, then said, nodding her head affirmatively, "Like we talked about before, we're gonna have to walk a fine line between the planters, the sharecroppers and tenant farmers, especially now that there's the STFU." Speaking slowly, Mother reiterated, "The Southern Tenant Farmers' Union."

. . . . .

I thought July was hot, but August was even hotter. The humidity was so thick you felt you were underwater. That first weekend of the month, because of the workload at the gin and out in the fields, I stayed Saturday night with Mother at Uncle Bob's new house, which had been an elegantly furnished plantation house. Everything inside now was old and worn.

"Minnie, you're eatin' skimpy t'night," said Uncle Bob's wife, Dora.

"It was mighty good, ma'am. I think I'm jus' not so hungry."

"Well, I declare, Minnie, you'll jus' melt away," quipped Will's fiancee, Ellen.

"Oh, I don't think so. I jus' think it's the heat."

"Yes, could be. Affects me like that, too—sometimes."

I really liked Ellen. She and Will had gone together since grammar school. Small, blonde, and petite, she was perfect for Will, showing all the signs of being ladylike but knowing how to work hard—in the fields if necessary. Though she was outgoing, she was a deep and thoughtful person. Of all the people in the family she, I felt, understood me best. She knew what it was like to struggle, having been abandoned to her aunt and uncle early in life. Fortunately, her relatives were upright, responsible people, and made sure she got an education.

Will, the eldest of the three brothers, was hardworking. He could be a hell-raiser if given half a chance, but Ellen kept a tight rein on him. She had plans for them, and was not about to let anyone or anything derail them from making a good wholesome family of their own.

"Cousin Minnie, you ailin' or . . . somethin'," said Will in his lazy jaw speech.

"Not at all. By the way, Will, I still remember the time you visited me at Grandpa's. That's when I got typhoid fever. Meant a lot to me. Thanks."

"You're welcome."

I pushed my chair away from the table only to hear, "Minnie, how 'bout a piece of pie?" Will's mother had offered me more, concerned she might be viewed as inhospitable to a guest.

"I jus' can't do another bite, but I thank you, ma'am. Gonna go if you don't mind."

"Not at all, you know where you can find us—around the pies."

Going out to the porch on this hot, sultry, muggy night, I walked away from the house. On a whim, I got into the truck and drove to a Union meeting in Tyronza. What I saw there were poor, desperate, dispossessed, or soon-to-be dispossessed people. Powerless, they'd come together, black and white, to save themselves and their families. This, I was told proudly by a man sitting by me, was the first integrated union in the nation.

Two—actually four—speakers caught my attention. One, H.L. Mitchell, a good-looking man in his late twenties or early thirties, was an articulate and well-disciplined orator, whose shock of thick blonde hair would fall forward as he moved around, which would force him to swipe back his hair unconsciously with his free hand. He was one of the two founders of the union.

In contrast to Mitchell's looks, Ward Rodgers had an equally thick mane of hair, but it was dark brown, along with his almost black eyes, and intense stare. Partly because of his personality and possibly because of his degree in Divinity from Vanderbilt University, his argument was laced with language from the Bible. Both men were young, healthy and attractive in their own way.

The audience responded enthusiastically to both of them, but it was when an elderly colored man, John L. Handcox, began to recite his poetry and song in that little colored church that everyone—white and colored alike—responded at a deep, feeling level, different from the previous speakers' arguments. There was something profound here. I felt like I did when Bonnie and I were kids. We sat on the steps of the colored church in town and listened to the singing of spirituals by the choir.

Finally, and unexpectedly, the mood changed. One member of the union, sitting in the crowd of both men and women, rose and spoke to us. The undertone of what he was saying was resentful and bitter, explaining to everyone how the planters had—for hundreds of years—sowed dissension among poor whites and coloreds.

A lean man with a creased, sunburned face and neck, hissed, "It's the planters who got all the land. It's the planters who work us from sunup to sundown, giving us barely enough to feed our families."

People nodded in the room, some calling out, "Yes, tell it the way it is!"

"The planters have used the ol' 'Divide and Conquer' for generations. That's how they keep us in our place."

"That's right, brother!" cried another voice, followed by others echoing the same words, this time with more force and resentment in their voices.

"We're taught to hate each other—not to hate the people who exploit and hate us. We're all little better than their slaves."

I had heard enough. I understood the pain and frustration of the people gathered in the room. I looked around myself, seeing sharecroppers and tenant farmers seated and standing along the walls of this dilapidated one-room church, grasping at hope. Something inside of me said they'd fail. They would fail and be swept away like so many falling leaves. I left shortly before the end of the meeting.

Having sat in the back of the room, I went unnoticed as I walked out into the light of the full moon. As I went toward my truck, a group of men got out of cars and trucks, and came between me and my truck, blocking my way. *Night riders*, I said to myself. I stopped. About fifteen feet separated us.

"A damned communist," snarled one.

"Please, let me pass."

"You come with us."

Remembering what happened to one woman, bruised from a beating, I stood straight and stood my ground. Unwavering, I pulled my Derringer out of my purse and growled, "Get out of my way."

There was a moment of silence. Suddenly some of the men laughed, then one insolent man said in a sinister tone of voice, "Come right this way, little lady. We ain't gonna hurt you."

"Do NOT put your hands on me." I knew if someone touched me, I would fight to the death.

"So you don't like to be touched, do you?"

"Get out of my way! I commanded."

"You're an uppity little thing, ainn't you?" sneered the same young man.

"As uppity as a planter's daughter can be!"

That seemed to confuse them.

"My Grandpa Coymen shot his fair share of men in the Delta, and his mother, Anna Keghel Coymen, stood down Yankee soldiers at her doorstep. I'll be damned if you mess with me! Now I'm warning you for the last time, get out of my way. Now!!"

There was a dead silence until one man spoke politely, "You wouldn't be Nora Belle Gibson's daughter? Daughter of Charlie Coymen, ma'am?"

"I am." I said with a deadly intensity in my voice.

"Her mother shot Frank at the fire station," rejoined an older voice.

"Now let me pass," I said slowly, not mincing my words. I'd brook no more fear mongering from this trash.

The man who asked about my family turned toward the men and ordered, "Let the lady pass! Git outta her way."

The men parted, one man asking me politely, "Why would a lady like you be hyere?"

"I wanted to hear what is being told to these people. What they're thinking. Now, let me pass."

The men drew farther apart, one man hurrying to open my door. "Sorry, ma'am. It was a mistake."

"Yes, a mistake." I got into the truck. The door was gently shut behind me. "Thank you."

"You're welcome, ma'am. No offense meant."

"None taken."

I laid my revolver on my lap, put my key into the ignition, and drove away into the night.

CHAPTER 29
COMMITTED

A week later, I pulled the truck into Clay East's gas station and let the attendant fill the tank. I knew that this was more than a visit. It had a lot to do with trusting myself, as well as trusting a man I found attractive. I thought long and hard about what I was about to do: I went into the dry cleaners attached to the gas station, which was in the part of town unofficially called "Red Square." Just as I planned, I found Harry Leland Mitchell moving along a line of clothes on hangers.

"Hello," he said when he saw me standing there quietly.

"Hello."

We each seemed equally struck by the same intonation in the other's voice. The same recognizable underlying emotion was detected in that one simple word. An underlying and unmistakable assurance and intensity passed between us in moments.

He casually walked over and cupped the edge of the counter, his arms outstretched, the veins thick and protruding from his white, slightly freckled skin. The white shirt around the armpits had dark rings of sweat, the neck of his shirt opened wide, revealing the upper part of his hairless chest. He was lean, but muscled. All of this I took in within seconds during our brief eye contact, confirming my feelings about him during the

Union meeting. The thick shock of blonde hair had at times fallen across his brow, giving him a somewhat boyish look, which could have obscured the nature of the man were it not for the passion and command in his voice. On stage he railed against the injustice and greed of planters and the plight of the overworked and starving sharecroppers and tenant farmers.

"I thought—"

He waited, the slightest smile curling at the ends of his wide, full lips.

"I thought," I began. I was so sure of myself when I drove away from the plantation, but now as I stood before him I may have overestimated myself. Perhaps it was his penetrating stare, because I hadn't sensed that when he was on stage, delivering his impassioned speech to the men and women of the audience. Then I was more aware of him striding back and forth across the stage with the almost constant movement of his big hand swiping his hair backwards, which within seconds flopped back across his forehead.

He didn't embarrass me by letting me make a fool of myself. Instead, he smiled and what a smile it was—incredibly warm and welcoming. "I remember you," he said softly, the softness of his voice contrasting so considerably with the openness of the smile.

"Oh, yes? I don't see how. I thought I was invisible in the back of the meeting there."

"You left early. If you had been watching me, you would have seen that I watched you as you went out the door."

"Why?"

"I—I don't know why, entirely. Let's just say there was something in the way you moved." He thought for a moment, and pushed his hair back. "As careful and considerate as you were, there was something that said, "I AM LEAVING. Please, get out of my way, now."

"I try not to be—"

"You are . . . and it's an attractive quality. On the other hand, that determination could get you into trouble."

"It nearly did."

"I know. One of the women in the back followed you out the door."

"Oh, she saw the night riders." I paused. "Them," I said, dismissively.

"Before she could get any of us, you had handled everything yourself."

"So she heard the dust-up."

"She did." His eyes were not playful in any way now. He was dead serious.

"Well, then you know I'm a planter's daughter."

"I do, and . . . I'm glad you came back." He held out his hand. "Leland; Harry Leland Mitchell. I'm pleased to meet you, Miss Coymen." Or, should I say, "Mrs.—"

"It's a long story." I dropped my eyes.

That is when I saw his wedding band. *He is married.* I felt a change of mood come over me, which brought me back fully in possession of myself again. Whatever had been roused was doused by a bucket of cold water. The reality of the moment all but destroyed any earlier thoughts or feelings I may have had. I looked directly at him.

"No, that's my mother's maiden name and my grandpa's name." I stood there, feeling slightly embarrassed by my miscalculation, which I could tell he was aware of. I said levelly, "Minnie Beck." Trying to regain my composure, I continued, "Minnie . . . Minnie is best."

"Good. Very, very good, Minnie. It's been a long time since—" He closed his eyes momentarily. When he opened them, he did not finish his sentence. Instead, he looked at me with his fixed stare, both appraising and absorbing the feelings coming from me.

I took another look at his wedding ring, which he didn't fail to notice.

Whatever feelings he may have picked up moments earlier had evaporated. He knew it by way of my stance (I took one step back from the counter), by my eye contact, and that indefinable sense we have of someone's emotions.

"I came back to let you know I really admire your courage and your convictions. You really care about people."

"Thanks, I appreciate that."

"Even from a planter's daughter?"

"Yes," he said, dead serious, "even from a planter's daughter."

Everything had changed so quickly in the general atmosphere.

"I felt the best thing I could do for you under the circumstances is to give you my business."

Leland nodded.

"I know it's just one person's business, but it's better than nothing, especially when there's a general boycott that has been called by the planters against your business. A lot of people, though, are sympathetic to you and your cause."

"I'm not one to turn down business, Minnie. I'm sure your family has heard the talk about some planters being retaliated against."

"Well, I am not my mother; so—"

"So?"

"So, until something is said to her, I don't have to deal with that."

"I guess you won't."

"But there's nothing that prevents me at this time from patronizing your business."

"You would do that?" Leland said, surprised at my willingness to possibly create problems for Mother and the business.

"I will," I said determinedly.

"Minnie, didn't I tell you that your determination may get you into trouble?"

"I guess it already has, and I'm still here."

"Indeed! You are, Minnie. Like I said, I would definitely appreciate your business."

Unsaid at that moment, I had already made a decision. I would withdraw some money each month from my bank account, and I would make a small donation when I came to pick up my dry cleaning. Even I was a bit surprised at myself. Normally, I was very frugal, knowing how hard I worked for every penny I earned. Frivolous, I was not. But I had come here with a desire to test the waters—to see how I felt about Leland. My instincts now told me he was a decent man, and needed help.

"Well, Leland, the next time I drop in, it will be with some clothes."

He nodded slowly. The expression on his face I would have sworn showed disappointment. "Thank you for your business, ma'am."

As I walked away, I turned and called back. "By the way, congratulations."

"Congratulations?"

He came around the counter and was within arms' reach. I was aware I was looking up and into his eyes. "Yes, congratulations for being elected as the Executive Secretary of the Southern Tenant Farmers Union."

"That only happened—"

"I assure you, we got the news the next day at the gin."

"You don't say," he said with that slightly enigmatic smile.

"Oh, I do say." I extended my hand, wanting to make physical contact. "Again, congratulations, Leland."

CHAPTER 30
KINFOLK

W e were all gathered around the dining room table at the Big House of what had once been the Jackson plantation. Uncle Bob, Aunt Dora, and I, along with their three sons and Ellen were making an attempt to cope with the late August heat. A desultory conversation about Will and Ellen's marriage plans had slowly petered out.

I was glad Mother wasn't here. She had given Uncle Bob two place settings of silverware from Grandpa's set of twelve. Afterward, I would have had to listen to her rant about how she should have kept it all, since country people like them made a mockery of its use. It was even tarnishing, which certainly would have ruined her dinner.

Actually, another bone of contention for Mother had just arisen: their recent purchase of furniture. It was new. I recently had heard Mother's complaint after we'd paid them a visit: "What a waste of money!" Then came the harangue and the regret that it could've been used to buy more land and more equipment—or just plain saved for the inevitable rainy day of farm life. Weather was always unpredictable and cost many a farmer his land. I could hear Mother now: They could've used what they had or gotten secondhand furniture from all the folks losing their homes to foreclosure. I knew I should have kept tighter control of his money—or just kept it for myself!"

Her fury didn't end there. "It's not only new, but also mismatched styles." Disgustedly, she went on, "Just look at that house. You've got early American up against French provincial! The damn fools just grabbed whatever caught their eye. It's a damn embarrassment—an embarrassment of riches."

If I had tried to say something in their defense like, "Well, it's pretty for them," she would have mercilessly lit into me. No, the best course was always to keep my mouth shut. Anyway, there was nothing to be gained by contradicting her.

"Gawd, but it's hot! Don't think I've ever seen an August like this," whimpered Dora, fanning herself with a tattered store-bought fan. "Minnie, sure ya don't want a beer? I got a nice cold one in the Frigidaire."

"No thank you, ma'am." And I meant that too. I'd had had enough alcohol around me to last me a lifetime. When I was young and Dad was drinking—those were awful days, let alone the nights. One night nearly cost me my life. Another, the man I loved.

I saw Ellen looking at me. She understood. I could see that in her eyes.

"Dad," said Roy, second oldest after Will, after having filled his plate for the third time and downing four beers, "I need some money for—"

"His carousin', Daddy. Don't give 'im nothin'!" Will blurted out, forsaking momentarily his country drawl for the irritation of the moment.

"You weasel tryin' to git everythang out of the ol' man you can. You ain't foolin' nobody, Will."

Other than Ellen, everybody on this side of the family spoke country. What's more, they spoke the lazy jaw dialect except when riled. However, it wasn't Roy's accent, it was his lack of respect for his Daddy that annoyed me.

"Boys, stop your arguing!" pleaded Aunt Dora. "Cain't you see I'm near expirin' from this heat?"

"I oughtta beat the livin' hell out of you," Will roared.

Roy stood up, slightly weaving back and forth. "Then, c'mon, step on out. I'll pound your ass into the ground."

I watched the arguing escalate, preparing myself. I didn't take anything or anyone for granted.

Ellen had been observing everyone carefully before she coolly said, "Will, this isn't goin' to accomplish anything."

Will clenched his jaw and didn't bite at the bait. He knew Ellen was right. He knew she had a high school education and thought things out carefully. She kept her self-control. In short, Will loved Ellen and there wasn't anything he wouldn't do for her.

Staggering over to the frig and grabbing another beer, Roy saw he was not going to get a fight out of Will—not with Ellen around. He turned his sights on me. "Well, Cousin Minnie," he grumbled as he took a couple more swigs of beer, "haven't heard a peep out of you all night."

"Now, son, don't go after Minnie. She's our guest." Dora waved her fan, trying to cool herself.

"There you go takin' their side again," slurred Roy, first looking at his mother, then his daddy, before turning back to me. "Minnie," he grunted, "Y'all been featherin' your nest, ain't that so?"

I remained seated and quiet, but I was starting to get downright mad at Roy.

"Now, son, leave Minnie alone. She's our guest . . . our kinfolk. Nora's just been takin' care of business, lookin' out for us," assured Uncle Bob.

"Yeah, yeah, Nora's been wheelin and dealin', that's for sure."

Dad had continued to have talks with Mother about not getting too involved with Uncle Bob's money. Despite his counsel, Mother had set up three bank accounts for Uncle Bob. One was almost empty squandered by two of the boys; the other two were untouched, needing Mother's co-signature.

"Well, Counsin? Thar's talk nobody can fart in town without her knowin' 'bout it. She's got the city council and . . . everybody and everythang else under her thumb."

I nodded my head and just glared at him, saying flatly, "Roy I stay out of Mother's way. The plantation and gin don't belong to me."

I glanced over and noticed Ellen was nodding her head, but it was the expression on her face that said she admired Mother's control over everyone. She admired Mother's power in town and, I suspected, she wondered just how much more control Mother had that was a secret.

"Roy," I repeated slowly, "I stay out of Mother's way. The plantation and gin don't belong to me."

"Well, you're there every weekend, ain't 'cha?"

Now he was getting personal and testy. I would not be bullied. Normally, he kept his distance. He knew I could hold my own. I had more than a few fistfights with him at Grandpa's and won! "Roy," I said, trying to control myself, "I work for free. Mother doesn't pay me. Never did and never will."

"That's your problem, Cousin Minnie. We all know Aunt Nora controls part of our Daddy's money."

"Roy, pipe down. Nora's my sister and has been good to us." Uncle Bob nervously looked around the table for support.

"You'd think she'd be content with owning half the county, but she's gotta have the damn phone company and . . . even the lights and gas we use—the utility company! Hell, you'd think, since we're kinfolk she wouldn't even charge us for that stuff."

'Nough of this talk, boy," barked Uncle Bob, rising from his seat, trying to establish his authority.

"Who says," slurred Roy, and he started to get out of his chair when the other two brothers rose and reached over and shoved him down on his chair. At that you'd think he'd been slugged, and he started to twist violently trying to stand, when Aunt Dora called out, "Honey, please—"

Wiping her forehead, she pleaded, "Give yer poor daddy some peace."

"Yeah, git off off his back," growled Will.

"So, you gonna make me?" slurred Roy, menacingly.

"Yeah. Yeah, if that's what it takes, you little piece of—"

"Hold on thar, boys. 'Member we're 'round the dinner table. I don't want'cha arguing. Hyear me? 'Specially with two guests hyear," begged Aunt Dora wearily.

I was still watching intently, figuring out what I'd do if a ruckus broke out, and a punch came my way. That's when I saw Dade, youngest of the three boys, slowly stand up and say, angrily, "Mama done spoke. I'm tared of ya flappin' yer jaw. I will do ya harm. Now keep yer yap shut?"

Dade, quiet and intense by nature, was a sweetheart until he got some drink in him or felt his mother or father were threatened. He was lethal like a water moccasin hiding at the water's edge. Like me, once his rage was released, there was no telling how much damage he could do.

It was Ellen who brought an end to the row. "Y'all are brothers; be good to each other, please." Turning to me, she said, "Minnie, what do you hear of the government programs for us farmers to get money?"

"Money! More money is what I hear." I knew that would quiet Roy down, and also get everyone else's attention, especially Will and Ellen, who were planning for the future and trying to guide Uncle Bob along the way.

Roy started to act up, but Aunt Dora put her hand on his arm.

"If we use the AAA program right, it'll benefit us all as planters. Look at the average net income of planters compared to doctors. Delta planters make about $1,000 more per year than a doctor's yearly income of over $3,000."

"Huh," garbled Roy. "Speak English!"

"Planters make more money than doctors—a lot more."

Do ya make that much, Dad?" asked Roy.

I could see him already deciding how to spend the money. If he found out the ways to cheat the system by not sharing the government subsidies with the hopelessly poor tenant farmers and sharecroppers, he'd do it.

Flustered, Uncle Bob fumbled. "I don't rightly know. Ya know, Dora?"

"Nope. It's all I can do to try to run this hyear house 'n all."

I really felt sad for Uncle Bob and Aunt Dora. I knew they were doing their best, but they didn't have the education, the smarts or the cooperation of all of their boys to act as a team. I looked over at Ellen, who was nudging Will.

"Well, then," Will said, "we oughta damned well find out, and make sure we use that gov'ment money right, like Cousin Minnie's sayin'."

Immediately, I saw Roy about to say something, when everyone around the table started chimin' in, "You're right, Will. That's right. That's what we need to do." And so it went.

When I got a glimpse of Ellen, she was smiling. She knew they won the battle. She knew eventually Will (and she) would have control. All they had to do was think smart and plan ahead. Yes, Ellen was the best thing that could happen to this side of the family. There'd be no more riding the rails for Will if Ellen had anything to say about it.

It was strange. I intuitively knew and understood Will's personality. He was like me: Pride, honor and self-confidence mattered. Unlike Will, though, I was aware of a quality in myself that was like Ellen: deep, passionate feelings that were hidden and secretive.

As far as our blood was concerned, I knew I loved Uncle Bob and Aunt Dora. I knew they would always welcome me under their roof. They cared for me as kin, and would do right by me. Will and Ellen, well, they were family. They were allies, but they share a bond that did not include me. They were planning ahead, and as long as I wasn't an obstacle, everything would be all right.

. . . . .

Two months to the day—in this case, night—after having dinner at Uncle Bob's, I said my goodbyes and walked out the door and onto the porch, when I heard the door open and close behind me.

"Minnie, you almost got away before I could thank you."

Coming up to stand next to me, it was Ellen.

"What are you talking about, for goodness' sakes?"

"You know how to stand up to Roy, and put him in his place."

"When it comes to that banty rooster, he and I have hit the dirt more than once at Grandpa's when we were kids." I shook my head and snorted, "It was always him who got the whoopin'. 'Guess he hasn't totally forgot it."

Ellen laughed softly. "Whoopin'. Minnie, I declare you're speakin' country.

"Oh, you've known that all along, Ellen."

"True, but it was fun to hear you use it."

"It just seemed like the right word when I thought about fighting Roy."

"Yeah, I heard about those fights from Will."

"Oh, Will and I never fought."

"No, no, he meant you and Roy. I think he was always proud of you, being a girl and all. He said you'd never go lookin' for a fight; but once somebody laid a hand on you, then watch out."

I met Ellen eye to eye. She really understood me— certainly the quiet side—and never pushed or probed into my affairs or feelings. My secrets remained my own unless I decided to tell her.

"'Course, Ellen, to tell you the truth, I always knew Will could lick me. On a couple of occasions things got tense, but we had, I guess, a way of just lookin' at each other that said, 'best to back off.' And we did. We had a respect for each other's territory and went out of our way not to hurt the other's pride."

"Yeah, it's funny, Minnie. That's more or less how Will described it to me, that is, about the two of you."

I had a sense there was more to this conversation than just idle chitchat. Ellen left the table and had come out to talk with me—not to pass the time of day because she was bored with everyone inside. No, at heart, Ellen was a strategist. Though she was light and convivial in a social situation, she had more than one side to her, which made her interesting. I could feel when she wanted to say something personal to me. This conversation would be done in private when she was laying the groundwork for her plans.

"Will and I never took each other for granted, Ellen. Also, we knew how to have fun. Gosh, he nearly got me killed on the train trestle! That was one scary moment."

"He told me about that, too. It made me so angry, I boxed his ears."

"You didn't!"

"I most certainly did, Minnie! Someday that boy's gonna be my husband and the father of my children. I was just letting him know what it means to be responsible."

"I guess you were."

The thought of her hitting him said a lot about Ellen. She is what is commonly called *the steel magnolia*—sweet on the outside, but hard, if need be—on the inside. Hitting Will also said so much about him. He'd only have taken that from someone he really loved and respected—like his daddy and mama and . . . Ellen. Obviously, he loved Ellen with all his heart.

"Ellen, Dad was just sayin' the other day what a great job you do at the utility company. Said it's a real relief knowin' he can count on you."

"I appreciate that, Minnie. I do my best. You know how hard jobs are to come by, so it means a lot to us—Will and I."

"I'm glad it's worked out so well for you, Ellen. I truly am."

"Why, thank you, Minnie."

There was brief moment of silence as we looked out onto the dark, open land. The smell of earth was strong and binding. For some reason, I thought about something from the Bible: *Dust thou art, and unto dust thou shalt return.*

I heard Ellen clear her throat. "Mmmm, doesn't that breeze feel refreshin' after that terrible heat during the summer? I always thought if the good Lord was going to redo cotton pickin' season, he'd see that October is always a better time."

"I'll put your suggestion in the next time I'm talkin' with him, Ellen."

"Now that's a sweet thing to do." There was a brief silence, then she said, "You know, Minnie, Will and I really think Nora is taking good control of her plantation (that includes you, too)."

"How so?"

"To start with, you didn't waste any time on Frank when he busted into the gin. You shot him on the spot."

"Oh, that. I—I mean Mother, did what she had to do."

I could almost see Ellen smiling in the dark. She had gotten the truth out of me. That annoyed me. I put up my guard. I didn't want to be surprised or say something I hadn't intended to discuss.

"Will and I respect your gumption, and . . . your business savvy. Nora continues to increase the size of her plantation. It's the largest private plantation in the county, and I don't doubt it'll grow bigger."

Ellen waited to see if I would reveal our plans but I remained quiet, other than to say, "Thank you for the compliment. I'll let Mother know how you feel."

"Well if you do, please let Nora know if there's anything either Will or I can do for you, to let us know immediately. You can count on us."

Finally, I sighed. She had gotten to the point: "You can count on us." Actually, what she was saying made sense. They were family. Who knows, but there may be a time in the future when we might have to take them up on the offer.

"Ellen, what a comforting thing to say. I'll let Mother know." I could tell she was happy that the foundation had been laid between us. I was receptive.

"Thank you, Minnie."

"Well, it's gettin' late, so I need to go. See you soon."

"Bye-bye, Minnie."

"Goodnight."

CHAPTER 31
SILK

The truck bumped down the dirt road. I was collecting rents from tenant farmers on the far end of our plantation next to Uncle Bob's lands. I drove along the edge of what had once been the Higgins' plantation, now part of our own small empire. The tenants had actually taken to us and told us repeatedly they liked us better than their previous landlord.

The first few weeks of October were already cooler than the preceding months. The cotton crop had been harvested. The leaves of the soybeans were now slowly changing from green to yellow and brown.

Suddenly I was startled when I heard a volley of gunshot in the distance. A flock of fearful ducks scattered over the trees by the river. I barely heard them quacking in panic. Another volley of gunshot sent many of the dead birds dropping from the sky like rocks. A few, injured, one wing extended, twirled downward like leaves, disappearing behind the treetops. Dogs near and far began yelping or baying, depending upon whether they were guarding a house or retrieving a duck.

Someone, I thought, would have duck for dinner. This, in turn, reminded me of many a succulent duck dinner with Grandpa at the Big House. I was aware of a slight change in my mood.

As I rolled up to an old shotgun house with a covered porch, an elderly woman rocked in her chair. She had, I imagined, spotted me from afar. Maybe it was the dust raised by my truck. She knew why I'd come. Though I'd never met her before, Tom collected the rents over here on this particular day of the month.

"Howdy," she shouted, hoarsely, as I pulled up in front of the house.

"Howdy, ma'am."

"Yeah, I been expectin' the rent collector, but I wuzn't expectin' it'd be a girl. I thought Tom wuz comin'."

"Hope you're not disappointed. I know he's better lookin' than me."

She rocked back and forth heehawing. I knew I'd gotten her funny bone.

"Ya might jus' have a point, young lady." She thought a moment, then said upon reflection, "But ya seem t' have a right nice disposition."

I was taken aback by her candor.

"M' grandbaby's out huntin squirrel or whatever he can git down by the river. His boys are fishin'. He's got ten of 'em, but no girls." She rocked back and forth without a word, but finally said, "I sure would've liked a purty lil' girl." She shook her head. "All my kids died on me."

"Sorry to hear that, ma'am."

"That's mighty kind of ya, miss, but when the good Lord's callin', ya gotta go. What'd ya say yer name was?"

"Minnie, ma'am."

"Right nice name, Minnie."

She started heehawing again. Between breaths she gasped, "Minnie, Minnie Mouse. M' son took me to one of those picture shows, and I seen "Steamboat Willie" with Minnie Mouse and Micky Mouse." She let the rocker slowly come to a stop. "What a hoot that was."

"It's one of my favorite cartoons, ma'am."

"Glad to hear that. Well, young lady, I'm Alice Cooper, but you can call me Alice."

I felt uncomfortable with the idea of calling an elder—even if she was poor—by her Christian name. And, she saw that!"

"Don't stand on formalities hyere, young lady . . . I mean, Minnie.

"As I wuz sayin', all my kids died. I could feel sorry fer m'self, but who am I to question the Lord when he calls 'em home. He left me my grandbaby and his kids, so . . . I'm grateful."

To cheer her up, I asked, "You say your grandson's down at the river huntin'?"

She nodded, and continued to rock.

"Well, ma'am, I think you're havin' duck tonight. Saw a mess of 'em brought down by gunshot."

"Ya don't say. Been a long time since we've had duck. Even squirrel's in mighty short supply these days. Hope they git more 'n one bird, 'cuz they'll be a ruckus around the table unless I make a stew with it." She thought another moment, asking, "What'd ya say yer name was, honey?"

"Minnie, ma'am, Nora Gibson's daughter. Charles Coymen's granddaughter."

Alice looked down and chuckled to herself; she looked back up. "My goodness that wuz a long time ago. I knew that man when he wuz one young buck. Gawd, that thar man could stop a woman's heart. He sure wuz a handsome devil. Hope ya don't mind me takin' liberties and speakin' m' mind."

"Not at all, ma'am."

Looking me over with those canny eyes, she called out good-naturedly, "C'mon up hyere and keep this ol' woman company. I'd sure appreciate it."

Even though Mother had me on a schedule, I felt sorry for Alice when she had said, "Keep this ol' woman company." Getting out of the truck, I came to the bottom of the stairs.

"Well . . . what'cha waitin' fer. C'mon . . . "

I heard the distinct accent of her people—mountain people, Hillbillies, who had come down from Ozarks when the land was opened up.

"Yes, ma'am."

"Pull that thar ol' chair up. Let's palaver."

As soon as I sat down, the chair wobbled. A few seconds passed. Seeing that I had settled squarely on it, Alice tugged on her nose and exhaled, "Well I guess it's gonna hold ya."

Seeing my expression, she went on, "Hate to say it, Minnie, but I was wonderin' if I wuz gonna have to pick ya up off the porch. That thar chair tipped over the last time. M' grandson put a couple nails to it, but said not to expect the impossible—that it'd hold."

"'Guess it did hold, ma'am, but a few more pounds, and I'd prob'ly be spread out with my legs in the air."

Alice started cackling, appreciating my humor.

"My names Alice—Alice Cooper to be preee-cise." If m' mem'ry serves me right, didn't ya say ol' Charlie Coymen's kinfolk of yers."

"My grandpa, to be precise."

"Mmm hmm, his granddaughter." Nodding her head, she sighed, saying "Yeah, I can see you're his blood: same high cheek bones, nose—especially his nose, and blue eyes, but to be sure, mind ya, the blue's not the same color. Nope, it ain't."

I smiled, recollecting not only the color of Grandpa's eyes, but also trying to reconcile the man I remembered to Alice's memory of him.

"Ya both have the hawk's stare," Alice said through what once must have been full shapely lips, but now because of age, time and the weather, had wrinkled into what looked like crepe paper. When she smiled, her teeth were few and far apart. "Yessss, that's it—the hawks stare! When ya fix your eyes on a person, it's to see in t' 'im. No nonsense it is." Taking a moment to cogitate, she went on, "'Course, I ain't seen yer mama, so I can't say if she's the same."

I didn't offer her anything to hang onto.

Taking a deep breath and shaking her head, Alice chuckled, "Listen to me go on. I declare, just some ol' fool woman. I didn't mean no offense, honey."

"Ma'am no offense taken. Nice to hear your thoughts."

"Really?"

"Really."

"Well, I'll be. Ain't nobody told me that in ages. I'm mighty obliged fer yer kind words, honey."

I gazed at her withered little body, rocking away rhythmically in the chair. The thinning grey hair exposed some of her scalp, while the almost translucent skin showed the blue veins at her temples. Wrinkled folds of skin draped her neck. Grasping the arms of the rocker, her hands and her twisted fingers said she'd worked long and hard in the fields.

Alice saw me looking at her hands.

"Got rheumatism. Never stops hurtin'," she moaned.

"It sounds like it pains you a lot, ma'am."

"Oh, it does . . . but what pains me most is m' funeral and goin' to Glory Land."

"Your funeral, ma'am." I asked, surprised, then concerned.

"Well, not on the 'morrow, it ain't, but . . . it's a comin'. When ya git m' age, ya know those thangs. That ain't m' big worry; it's this." Alice reached down, pulling up her old cotton dress that had been patched and mended time and again. "See, it's this hyere burlap."

"Yes, ma'am, I see." Alice was wearing a burlap slip. I watched as she rubbed the rough cloth between her forefinger and thumb. I felt the slight shudder of remembrance, reminded of the years of my youth working in the burlap factory. I didn't have to touch the cloth. I knew exactly how it felt against the skin.

"Ma'am, might I go inside of your house?"

Assuming I wanted a drink of water, she said, "The kitchen's straight on through. Water's sittin' in the jug.

"Thank you, ma'am."

Once I closed the door, I pulled my dress over my head and pulled off my slip. Minutes later, I was back on the porch and took my seat. She didn't miss a thing. "What'cha got thar?"

"I didn't want you meetin' your Maker in burlap. Here you are, ma'am."

"But . . . but . . . I don't know what to say. I ain't got no money for a luxury."

"Take it, ma'am. It's a gift."

"Well, I declare," Alice fumbled, groping for the right words. "It's prob'ly the only time in m' life when I wuz at a loss for words."

I watched her as she caressed the material lovingly. Then, she ran it across her weathered cheek and closed her eyes. "Oh, my, jus' what is it, honey? It's so white, so smooth, so—"

"It's called silk."

"I—I—"

"Don't worry. I got another one."

A big smile spread across her face. Alice exclaimed, lifting the hem of her dress and placing the silk next to her leg. "They're all gonna be mighty surprised—mighty, mighty surprised, 'cuz in the pine coffin whar I'm laid out, I'm gonna have m' grandbaby lift my dress up hyere, so all the folks can see I got this fine . . . fine silk garment."

CHAPTER 32
POWER

November brought good news. Mother accomplished two major goals—political goals. She had by way of her vocal and financial support seen two of her candidates win elective office. Mayor Peter Church was elected from our district to the House of Representatives in Little Rock. Lawrence Burgess, a city councilman and ally of the mayor, was elected as County Judge. Having that position, Burgess could affect projects that benefited the plantation directly. Drainage and levees were major concerns ever since the Great Flood of 1927 devastated the Delta. Mother's money bought another sitting councilman, Ross Conyers, a seat on the Drainage District as one of the directors. The judge and the councilman were both dependent on Mother for ginning their cotton and for their utilities.

Surprisingly, Mother didn't go to the men's swearing-in. She did not want to raise her profile among other planters, so she sent me instead. Her only admonition to me was, "It's best not to let the left hand know what the right hand is doing."

Today we worked at the gin until late and were exhausted by the time we left and walked over to the house. When we came through the door, Delia was there to meet us.

"Mrs. Gibson, I cooked up a real nice dinner for y'all."

"Thank you, Delia."

"You'll have a nice green salad, followed by a navy bean soup with grated carrots, followed by chicken and dumplings."

Mother seemed pleased. "My, sounds like a feast."

I was tickled. Delia was a good cook—a very good cook. Having spent years in the kitchen with Marie, she observed and learned many of Marie's recipes—unbeknownst to Marie, who jealously guarded her cooking secrets.

"I thought y'all deserve it. The way you work, I declare."

As we walked into the dining room, Mother exclaimed, "My goodness, Delia, I didn't expect such a formal dinner."

Delia had already set the dinner table, and was now standing in the doorway to the kitchen.

"You set out all of the dinnerware."

"Learned me that from Miz Marie, ma'am. You know how she was."

"She was a real stickler for details," replied Mother, almost sympathetically.

"Was she ever," muttered Delia, taking a deep breath and exhaling it slowly. She remembered the heavy hand of Marie.

I particularly knew what Delia meant. Marie oversaw everyone who worked at the Big House like a hawk. Delia was always being pushed by Marie to do more, but I could see where it paid off. Delia absorbed over the years so much of the finer ways to run a household. She knew what she was doing.

"Y'all want to eat now?"

"That'll be fine."

"Miz Minnie, got a treat for you—apple turnovers."

I broke into a smile. Just something Marie would have done. It warmed my heart. "Oh, Delia, that's perfect."

Mother and I sat down at the table when almost at that exact moment there was a knock on the front door. We looked at each other, still a little wary from our experience with Frank crashing through the door of the office and firing his gun. Even with our guard dogs and the Deputy Sheriff next door, we still didn't take our safety for granted.

Delia came through the dining room to answer the front door. When she opened it, I heard a familiar voice—the mayor's. Mother must have heard him, too, because she called out, "Delia, you let that boy in."

Mother stood up, which was my cue to stand up, too, just as Delia led Peter and his wife into the room. "Norma Mae and Peter, y'all sit right down and have dinner with us."

They hesitated until Mother said, "I insist."

The Churches were now on a first-name basis with us, since Peter won the election to the Arkansas State Assembly as an assemblyman representing our district. This was Mother's signal that they were now friends.

"Well, if you insist, Nora," responded Norma Mae. They sat down, just as Delia brought our salad bowls, then quickly made two additional place settings.

"What brings y'all out?" teased Mother.

"We wanted to thank you personally for what you've done," said Peter. "I had no idea I'd ever be much more than a mayor—if that."

Mother arched her eyebrows as if to say, *Really?*

Norma Mae said, affirmatively, "I never had any doubt, Peter, you would rise like cream to the top—none at all."

I cast a glance at Mother, who looked at me, now all but saying, *I knew he'd go far. I don't back losers.*

"I'm sure y'all must be very excited," I offered, watching carefully to see how their behavior might have changed. Certainly, their position in town demanded a new level of respect from their colleagues and ordinary folk alike.

"Oh we are, indeed, but I—and the city council—have decided that I'd keep my job as mayor, as well as my new position in Little Rock. They felt I'd be more helpful to the town that way since I'd have a stronger voice for our town in the Capitol."

"I think they were very wise. Don't you, Minnie?"

"By all means, Mother." What I didn't indicate was the Council's decision had been a foregone conclusion, once I had explained to them what Mother and I thought would be best for the town. Of course, no one would say or do otherwise—even if one of them wanted the position. Unspoken, the councilmen and I knew that *what was best for Mother was best for the town.*

Norma Mae's pedigree and diplomacy came to the fore. "I know Peter will do his utmost best for everyone."

Mother looked in her direction and smiled.

Peter picked up his wife's meaning. "I'm looking forward to working with the legislators—and the rest of the government—in Little Rock to improve conditions for everyone here."

What Peter didn't say was "everyone" seated around the table, which was already understood by us. Some things don't have to be explained.

"It's wonderful that another one of 'us' was elected," said Norma Mae. "This way you'll be so much more effective, honey."

I looked over at Mother, who fully understood the implications of Norma Mae's statement. Mother now had allies: Burgess, a County Judge, and Conyers, a director on the Drainage Board.

Responding to Norma Mae, I said, "Already having a good working relationship with ex-councilman Burgess will definitely be an asset."

Mother loved that word "assets," and spoke up. "Definitely!! They will definitely be assets to you, Peter, and to our town."

"I believe you're right, ma'am."

"Nora is right. We'll have to have one of those special dinners with them and bring out our new silverware that Nora so generously gave us. I just can't wait to use it." Turning toward Mother, Norma Mae continued. "Matter of fact, we'll all have to get together real soon. They'll be so much to talk about." Shifting to a lighter note, she said, "I think I have a few Virginian recipes you'll enjoy."

"That'll be just lovely—just lovely," purred Mother.

I observed Peter as the salad was brought out. Ready to eat, Peter picked up the wrong fork, when he heard his wife clear her throat. He watched her as she first put her napkin on her lap; then, she picked up the salad fork. Quickly, changing course, Peter grabbed his napkin and picked up the right fork. I glanced at Mother. She was fully aware of everything.

When the soup arrived, I watched as he picked up the soup spoon but when he bent over the bowl, Norma May cleared her throat again, straightening up in her chair, which was a signal for Peter not to slouch and to pull his shoulders back. Carefully, he lifted his spoon from the bowl to his lip. When he dipped the spoon into the bowl, he titled the bowl away from himself and filled the spoon with the soup.

In some ways it seemed almost painful to watch Peter try so hard to observe proper etiquette at the table, but he looked determined and not at all uncomfortable, obviously wanting to learn from his wife. Clearly he admired his wife's breeding, and was trying hard to please her. I could see the power of his wife. She was molding and shaping him right before me.

Norma Mae redirected our attention away from Peter by discussing issues at the school. Mother had already acquired a teaching certificate for her, so now she had a solid and secure position at the school.

. . . . .

The Saturday morning following the election this past Tuesday, I arrived in town early and started out of the station, when a truck pulled alongside of me. On guard, I instinctively slid my hand inside my fur coat and gripped my Derringer.

"Don't shoot, Lady!" came the familiar voice. "It's me, your ol' fishin' buddy."

"Tom, don't you go playin' with me, boy! You could get yourself shot." I looked straight ahead and continued walking. I was really annoyed. He not only scared me, but I was within a hair's breadth of pulling the gun out of my pocket.

"Minnie, look at me."

Not stopping, I turned and glared at him.

Tom was leaning out of the window of the truck. "Y'know, I think you actually would—shoot me."

"Only if I had to." I was cooling down. "Right now I'm not feelin' too kindly toward you racin' up on me the way you did."

"Awww, Minnie, I apologize." Tom smiled.

"Uh huh. You do, do you, with that big ol' grin plastered across your face. I have a mind to give you a lashin'."

"Really? Well, then, that'd mean I'd have to take off my shirt, and—"

"Okay, Tom. Just stop the truck and carry me over to the gin."

"Yes, ma'am! I am your willin' servant."

"Tom . . . enough, okay?"

"Since you put it that way, I got something important you might want to hear."

"What is it?"

I got in the truck, and Tom drove me over to the gin. I sat there, listening to him.

"So, that's it. Roosevelt has set up an agency to help people get a house on a two-acre cleared plot of land, along with—"

"There's more?"

"With a barn, a smoke house, a chicken coop, and the right to farm twenty acres of land with tools supplied by the government," Tom said forthrightly.

"Where's this happening?"

"The town's named Dyess Colony. Eventually, there will be five hundred houses there."

"No! That many houses?"

"Yep, with a hospital, schools and stores."

"It's hard to realize the government—"

"The government's building the town in Mississippi County—just north of Lepanto. They got men workin' on it in

May of this year, draining 16,000 acres of swamps and turnin' the land into bottom land."

"That's backbreaking labor. Also, if the snakes don't get you, the diseases will."

"Minnie, these men are just happy to be workin' and bringin' in money to feed their families. I reckon for them that other stuff's the least of their worries."

"I suppose you're right."

Tom just looked at me, letting what he had said sink in. He snorted, "Nobody's gonna let his wife and kids starve. From what I hear, some houses are gonna be ready by February."

"Tom, wouldn't it be great if," I caught myself. "Tom, you sly old fox, you led me right to where you wanted me to go. Didn't you?"

"Maybe I did; maybe I didn't," Tom said, rubbing his chin between his forefinger and thumb.

"Okay, you baited the hook, now I'll bite. Wouldn't it be great if some of the folks being evicted off our plantation were able to get a place?"

"It would."

"Well, go on. What do we have to do?"

"Not me, Miss Minnie, but you?"

"I get your point."

First I had to get Mother's attention, hold it long enough to let her know about the place. Then I had to dangle a carrot before her—what's in her self-interest. I saw Tom looking at me, waiting for me to ask the next question.

"What're the details?"

By the time Tom finished, I was ready to talk with Mother. "Imagine that," I told him. "I'd never have guessed the government would do something like this. Just wait 'til I tell Dad!" I paused, turning the idea over in my mind—telling Dad. No point in rousing him up, and having to listen to the harangue about his "isms."

"No, on second thought, I don't think I'll tell Dad. Mother's the 'decision maker'."

Tom winked at me.

"I declare, give you an inch and you'll take a mile."

"At least a mile, Minnie," Tom said, his voice dropping and his eyes narrowing.

I felt like he was looking right into me. "You're just impossible sometimes." I opened the door and scooted out. "Thanks for the ride."

"Anytime, ma'am." Tom touched the brim of his hat and nodded. "Anytime at all."

I failed to knock on the door to the office, and found Mother pouring over some paperwork, running her fingers through her hair. Not wanting to upset her, I knocked on the door and she looked up, with me standing inside the room. Evidently she was distracted by what she was working on, so she didn't take notice that I had not knocked before entering the room.

"You're here early, Minnie."

"I couldn't sleep in. Our neighbors and Dad were going at. They were yelling and cussing, so I just got up."

"They'll get a talkin' to from me. I won't tolerate them arguing with Dad and you not gettin' a good morning's sleep when you've worked all week. I'll have somethin' to say to them, all right!" Mother took a deep breath, leaned back and exhaled. "Oh, hearin' that just comes at the wrong time."

I looked quizzically at Mother.

"This is the list of evictions I'm goin' over. Some folks are more bother than they're worth, but others—they're good, sound, hard-working folks, but they're on land we'll be mechanizing next year. So we'll only need a few of them."

This was the moment. As I was putting my gun in my purse, I looked up and said casually, "Maybe they can go to Dyess Colony."

"Dyess . . . Colony? What or where is that?"

"Oh, it's a town being built for people who have nowhere to go. The government is building five hundred homes with farmland for people—just north of Lepanto."

"That's all swampland."

"They're clearing 16, 000 acres."

"And?"

I could tell Mother was really interested. "A family will be given a house on a two-acre plot of land and all the tools to clear the stumps from twenty acres. It'll cost them $3 an acre with a mortgage that doesn't start for three years."

"Is that right?"

"It's hard to believe, but it's true. They just have to qualify to be accepted."

"Accepted by whom?"

"By a government representative there. The family has to be healthy, have a husband, wife and kids who can work, and know how to farm."

"We certainly have folks here like that," responded Mother, her eyes brightening.

"The government will provide a hospital, schools, a barn, a smokehouse, and a chicken coop."

"Well, I declare, who'd 've thought?" Mother said, more to herself than to me.

"The key is the family has to be on public relief."

"Mother's brow furrowed momentarily, then she smiled. "Well, that shouldn't be a problem. Now that we got 'our boy,' Mr. Church, in the House of Representatives, and Burgess as the County Judge, let alone the City Councilman, I—no, you— ought to be able to move that along."

"Some of the houses will be ready this coming March."

"March, huh?" Mother looked down at her list and began to make checkmarks by some names, then picked up the telephone. "Give me the Church residence, please."

Mother held the receiver against her chest. "It's time to collect, Minnie."

I knew what she meant.

A smile came to her face. "Good morning, Norma Mae, how're you, honey? It's Nora . . . Yes, we're fine. I was hoping you and Minnie might do lunch . . . No, I'm tied up . . . Uh huh, fine . . . Noontime . . . I'll tell, Minnie. I'm letting Delia know to expect y'all for lunch. Yes, not today, but we'll do something soon . . . Bye-bye."

. . . . .

That evening at dinner, I volunteered, "I had a nice lunch with Norma Mae. She already had heard about the Dyess Colony and was able to fill me in on some things I didn't know. It seems, Mother, she has a feeling for the homeless and soon-to-be dispossessed (I guess because of her own circumstances when she met us). Anyway, she *wants* to be helpful."

"Does that mean she'll talk with Peter about it?"

"Oh, she is definitely on a mission now. Not only does she plan for Peter to make his mark in Little Rock, she sees how this project can help him with the Roosevelt Administration and benefit the people around here who need it most."

"And?"

"And you, Mother. She wants to please." I knew that was what she really wanted to know: Norma Mae and Peter were assets.

"Thank you, Minnie. Good work."

I realized just how keen a judge of people Mother was. She not only saw an ally in Norma Mae that first cold morning, but also she saw the potential in this woman to be of value to her way beyond the school board. Mother had just been biding her time, especially once Peter was elected as a state representative. As smart as Norma Mae was, she had no idea she was a pawn in Mother's overall plan. Instead, she thought of herself as Mother's friend and ally. I decided to test the waters to see if what I was thinking was right.

"Looks like you've got both an ally and a friend, Mother."

"Minnie, you still have a lot to learn. Yes, Norma Mae is an ally, but a friend," Mother slowly shook her head, "a friend is something else."

I was right. That's what I had been thinking. A friend? I could only think of two women Mother considered friends, both in Memphis: Mrs. Fitzgerald, who stored some of our possessions when we lost The Big House in Memphis, and Louise, our neighbor next door, who was always helpful and never a bother. Most importantly, she made Mother laugh.

Mother would be on guard a long time before she counted Norma Mae as a friend. Too much could happen to sour the goodwill she'd established with this woman. There was a loaded gun, so to speak, Mother had placed inside that home; a loaded gun which could go off unexpectedly at any time. That gun's name was Peter Church, Norma Mae's husband.

CHAPTER 33

WHEN CHICKENS COME
HOME TO ROOST

Sunday evening after Mother and I had eaten, we went out to the living room and settled into some comfortable chairs before the fireplace. A wonderfully cozy and contented mood settled in around us. Mother had sent Annie, Marie's daughter, a train ticket in Los Angeles to join us. At noon, the train arrived. Of all things, Annie later insisted on helping Delia serve us dinner.

Now Annie was free to join us when Mother presented her with the jewelry and cash, which Marie had entrusted into Mother's care for her daughter. Rather than waiting until Mother could get to the West Coast, she decided to send for Annie. As Mother said to Annie once she was here, "I couldn't sleep, knowing what your mother wanted me to do."

Earlier that day, I had no idea who was coming to visit. Mother had said it was a surprise. When Annie stepped off the train, I all but fell into her arms. I felt like that same child protected by her from my Mother at the house years ago. Annie stroked my hair while I cried aloud. I tried to stifle my emotions, knowing Mother stood next to me.

Later that evening, she would go and spend the night at Delia's house; then leave the following morning to go visit her father in a nearby town. After a few days with the family, he would take her to the train station, where she'd leave for Los Angeles. As happy as I was to see her, I felt an underlying sadness knowing that she would be with us for only a few hours.

"Oh, yes, Miz Nora. I do miss y'all, but now I got my own family out there: six boys and a girl. The youngest girl, I named her Marie, after my Mother. By the way, thank you for sending me those pictures of Mama and us. This way my children gonna know who their grandma and granddaddy look like. Yezum, it's somethin' special. Can't git over how my girl favors her grandma."

Mother took a sidelong glance at me and shook her head. "There's jus' no accountin' for those things," she said to me, as much as to Annie.

Annie now wore the tiny ruby earrings that belonged to Marie. Every so often she would reach up and tenderly rub them, to make sure either that they were real or that they hadn't fallen off. It was about then the doorbell rang. Annie stood up immediately; Delia already raced for the door. Annie had just enough time to step back a few steps from our chairs. Annie hadn't forgotten her Southern ways.

"Miz Nora, it's the Churches come callin'."

Mother called out, "By all means, ask them in."

As Peter and Norma Mae walked into the room, Mother hugged each of them. I could see that they were pleasantly surprised. Mother had defined a new level of intimacy between the Churches' and the Gibsons'.

"Please, please, y'all take a seat by the fire."

Norma Mae spoke up. "Thank you, Nora, how nice of you! As I told you yesterday, we're leaving on the train tomorrow for Little Rock to set up a second home. But we couldn't leave y'all without thanking you again for everything, and wishing you a very early Merry Christmas."

Mother returned the cordiality. "Why, how very, very nice y'all." Turning to Delia and Annie, she said, "Would you please bring the guests something to drink, as well as serve them a dessert?"

"Ma'am," Peter asserted, "we just had that going-away dinner by the town council and their wives, so—"

"Yes, we did, Nora, but a drink would suit us both. It's a time to celebrate!"

"Minnie," Mother said, uncharacteristically gracious to me, "maybe you can show Annie where the liquor is."

As we left the room, I heard Mother begin to explain the relationship of Annie to our home in Memphis before she and Dad went to California.

Annie followed behind me into the dining room and to the liquor cabinet. "Annie, would you get the tray there? I took down a bottle of whiskey and placed it in the middle of the tray. One by one, I placed four snifters around the bottle. "Annie, in the refrigerator in the kitchen there is a bottle of Coca-Cola. Go get it, and fill one of the snifters half-full with it. That one's mine."

"Yes, ma'am."

"Please pour my glass half full, then bring the tray into the living room. Serve me first, since I don't drink alcohol."

Knowing the family history, especially one awful night years ago, when Dad was drunk and nearly killed Jeanette and me, Annie nodded. "Yes, Miz Minnie."

After I entered the room and found an empty chair, Annie came in and I took my Coca-Cola. Not realizing Norma Mae had been gazing at Annie as she was serving us, it was when Annie came to Norma Mae that she looked up. Carefully she examined Annie's face, saying, "I just don't know where, but I feel like I know that face."

At that instant, Peter nearly choked on his drink, the blood quickly draining out of his face.

"Peter, I declare, use your napkin," Norma Mae rebuked him. Softening the tone of her voice, she declared, "Honey, you're white as a ghost. Are you feeling all right?"

I looked at Mother and she looked at me. We both then looked at Peter. He was, as is commonly said, *the image of death warmed over*. We both knew exactly what had happened: Annie had happened. Their same birthdays, their same unmistakable family resemblance—high-bridged noses, full lips, even the shape and expression of their eyes cried out *family*. Only the shade of their skin and the texture of their hair separated brother from sister.

Two people in the room were absolutely oblivious to the situation: Norma Mae and Annie. The two people who were most directly affected: Annie by blood, and Norma Mae by marriage, were oblivious to their respective positions.

Neither Mother nor I anticipated these two people—whom now I could see indisputably were fraternal twins—would meet, and certainly not in our house. In one brief instant, I realized that Peter, as soon as he'd seen Annie, either recognized her from what had been a one-way, secretly arranged encounter by his/their mother in town (unbeknownst to Annie) or tonight he'd—only by some strange, intuitive sense—knew he'd come face to face with *his blood—his sister*. Though Mother and I hadn't anticipated this meeting, I was fairly certain that Peter felt otherwise: A trap had been set and he was caught.

Peter was uncharacteristically quiet the rest of the visit, looking into the fire and looking down at this hands.

Once the Churches had taken their leave, Mother watched them walk down the street, Norma Mae's arm in Peter's.

"Mother! Did you—?" I said sharply, surprising myself.

Keeping her gaze on the couple, she said, shaking her head, "No, Minnie, I did not. Believe me when I say this. But you know, sometimes . . . sometimes things work out better than you could have conceived. Peter had been on the end of my leash; now I've got him by the collar. No, I couldn't have planned this any better."

I felt sick to my stomach and knew I had to get away from her. "I don't think dinner agrees with me. I'm going to bed."

"Of course, Minnie. You've never really had—shall we say—a strong stomach. Have you?"

"Strong enough! I lived for years on oatmeal and peanut butter sandwiches after you abandoned me."

I turned and went inside, leaving Mother speechless—for once.

. . . . .

The next morning the phone rang. Mother picked up the receiver. Other than saying, "Hello, James," and "I understand," she didn't say anything except those few words. Mother hung up the phone and came back to the breakfast table. "Minnie, Daddy said that he got a call from his sister and that she is sending Jeanette home after the holidays." Mother paused. We'll know more once we get back home."

December 25, 1934

Dear Journal,

This year was more of everything. More money—cotton prices were higher. More modernizing—more tractors and trucks with more tenant farmers trained to drive them. More evictions.

Last year and this year, Mother made the decision to evict first the sharecroppers, followed by some tenant farmers, based upon how much land could be brought under cultivation with new equipment. This year it was more of the same. It would take careful planning to know how much money to spend, and how many farmers with mules to keep.

Mother's intuition about more trouble from the union and planters was accurate. When the State Supreme Court went against a sharecropper protesting his eviction by a planter, the U.S. Supreme Court refused to hear the case. Sad. There would be no help from the courts for the poor.

Things got really bad for union members when their meetings were broken up by night riders, ruffians hired by planters to terrorize people. Both men, as well as women, were beaten up. When people were killed and their bodies ended up alongside the road, it brought the FBI into the area.

On a personal note, I met and became more acquainted with Leland Mitchell. I did feel some disappointment about the experience, but it wasn't because there was something wrong with him. That is all I will say about it.

Mother had the chance to buy the rest of one of the farms I negotiated a partial purchase of the previous year. They were good people. I negotiated a rather fair settlement, considering it was during the Depression. Mother added 500 acres more to the plantation, now standing at 7,400 acres exactly.

Marie's daughter, Annie, arrived in town unannounced. That same night at the house, Peter and Norma Mae Church came by. Annie unknowingly met her fraternal twin brother. Peter realized who Annie was, and he nearly choked on his drink. Mother was pleased. She has even more control over him now.

On quite a different note, most gratifyingly for me, my French lessons with Miss Virtue continue. She said that next year next year I will start what would normally be considered my third year of French. I've never told Mother about the tutoring. Best to keep this a secret; otherwise, she'll think I'm wasting her time.

I received a Christmas card from Grace but she didn't say much, except her mother wasn't feeling well. She seemed down, so I promised myself to send her a cheerful letter in the next few weeks.

Unexpectedly, we received a call from Aunt Ethel, telling Dad to expect Jeanette on January 4th. Dad really didn't say much—at least to me—about the call. Mother had let slip that Jeanette had been a "handful" for Ethel. I guess, I just have to wait to find out the particulars. I have a pretty good idea the problem had to do with boys.

CHAPTER 34

SENT HOME PACKING

Almost as soon as Jeanette came into the room, the phone rang—again. Dad grimaced. Each time during the day, it was the same call, though not necessarily the same caller, with the same question: Is Jeanette home? I could see that he was sick and tired of the calls. "Evidently," he said, "Jeanette must have sent out letters of her arrival and like a wildfire, a few messages turned into scads of messages passed from one friend to another."

Dad jerked out of his dining room chair and bolted over to the phone. "Enough," he muttered. Picking up the receiver, he snapped, "She's not here."

"But Daddy—"

"You're not here. We're going to have a nice— uninterrupted!—dinner. Afterward, you can talk to your heart's content on the phone, but NOT now!"

Jeanette's flame flickered, but it wasn't really diminished. She knew—we all knew—Jeanette did not lack for friends. Even her two-year absence had not dimmed her popularity. The girl from California was back!

The short nap rested her after her three-day train ride. That was apparent. What was an unexpected surprise for me was

Jeanette—the changes in her physical appearance and personality. She was *Miss Personality Plus!*

"Hello, everyone." Jeanette went around the table and kissed all of us on the cheek, then settled into her customary chair around the dining room table. Unlike the bubbly, effervescent youngster, who struggled at times to hide the sensitive, shy side of her nature, now at sixteen and a half, she was more of the woman she was to become: radiant and charming, with a figure and face to match. The baby fat was all gone. Yes, there was a twinge of jealousy on my part.

It certainly didn't help my mood that I worked all of last week, including Saturday, at the plantation. I was tired. Normally having her back home, I would have been more excited. Instead, I braced myself for the onslaught: Jeanette regaling us with her ceaseless descriptions of her California experience and all the Californians she met, both in and out of school.

"Now, Jeanette, I've prepared a nice meal, so—" said Mother, trying to encourage Jeanette to calm down and enjoy the food and company. But this civilized atmosphere was not to last. After eating half her dinner, she began non-stop. Like a locomotive gathering speed from the burning coal, the fuel for her was our attention—actually, anyone's attention would have been sufficient.

The phone rang. Jeanette bounced up and made it to the phone over Dad's protestations. After a few brief words, Jeanette signaled abruptly, "I'll be going out with some friends."

Just as quickly, Dad shouted, "Tell 'em NOT tonight."

"Awww, Daddy, but—"

"Not tonight, I said!"

Jeanette reluctantly hung up the phone. I guess, second best—that would be us—would have to do. Almost as soon as she was about to sit down, there it went again! The telephone rang. Both Jeanette and Dad ran for the phone, but Dad got there first and said sharply, "Call back, tomorrow!"

Jeanette looked like he had lost is pants in public. She was mortified. "How could you, Daddy?"

"How could I what?"

"Well," Jeanette weighed what she was about to say, "be so . . . so rude?"

Well done, dear, I thought. I know what was on the tip of your tongue: "How could you be so rude?" Good judgment prevailed. She realized she was back home—back in the South, where manners were everything. "Smart girl," I said under my breath.

"What did you say?" asked Mother.

"Oh, I was just marveling at how much Jeanette has changed."

Mother looked like she was about to leap to Jeanette's defense when I said, "She's so pretty. Her blonde hair is platinum."

Nodding her head approvingly, Mother said, "Hasn't she? Our little angel is growing up."

Gawd, if Mother (and Dad for that matter) only knew how I detested that name—Angel. I'd lived with it for all these years, Mother and Dad cooing over their "little Angel."

As I was trying to enjoy my dessert, Dad and Jeanette came back to the table and took their seats. Immediately, Jeanette started. "They've rebuilt Poly, the new high school that was destroyed in the earthquake, so everything is new and clean. The students are happy, the teachers are happy, everybody is happy. Of course, everything can't be perfect."

"With a new school, what else did you need?" asked Dad. "I mean," Dad paused, "things can't be perfect."

Well, Daddy," Jeanette said, almost confidentially, "When I entered that contest, the one where I imitated Mae West at City College, well, I'll tell you the boys went wild. I won hands-down, until they found out I was in high school. It was sooo unfair—they actually took back the award and trophy."

I groaned. I'd heard the story before. *My Gawd*, I thought, *get over yourself, girl*.

Dad, lifting his eyebrow, objected, "What was unfair about it? You won it under false pretenses."

"Ohh Daddy, but I was the prettiest and the best; everyone knew it."

Dad didn't say any more, but I could tell he was annoyed.

"And, then, would you believe it, my high school teachers (the women, mostly old maids) were all cold—cold, mean old biddies. They were really jealous that I won the award. It was very unfair, but—" now Jeanette's eyes gleamed, "I still had the last laugh (I think that's the way you say it?), since a big fraternity (maybe a couple of them) got donations to buy a trophy for me. They presented it to me with this swell letter, saying I was their choice, and pledged their undying love and servitude to me."

Jeanette magically presented the letter and passed it around the table for all of us to read. Mother read it, beaming with pride; I read it with mixed emotions; Dad took one look and handed it back to Jeanette.

"So, what else happened out there?" Asked Dad. Jeanette, sensing something possibly unflattering behind his question, just barreled ahead with one story after another, avoiding what I suspected was a sensitive topic. They both weren't talking about the issue.

"Ethel was going through some family albums and stopped when she got to one man's picture—Uncle Lyle."

Dad didn't say anything, but it was if someone had hit him in his stomach.

What a little manipulator, I thought. *She deflected by changing the topic.*

"Aunt Ethel told me it was both strange and sad about the baby of the family. Her brother, Lyle, one day went off to work and never was seen again. It was a real mystery. She said Grandma spent thousands of dollars having detectives search all over the city—actually all over the country." She sighed, dramatically, "They never did find any trace of him."

262

This must have been the first time Mother heard about Lyle because she said to Dad, "James, is this true?"

Nodding his head slowly he said, simply, "Yes, it's true, Nora."

Jeanette now moved on to another topic. Guess what? Aunt Ethel bought a car, and we were able to go all over the place. We still took the Red Car trollies for long distance trips, but the car really made everything so convenient: shopping, sightseeing, going into Los Angeles. We still took the trolley up to the mountains—up to Mt. Lowe, where Aunt Ethel rented us a cabin at Christmas time.

"So, Ethel," interrupted Dad, "has a car now, does she?"

"Yes. She said she planned to 'kick up her heels' with a little traveling. Of course, that didn't include the little ocean cottage she bought near a place called Pismo Beach, which is way up the coast. The place is right on the water. Wow! What a cold and wild ocean that is up there. You can't swim in it. All you can do is watch the waves—breakers—roll in, but it is gorgeous. Something else that was lots of fun: clamming. We got to search for clams along the tideline and make clam stew. But . . . I only got to go up there once. Most the time, she and her friend, Alice, would go up there for a long weekend or holiday."

"You mean she abandoned you? How irresponsible—"

Mother had hit a nerve. I felt like I'd been shocked. She's feeling concerned about Jeanette being abandoned for a few days, after she left me at thirteen to be on my own for years!

"Oh, no, no, she didn't. She left me over at Betty's (my best friend's) house—the one her family rents from Aunt Ethel, so I was always under "supervision." She knew that would be important to you. She said it also brought her "some peace of mind.""

I saw Mother nod her head approvingly, saying, "What a relief."

Jeanette went on. "Aunt Ethel tried to entertain me—and Betty—but she was becoming an ol' fuddy-duddy."

With that, Dad started to interject something, but Jeanette hurried along, saying, "Even though Aunt Ethel got boring, the boys weren't—they were real spiffy; the guys from school with their jalopies and roadsters raced past our house, wanting me to come out to the porch and chat, but, I had to act like some old spinster. Aunt Ethel put her foot down and refused to let me go out for a spin. Would you believe it?"

"Dad was about to blow his top when Mother came to Jeanette's rescue, saying, "No, I have to agree with your Aunt Ethel. I would do the same thing, and—*I know*—your Daddy would agree." Mother looked over at Dad, who was appreciative of the support and agreement, which was enough to keep him from reprimanding Jeanette severely.

Mother really understood Dad well. She mollified him and kept peace at the table, but I could tell things weren't going to be the same around here. No, Jeanette was "feeling her oats," as is commonly said, and this was just a warning of things to come, that is, unless Dad put his foot down firmly and fast. I would just wait and see how he handled himself. I suspected Mother and he would have a serious discussion about Jeanette tonight in the privacy of their room.

For me, I would sit back and watch the ongoing saga unfold. Yes, I was glad to have Jeanette back and to feel the energy and excitement she would bring around the table. I wondered about the secrets being withheld, which weren't being discussed. Why exactly was she sent home by Aunt Ethel? I also wondered if California was a lot looser than here. It would be interesting to watch her adjust back to Southern ways and Southern living.

· · · · ·

February 3, 1935

Dear Journal,

I was really missing music—beautiful music—in my life. Between the telephone company and the plantation (if you don't include an occasional movie), my life was nothing but work. I realized I needed beauty to nourish something deeper in myself.

I bought a ticket for a matinee concert that featured Rachmaninoff's music. Knowing Norton was now married and living in New York City, there would be absolutely no danger of a chance meeting. I hadn't foreseen I would have this wild fantasy as I went into the concert hall: Norton is there, waiting. He rushes up to me and tells me he never did get married, and he is madly in love with me, and can't live without me.

Living the fantasy, I listened to the music, forgetting the reality of my life. I let myself be swept along by the pianist playing a series of short preludes, just as I had when Norton and I listened to the magnificent Second Piano Concerto. It wasn't until the last one, entitled, "The Song of Destiny," that the somberness and finality of its theme brought back the pain I had purposely buried. I felt this deep well of emptiness and left the hall just as the last notes were struck.

I was crying. What had I done? I was so stupid to think I could go back there, listen to that music by myself and think I would be all right. Then I became angry with myself for opening the wound. What a fool! What a fool I am!!

CHAPTER 35

THE DYESS COLONY

The last of the six sharecroppers jumped into the back of the truck only weeks before spring planting was to begin in March. I drove down the dusty trail on our plantation until I came to the paved road. I turned onto it and headed toward Lepanto and this new town, Dyess Colony, built by the government.

Norma Mae—as importantly as her husband—had, as Mother said, "delivered the goods," and gotten the croppers on government assistance. A few of them initially rejected it as an admission of weakness, their shame replacing common sense, until I explained it as an unforeseen opportunity for them and their families. They would be only among a few farmers selected who (we hoped) would qualify for the program and become homeowners and farmers on their own land. They realized the seriousness of their situation, since they already had been given notice by Mother to quit our land. They were being evicted.

A few hours later, I pulled into Dyess Colony. There was a sign, which pointed to the administrative building. Once I stopped and we'd gotten out of the truck, I could see the earlier suspicion of the croppers had been replaced by anxiety. My interpretation was they could hardly believe what they were seeing, and they desperately hoped they would qualify to live here.

Before we left I had explained the program, and what I knew of the benefits and the procedures. Still, once we went into the building, it became intimidating to everyone, including me. Clean carpet covered the floor; a couple of sofas and four wooden chairs filled the room, along with a coffee table with some magazines. Such luxuries these men had never known.

I took charge, walked up to the desk, and spoke politely—but directly—to the secretary, at least I thought she was. "I have six sharecroppers from our land who are being evicted soon, and they want to move to the Dyess Colony."

The young woman nodded, placed six forms on six clipboards with pencils. "First, they need to fill these out."

I glanced at the men, who either worriedly looked at one another or simply kept their eyes glued to the floor. I realized most—if not all—of the men couldn't read or write.

"Thank you. We'll be back shortly." I turned and started to walk out the door.

Obviously having seen this problem before, the secretary said kindly, "If y'all will go through that door, you'll find tables and chairs. You can fill out the questionnaire in there. As soon as one of the men is finished, he can come to me and I'll send him on to a field worker for an evaluation."

That's when I saw the fear in their eyes—the fear of the unexpected and the fear of being found unable to read or write which, I suspected, they concluded would disqualify them.

Fortunately, the secretary had dealt with this problem before. "Gentlemen, your field worker is here to help y'all. We're looking for men who know how to farm and have a family. That's all."

Chests heaved in a sigh of relief.

One by one, I helped each man fill out his questionnaire, sending him in for his interview. By the time I finished with the last farmer, I went with him into the waiting room, to find four men sitting there with smiles on their faces, having had their interviews. It looked to me like things were going well. At that moment, another of our group came back into the room, while the field worker called out one of the three men left unevaluated. I would have sworn I detected a general lessening in their anxiety.

One farmer, William Jones, had been explaining the program to each man before the sharecropper went in for his interview.

"Y'all are in good shape. Sure was smart to bring proof yer on gov'ment assistance."

I nodded my head. Looked like Mother prepared well, making sure Peter and Norma Mae Church had gotten these men on assistance. Otherwise, they wouldn't have stood a chance.

It wasn't long before a door opened onto a long hall, but this time it was a middle-aged woman who asked, "Would Joe Long come this way?"

Joe stood up hesitantly, stared straight ahead as if he were going to a firing squad. Then he disappeared behind the door and into the hall, the door slowly closing behind him.

It wasn't long before the same door opened again, and a middle-aged man stood there and called out, "Warren Culpepper, you're next." Warren stood up hesitantly. He, too, disappeared behind the door and into the hall, the door slowly closing behind him.

After the door closed, William Jones started to tell Hank Paulson everything he knew about the program. Occasionally, one of the other men filled in the details.

Said William to the wide-eyed farmer, Hank, "Ya won't believe it but if you qualify, which you will, Hank (sure as the sun sets in the west), one of those 500 houses in this here city— some of 'em with two bedrooms, some with three, is gonna be yers. The gov'ment gives ya that house with a couple acres for a vegetable garden, as long as ya can farm. Then ya can git 20 acres to farm. They'll give ya a cheap mortgage."

"He's tellin' ya the truth, boy," said a youngish man with the calloused hands and parched skin of a farmer, who—like all the men—looked many years older than he actually was. I knew his age from the records Mother kept on her renters.

"Thar's more—a heap more. Gonna give ya tools and equipment, a donkey to farm with. Plus, ya git a pig, chickens, and a cow."

"Ya take me for a fool, Will?"

At that point all the men shook their heads, saying everything from: "He's not messin' with ya, boy," to "As the Lord is my witness, he's talkin' truth to ya."

Even I was having trouble taking it all in. It really sounded too good to be true, but I realized William wasn't joking or pulling anyone's leg. It was the truth.

"Also, Hank, thar's schools fer the kids; a hospital, a theater, and a commissary whar yer wife can buy what she's needin."

Hank now was shaking his head, saying after each new revelation, "Ya don't say."

William would say at that point, "I do say, and—"

Another wizened old farmer croaked, "Even got a cannery whar ya bring yer vegetables; keeps 'em 'fer a year or more."

I was positively dumbfounded by everything I was hearing. This was turning out to be better than anything I could have possibly imagined. I was so glad to know these men and their children were going to have a chance—a future.

It was then I noticed the startling change: These men left our plantation with suspicion, desperation, and doubt written across their faces. Now I saw hope in their eyes.

CHAPTER 36
THE POTBELLY STOVE

This last weekend in February turned bitterly cold. I was glad I'd taken the farmers up to the Dyess Colony the week before; otherwise, they would have frozen in the truck. Today was miserable. There was no other word for it. First came the rain, followed by sleet. Driving was hazardous. No one wanted to be outside.

I pulled the truck to a stop near Smith's General Store. Near, because there were already trucks and a couple of cars pulled up in front. I had a pretty fair idea what was happening inside.

As I came in—quietly—I heard one grizzled ol' farmer say in lazy jaw, "Yep, gonna be trouble wit 'em; planters ain't gonna tolerate it."

There was a general consensus of opinion. I watched as heads nodded and listened to a chorus of "yeps," "ahh huhs," "mmmm hmms," grunts of the men sittin' around the pot belly stove. Passing around the spittoons, the men took sips of coffee, the steam rising from their cups.

A better-educated voice chimed in. "I heard Lucien Koch, director of Commonwealth College—"

"Ain't that over thar in Mena—on the other side of the state . . . right off the Texas line?"

"That's the one," volunteered an unschooled voice. "Been teachin' all sorts of radical ideas."

Coughing and spitting, a middle-aged farmer interjected, "Damned bunch of communists over thar. Wanna grab our land, from what I done heard."

I remember Dad reading on the last day in January in the *Memphis Commercial Appeal* about foreign influences spreading into the STFU in the Arkansas Delta. Confirming his worst fears, he handed me the article. The headline of the article, "Red Flag Spreading," maintained that "un-American" agitators were attempting to infiltrate the union, which I knew was being vigorously opposed by Leland and the union leadership. True, Leland was a socialist, but he was not a communist.

"You been listenin' to the planters, Bill," challenged the educated voice.

"Yeah, I have, and those boys are damned upset with this here communist agitation; damned troublemakers they are, Riley."

"I suppose they got their rabble rousers like most groups."

"What'd 'ya wanna say? Seems purty clear t' me that this boy Koch's meetin' with the union. He got idears—"

"Idears, Bill?" asked the youngest of the group, kicking at the floor with his boot.

"Yeah, sonny boy. Idears! He wants t' git hold of the union. Ya know, take control and git real strong once he gits workin' men, not those damned eggheads from the college."

"Then," warned a new voice in the group, "once they take over the union, the reds gonna shoot the leaders, ya know the guy's that got the STFU goin'."

"Are you talkin' 'bout Leland Mitchell and that fella, Ward Rodgers?" asked Riley, the farmer with the intelligent voice, obviously, someone who'd gotten a lot better education than the rest of the men around the stove.

"Yeah, I guess that's 'em," replied the farmer. "Those young'uns' days are numbered. They jus' dun't know it. Reds'll line 'em up again' a wall, den pow! Shoot 'em dead like they do in Russia."

"Russia, you say?" Again, that same man with a voice that said he knew a lot more than he was letting on, in order to fit in with the group.

"Uhh huh, one and the same."

"First," pointed out Riley, "they got to get him out of the Jonesboro Jail, where they arrested him for trying to overthrow the government and speakin' with profane language."

"Ya don't say?"

"I do, Bill. Ward told the crowd if the planters try to use the kind of violence like the Ku Klux Klan, he'd get lots of men to hang the planters. 'Course he told 'em he didn't intend to do that."

There was more grumbling among the men but no one voice rose above the other, so I could make out what they were saying or how they were feeling about this latest statement.

Bill, the man with the most to say, cleared his throat and cleared it again. He grabbed the spittoon while the rest of the group waited to hear what was on his mind.

I continued to pretend to shop with my back to them, getting an idea of how strong the feelings were when it came to the union, especially when the common folk thought there were communist agitators involved—people who wanted to take their land. That sort of talk could get people riled up. I heard enough of the beatings and maimings of people who'd gone or led the meetings. Feelings were hardening. I knew some of the planters with their men, the night riders, were scaring a lot of people.

"I done heard—" rasped Bill, clearing his voice again, "I done heard from one planter that it's getting downright dangerous what's happenin' right under our very noses."

"How so?" queried Riley's educated voice.

"Well, those agitators actually been carrin' red flags. And red flags mean—"

"Re-vo-lu-tion," spit out the hoarse voice of the grizzled, old farmer I saw when I came into the store.

"Not here it don't!" shot back still yet another new voice. "We know how t' deal with those folks."

At that moment I heard Mr. Smith call out, "Howdy, Minnie, can I help you find something, honey?"

I knew I had been identified. The men grew silent. I might as well turn around. "Thank you, sir, but I believe I've got what I want." I picked up a bar of chocolate candy and walked to the counter.

All of the men stood up and tipped their hats. I heard the muffled voice of the grizzled old farmer, "She's a planter's daughter."

. . . . .

Dad was at the office when I got there. Mother was on the telephone. "Ellen, Minnie and I are coming over." There was a pause. "Good, we'll see you over there in a few minutes."

Dad said, "If I'm going to catch the train to Memphis, I need to leave now."

"We'll drop you off."

"Nora, I'd prefer to walk. It's only a short stroll over to the station and I've been sitting too long. Thanks anyway." Dad pecked Mother on the cheek, and was out the door.

"Minnie, drop me off at the utility company. I want to go over some things with Ellen."

"Okay."

We walked out of the office and got in the truck. As we were driving along, Mother spoke, "I went to a funeral this past week."

"Whose?"

"A sharecropper's."

"A sharecropper," I replied, obviously surprised by the news.

"Yesss, an elderly woman. She had known Daddy." Mother sighed, "There aren't many of those old-timers left now. I only felt it was fitting for me to show up."

I didn't say what I was thinking: "I'm surprised you took the time for someone like that, even if she had known Grandpa. Let alone, I know you don't like funerals."

"Lot of folks there?" I responded, thinking I should say something.

"Not many. Mostly just her family. I couldn't help but chuckle when I saw her laid out. "Her grandson hadn't pulled her dress down all the way and left her slip showing. Would you believe it? A sharecropper had a silk slip. I was kinda flabbergasted, not just that her slip had been left showing, but it was silk. I'll be." Mother shook her head, seemly astonished by the oddity of the situation.

I had a pretty good suspicion who she was, but I asked the question anyway. "What was her name?"

"Alice; Alice Cooper. You know, you went out there once to collect the rent some time ago. I remember because you were gone so long."

"I remember."

"They are on my list to be evicted."

I saw from the corner of my eye that Mother had turned her head and was looking at me to see, I suspected, what my reaction to her news would be. I waited. I was prepared to come to the family's defense. But my instincts told me to wait.

"I reconsidered. Maybe it was because she knew Daddy, and I knew he wouldn't have wanted 'em evicted. Maybe it was just business, since all those boys might be helpful, especially if Tom shows 'em the ropes with the machinery and things."

I felt the manipulation here, but I did not react other than to say, "I'm sure you made your decision for the right reasons, Mother."

She turned her head and stared out the window, laughing. "Imagine that: a silk slip on a sharecropper? What a hoot!"

CHAPTER 37
GOOD YEARS FOR A FEW

APRIL 1, 1935

L ying in bed, I was thinking about what Dad had said as soon as the New Deal came out, especially as it related to farming. Dad has been proved right. Some of the planters and small farmers misused the Agricultural Adjustment Administration program. Not only did most of them not share the rent money President Roosevelt intended for their tenant farmers and sharecroppers, but also—from what we were hearing—many of them actually cheated the government by planting cotton on the land they promised to leave fallow or plow up. Some greedy planters, on the other hand, harvested other crops such as soybeans or corn; made a profit, yet didn't share any of the rent money from the government with the poor on their land. "Human greed will always win out," asserted Dad.

I was hearing much the same thing from the farmers around the potbelly stove over in Arkansas. Those farmers who were struggling to survive—even with the government program—didn't hesitate to use the names of those farmers they suspected of cheating.

I was reminded of Riley saying one day, "That Pickens up on the St. Francis River, you know who I mean? Everyone nodded. "How'd he buy another four hundred acres when only three years ago he was dirt poor, whining he was about ready to lose his land—500 acres? I know how. So do the rest of y'all." Everyone nodded and agreed that Pickens was cheating the government. As I listened to the men, this was one time I wished Dad had been wrong about his predictions.

Though I popped into my bedroom before dinner to take a nap, I left the door open. Jeanette had the radio on while Mother was preparing our Sunday meal. The music was loud enough that I could hear the song clearly. Though the beat of the music was catchy and words made you want to sing and dance, for the first time I really listened to what the words meant. "Ain't We Got Fun" got you right from the start. This time the lyrics took on a different meaning for me:

> *Ain't we got fun! The poor get poorer, and the rich get richer, ain't we got fun . . . .*

Lying in bed, I realized there wasn't anything funny about the music. The reality was everyday life was becoming more and more desperate for the poor. True, we, just by chance, were living better. Still, we worked like dogs.

Mother, as a planter, having already said she had to walk a fine line between other planters and the STFU, knew how precarious our position was. Those planters who agreed to pay workers a union wage found they were being retaliated against—gins wouldn't bale and market their cotton. Stores were out of seed, fertilizer, and other vital supplies they needed, and the list went on.

I recognized the predicament we were in: needing workers while needing not to create unforeseen problems for ourselves from powerful planters. I felt deeply the desperation of the poor. That's when I thought of a plan that would help the people and not hurt us in the process. Knowing Mother, I couldn't approach her with my idea directly. But I could lead the horse, in this case, Mother, to water and hope she would drink. I began to drop hints along the way until *Eureka* she had the idea!

Mother conceived of a plan—"her" plan. She would pay the wage laborer at the end of the day not the 50 cents an hour he was striking for, and not 30 cents the planters wanted to pay him, but she'd pay him 25 cents an hour! Yes, 25 cents an hour, but—and this was what made the plan work—their pay would be supplemented by foodstuffs worth 20 cents an hour. This way it was a little less than the union wage, but certainly more than the planters' wage. Flour, sorghum, potatoes, bread and beans, along with a few other sundry things, became the supplemental wage.

The plan worked well for a couple of weeks until Tom, who met me at the station Friday afternoon in mid-April, warned me, "Minnie, there's a problem."

"What kinda problem?"

"Distributing food at the end of the workday."

Having a couple of hours of daylight left, I said, "Take me over there. I wanna see it for myself."

"But your mother—"

"I have my suspicions about this situation. We'll tell her later."

Tom loaded my suitcase into the truck and we headed out to the farm.

Not long afterward, we'd come near the station when I told Tom to park down the road by a tree, partly hiding the truck from the field hands who were just visible, trudging down the rows toward the station, where they'd drop off their tools, seed and get their supplies.

A number of seconds passed when we'd come into the clearing. I motioned for Tom to follow me behind some bushes next to the supply house. Now we waited and watched. It was just as Tom described it. Most people stood in line patiently as supplies were passed out to them until two fellows started a row, yelling and pushing some other workers, trying to take more than their fair share.

Tom went over and the dispute was settled quickly, though not without Tom appearing to me to be on edge as he walked back over to where I was standing.

"It's what I suspected. I saw a couple of faces I recognize."

"Who?"

"The guys causin' the trouble."

"Huh?"

"Yeah, it was them all right—two of the same group of men, night riders, who thought they'd rough me up . . . scare me."

Tom was silent and gazed intently at me. "They meant to harm you, Minnie?"

"Well, I can't say for sure 'cause I didn't let 'em get that close. I pulled my gun out."

"Minnie—" I could see Tom was really upset. "Those two men, who jus' walked by us, were part of that gang?"

"Tom, nothin' happened. I didn't let it get that far."

"You didn't let them get that far?"

Now I saw admiration in Tom's face, and something else I'd have preferred not to see: protectiveness, caring, love. In order to avoid us getting into dangerous waters, I said quickly, "Tom, I'm goin' to discuss what happened here with Mother. We'll let her decide what she wants to do about this."

At first I could see it in his face and his clenched fists. Tom seemed reluctant to accept my suggestion before he gave the men a beating. That is, until I ordered, "We are going to Mother. She's the decision maker here, and would be mighty put out if she thought either of us was acting on something like this without her knowing about it."

Tom caught himself from saying whatever he was about to say and instead nodded his head. "I guess you're right, Minnie."

"I know I'm right, Tom."

We drove back to the gin in silence. Once we got there and went to Mother's office, I knocked on her door. "It's me, Mother."

When I entered the room her first words were, "You weren't supposed to be here 'til—" Then she saw Tom and stopped speaking, looking at the both of us.

"I'm sorry to tell you, Mother, you were right about us being caught between the planters and union."

Mother shifted her gaze directly to me. "Exactly what are you saying, Minnie?"

I explained the situation out at the station in detail, including my trip to a Union meeting, which caught Mother off guard. At first she was visibly angry with me, but cooled down once I told her that I'd never have been able to identify the night riders if I hadn't gone to the meeting. Mother understood the logic of my explanation and didn't chastise me—even though it had been a risky venture.

"Well, when that news got back to whomever hired those boys, it might have raised more questions about our intentions. I can't, however, bother about that right now. Tomorrow we'll be there—me, you, and we won't be packin' these little things in our purses," Mother said emphatically. "As for you Tom, you bring your brother."

Mother called Al in and explained what she wanted. Al assured Mother he'd get hold of Ben. Mother's instructions were clear: We'd meet at the gin, go over her plan, and drive out to the station. "Guns loaded," she said, her voice dropping ominously.

. . . . .

All went according to Mother's plan. We met promptly at four. Two of the trucks were pulled to the side of the road while I let my engine idle. Quickly, the four men got out of their trucks and hopped into the back of ours, and I drove to the tree near the station. They jumped out quietly and walked over to the clearing. No one was there except Willy and Clem, who were ready to hand out supplies and the men's pay, when they caught sight of us. Mother put her hand to her lips, motioning for them to stay put and do their job.

We hid behind the same bushes that Tom and I had the day before. This time, we were a total of six. Concealed, we watched and we waited silently.

There was the smell of the freshly plowed earth. My eye caught one little wildflower, hiding along with us behind the bushes. I reached down, picked it and inhaled its sweetness. Suddenly Mother reached over to hit my hand when I caught sight of her hand and grabbed it with my free hand. The two of us just glared at each other. Then I slowly let go of her wrist.

Mother hissed, "This is no time for foolishness!"

I nodded. What she said was true. We were armed—the men with shotguns, and Mother and me with revolvers—.32's.

Then came the sound of the voices as the men came into the clearing and began to line up in single file. Within minutes a ruckus broke out among the men. "Are those the men, Minnie?"

"They are!"

Tempers having flared, a few punches were thrown. A fight broke out. At that moment, Mother commanded, "Okay."

We stepped from behind the bushes. Mother lifted her gun and nodded to us to do the same. "Now." On that command we fired in unison. The sound of the guns going off was deafening; some workmen hit the ground, a few started to run. Mother yelled out, "Y'all stop right now! Hyear me?!"

Mother motioned for us to lower our guns, and for us to follow her. She walked over to the men with her gun still titled up and said, "I'll have no more of these shenanigans." Approaching the two "night riders," she said loudly and harshly, "Y'all get your things. Now!"

Still shaken, the men got their pay and supplies, and walked humbly toward their car. That was when Mother shouted out, "Y'all tell whoever hired you, I'll not put up with this troublemaking. You're wasting my time! Y'all hyear me? I'm gonna make me a telephone call, and settle this funny business one way or another."

The two men got in their car, drove off, and did not look back.

I watched as the dust rose from behind their car, when I heard Mother shout, "Y'all forget this happened and go about your business." She looked at the field hands as they silently got their pay and picked up their supplies, with hardly a murmur between them.

Mother nodded at us. "Let's go. Minnie, you and I are going back to the office. I've got a call to make, and I know exactly who I'm gonna talk to." Turning toward the men, she said appreciatively, "Y'all, thanks for the help. Now, go on home and get dinner." The lids of her eyes slightly shutting, Mother declared, "Everything's under control! Everything!! Now, let's get you fellas to your truck."

. . . . .

The house was beautiful, outside and inside. A large two-storied house with two large pillars that reached to the roof, it reminded me of Grandpa's antebellum-style home, but it didn't quite have the grandeur and presence of the Big House. Also, the house didn't look as big, which diminished—at least for me—the imposing quality of it. Nonetheless, the house said wealth and influence.

Once the maid had shown us into the parlor, eight men, all planters, sat in a semi-circle around one elderly man with white hair, a white mustache and beard, and a white double-breasted suit. All men rose to greet us. The elderly man was every bit the Southern gentleman and treated Mother accordingly. After the formalities, Mother and I were shown to one of two down-filled sofas, covered by a beautiful damask fabric. Some leather chairs of brown and green, and a rocking chair, along with elegant, comfortable-looking Queen Ann chairs completed the circle, with planters of various ages seated nonchalantly as if they were paying a social call. But this was no social call for Mother.

"Nora Belle, how many years has it been since I last saw you?" graciously mused Mr. Dawson, the elderly planter. Before Mother could answer, he recollected, "Not since you were a young lady—a mighty pretty young lady—going to boarding school."

"I believe you are right, sir." Mother smiled, showing an amiable and well-bred side that I seldom witnessed in her every-day behavior.

We were served sweet tea while all of the men had drinks. None of them betrayed any sense of having drunk too much. None showed any sign of inebriation, though I suspected they already had a couple of drinks before we got there.

"Nora Belle, I've been thinkin' about the call I had from you. You indicated you wanted to have an opportunity to meet everyone—people like yourself. Of course, all of us were delighted with the idea."

Of all the men, only one came from our county. Most of the rest of them lived in surrounding counties. One older gentlemen sitting near the host had been driven down from his place near the Missouri border. All of the men were plantation owners. Though some had plantations of long standing, like Mr. Dawson, others had held their land only from the first decade of the century. If I looked deeply enough, all of them showed the signs of worry and anxiety: one man rubbing his fingers together, another tapping his foot, while still another had a twitch on his face. I was aware that underlying anxiety belied their relaxed postures and whatever concerns they had for the future. The men, I suspected, were trying to avoid thinking about the fate of men they once called friends, who had lost their land in the chaotic years of the Depression and slipped beneath the surface of polite society.

"Of course," Mother said pleasantly, "I'm glad to see friends and make new acquaintances. One can never have too many friends, don't you agree, Minnie?"

I knew what Mother wanted: I was expected to play my role as the dutiful daughter and the young Southern lady in the room. "Oh I do, Mother. If there was one valuable lesson I learned at boarding school, it is one can never have too many friends." I looked around the room, smiling at and catching the eye of each man in the room.

"Mr. Dawson said, engagingly, "Oh, I see you have a wedding band on. Is he by any chance one of us?"

"No, sir. My husband and his family are in the energy market."

"Is that right?" Mr. Dawson replied with sincere interest. "And your married name, honey?"

"Beck, sir. Mrs. Beauregard Beck. They've got holdings all over—even in Cuba."

"I'm familiar with the name, but I've never had the pleasure of meeting them."

"Oh, they're a little different from us Delta folks, but after a while they start to warm up and get off their high horse."

I could see by his expression Mr. Dawson not only knew the name—he nodded his head approvingly. The name was known by some of the other men in the room, too, one man leaning over to tell another of the pedigree of these people. There may have been envy in some of them, but it didn't show on their faces. Rather, they were impressed; I could definitely see that. I knew it'd be a topic of conversation once we left. More importantly, it would be something that would be considered in whatever happened or did not happen in this room while we were here and afterward. I glanced at Mother, and saw immediately her approval for the weight this information carried with everyone here.

"Well, Nora Belle, this explains a lot." Mr. Dawson paused, ever so briefly.

Mother raised her eyebrows as if to say, "How so?"

Mr. Dawson, taking on the role of the patriarch and spokesman for the group of landowners, smoothly said, "It explains all of your charitable works, which we all commend you for."

"How nice of you to say that." Having picked up her tea and taking a sip, Mother said sweetly, "Don't you think so, Minnie?"

"Why, of course. Like you say, Mother, whatever benefits one, benefits all, especially friends."

Mother almost looked surprised by what I'd said. She knew they were aware that we now considered them as friends. As friends, there were potential opportunities that hadn't been there before. They had something to gain from courting our friendship.

That's when Mother nonchalantly explained, "I believe there may be a misunderstanding of our intentions." She waited.

There was a stillness in the room, when Mr. Dawson objected in an avuncular tone of voice, "No, no, Nora Belle. I'm sure that words like intentions and misunderstanding are not something any of us would ever use. More broadly, I think all of us—I'm sure this must have been something that's crossed your mind too—are concerned about this union business."

"Oh, I'm totally in agreement, sir."

Mother's comment appeared to be something he wasn't expecting. It took a few moments for him to regain his train of thought. "I, like the gentlemen in this room, are worried these rabble rousers are working up folks and mean to bankrupt us and destroy our way of life, honey."

"Completely," agreed Mother, catching Mr. Dawson and the rest of the room off-guard. "We've all had to adjust to the changing times, and try to come up with solutions to this problem. I for one, some of you may know, am trying to modernize my operation with new equipment."

Now I did see through the smiles and pleasant expressions, their envy of Mother's business operation, which required capital—cash, which many of them did not have in abundance. Yes, the envy was there. We have the money to modernize. They felt we not only have an unfair advantage, but we were possibly collaborating with the enemy.

"Nora Belle, we have heard about you modernizing your operation. It sounds quite interesting. What we don't understand is—is just all of the aspects of it. Some things sound almost revolutionary."

Mother picked up on the word "revolutionary," which was shorthand for communists. "Oh my, those damn communists." Now Mother's voice dropped to a low growl and her eyes squinted. She lifted her clenched fist high. "Most of them are just Northern agitators," she almost shouted. "I just can't stand the thought of them! I'll not have them—or anyone else for that matter—coming in and telling me—or any of you for that matter—what we can and can't do. It's just not the Southern way of doing things."

I saw all the men nodding and murmuring in agreement with her—but one. Mr. Dawson was looking very carefully at Mother, appraising her.

When I saw that, I realized Mother was putting everyone on notice both by the tone of her voice, her raised, clench fist, she was not a woman to be trifled or interfered with. She'd fight. I surmised they must've heard about Mother shooting Frank the fireman.

"That's why," now Mother's voice rose to the reasonable, confident business woman, "I decided to outsmart them."

"And pray tell, Nora Belle, just how are you doing that?" asked Mr. Dawson, leaning slightly forward.

"Well, I pay laborers below the hourly rate, and give them a few supplies to pacify them. So it all comes out to be just about the same rate, more or less a few pennies. Like y'all, I've got to have workers, and they can't be starving."

"No, of course, they can't be starving, but some are just downright lazy, not wanting to work, hanging around trying to get free handouts, and get other folks riled up."

"Absolutely!" said Mother, with certainty. "Absolutely. That's why we must work together. Don't you agree?"

"Why, yes," said Mr. Dawson, hesitantly.

"Working together is crucial. We must learn from each other what is best, and yet not create problems for one another. The key is cooperation. One crucial thing is we mustn't give in to those union thugs," Mother declared vehemently.

Everyone was nodding their heads in agreement, some more vigorously than others. However, one man, Mr. Dawson, just smiled. I would have sworn I heard him chuckle.

"Nora Belle," he shook his head in amazement, "you are your father's daughter. You are indeed. Did I ever tell you some of the crazy things your daddy and I did when we were young bucks?"

"I don't believe you have," Mother purred, inviting him to begin the storytelling.

"Well—"

The rest of the afternoon went on pleasantly enough, stories shared by all. I sat there and enjoyed the tales, knowing Mother had won this one. I marveled that, besides me, only Mother and Mr. Dawson knew it.

. . . .

On the way to Uncle Bob's house, there was only the sound of the truck's engine, the feel of fresh, country air blowing through the opened windows, and the occasional bump in the road. Mother was looking out her window as we passed by plowed land, ready for the seed, pastures, and the rare clumps of forest still left standing.

I stared ahead, sometimes glancing at whatever caught my fancy. This quiet time was good. Both of us kept to our own thoughts. Possibly for Mother, she was happy not to be thinking about anything. Enough was enough!

Those last minutes of the social engagement with the planters still preoccupied me. Mr. Dawson could have no idea that his invitation for me to come and visit with his granddaughters and the families of other planters had fallen on deaf ears. His words, "young ladies more your own age, that you have something in common with—not us stuffy old men, talking business," had left me cold; absolutely ice cold. At some level, I almost felt insulted but I had to remind myself, he was inviting me into their social world and meant no offense. He had no idea how I really felt about talking with silly young women and their meaningless fripperies.

I, like Mother, was engaged with those very things he held dear: business, management, money, and power. Catching myself puffing up, I laughed aloud. I had no real control over any of those things.

"What's that, Minnie?"

"I was just having a foolish thought."

Mother didn't even bother to nod, but turned back and stared out the window.

The fact exists, I realized, that I was different. Whatever is that world of genteel affectation, carefree social blather and gossip, it had passed me by long ago. Being on my own and working in a burlap factory created a very different person than the young women of the planter class—or any other class with money.

On further consideration I realized Mother and I were both similar and different. Mother had shaped my social graces with a heavy hand—and I mean heavy—during the years of my early life. Near the end of that period, she sent me off to boarding school. She, too, had gone to boarding school but she'd grown up without a mother. Under Marie's benevolent supervision and exposure to what Marie knew to be the better things, Mother had learned the proper etiquette of a Southern Lady and how to handle herself. Though Marie had been hired by Mother's mother to be a governess, Marie, along with boarding school, shaped an important part of Mother's life. I guess, another odd similarity was work. At thirteen, I went to work at the burlap factory and the flower stall. Mother, at her father's insistence, spent her summers in a hot kitchen, cooking breakfasts for the field hands, and learning the ways of managing a plantation and the men who worked on it. Life at the Big House was not a life of idleness and social gatherings. She—like myself—had been expected to work—and to work hard.

One difference between us—among others—she lived the life of a society matron until Dad's bankruptcy brought that to an end. I never really had that experience, unless I consider a six-week taste of it when I was married to Beauregard. Unlike Mother who loved and loves Dad, I detested every moment I spent with Beauregard and his friends. Admittedly, I became very fond of his parents, but those experiences with them wasn't enough to open up the world of the very, very rich for me, let alone for me to become accustomed to and to enjoy.

Before I knew it, Mother called out, "Minnie, you went right past the house."

"Sorry, Mother."

I turned the truck around and headed to Uncle Bob's, looking forward to a good country dinner with *our own* people. Given the thoughts I had been turning over, I realized the way of life in the delta and the simplicity of Uncle Bob and his family were something that I truly valued. In that sense, I was lucky.

CHAPTER 38
NO!

On a fine June day—two months to the day of our visit to Mr. Dawson's, and less than a week to the official day of summer—I drove from what had been the Jackson plantation (now ours) to the gin. Along the way, I was aware of spring flowers giving way to the gorgeous white blossoms of magnolia trees as I came into town. The scent of the blossoms was heady and almost overpowering. Occasionally, the whiff of honeysuckle drifted through my opened windows, bringing me a sense of joy, then a sweet sadness. I couldn't help but recollect the time when Marie's mother visited at Grandpa's and the grand dinner in the evening, where the savory smells of Marie's cooking gave way to the fragrance of the honeysuckle, which wafted in on a light breeze into the room.

Strolling into the office, I was momentarily surprised to see Dad. Normally he would have been in Memphis, but there he was, sitting across from Mother. As I went to take a seat, I realized they had abruptly stopped talking and were staring at me. My guard went up.

"Minnie, good news. The telephone company in town is for sale, and I am going to buy it! Mother was excited, and hurriedly continued. "When can you give notice, and start to work here?"

"You want me to—"

"Of course! Of course, *we*," coughed Mother, "of course, I do. Who else is better qualified and can be trusted than you—family? This will give us control of everything but Smith's General Store and Solomon's place—businesses of no interest to me. Though, if you think about it, more than a few planters own the company store that all their hands are forced to patronize; so owning them would have its benefits."

At that point, Mother was interrupted by Dad, who had watched me as my initial shock turned sour. "Nora, the acquisition of the company is, as we discussed, a sound idea. However, bringing in another family member to run things has its drawbacks."

"Drawbacks? Oh, who cares what some of the people think in town. We've got the money." Hesitating to organize her thoughts, Mother said, indignantly, "We got the RIGHT to do as we please!"

I watched Dad start to say more, when I decided enough was enough! I knew Mother was fired up, and this would end up in a long and drawn-out struggle. In a sense, it would be a test of wills. Instead, I would nip this in the bud and fight my own battle, but I would let her think the idea not to involve me was her own idea.

"No, Mother!" I saw the shock; she'd actually heard me say NO to her. I hastened to add, "There are a couple of reasons. Jeanette needs me right now—more than ever. You know she cannot pull the wool over our eyes to get her way, but," I shook my head, "I'm sorry to say Dad, "you, you're a pushover."

"I, I—" reacted Dad defensively.

"James, what Minnie is saying, is that you don't understand girls the way we do. It's a female thing."

Dad opened his mouth to say more when he stopped and looked over at me, nodding his head. He picked up my scent and where I was going.

"And, it's not much, but I do bring in a salary from the phone company in Memphis."

"I could pay you as much, if not more."

"As you said, Mother, 'I could pay you as much, if not more'."

"Well, I can," responded Mother, quickly.

"Indeed and, at the same time, you'd be taking hard-earned money outta your pocket for me, when I'm already bringing in a wage."

I saw a twinge in Mother's face at the thought of that.

"Money's hard to come by and, as you've said, 'With farming we never know from year to year what to expect.'"

"That wasn't me, that was your grandpa. There wasn't a day that would pass when he didn't say those exact words," muttered Mother, shaking her head.

"Yes, Grandpa was forever saying it."

Mother shook her head at me, "It doesn't make it any less true, no matter how many times it's said. It's a good reminder not to count your chickens until the eggs hatch. A sly fox can usually get in."

Mother was becoming more cautious by the moment.

"You told me Ellen is doin' a great job at the utility company, still she doesn't keep busy enough."

"I did and . . . she doesn't. I do hate wasting money, even if it is for a soon-to-be family member."

"No, Mother, I want to keep my job. It wouldn't be wise for me to quit and mooch off of the family. Instead, if you want me to, I'll help train Ellen to be an operator. You can see if she's fit to take on more responsibility. You've always said, "Responsibility and work never hurt anyone.""

"I'm glad to see all my training hasn't gone to waste. You've listened to me."

"Oh I have, indeed, Mother. Indeed, I have," I replied, my voice dropping unnoticeably to everyone but myself.

"Well good, then it's about time Ellen did more. I'll have her come over here when she finishes up at the utilities." Mother picked up the phone and dialed. "This is Nora Gibson. Let me speak to Ellen."

NO!

I looked over at Dad. He smiled, and shook his head ever so slightly. We were in accord. I could imagine him saying to me, "Well, done, Minnie. You've learned the 'secret'."

CHAPTER 39
DOWNSTAIRS, UPSTAIRS

Autumn was in the air, though it wasn't quite October. A few leaves were turning yellow, harbingers of vibrant colors to come—gradations of gold, stand-alone orange and flagrant crimson. I looked out of Miss Virtue's opened window to feel a slight breeze, then to see the lace curtains gently flare out almost at the same moment I heard the tea kettle begin to sing.

"Miss Minnie," came her voice, "tea's almost ready."

I stared at the thin, overlapping slices of pound cake on a lovely porcelain plate, which was a gift from Marie. I could all but taste the tang of the lemon glaze that oozed over the sides of the moist cake. Miss Virtue served me the same dessert after our French lessons. I bought the lemons and she made the glistening, tasty glaze.

Sitting there quietly, my French book closed and to my side, I found myself musing over my visits to her home. Among the many qualities I admired about her were both her frugality and her generosity. Miss Virtue must be the only colored person in town with a small refrigerator that provided her with iced cubes (one tray filled with lemon juice cubes), which guaranteed our drinks were cold, even if the ice was half-melted before we were able to take our first sip during the long, hot summers. Times were hard, yet she still found a way to have a dessert and beverage for me. "Genteel" was the word that came to mind immediately when I thought of Miss Virtue.

"First the teapot," and she found a place next to the tray, followed moments later by, "and now our teacups, along with the sugar bowl and creamer," which actually held milk that was better than cream with tea." These she carried on a pewter tray, which she set on the opposite side of the plate. Without hesitating, she prepared my tea with no milk and three lumps of sugar. Knowing my tastes, she did this from habit.

"Miss Minnie, your tea," and she handed me my cup and saucer with a grace befitting a formal occasion. "Please, see if it is to your liking."

One sip later I murmured, "It is, thank you."

"And now," Miss Virtue prepared her tea with milk and one lump of sugar, then took a sip. "I believe it is just . . . perfect, if I do say so."

I smiled agreeably, nodding my head in accord.

"If I've learned your ways, Miss Minnie, I'll serve you two pieces of cake." She did, handing me the small, delicately flowered plate with two slices of cake and a small fork.

Dispensing with ceremony, I took first one bite, then another, then one more. By now I knew my pleasure suited Miss Virtue just fine. As I was eating, she served herself a slice of cake, but before taking a bite, she said, fork in hand, "Did I ever tell you about my visit to New Orleans with Marie, and our stay at her cousin's?"

I shook my head, since my mouth was full.

"I'm telling you about my experience, because it really changed my view of Marie and, I think, it may give you even a better understanding of her . In my case, I thought I really knew Marie until I visited her home and saw how she grew up. I think the details of the story will surprise you, too.

"As I said, we went to visit Marie's family's home. A cousin and her family were still living in the original house on the edge of the French Quarter, where Marie and her family grew up. Matter of fact, they inherited it, the house having been passed down from generation to generation from Marie's great-grandmother's side. When her great-grandfather married her, he inherited the house. You might remember, he came originally from Haiti in the late 1700s and had the name Francois Marchand."

"From what Marie said of him, Francois was a man who 'didn't waste any time getting what he wanted.'"

"I believe you're right. Those were her exact words."

Refilling and replenishing my teacup, along with another slice of cake, Miss Virtue placed her plate down on the table and continued to say, "Like I told you, our family histories were similar, yet different. Free people before the Civil War, my family were craftsmen of modest means from African and English backgrounds. Whereas Marie's family was *gens de couleur libre*, free people of color, who had French, Spanish and African heritage. Moreover, at least with this family, they were people of wealth, which could still be seen in her cousin's house. Not only were the furnishings expensive, since the Union soldiers didn't loot their home, but also it was big. The house was three stories high and made of brick. Unlike most Big Houses in New Orleans that had slaves, who lived in slave quarters built next to or slightly to the rear of their owners' houses, this house did not have slave quarters."

My interest was really piqued. I had seen old photographs of the Big Houses in New Orleans with the slave quarters, but Miss Virtue made a point to say there were no slave quarters. So I was left to assume the slaves lived inside the house. Yet this didn't seem quite right, so I asked, "Why was her cousin's house different?"

"I discovered the answer to that question in time, Miss Minnie."

"Ohhh—" I was truly confounded now, yet intrigued, and realized she would get around and answer my question eventually. She was telling a story of both times past, as well as one about Marie.

"Marie's cousin still had servants, but they lived only on the first level of the house and the back half at that; whereas the family lived on the second and third stories."

"Why on earth—?"

"It was somewhat on the English class model, with the live-in servants occupying the back of the house. Once, when I did accidentally wander back to the kitchen, I was shown the servants' quarters.

"They kept the downstairs rooms for people—colored or white—they had to see for one reason or another, who were invited into the house. The uncovered wooden floors were scuffed and unpolished. The furniture was simple. It's hard to believe but these conditions were in keeping with their intentions. The fabric on the few pieces of furniture was worn, torn and stained in the parlor where they brought their guests. A simple wood table and chairs was in the dining room, with a narrow cabinet without doors that held mismatched plates, cups, and saucers on one shelf, along with a second shelf with mismatched spoons, forks and knives, laid out in a row."

I watched Miss Virtue take a sip of tea, then cut her cake into bite-sized pieces, which she moved about the plate. About to continue her story, instead she took a bite of cake. "Oh, that is good if I do say so, *n'est ce pas?*"

I smiled and said, "It is excellent, I agree. Thank you, again."

"You're welcome. May I serve you another?"

"It was delicious, but I'm full, thank you."

"Well, Miss Minnie, to get back to our stay in New Orleans, there was a much smaller room next to the dining room, which was all but empty except for a rocking chair and two chairs piled on top of each other. Oh yes, inside this small room was a stool and some cleaning buckets and mops. (Again, in a cupboard, books, paper and such were stored for the servants.) From there, we went down the hall to another room that had three old iron beds with simple bedcoverings. Cheap, tattered curtains barely covered all of the windows."

I saw she was reading me correctly. I was thinking that they must have fallen on hard times. How sad for Marie, my expression said, maybe even embarrassing since her best friend was seeing how far the family had fallen into poverty.

Along the same vein, Miss Virtue sighed, "The paint was peeling, both inside and outside of the house. Once upon a time it had been a grand house."

"It sounds kinda—"

"Dreary and poor, I know. I assumed Marie and I would be sleeping in what looked like the downstairs bedroom. Oh yes, that room had a single lamp on a small table, along with a tiny dresser drawer.

"Well, at least on the positive side, you had a roof over your heads and something to eat," I said, trying to be upbeat, given their circumstances.

Miss Virtue nodded, smiled slightly and mysteriously.

"Instead of that room, we were told by the butler to follow him upstairs where we would find our bedrooms, which sort of caught me off guard. Without further ado, we followed the elderly man up the staircase to the second floor, which, he said, wound around to the third floor above us. Above, at the very center of the ceiling, there was a lovely medallion of plasterwork. Around the medallion were sculpted mouldings shaped like leaves, which created the image of a sunflower. As we climbed the stairs, I was aware of the poverty that had befallen the family. The steps were uncovered, unpolished and scuffed. Surprisingly, when we reached the floor, two very large dogs came forward and slightly growled, which was very scary.

"'Rufus, Ginger, we got guests. Now you be nice,' said William, the manservant.

"Once we reached the dogs, they sniffed us, then started to wag their tails. They now knew us. We were welcome in the house and to the second floor. As we went down the hall, which was now carpeted, we were shown into the first room, where the door was already open. There, inside were two four-poster beds that had mosquito netting tied to the side. Later, I would find that beneath the lovely bedspread, there was a down-filled mattress and pillows, with laced pillowcases.

"My goodness!" I said, suddenly amazed.

"That's right, Miss Minnie. We entered a world few outsiders were admitted to. Just to finish telling you about our bedroom, let me say that the room was painted a soft peach color, with antique furniture and a lovely gold-rimmed mirror. The furniture had been in that house for generations. True, it was worn with age, but it was beautiful!

"My Gawd," I uttered, feeling even more surprised than I had initially.

"I had never been to a house like this, so it was quite an experience for me. Marie and her people had grown up in this very place. I saw so much just on the second floor. Incidentally, the third-floor bedrooms were closed off to us, since Marie's cousin, her son, along with his family, were out of town visiting kinfolk in Baton Rouge."

"What did you see?" I asked, genuinely interested.

"Miss Minnie," she said softly, "there were oil paintings of family members and lovely European scenery, an old gold and silver clock in our room, along with one almost identical to it in the library where most of the books were in French. Dear me, the chairs in the library were so plush, and the desk was some rare wood I didn't know existed."

I thought of Grandpa's Big House but stopped myself, since I knew I'd slip into a dark a mood. Rather, I said, "What a wonderful experience."

"You're right, Miss Minnie, but let me say the rest of the second floor was really impressive, too: the parlor, the dining room, where we ate off of beautiful old porcelain, along with real solid silverware. The furniture was French provincial. My goodness," Miss Virtue mused, "it was an experience I'm not likely to have again."

"Why not?"

"Without Marie, they wouldn't know who I am. Having successfully kept the prying eyes of the world away for all these years, the family is very, very private. I suspect most of their possessions had been acquired before the Civil War, given what looked to be their age." Shaking her head in amazement, Miss Virtue said, "Only the cleverness of the following generations during and after the war, guaranteed the survival of this house and their way of life."

I nodded my head, understanding the reasons for the way the family lived life in that house. I thought of Marie and realized she had been raised as a member of the upper classes. She and her people were every bit as cultured and well-bred as any whites.

"The reason I mentioned the generations that followed is because they adapted to the changes after the war. They lost the plantation house and most of the sugar cane fields because of carpetbaggers, and people operating under the cover of the Jim Crow laws. Those things were obvious assets that belonged to the family; they couldn't be hidden. But the Big House in New Orleans was different. They let it look run down years before the Civil War, so as not to draw attention. Afterward, the sons went into business and educated their children, some of whom went North. This way, I was told, they could expand their business."

"Imagine that," I said, continuing to be amazed.

"By the way, I never did see the third floor, where the bedrooms of the family were. That space remained private and out of bounds for me."

"I declare, I never would have guessed you would be telling me this."

"Miss Minnie, it isn't out of jealousy or spite on my part, but genuine admiration of what lengths this family had gone through to protect themselves from both the coloreds and the whites. Like I said, if the whites had but known what was inside the house, and how these people had lived and live today, well—"

"Well, who knows what might have happened to them," I said, fully understanding their precarious existence.

"Yes, only two extended family members were brought into their world: Marie's mother and nephew when they visited from Canada. That's all."

"Oh, yes, I had the pleasure of meeting them at Grandpa's Big House," I said.

"Marie told me what a gentleman and generous man your grandfather was while they stayed there."

A silence ensued, neither of us speaking until finally, Miss Virtue continued her story of New Orleans. "I remember the experience so well. I'll always think of it as my New Orleans experience."

Yes, in all truth, I was stunned by what Miss Virtue described and she must have noticed it, saying, "But it was the servants and the service that was unique."

"Servants? I don't know why I seemed surprised, given what you've described."

"Oh, the servants weren't just any servants. That's what makes my experience truly unique. I say this because I know there are other wealthy colored families who live well, but coming back to the servants, this is what is so fascinating, Miss Minnie."

"How so?"

"It goes back to the founder of the family: Francois Marchand. He abhorred slavery, but he needed slaves to work his sugar plantation. However, he refused to have slaves inside The Big Houses, either on the plantation or in New Orleans. He only hired *gens de couleur libre*, that is, free people of color."

"Really, no slaves?"

"No slaves in his houses. That's why many of those servants and the children of those servants stayed with the family over the generations. They've also taken it as a point of honor—as well as their security—to keep secret the true nature of this family's home, which sheltered them, even hiring them into the business. Some of those children were sent to Howard University at the family's expense."

"I had no idea about this part of Marie's family history, other than Marie did mention they owned slaves."

"Well," Miss Virtue paused, "it was a delicate issue. No matter how you explain it. I guess Marie didn't have the inclination to try to explain it."

"I sort of understand."

"She didn't, Miss Minnie, really want to—as some say—'sugar coat' it."

"Ohhh, I never would have thought about it that way. Matter of fact, I had no idea that society then was so complex, making these kinds of careful distinctions."

Miss Virtue shrugged, saying, "In the long run, I believe it saved them. Marie also said that it gave employment to *gens de couleur libre*, who might otherwise have had to sell their services to whites. Some of those folks would have treated them little better than slaves.

"While I was staying there, Miss Minnie, I couldn't help but think about all of the servants who worked for generations for Marie's family—in that same house. Kinda hard to believe, but it is true."

I was truly fascinated by Miss Virtue's story. "Marie, her family history and the history of all of those people over the generations are really unique, aren't they?"

"It certainly is amazing. It was quite an experience for me to be in that house with so much history that belonged to colored folks all these hundred-plus years. Everything about that house, her cousin, and her children were a world apart from the world outside that most colored folk have known."

"It sounds like you're describing a way of life no one—white or colored—has any kind of idea of the way this family has been living and is living to this day. It was if the Jim Crow laws didn't exist inside this tiny piece of the world in the South."

"Did you like the family? Oh, that's right, you said they were out of town."

"Yes, Marie's cousin left the day we arrived; the others had already gone. One grown son had left for Haiti, where he'd married a woman from the upper class—*gens de coleur.*"

"*Gens de coleur,* there?"

"Yes, they run the country."

I waited to respond, trying to absorb all that I'd heard. Finally, I said, "Marie came from an educated family that was very rich. Now I know what *gens de coleur* really are."

"Miss Minnie, you are right about Marie, but keep in mind there were very, very few *gens de coleur* like Marie and her family."

I thought about what she said, and determined what was ultimately most important, what related directly to me and why she told me the story.

"My family—and I—were so fortunate to have had Marie in our lives."

Suddenly, not to embarrass me by sensing my sadness, Miss Virtue looked down at the teapot, lifted it, and began to pour what turned out to be dribbles. "Goodness me, I think this is the last of our tea." It was as if Miss Virtue was trying to squeeze the last few drops out of the teapot into my cup. "Give me a few minutes, and I'll—"

"No, thank you. I know Mother will be wondering what's happened to her 'free labor'."

CHAPTER 40
THE IRONY OF BOUNTIFUL

Mother and I stood in the last field to be cleared in late September. The cotton had been tromped. Tom walked over to the truck to haul the load in the trailer to the gin. Mother patted her brow with her handkerchief.

"Whew, another good year—actually a very good year."

"It is. Your intuition paid off."

"That and a lot of hard work—teamwork."

Mother continued to look out and down the now barren rows, which only six weeks earlier had been a huge white blanket of cotton, to what now looked like low hedges of tiny semi-barren bushes that reached far into the distance to the stately pecan trees that overlooked the winding river below. Transfixed and held fast by the land, Mother, too, may as well have been an oak tree, rooted in the soil.

I turned and walked over to the truck as Tom climbed in. When he went to start the ignition, he looked around and saw me coming toward him. His shoulders relaxed. A weary smile spread pleasantly across his suntanned face. Even under the broad Stetson, I could see his large blue eyes absorbing the moment of this encounter.

"Howdy, Miss Minnie," he said ironically, placing his two fingers on the brim of his hat.

Capturing his layered meaning, I replied, "Howdy, Mr. Tom," and curtsied ever so slightly.

His chuckle turned into a laugh. I was glad to see him laugh. He was always so serious, which under the circumstances of the harvest was quite appropriate. Yet, whether it was the harvest or any other time we met, seldom did he laugh. I could only tease out of him the occasional chuckle.

"So when you comin' over to see us?"

I hesitated.

"At least you oughta see what your mother's done with our house. Built another bedroom for us—"

"I'm sure it comes in handy at the rate you're goin'."

"A man's gotta do what he's gotta do."

"Yeah, but maybe you're tirin' out your woman."

"Could be. I'll give that some thought. You got any ideas?"

"Ideas I don't. I'm plumb give out." I realized I'd let this light-hearted banter get out of control. It was heading in the wrong direction. "I heard you got yourself a proper portico on the front of the house now . . . with columns and all. Won't be long before you got yourself a plantation, sir."

"Don't think so, Minnie. Things and people don't change that much. I am pretty much who I am."

"I believe you're right."

Tom stared at me with a quizzical expression on his face, not quite sure if what I said was approving or disapproving of him. To clear up any doubt, I said clearly, "Tom, you're one of the most genuine and true *friends* I have." I emphasized the word, "friend."

"I was afraid you might say somethin' like that, but Minnie, I still trust my feelings and know what I know. However, if it's a friend you need right now, then I'm that friend."

I averted my eyes. I felt the emotion behind his words and took two steps back from the truck.

"You know, Minnie, I still read to improve myself, though nobody would guess."

"Tom, I notice you don't say 'ain't' anymore."

"Yep, that's because I listen to the radio."

"What're you reading now?"

"I just finished reading Jane Austen's *Pride and Prejudice.*"

"I have, too."

"It was a mighty hard and long read, but it was worth it."

"Why do you say it was worth it?"

"Because it has a happy ending—love wins out."

"I'll have to reread the ending."

"Might not be a bad idea, Minnie."

Tom gazed at me, then started up the ignition.

"Well, I guess I best get this cotton to the gin. See ya, Minnie."

"Goodbye, Tom."

I watched as the truck turned and went down the dirt road, a small dust cloud rising behind it and the trailer.

"He's a good boy. I like Tom. He's one of the few people I really trust," said Mother, now standing beside me. We both gazed into the distance as the truck finally turned onto the paved road toward town and the gin.

"I'm glad you kept him on, Mother. He's been a real asset to the plantation."

"Yes . . . a real asset." Mother paused. "It serves us well to protect our assets. I hate to see waste. I like to keep things simple. For example, Tom is and always will be a country boy. That's his virtue, but his liability. That's why *we* want to protect him."

I looked around at Mother. Our eyes met and held. "I've had a long time to realize that from now on I choose the man; he doesn't choose me. I'll never allow myself to be in that position again." There was a heavy silence. "I've also been wrestling with the idea of whether or not to stay married."

"And?"

"I've decided to keep the arrangement, unless Beauregard chooses to divorce me." I took a deep breath. "Quite simply, Mother, it's a matter of practicality. I have more to gain by wearing this wedding band than not. I don't want questions asked here or at work. More importantly, I don't want any complications from men, most particularly Tom, if I take it off.

Mother nodded, sighing, "Let's get back to town, Minnie."

. . . . .

When we went into the office, the phone was ringing. Not liking to miss calls, Mother rushed over and picked up the receiver. "Yes, it's Nora." There was a pause. "I'll send Minnie over with the list of evictions. Thank you, Bill."

My heart sank, as it always did when there were going to be mass evictions.

"Minnie, Bill Peterson, the lawyer, is ready to take care of the rest of this year's evictions. Here take a look."

Mother handed me the list. I started to let my eyes travel down the page when Mother said abruptly, "Minnie, don't make this any harder than it is. Now take it over to Lawyer Peterson. He's waiting. I don't like my time wasted, and I'm sure it's the same for him." Uncharacteristically, Mother ended with, "Please."

By the time I reached Bill's office, I'd had had time to review the list. I counted the families, realizing this left 40 families on the plantation. These 40 were what were left of the 135 in 1932, not counting the families on the Jenkins and Jackson plantations—half of whom had been cleared off by 1933 after the harvest.

"My God," I groaned. I had spent the last few years collecting rents from many of them when Tom was busy. I knew the children by name.

The only people left off the list were those who had learned to operate the new machinery. Others would farm the sloughs with mules. Neither race nor union membership had been a factor.

I took a deep breath. At least dear old Alice's family had been spared. I guess Mother had found a use for the grandson and some of the kids. Maybe, since she'd gone to Alice's funeral, she held a certain feeling for them, since the old woman had known Grandpa.

I was upset. I just couldn't let this stand without doing something. I went back to the office.

"Back already?"

"Mother—"

She saw the list in my hand. "So, whom do you want to save?"

I wasn't expecting that response. I hesitated. "Well, I—"

Mother sat there and stared at me.

Collecting my thoughts quickly, I blurted out, "We could get some of those folks into the Dyess Colony—like we did the others."

"Not we, Minnie, but *you*. First, deliver the list and let the evictions sink in. You'll be more effective that way." Mother dialed the number, then shoved the phone to me.

I listened to the phone ringing, wondering if anyone was home. After a few more rings, I heard the click and a familiar voice at the other end of the line. "Mrs. Church, this is Minnie . . . yes, ma'am, everyone's fine . . . I'd like to talk with you in an hour. Will you be available? Thank you, ma'am. I'll call you then . . . yes, Mother's fine . . . bye."

"Now, get the list over to the lawyer," said Mother. "Don't keep him waiting any longer."

I realized that I'd walked over to the lawyer's office almost never taking my eyes off the list, thinking about the various individuals I knew which ones were the best candidates. By the time I knocked on his door, I had made my choices.

"Why, come in, Minnie." We'd long since been on a first name basis. "Nice to see you."

I dispensed with the pleasantries. I was in no mood to be social. "I've got the list of evictions."

I saw a momentary sadness cross his face, but he bounced back. "Tell Mrs. Gibson that I'll start to work today and deliver them at the beginning of the week."

Looking at him with a straight face, I said, "She'll be glad to know that. She doesn't like to waste time."

He nodded.

"Well, I've got to get back to the office to make a call, then go back to Memphis."

God, I was never so glad to be going back to Memphis as I was now. I didn't want to have to be reminded of this 'business.' I was certainly glad I wouldn't be here next week when some of these folks would plead with Mother not to be evicted because they had no place to go. However, I would do my best to save a few of them. Gathering my thoughts, I rushed over to Mrs. Church.

· · · · ·

Monday, the following day after I met with Mrs. Church, work was typical, that is, customers made the calls either they had postponed or didn't have time to make on Friday. However, there seemed to be something in the air that was different and unnerving. Something was going to happen.

As usual the supervisor was berating someone. Unlike dear Mrs. Sullivan, who had been replaced for not being strict enough, Miss Drummer marched up and down the aisles, waiting for a girl to make a mistake. Once she had her victim, she was merciless.

Today was no different, except Jill started crying loudly, "I just can't take it any more. No more. No more. Please . . . please."

"If you can't do the job, you're through. Get out."

I turned around to see Jill stand up. She stood there, ramrod straight her eyes glazed over, not moving.

Drummer poked her finger into the young woman's chest and sneered, "Get outta here." Her coarse New York accent cut through the room like a knife.

Jill snapped like a branch. She started screaming and hitting Dummer again and again until Dummer lay on the floor, bleeding from multiple lacerations.

I, along with some other girls, pulled Jill off. Once she stopped struggling, Jill just stood there rigidly, gazing at us with a fixed stare, an uncomprehending look in her eyes. She had, I realized, "lost her mind."

Drummer lay on the floor, muttering, "The police. Get the police."

I intervened and shouted loudly, "No police. Call for two ambulances. Jill's had a mental breakdown. The other one's for Drummer."

Neither Dummer nor Jill returned to work. Dummer was fired. Jill was catatonic in an institution for the mentally insane.

. . . . .

Normally the beauty of autumn in October would swell my love of the season to the bursting point. However, the violence by the night riders was a constant source of anxiety and apprehension. Today was no different. I had been urgently called over to Otis' house by one of his young daughters.

As soon as I walked through the door, I heard the screams of a colored woman with a yellow bandana wrapped around her head. Immediately, I recognized Liza Green, who'd warned me about the mayor's car in front of the house with the girls.

"Oh, Lordy, somebody, anybody hep me."

I rushed over to the overwrought, elderly woman to see the other side of her scarf stained with blood. Her left hand was covered with blood, trying to stanch the bleeding.

"Oh, it's you, Miz Minnie. Pleaze hep me."

I almost said, "Oh, my God," but that's the last thing I knew was needed. Instead, I needed to keep my head and not create even more hysteria. I must control the situation as best I can. "Let me see what I can do." I started to peal away the cloth, I realized part of it was stuck to her skin and pulling it away—beside the pain that was caused—only caused more blood to flow.

All the while Liza wailed and cried, "They done cut ma ear off. Cut it off. Lordy, me. Please, hep me!"

"Miz Minnie, it was the night riders that done this."

"What?" I said, pressing my hand against the wound. "Who's responsible?"

"Ma'am, it be the night riders; they got her as she come out the union meeting," cried, Otis. "They did it. They cut her ear off."

"She promised a friend to go to a meeting."

"She what?" I gasped.

While he was speaking, I was trying to listen to him and figure out what I could do. "Otis, this is an emergency, help me get this poor woman to my truck. I can only do so much. She's got to be seen by the doctor."

The old woman began to shake all over. "You promised me the white lady would . . . oh, no, I cain't see no doctor. Maybe he be one of 'em. He'll kill me fo sure."

"Otis, get her into the truck and you come with us. This requires a doctor's skill—to do some stitching. Let's go."

As I rushed to the truck and Otis all but carried the poor woman in his arms, she continued to cry, "Oh, pleeze, ma'am, don't hurt me."

"Ain't nobody gonna hurt you, ma'am. Jez cum along wit us," comforted Otis.

Fortunately, the ride over to old Dr. Jones was short and he was in his office. I assured him that I'd cover the cost, but he shook his head, saying, "Bring her in through the back door."

"Minnie, you studied nursing. Well, you're gonna assist me, honey."

Otis carried the elderly woman in his arms into a room and helped stretch her out on the table, assuring her everything would be okay.

Dr. Jones had already filled a syringe, while Otis and I held her tightly. Then he gave her a shot of what I presumed was morphine because it wasn't long before her loud cries became a low moan.

"Otis, go back to the truck and wait."

He nodded as he backed out of the room, glad to get out of the office.

Reaching over to a low-lying table, the doctor handed me an opened bottle of saline solution. "Minnie, you pour this slowly over the cloth, and I'll pull it away easy-like. Now! As he started, blood began to flow. "Minnie, there's going to be a lot of blood."

"I'm fine."

And the blood began to flow. "Minnie, grab those cotton pads and soak it up." When he'd removed the cloth entirely, he commanded, "More pads quick." Then, he reached over and got a bottle of mercurochrome, handed it to me, saying, "All right, I'm ready to stitch her up. Soak up a little more of the blood. Good! Now swab the gashes with mercurochrome. Quick! Great!" Now he began to stitch together the skin, the patient twitching. She obviously still felt the pain of the needle piercing her flesh and pulling the skin together.

I continued to soak up the remaining blood, then took another cotton pad and wiped off his brow.

"Now, swab the area again."

Dr. Jones reached into a drawer and pulled out a bandage. "We'll put on a crown bandage." He wrapped her head, telling me to keep pressure on the wound.

I looked up at him, waiting.

"Are we done?" he said, questioningly.

"No, sir. I believe you need to give the patient a tetanus shot."

"That's right, nurse!"

By the time we had finished, I had had what I dreamed of in nursing school—to assist as a surgical nurse. It was a horrible, bloody ordeal, but I did not flinch or let him—or this elderly woman—down.

After the surgery, Dr. Jones said he'd look in on the patient in three days.

I drove Otis and the old woman back to his place. Remembering the healing herbs like white willow bark for pain that Marie used, I said to her, "I'll be back. Don't worry. I'm not going to abandon you."

As I was leaving, I heard Otis say, "I told you, ma'am, you'd be safe with Miz Minnie." I felt a lump in my throat. Then came the anger. I was furious at those men who savaged a helpless, old woman.

$\cdot \ \cdot \ \cdot \ \cdot \ \cdot$

December 25, 1935

Dear Journal,

The year is almost gone and what a year it has been! I can't believe how fast the world is changing around us. Whether it's the world, the government, my job, or the plantation, there's so much that has happened this past year, it makes my head spin.

First, the world—the thing I understand the least. Between my history book: "The Story of Mankind," and Dad, who keeps me up on everything, I have an inkling of the problems. For whatever reason, the thing that comes to mind most is Germany. Seeing the newsreels of their soldiers marching worries me. Dad says Hitler is going create another war.

Secondly, the stuff with the government never ends. There's always lots of wrangling between the two parties. The Democrats have control, so at least things get done. From Dad, we hear the same thing, "Let the market work without government, which only makes things worse." I don't agree, but what do I know. I don't have Dad's education and knowledge. Still, I draw my own conclusions, based on what I hear, read, and—unlike Dad—see. He doesn't experience the very real problems and struggle in the Delta.

Since Mother and I voted for Roosevelt, we trust he'll do the right thing, but Dad has continued to be right about human greed. The Farm Bill, that is, the money intended to help the planters, tenant farmers and sharecroppers, by and large, has stayed in the pockets of the planters and the small, independent farmers. The poorest of the poor are even worse off because of the mass evictions of so many others. This isn't to say, though, that the union didn't win a big victory. They called for a strike, asking for $1 for a hundred pounds of picked cotton. Planters offered forty cents, and planters agreed on 75 cents, which meant that a good picker could make a little less than $2 for a day's work.

I do feel good about something I was able to do about Mother's evictions of farmers. I was able to get 15 families relocated into the Dyess Colony. I had to make three separate trips to do it. I have Norma Mae to thank for getting these farmers on public relief.

I think one of the worst things to happen is the terror of the night riders— thugs hired by some planters. Men and women have been badly beaten, while others have been murdered outright. Nobody is prosecuted. One thing that sent Dad over the top was a national broadcast by Norman Thomas, whom we listened to. Thomas declared that the situation in the Delta was no better than slavery for modern men and women— white or black.

I have continued to do my healing of the poor, which I am glad to do. There was one awful experience that really tested me—an elderly colored woman had her ear cut off by a night rider. When I saw the horrible mutilation, I took her to Dr. Jones. I assisted him in his office as he did the best he could to stitch up the gash across the side of her head. Later, I brought her honey to try to prevent infection, and a healing herb (that aspirin is made from) to dull the pain. Now she wears a headscarf to cover her missing ear.

My job at the telephone company becomes harder with each passing week. It's a terrible work environment for us. Anyone seen not working fast enough is taken aside and given a warning. Quite honestly, I've considered quitting and working on the plantation, but I refuse to allow myself to be under Mother's thumb. I would be if I quit. So, I just plug away, even though I know I have options. I just don't take anything or anyone for granted. In a strange way, the company makes me look forward to going to the plantation and working.

Today, Christmas 1935 has been a very real blessing. I may be tired, but I am okay. Everyone is in good health, money isn't an issue, and our home is quiet and secure. It seems strange with our resources, neither Mother nor Dad have indicated any willingness to spend money on a house of our own.

And Jeanette at seventeen. What can I say? She gets more and more beautiful and popular with every passing month. What bothers me is she knows it.

I had a note from Grace, my friend from nursing school. She seemed depressed. I must send her a card.

To end my entry to you on a positive note, I am truly grateful for what I do have. That most definitely includes you, dear Journal, with whom I can share my thoughts and feelings—and secrets.

Part Three

CHAPTER 41
THE CART

"My God, it won't be long before we're halfway through the month of April, nineteen thirty-six," exclaimed Mother. "It's hard to imagine so much has happened." Ruminating, Mother took a deep breath and exhaled, exhausted by what she was about to say. "It's time to collect—"

"I'll take the truck over there and get the May rents," I said.

"I could wait for Tom to do it," Mother said wearily, "but I want to get it out of the way and not have it hanging over my head."

"Most folks ought to be either at home or out in the fields, so I won't have any problem."

Mother nodded her head and went back to counting cash from rents already brought in by her help or by the renters themselves. She had a deposit slip already set out, and would want to get the cash to the bank before the close of the day. It wasn't wise having that much money in the office overnight.

After I left the gin and crossed the bridge over the river, I decided to take an unpaved road to what had been the land that belonged to Grandpa forty years ago. Then it went to the sheriff because Grandpa had killed the bushwhackers, then half of it was bought back by Grandpa a couple of years into the

Depression, along with a few hundred acres from an adjacent farm.

The road I wanted to take was a shortcut. Even though it would be a bumpy ride, I was looking forward to it. The spring day was beautiful. A cloudless blue sky gave me a feeling of boundless freedom. The smell of the freshly plowed earth was familiar and comforting. A spring breeze brought the scent of countless wildflowers through the truck's open windows. Alongside the road and in some untilled fields and pastures, there was a blaze of colors—the brilliant orange-red of Indian Paintbrush scattered among snow white blossoms of Thimbleweed and Queen Anne's lace, its tiny umbels tinged with pink. Interwoven in the tapestry were the Poppy Mallows, deep, rich purple, and the tawny orange of the Ditch Lily. Not far off the road, the first yellow black-eyed Susan lifted its head toward the sun. I felt my spirit fill with exhilaration and pleasure. I felt so alive! "God, the world is a beautiful place!" I shouted aloud.

Moments later, I slowed down and turned onto the shortcut. It wasn't long before I saw something coming toward me. The closer I got, I realized it was a mule-drawn cart, so I pulled to one side of the rutted road to let it pass.

The cart and mule slowly drew closer and closer. I could make out a woman and two small, shirtless boys sitting on a bench, while behind them stood a young girl about twelve years old, holding onto her mother's shoulders to steady herself. She wore a faded yellow cotton dress.

It wasn't long before I could hear the wheels of the cart rolling toward me. The wheels, unable to always follow a rut for long, slipped out, which gave the appearance at times of the cart swaying back and forth 'til the wheels found another rut. Looking at the jostling of the people, I knew that they couldn't be very comfortable. Feeling not at all friendly by keeping myself inside the cab, I got out and leaned against the door.

Closer and closer they came. They couldn't be more than a stone's throw away, when I saw all of their worldly possessions in the cart—a simple wooden table with four chairs, and crammed between these on the side panel were burlap bags of what little clothing they had, some sundries, bedrolls, and maybe a little food. A large can probably held their drinking water. Up front, my eye caught their one piece of art and inspiration—one of the little boys held a picture of Jesus that had probably been cut out of a large magazine and had clumsily been framed within uneven pieces of wood.

Whatever joy and freedom I felt earlier had evaporated. I watched with a growing intensity the misery of these country folk, traveling down the road toward me, knowing in my heart that they had no place to go.

Just as I heard the hooves of the mule and its heavy breathing, the woman looked at me, expressionless. What I saw in her eyes and her face was hopelessness. Were it not for her children, I suspected she might have thrown herself into the river like so many others before her had done, but she was a mother and with whatever little strength and fortitude she had, it was for her children's sake she was still alive.

"Howdy, ma'am," I said hospitably.

She drew rein. "Howdy," she said flatly.

"I can see y'all are travelin'?"

"Uh huh," she said, swaying back and forth slightly.

In a glance I saw they hadn't been eating much for some time. Rail-thin, the girl stood stoically. The straw color of her hair was dull and lifeless. The two little boys' ribs stuck out, while their mother's gaunt face attested to the fact she was obviously giving them much of the food she needed for herself. When she started a fit of coughing, I wasn't sure if it were the result of having inhaled so much dust along the road, or if she had a more serious respiratory problem. Her sunken eyes, sharp cheekbones, and hollow cheeks gave me more cause for concern about her health. Yet her complexion was good and her skinny, yet sinewy arms and veins, told me she was tough. She had worked hard all her life.

The mule didn't look like he was in any better shape. He'd lost more than a few meals. His bony ribcage bulged and his hips scarcely had any meat on them other than the hide. The white and grey hairs around his mouth said he was old and tired. I wondered how much farther he'd be able to get them.

I was aware that I was being stared at when the little boy's eyes met mine. Breaking into a sweet smile, he held out the picture of Jesus and said bravely, not altogether sure of what he was saying, "He's the Lord. He's watchin' over us. He'll protect us."

I felt this great upwelling of emotion. With nowhere to go, no work, no income, and no one to welcome them or help them, they were on their own. I could only imagine what might happen to the children. The poorhouse—maybe? Yet, most likely not. An orphanage more than likely would be their next home. A mother unable to support her children would be forced to give them up. They would be separated.

These people's way of life had been snatched away from them. I was certain that they and their people had lived on the land for generations. It was all they'd known. Thank goodness it wasn't from our land they were coming. Mother had not evicted anyone on the land across the river, so it had to be from the sheriff's land or someone else's. Sadly, they had been evicted during the planting season, so they had no chance to make any money until cotton picking in August.

"Good weather for travelin'."

Taking a deep breath, the woman, somewhere in her thirties but looking more like fifty, said, "Yep, 'guess it is. 'Guess it is, ma'am."

Mother told me incessantly these last few years not to let sympathy get the best of me; that business is business. It's either them or us. I knew all the words and phrases, even the one from the Bible: "You will always have the poor among us." I remembered, however, that I'd seen Mother melt on more than one occasion when she saw something that pulled at her heartstrings, and she couldn't help herself—she gave.

"Ma'am," I opened my purse and grabbed nearly everything I had from yesterday's paycheck: $19.75. Handing the money into her trembling hands, I kept enough money for the train back home and carfare to the house. Considering a good picker—a man—could make almost $2.00 for twelve hours' work, this was worth almost ten days of hard work under the hot sun (if you could find the work). Seven cents would buy a loaf of bread for her and the children. At least, I reckoned, it would help feed them. At least the money would sustain hope, and encourage the little boy's simple belief that "He will protect us."

She looked at me, the slightest smile creasing her cracked lips.

"Please . . . please take it; might come in handy."

"My children . . . my children," she croaked through her blistered lips.

Nodding my head, she knew that I understood: *My children will eat.*

"Thank you," she said, saying nothing more. She looked straight ahead, pulled on the reins of the old mule. He started to walk slowly down the road, the sound of the wheels and cart creaking and groaning.

"Nineteen dollars," I said to myself. "I only had $19.00 for them."

CHAPTER 42
THE GARDEN PARTY

"Well, I declare! You must be the famous Minnie Beck my grandpa's been telling us all about."

God, how I hate this! It's everything and more of what I dreaded about socializing with the planters and their families, but Mother insisted it was an invitation we could not turn down.

"I'm sorry, but I don't believe we've met."

"Lordy me, I'm forgettin' I didn't introduce myself! I'm Lucy Dawson, and we're at my grandpa's house. Isn't it simply gorgeous?"

"It is beautiful," I said, quite honestly.

Flipping her hair with her hand, then patting her perm down, Lucy was exactly what I expected of a planter's daughter or, in her case, granddaughter—someone I was supposed to have so much in common with. Seeing I didn't have a drink in my hand, she volunteered, "No one's gotten you a drink. Johnnie, over here."

A nicely-attired young colored man, dressed in a short white waiter's jacket and black slacks, held a tray and came over at her beckoning.

"Yes, ma'am."

"My friend needs a refreshment."

Dutifully, he held out the tray with glasses of lemonade on it. Straight-backed and very proper, he said simply, "Ma'am."

"Does this have alcohol in it?" I inquired.

"Well, doesn't everything worth drinking have alcohol?" giggled Lucy.

"I'm sorry, but I don't drink."

"Then ma'am, I'll bring you unadulterated lemonade."

"Un . . . a . . .what?" Lucy asked, thoroughly perplexed and possibly somewhat exasperated by his use of the word.

"Yes, I'll have that," I said, not to embarrass the man.

"I'll get you a glass, ma'am."

"I declare, there he goes using a word he probably doesn't even know the meaning of. Did you understand him?"

"I sort of got his drift. It's fine, Lucy." In order to get her mind off of the servant and her annoyance with him, I redirected the conversation to something she could understand. "My, what a beautiful dress you're wearing. Just where did you get it? I'm just green with envy."

"Oh this, you like it, honey? Well, let me tell you—"

I listened to her go on, catching every other word, until the servant arrived with my lemonade. Trying to be quick to wave him on, I was a little too late to prevent Lucy from venting her spleen. "Don't go usin' words that make you sound uppity. That's not why you're hired. Be careful. Jobs are scarce."

"Yes, ma'am. Of course, ma'am. No offense intended."

"Well, then, you can go."

His head held low and his eyes still lower, he slowly backed away. In that instant when Lucy turned her attention back to me, he made eye contact with me and saw me shake my head. I wanted him to understand I didn't approve of Lucy's behavior.

"That's what my daddy says, Minnie, 'Give 'em too much book learnin' and they'll be thinkin' they're our equals'. 'Course, to be fair, that applies to the sharecroppers and all the rest of them living off us. Gracious me, how many words do they need for field work anyway?"

As if Lucy hadn't pondered the subject deeply enough, she came back to the waiter. "Would you believe," Lucy said, obviously still annoyed with Johnnie, "he's actually goin' to college? What a waste if you ask me," she drawled.

At that moment, I had the strongest urge to blurt out, "I'm not asking for your opinion. I don't want your opinion. I'm embarrassed by your behavior." But I held my tongue.

"Could you direct me to the 'little girls' room'?" I asked, knowing that this is the proper term a young woman of breeding uses to refer to a bathroom.

"Oh, sure. Go through the French doors and down the hall."

"Thank you, Lucy." We both went our separate ways.

I wandered into the house and back out into the yard, where the cooks were serving barbecue to the guests.

"So you were able to come," said a somewhat familiar voice.

"Mr. Dawson, how nice to see you again."

"I noticed you were chatting up a storm with Lucy." He must have noticed the subtlety of my expression because he continued, "or she was—"

"Sir, what a beautiful home you have."

"As nice as your grandpa's?"

"Well—"

"How could you be impartial, Minnie? Charley had a classic antebellum home. I was there—goodness, over thirty years ago—shortly after it was built, if my recollection serves me right."

A nice smile of remembrance passed across his face. With his thick white hair, beard, white linen suit and Panama hat, he was every bit the Southern gentleman and grandpa. I felt warm toward him, which made me think of Grandpa at the Big House—Grandpa, Marie and all the good times we had had together.

"I've been having a nice talk with your mother—charmin' woman."

I nodded my head in agreement. If he was trying to draw me out about Mother, I wasn't offering him much information.

"I don't think I've ever met a woman quite like her before. She's intelligent and—"

Finally, I decided to give him something to chew on. "My mother is a very determined woman."

"Intelligent and determined," he mused. "I might also say, *a force to be reckoned with.*"

"Do you think so, sir?"

"Oh, I do. I do, indeed, Minnie." He paused. Then, he asked me quite properly, "May I call you Minnie, or do you prefer to be called Mrs. Beck?"

"Minnie is fine, sir."

"I'm sorry not to see your husband here. Business?"

"Always."

"I haven't heard if the Becks plan to move into the Delta."

"I am here," I said, demurely, not answering the intent of his question, but sowing the seeds of doubt. The Becks were allied to Mother by way of my marriage. If such a rich family as the Becks moved aggressively into the Delta, we could create serious problems for other planters. In a sense, we could gobble them up.

"So you are, honey."

"Sir, my husband's family is preoccupied with developing a major project in Cuba, so—" I decided to terminate this discussion. I changed the subject, leaving Mr. Dawson to speculate on my reasons—especially since I couldn't carry the topic much further. "But as you know, Mother, she's been busy here in the Delta."

"I believe that might be an understatement."

"I beg your pardon, sir?"

"Well," he said, still smiling, "besides more than doubling the size of her plantation—"

"Tripling, and then some," I interjected, modestly. I regretted immediately what I'd volunteered.

"I haven't been able to keep up with Nora's expansion— mechanizing farming, expanding the gin, buying the utility and telephone companies, I'd say she's putting the rest of us planters to shame. Am I leaving out anything?"

"Mother's always been about progress."

"I can see that. It was sad about the banker, but then luckily the Memphis Bank came to town and picked up the slack."

"A town's gotta have a bank, sir."

"All very true, especially if they want to branch out." Clearing his throat, he dug deeper, "Gives them the opportunity to work more effectively with Nora's other friends—I mean, associates."

"I'm not sure I understand."

His eyes narrowing, the canny old man looked directly at me and said, "When you think of your mayor, who's now in Little Rock, along with his wife, who's known as the Virginian aristocrat." He took my measure and decided to go on, finally saying, "Nora's councilman is now the county judge, and another one is on the District Drainage Board. My goodness, your mother's reach goes way beyond the town now, wouldn't you say?"

I heard both resentment and fear in his voice. "Oh, I don't really follow politics. I'm like the other girls here."

"Minnie, not to embarrass you, but you are nothing like any of the girls here."

"Sir, do I not measure up?"

"That, my dear, was a compliment. I'd be proud to have you in the family. You're nobody's fool, which, unfortunately, I can't say is true for most of the people at this party."

"Sir, you honor me."

"I meant to, Minnie. I just hope that husband of yours realizes what he's got in you."

I did not say anything. Mr. Dawson had hit a nerve. He must have known it by my silence.

"On a lighter note, I hope you'll enjoy the barbecue. Our cooks really know how to do barbecue. Please, go and enjoy. You need to be around young people your own age."

"Sir, I learn ever so much more from someone like you."

Taking a long look at me, then winking, he urged, "Shush now, Minnie. Go and have fun. You don't have to be responsible to anyone, including yourself. Go, honey, be free."

He started to walk away, then turned around. "See those folks under the magnolia tree? They're crowded around Pauline Hemingway, the wife of a famous writer. She's one of us—from the Pfeiffer plantation. Ernest, her husband, is at their home in Key West, unfortunately. Anyway, you'll find her interesting, perhaps fascinating."

I watched Mr. Dawson turn and amble off to a small crowd gathered under another ancient magnolia tree, its branches spreading out and creating shade for the guests, the fragrance of its blossoms wafting over to where I was standing. Throughout the garden, flowers were blooming in front of what looked like ancient marble statuary set back in sheltering coves among the bushes.

Wandering over to the outdoor table set up next to the cooks where the food was being served, I stopped suddenly to bend down and smell a gardenia when a youngish man, one of the planters I remembered from our last visit here, cut across my path.

"Hello, I believe we've met before—the last time you were here. Perhaps you may have forgotten?"

"No, I haven't forgotten you."

"That's really nice to know. I was lookin' forward to you and your family coming to the barbecue so we could get better acquainted. I believe you said you can never have too many friends."

"I believe I did."

"Lawrence Bullock, ma'am, at your disposal." He bowed deeply and stretched out his left arm, his right holding his drink. Chivalry, No! A Southern gentleman would never have been holding a drink and making that grand gesture. He had no idea how ridiculous he looked to me.

I pulled out my handkerchief and patted down my forehead, making sure he saw my wedding band. He got the message immediately and after a little small talk, wandered away.

Just as I was placing some potato salad on my plate, I heard a pleasant voice. "I saw how you got rid of Lawrence; he can be a pest." Startled, I recognized the guest when she extended her hand. "I'm Pauline Pfeiffer Hemingway."

"I'm pleased to meet you. My name is Minnie . . . Minnie Prescott . . . Beck." I noticed she was a very sensitive person and heard me hesitate before I used my maiden name. To clarify myself, I added, "My mother is Nora Belle Coymen."

Nodding her head, she said, "I really wasn't familiar with the Coymen plantation until your Mother took over and began to expand it. I guess there's been a lot of talk about it, but then, when are people not talking? I think it's wonderful that a woman owns and runs a plantation."

I looked at her, hair cut short in a no-nonsense fashion, she was thin without being gaunt. I listened carefully to this very intelligent woman as she spoke, allowing me to fully appreciate the sincerity of her thoughts. The more I observed and listened, I couldn't help but feel behind this very comfortably assertive exterior, there was a somewhat shy and retiring nature—definitely introspective and deep, which contrasted with so many of the guests at the party.

"Oh my, your mother was the woman who shot the sharecropper who tried to kill y'all? Now I remember. As an aside, my husband loves guns. He'll be up here in a few weeks to hunt with our boys." Pausing to see how I received what she said earlier, and seeing I had not taken offense but that I chuckled and shook my head, she went on. "Sounds like it could have been a scary moment for y'all?"

I think she had taken my measure and figured I had done the shooting, having said "y'all." There was just something about the way she looked at me and waited; again, not probing or crossing any boundaries, which put me at ease. I knew that I liked her.

"Neither my mother nor I am going to let trash or anyone else run roughshod over us. We're just not made that way."

"I can see you don't do the Southern belle thing, unless . . ."

"Rarely. Very, very rarely," I said, feeling light and forthcoming. Pauline just had a certain way of drawing me out and making me feel good. I thought I'd extend myself and see how she reacted. "You'll excuse me for not asking after your husband, and how does it feel to be married to a famous author and all, but I know just how boring that is for me. I'm not an appendage of a man, and, I suspect, that's true for you."

Pauline smiled, took a deep breath as if someone really understood her. "Minnie, you are so right. I'm bored silly talking about *my* husband. Instead, let's you and I have a real, honest-to-goodness conversation."

Who would have guessed, but we did. Pauline's relaxed posture, the down-to-earth joking and sharing of her life, really gave me a chance to be myself, but it was not to last. Suddenly, a couple of women called out, "Oh, it's Pauline; Pauline Hemingway."

I saw the faintest shudder cross her body. "Minnie, promise me we'll stay in touch," Pauline said hurriedly. "I like you and, I believe you like me. Ernest will be very comfortable as well. Here!" She opened her purse and handed me a card. "Of course, his name is on front, mine's on back with our phone numbers up in Piggott, and out on Key West."

The moment was gone, the voices were insistent and upon us, clamoring for her attention. "Pauline, it's jus' sooo won-der-ful to see you."

"Caroline and Melba, imagine, my goodness, just to see you in the flesh again." With a shrug and a sigh, Pauline whispered, "You'll excuse me, Minnie," and she turned her attention back to the two chatty women.

Looking at the assembled guests, the laughter, the giddiness, and the abundance of wealth displayed, I found myself comparing this moment to the week before, when I stopped on the country road to see the homeless sharecropper and her children rolling down the rutted road, pulled by the half-starved mule; rolling along in that cart with all of their worldly possessions; rolling down the road with nowhere to go.

However, these guests' leisured stances, their smiles and dalliances, contrasted sharply with the poverty and starvation around them; their lives left me cold and angry. I went to bed thinking about work the next day and woke up thinking about work, whether it was at the telephone company or the plantation. I thought of Mr. Dawson's comment: *You don't have to be responsible to anyone, including yourself.* If he only knew, I thought. But then, I suspect he must have sensed it, because he wouldn't have said it otherwise. I felt somewhat exposed and did not like that feeling, which was one more reason I didn't want to be here.

I could hardly wait to leave. I wanted to be as far away from this place and these people as I could possibly get. I had nothing in common with them—nothing at all, unless one counts wealth, which, I always reminded myself, didn't belong to me.

CHAPTER 43
A REAL PLANTATION HOUSE

On our way home from the Dawsons, I glanced over to see Mother smiling and slightly nodding her head back and forth. I assumed she must be thinking about the garden party, or caught up in the loveliness of a beautiful day in May: clear, blue sky, new green leaves on the trees, perfect temperature, and the smell of freshly plowed fields.

"You thought Dawson's plantation house was beautiful; it was, but it was not really unique. You should've seen Lakeport Plantation when I did. Now, that! That was a real plantation house. When I say this, you have to understand, it did not have, the classic columns and furnishings of Dawson's place. Also his yard is much lovelier. Still, it isn't a *historical* plantation house."

Incidentally, from what Marie told me, her family's plantation was built in the style of what I saw of the Big Houses in Louisiana, but, mind you, on a smaller scale."

Mother's reference to Marie's family's plantation house really caught me off guard. I didn't really think Mother knew anything about Marie's family background and wealth.

"I didn't think Dawson's place was as beautiful as Grandpa's Big House," I replied, echoing what I thought were Mother's sentiments.

"No, it wasn't. However, what I am talking about, Minnie, is . . . is you can't compare something built before the war, and a Big House today. I know, because I've been in a few of the old homes when I was in boarding school. I acually went to stay with a couple of the girls who came from real planters' Houses. One was in Missouri, another in Louisiana. The Big House in Louisiana had been built on a really grand scale, though it was somewhat rundown, owing to the family's circumstances. From there— in Louisiana that Christmas holiday—we went to visit a few other planters' families that had survived the pillaging by the Yankees."

"I had no idea, Mother."

"How could you, Minnie, since I've never spoken of them—especially after what happened to Grandpa's."

I remained silent, waiting to see if Mother would want to continue speaking, after having mentioned our Big House and all the feelings that might have gotten kicked up. I looked over, just as she continued. "It was on my visit to Louisiana that your Grandpa came to fetch me in his riverboat and brought me back to Arkansas. Along the way, he paid a visit to the Lakeport Plantation, which was actually in southern Arkansas—in Chicot County."

"Arkansas?"

From the little I knew, there weren't any antebellum plantation houses left in the Delta. Even though planters had begun to move into the Delta before the war, what few there were either didn't survive the fighting or fell into total ruin later. That's about as much as I had heard and learned in school or from Great-Grandmother Keghel, an antebellum planter's daughter. She had said that—even if there were Big Houses here—we Arkansans, nonetheless, were considered to live in frontier land and looked down upon by other Southerners, who thought of us as wild and wooly barbarians.

The Johnson's plantation, Minnie, wasn't far from the river—"

"The Mississippi?"

"Of course, what other river is there?" said Mother testily. Obviously thinking about the sound of her statement, she backtracked. "Lakeport Plantation is the only plantation left standing near the Mississippi River and in the Arkansas Delta. You haven't travelled much, so I shouldn't blame you for your ignorance."

I wanted to say something snide to Mother but held my tongue, and let her get on with the story. Everything had been pleasant until her last remark, so there was no point in ruining things now.

"As I was saying, we spent the evening with the Johnson family—very genteel people. They are the same Johnsons as the people known in Arkansas as "The Family" or "The Dynasty.""

"They sound—"

"Very rich and very influential in the antebellum South, mind you. At the time they had fallen on hard times. However, before the war, they all but controlled the state, with one member a federal judge and state senator. Then there were the Johnson brothers from Kentucky, who bought 4,000 acres in 1830-something. By 1859, the plantation house was built but not fully furnished. Your grandpa told me one of them had over $200,000 in assets before the war; $17,000 afterward."

"Slaves," I said.

"Slaves," said Mother. "A lot of his money in Arkansas was tied up in slaves. Unlike a lot of folks who owned slaves, that didn't finish him. Since he came from Kentucky, he had other assets, including their city home in Louisville. According to your Grandpa, who learned it from his mother, the family up there was well-fixed, having had Vice President Richard Johnson as their uncle."

"Really?"

"You probably don't know who the president was."

I started to react when Mother said, matter-of-factly, "Van Buren was. In all truth," Mother chuckled, "I wouldn't have known either if we hadn't stayed there with the family, who was quite proud of their famous uncle. On our way home, Daddy went on to say that Van Buren called Johnson an amalgamator."

"A what?" I said, having absolutely no idea what that meant.

"It's because Johnson never married and had a free colored mistress, who bore his children."

"They certainly didn't teach us that in school."

I was surprised Mother had used the word, "mistress." I had never heard her acknowledge such a thing before. Yes, Mother is changing now that she is really back in the Delta. Or, she always knew about such things. Again, maybe she's just getting older and doesn't worry so much about what is and isn't proper for "young" ears.

"No, Minnie, I doubt that was taught in any school. Anyway, the nephews inherited a great part of their uncle's wealth. The other portion went." Mother hesitated, "to the children of his mistress."

"Is that so?"

"Indeed. Actually, I was surprised daddy knew that kinda history. It wasn't like him, given he didn't care a hoot about other people's lives, and what few books he knew were read to him by Marie.

"Mmm hmmm," I said, letting Mother know I was listening. "Marie, I bet, really got a chuckle out of him."

"Ohhh, she did for a fact! *Treasure Island, Huckleberry Finn* and *The Adventures of Tom Sawyer* were what he came to love. I remember as children, Marie would read those books over and over to us—after dinner—as our entertainment. Your Grandpa was—for a fact—her best listener. He could and would take over and 'read', so to speak, the rest of the chapter to us. It was the only time I ever saw him pretend anything in life, using different voices for each of the characters. Actually, he could be quite funny," remembered Mother, her voice becoming heavy with nostalgia.

"I would love to have seen—and heard—Grandpa then. My goodness—" I said, almost whispering, a hint of emotion creeping into my voice, which Mother did not detect. If she had, I knew all too quickly she'd reprove me and, maybe, end the storytelling altogether.

"Oh, if you could have *seen* him! He was one handsome, fearless devil. The women used to swoon all over—"

With that, Mother stopped abruptly. It was becoming either too painful remembering those years or she simply brought herself back to the story she was telling me.

"Anyway, as I was saying, when we arrived, the Johnson house was weathered—not grand at all from the outside, but once we were inside you could see what they had planned for the house—fourteen-foot ceilings with two great medallions moulded to frame the chandeliers. All in all, I remember that there were nineteen rooms, covering around seven thousand square feet.

"It must have cost a lot to heat it."

"'Course, since it was December, only a small, living portion of the house was heated. Nonetheless, we were shown through the house, even if it was a quick tour. The original Johnson must have had great plans for his plantation and that house. It had two parlors, two kitchens, drawing and sitting rooms, but . . . oddly enough, there were only three bedrooms. Would you believe that—just three that is, if I don't count the nursery."

"I guess they didn't want guests."

"Minnie!" Mother said sharply. "They were, as I said, very genteel to us, but you might have a point there. I never really thought about it much."

At that moment, the truck hit a pothole in the road and we were jounced severely, which definitely shook Mother out of her annoyance with my last comment, because she went on. "I still remember the cooks' names, Fanny and Amanda. I suppose I remember them because they prepared a real feast for us. Those women certainly knew how to cook. I was told it was because the plantation was only a few miles from Louisiana, and the influence of Creole cooking was second nature to 'em.

Can't remember where they originally came from, since they'd been brought originally to the plantation as slaves. The important part for the Johnsons was that their cooks stayed on after the war."

"I wonder if they cooked as well as Marie."

Mother thought about that for a moment, but evidently dismissed the idea of comparing anyone else to Marie and shook her head.

"That's kind of amazing when you think about it. I'm sure I would want to get as far as I could from a place that had kept me in chains."

"Minnie, they wouldn't have been kept in chains!" said Mother, indignantly.

"I know, but that's the way it must have felt to many people."

"I don't doubt you're right."

Mother paused (I think) to consider what it must have been like for people who were enslaved. "No, I don't think I'd have stayed after I was freed. I saw the slave quarters on a few plantations, including that one, and they were pitiful places."

We both grew silent. After a while, Mother said, "Would you believe they still had a mammy living there?"

"A mammy?!" I said incredulously.

"Yes, Mammy Charlotte Mitchell, who'd been a slave until her early twenties, then moved to the plantation to raise two generations of Johnson children. She took care of those children before and after the war. Yes," Mother mused, "she stayed on—just like the cooks."

"It still seems so—"

My thoughts turned to Marie. I wondered, though she was born after the war, if she had had a mammy who stayed with the family in New Orleans. After my visit with Miss Virtue, a lot of questions had arisen about Marie's household before and after the Civil War.

Not having a response from Mother, I repeated, "It still seems—"

"So unreal, today."

"Of course, Marie." I mentioned.

"Marie, Minnie, was *no* mammy!" said Mother, indignantly. "Marie was a highly educated and cultured person. Like I mentioned earlier, her family had been plantation owners and were a very special group of people. She loved—"

I waited to see what Mother would say, but she didn't finish her sentence. Mother did know whom Marie and her people were and had put Marie on a pedestal. I suspected, indirectly—whether Mother knew it or not—she thought of Marie and her family as people of her own class—plantation owners.

To smooth things over, I said soothingly, "Marie loved us, and we loved Marie."

Mother, still annoyed with me, said without hesitation and forcefully, "And we—none of us—should ever forget that!"

CHAPTER 44
A MOST WELCOMED VOICE

I had come home from work Friday, and just walked through the door when Dad mentioned I had received a call from what sounded like a young woman. Her name and number he wrote down on a piece of scratch paper next to the telephone. On the way to the kitchen to make dinner, he didn't stop to answer questions.

Having the intention of going to my bedroom and taking a quick soak in the tub before eating, the last thing I wanted to do was pick up a telephone after a full day—a full week—of answering calls. I started to ignore the message when, instead, I went over and picked it up.

Dad had written the name "Grace" and a telephone number with a prefix of Nashville, Tennessee. I almost laid it down to head to my bedroom when I realized it must be Grace—Grace Tyson from my nursing school days! Excited, I dialed the number and a man answered, "Phillip Paulson speaking."

"I'm calling for a Mrs. Grace Tyson." I paused, realizing that the speaker wanted me to identify myself. "I'm a friend of Grace's. She called my house and left a message for me to call her." I paused again. "I live in Memphis."

"Oh, yes. Grace said she called a friend of hers from nursing school. How are you? I'm her father."

"I'm pleased to make your acquaintance, sir. Grace spoke highly of you when we were at school."

"Did she? I'm surprised she was still speaking to me by the time she got out of high school. I guess my wife—bless her soul—and I rode her hard about her studies."

"I'm sorry for your loss, sir. Grace wrote me."

"Thank you. Let me find Grace for you."

I waited at least a minute before Grace came to the phone.

"Hi, Minnie! It's me, Grace."

"Hello! How nice to hear from you."

"My gosh, girl, you have a regular professional voice now. You almost sound like some sort of announcer or actress. Maybe I'm speaking to the wrong Minnie," Grace cackled. She thought that was so funny.

"Well, I declare. You may have the wrong Minnie, but I'm speaking with the right Grace. You sound like you always did, girl. How're you?"

"Well, more or less okay, given all that's happened and will happen."

"What do you mean?"

"I've got to be down in New Orleans Sunday afternoon for a family funeral. I'm not lookin' forward to it. I can say that."

"I'm sorry to hear it."

"But that's not why I'm callin', Minnie. My train will get into Memphis at 10:00 a.m. tomorrow. There'll be a four-hour layover. I was hoping we might get together for an early lunch or late breakfast."

"Just a moment, Grace."

Dad was standing nearby and didn't wait for me ask, but nodded his head.

"Yes, of course I can. I'll meet you near the ticket counter."

. . . . .

I arrived at the station half an hour early, in case the train arrived before ten. Luckily, I was more or less right. The announcer's voice crackled, "Inbound train from Nashville arriving." I looked up at the big clock in the station, then at my wristwatch: 9:42 a.m. I was so pleased to have the extra time.

I watched half of the train roll by me, then to a stop. Expectantly, I waited; then waited a while longer. Suddenly, from one of the cars near the front, Grace, appeared, hesitated, searching the sea of faces until she found mine. I lifted my arm and was waving it wildly. Hurriedly, we both moved through the crowd until we reached each other halfway.

Without thinking, she put down her suitcase and with outstretched arms we embraced. That must have been the longest hug I'd given anyone ever, unless it was the one I'd given to Grace the day I left nursing school.

"My God! It's really you, Minnie?" effused Grace, with tears in her eyes.

"In the flesh, in the flesh," I responded softly.

"Where shall we go, Minnie?"

"There's a little breakfast diner just outside the station. Let's go there. We can talk without all of this hubbub."

"Well, let's go, girl."

We talked nonstop until we got to the diner—mostly about the trip and the departure time—just little things. Once we were seated in the relatively quiet diner, since it was somewhat late for breakfast and too early for lunch, we had the place to ourselves. We had privacy.

Privacy was something we instinctively knew we needed to let our hair down. Almost eight years had separated us, but it felt like no time at all had passed, since we picked up where we left off the day I left the school.

"That was one of the toughest days of my life—leaving school, but I had to do it."

"I remember it as if it were yesterday, Minnie," said Grace, with great empathy.

"But at least I got to see Grandpa and the Big House."

"And Marie?"

"Yes. Dear, sweet Marie. I'll never forgive those men for what they did."

"What do you mean?"

"The KKK. They burned down the Big House—after Grandpa died—with Marie inside."

"Oh no!" cried Grace, "Not that, Minnie, not that!"

I was silent for a moment. "But Mother got nearly all of them—one way or another. I guess I did, too. I shot one of the perpetrators."

"No?!" exclaimed Grace.

"Oh, yes . . . yes I did." I took a breath and let it out. "As Mother said after the fire, 'I've got a score to settle'. And we did, one way or another."

Grace looked at me, fully understanding the seriousness of the situation and of the depth of my feelings. It was as if I were reliving the experience as I talked. Finally, exhausted, not having expected to talk so much about myself, I started to shift the attention back to Grace when she said, "So . . . y'all lost the plantation. How sad."

"No. No, we didn't. Actually, the plantation is over double the size as when Grandpa had it; plus, Mother got the gin up and running and bought a couple companies in town. She pretty much has taken control of everything."

"Except you?"

"Except me. That's why I kept my job at the telephone company. I earn my own money. I can—if I had to—move out at any time. I do, though, spend most of my weekends over in the Delta, working at the gin or going out with the manager and riding bosses to the fields. Actually, I really like that part. It makes me feel close to Grandpa."

"I'm glad to hear that, Minnie. I knew you always had it in you. One way or another, you'd rise to the top. You're one tough cookie!" said Grace, wagging her finger at me.

I thought that was funny and started laughing, which got Grace to laughing. "'One tough cookie,' I declare, I've never thought about myself as a cookie, all sweet and gooey or tough, for that matter, like a sheriff. I just do what I gotta do to get through things. Hell, Grace, think of yourself. As a nurse, you deal with real life and death issues all the time. You gotta make decisions that'll either heal someone or nurse them 'til they die. Now that is tough!"

Grace was taken aback by my statement and sat there, finally dropping her eyes to her hands, folded on top of the table. "Minnie, dying is one thing when it's a patient, but it's different when it's someone in your family."

"I can only imagine."

"No honey, imagining isn't it. I watched my Mother die of cancer. She died right in my arms at home. I nursed her. I felt guilty that everyone expected that I could save her because I am a nurse." Grace was struggling to tell me what had happened without crying. Still her tears slipped down her cheeks. "When my brother was shot by some drunken fool, he lingered for a few days in the hospital, then died. All of this happened within a couple of years. I wanted to help save them, but there was only so much I could do."

I realized how much Grace needed to talk with me as much as I needed to talk with her. We were still each other's best friend, sharing our secrets—or at least most of them on my part.

"I think one of the hardest things for me to accept was after the birth of my son, I'd never be able to have another child. Before him, I miscarried, as you know, and after him I miscarried three more times. My life was at risk. So I did what I had to do. Fortunately, I had the same wonderful doctor and nurse who were there when my son was born."

I nodded my head just to let Grace know I wasn't condemning her decision, and I said forthrightly, "I would have done exactly the same thing."

"Oh, thank you, Minnie. I haven't told anyone—other than my husband—and sometimes I felt so alone. I really had to wrestle with the guilt. I stopped taking Communion, since I couldn't risk telling the priest my sin."

"Grace, for a long time I stayed away from the Church. Now I go maybe once a month. Sometimes I take Holy Communion; sometimes not. I make my own decisions. Part of that came from some experiences where I saw that not all priests are holy."

I saw that this shocked Grace. What shocked me more was when she said, "I'm glad you told me that, Minnie. It's real helpful. You've always been strong and determined. I can see where it helps you make your own decisions. I see clearly now that you weren't forced to leave nursing school, but that you made your own decision there."

"I did, for better or worse," I smiled knowingly. "I'd have to say since I can't redo it, I did it, with all the heartache—and fun—that came later for the right reasons. I'll never know what could have been. I only know what is—what is true for me now."

Grace stared at me for a long moment. "Minnie, I'm so glad we've stayed friends. It means a lot to me. You're a real comfort."

"You're a real comfort to me, too. I think there's something else I want to tell you."

I shared from the soul. I told Grace about my love for Norton; my hatred for Beauregard; the legal separation; and the petty, little frustrations at home with Jeanette and Mother. I didn't neglect Dad. Surprised, Grace heard me praise and appreciate Dad.

There were tears for both of us when we realized we had to say goodbye, not knowing how long it would be until we saw each other again. Of course, we promised to stay in touch. Of course, we promised we wouldn't let so much time pass until we saw each other again. Our promises made us feel better, even as I waved at her as the train pulled out of the station.

CHAPTER 45
THE UNION

A couple victories occurred for the union. Why? One victory came because of the bullies hired by the planters. The beatings of a minister, Claude Williams, and W. Sue Blagden, a Memphis socialite, were carried in newspapers from South to North. I, like so many others, was appalled, even though I was no stranger to the danger.

The photos showed large, dark bruises from the severe beating on Mrs. Blagden's face and legs. This reined in planters. They had crossed over a line. In the South, damage was done to the myth of a Southern gentleman's chivalry and manners.

Yes, the union got a pay increase for tenant farmers and sharecroppers, but their income was based on seasonal work, which wouldn't cover yearly expenses. How, I thought, were these people able to feed themselves? In the first couple years of the depression, Marie had asked me: "When was the last time you remember seeing a squirrel or rabbit? The same is true today—rarely. Even birds are scarce.

I thought of Leland's involvement in the Union and the increasing danger to him and others. Every week I dropped off some of my clothing to his cleaners, trying to be supportive of his efforts. Today, my feelings said that something wasn't right, and I acted on them.

As I came through the door, I saw Leland standing behind the counter. Where clothing should have been hanging, the racks were nearly bare. Without a word, he reached behind himself, and handed my dresses to me.

Minnie, I was hoping you'd come in early. As you can see things are changing: We're moving out. It's just too dangerous around here. Whatever it was he heard, he leapt over the counter, and pulled me down to the floor, as a hail of gunfire shattered the glass of his storefront. I twisted around, opened my purse and pulled out my derringer while he dragged me behind the counter. We waited. Finally, we heard the sound of voices. Townsmen came rushing in. Leland must have recognized the voices and called out, "I'm all right."

He stood up, motioning for me to say put. "Everything's okay. Let's go out on the porch and the men walked out of the cleaners. I stayed in place until Leland poked his head over the counter.

"That was a close one," I said.

"Yes, too close. You just saw why we've got to move the union office to Memphis. It's too dangerous here."

I stood up, a little shaken, but alert and fully in control of myself. I nodded. "I believe you do, Leland. I'd hate to see anything happen to you."

"If it were just myself, I'd stay, but I have to think about my family."

"Has anything—"

"No, but I can't risk it—not just their safety, mine. They depend on me to feed 'em. If it were left to me I'd go hungry before I cowered before that scum, but I can't let my family starve if something happens to me."

I shook my head. "No you can't do that."

He took a deep breath and looked hard and deeply into my eyes, then shook his head.

I saw the fierce determination there, but also I saw the anger of defeat, or, maybe, just the acceptance of what was the wisdom of a tactical retreat. I couldn't be sure. I was running on my instincts now.

"If you need some cash, I could loan you something to get your business going in Memphis."

For the first time, I saw the intensity of his emotions rise to the surface of his eyes, but he quickly squelched any show of emotion. I knew he deeply appreciated my offer.

"No, that's not necessary. The Union will move its day-to-day operations over to Memphis. I'll get a small salary—enough to support my family. Things will work out."

"Yes, I'm sure they will."

I started to turn and walk out, when Leland called out to me, "Minnie, you forgot your clothes."

I went back and opened my purse.

Leland smiled, and shook his head.

"I'm not going to shoot you. I was reaching for my money," I said earnestly.

"No, this one is on me."

"Nooo, this is on me, and I pulled out twenty dollars. This is my donation to the cause—and to you and your family."

Saturday
May 1936

Dear Journal,

The Union is still swimming upstream.

Leland has been forced to move to a Memphis office.

Planters are continuing to evict sharecroppers and tenant farmers alike, turning them into little more than wage laborers—something these families have resisted and dreaded for hundreds of years. Some planters—like Mother—had been able to mechanize on their own, but it was the new government subsidies that got many planters and small farmers through. Though they vehemently said they were opposed to government assistance, they all took the money not to plant as much cotton. Some as recommended, planted other crops and made money from those while still evicting people wholesale, which further increased their income. Meanwhile, the planters maintained they were opposed to what Dad called "socialism." As a dyed-in-the-wool capitalist, Dad called them hypocrites because they benefited directly from social welfare for themselves at the taxpayers' expense. Strange, I'm not sure I understand his logic completely; whereas, Mother could care less whether the money came from the government or the buyers. "Money is money," to quote Mother.

Mother—with Dad's advice—continued to mechanize. Her plan was almost complete. Nearly all of the land was now farmed with tractors, trucks, and all the other necessary machinery for a modern farm operation, except for sloughs that needed mules and plows. It sure didn't hurt that "the increasing price for cotton and the other crops had all but offset her initial capital investment." (These are Dad's words, not mine.) More—a lot more money—was coming in than going out. Mother still acquired more land, putting her plantation at over 8,000 acres. This made it one of the largest family-owned plantations in the state if you didn't count a few large landholder companies, such as Chapman and Dewey, with 17,000 acres, and a couple of others that were considerably bigger than Mother's. None of them could boast that a woman owned and ran a plantation. Oddly, Mother has not cut down the trees or plowed up the Indian mounds on what had been Jones' land.

When it came to this question of the size of the plantation, it was on one of our nighttime walks after dinner that Dad let down his hair and said Mother worked to create an even bigger plantation than Grandpa because she was competing with him. She wanted, as Dad said, "her father's approval." It got me to thinking, whose approval had Dad sought? Whose approval was I seeking?

Uncle Bob was, for the most part, stuck to his old ways of doing things. Though he mechanized some of his land—the thought of tractors and trucks appealing more to his boys than to him— he hated evicting people he had known for years. As a result, there were still a lot of sharecroppers and tenant farmers left on his land.

Of course, after new cars for three boys and extras for his new house, his savings dwindled, though not to the point of creating a serious danger or crisis for anyone there. In spite of herself, Mother—at times—still had to give her opinion, which for the most part was sound advice.

Thankfully, modernizing at the gin occurred as well. The books had balanced the last couple of years. Now the gin was making money again, to everyone's satisfaction. Mother—when feasible—had collected a major portion of the debt owed to the gin. What was owed was owed, and no one was getting out of his responsibility to repay his debt. The utility makes a profit, even if Dad had to hire a couple of men to replace him. Mother's planning made the welfare of planters and others even more dependent upon her goodwill.

Ellen has taken like a fish to water managing the telephone company for Mother. Whatever debt was owed, Ellen was more tenacious than Mother in collections. Though the company makes a profit, it is small in comparison to the gin and the utility companies.

Jeanette helps me review my third-year of French, which has brought us closer together, and Miss Virtue helps me with my forth-year French grammar and conversation. This is personally very gratifying.

I continued to read a number of novels recommended by Dad. I realized one of the benefits of work, study and learning has been to help me not feel so self-conscious about my limited education. I could carry on a relatively good conversation with Dad and, if the opportunity arose—which it seldom did—with an educated person. Still, there was always the nagging feeling I'd embarrass myself by saying something stupid.

My Journal friend, I am always being cautioned by Dad not to appear to know more than the man I am interested in. It's a rare man, he said, who is interested in a woman's brain.

CHAPTER 46
THE LOST CEMETERY

"Miss Minnie, are you sure you really want to hear the story?"

I was determined to see Miss Virtue the next day, though not for my French lessons. It was just for the pleasure of having a cup of tea together, talking and listening about our experiences with Marie and Grandpa. Other than Miss Virtue, I had no one who knew Marie as well as she did. There was always some unknown tidbit from the past that might be offhandedly mentioned that got my interest. It was through Miss Virtue that much of the past was brought back and lived for the short time I was in her home.

"I do want to hear. I never knew about another family like y'all in Arkansas."

"Marie never talked about her vacations much, did she?"

"Nothing at all. On those occasions when a grandchild acted up and Grandpa decided to discipline both the culprit and the rest of us, he sent Marie away. We just figured that Marie went to see her daughter in a nearby town, where she also owned some property."

"No, she didn't always go there. Sometimes she went to see her cousins in New Orleans, but sometimes she'd go down to visit the Lafayettes in the lower half of the state, closer to

Louisiana. If we could arrange our schedules to coincide, then we'd visit the family together."

Hearing something new about Marie, I said, truly surprised, "I never heard her mention this family."

"Well, they were a colored family of means who lived outside Helene, which was located where the St. Francis flows into the Mississippi River."

"I've never been that far south in Arkansas," saying it as if it were another state, having absolutely no idea what it looked like.

"Well, the town and country have quite a history, but I'm getting ahead of myself. I was speaking of the Lafayette family. Like Marie's and my family, they were free people of color—or as Marie would say, '*gens de couleur libre*'—before the Civil War."

Taking a sip of tea, Miss Virtue set her cup back on the saucer on her lap, and continued. "As you might have already guessed by the sound of their name, they had a French Creole background. They had come up to Helene from Louisiana, and bought land before many white planters began to flood into the area. Fortunately, the Lafayettes had already established themselves because there was a lot of rivalry and antagonism toward them from the white planters who wanted as much land as they could get. Helene was becoming as important as Atlanta for its plantations and wealth. Oh, Miss Minnie, I see your cup is empty. Let me pour you another cup. I'm not much of a hostess once I start talking. It must be the teacher in me."

"I wasn't suffering in the least. I must have drunk most of your tea, anyway."

"Oh, no. I always keep more on hand. Shall I make us another pot?"

"No, thank you. I'm fine."

"Okay, then. I'll get on with my story."

I settled back into the nice, soft leather chair. Miss Virtue set her cup and saucer on the coffee table and slowly rolled back and forth in her rocker.

"The Lafayettes have a nice, comfortable house, but it's nowhere near the size and grandeur of what the white planters were building, because they knew that it would only create envy toward them and make life difficult. So they maintained a level of modesty to avoid problems. However, like many of us after the Civil War, taxes were raised so high on all planters whether you were white or colored. Then came the Jim Crow laws after Reconstruction, when they lost even more land—a little more than half their holdings."

"More than half of it?" I said, wondering how much that had been.

"They were left with seven hundred acres and their home. Enough to maintain themselves and get their children educated, but still it hurt to lose what they had, because it meant they struggled even harder just to keep what they have and to keep away those elements—the ones who were looking for any excuse to hurt them."

I nodded. I knew exactly what she meant by "those elements." They were the same people who had destroyed the Big House and killed Marie. Miss Virtue didn't have to spell it out for me, and I'm glad she didn't. It was still a raw wound. I took a deep breath, and waited for her to see that I was ready to hear more.

"Anyway, as I said, we would go down and visit. They always made room for us. Even though they had four bedrooms, they had a large family, so the house was full. It is a nice house, though. Besides four bedrooms, there's a nice, big dining room and kitchen, and a lovely sewing room where we'd take tea. Behind the house was a backyard with a vegetable garden and fruit trees—much like your Grandpa's. But they didn't paint the house."

"Why?"

"Oh, Miss Minnie, they didn't want to draw the attention of their white neighbors."

"That's understandable."

"As I said, I spent many summers with the Lafayettes, since I gave the children French lessons. Their grandparents, having been born in Arkansas, had not studied French, so the parents of the children had lost the language."

Miss Virtue smiled. "Matter of fact, I spent late last summer down there. Funny, when I taught those children, they bent their ears in my direction and studied." Miss Virtue shook her head, bemused. "I guess it's always that way. Children don't particularly want to listen to their parents."

I nodded in agreement, but I doubted those children had the heavy hand of a mother like mine.

Suddenly Miss Virtue's expression changed and grew very sad. "Unfortunately, when I was there, the family and colored folks all around were grieving."

I expected to hear they were upset at Marie's passing or some family member's death, and prepared myself emotionally.

"Remember, Miss Minnie, I said that the family had lost more and more of its land?"

"I do."

"Anyway, on their original plantation they had a cemetery for their own family, and allowed other colored families to bury their kinfolk on the same plot of land. Well, when they lost some of their land, they lost the cemetery. This past spring, the new owner of that land plowed everything up to plant crops."

"No," I said, feeling the pain of having your loved ones' graves destroyed.

"Yes. The owner just plowed them up, like no one was there. I'm sure from his way of thinking, there was no one there. Just a bunch of old bones, old colored folks' bones. Nothing more."

"So, Miss Virtue, in a sense they lost their people for a second time. They have no place to pay their respects. Their people are forgotten."

Miss Virtue stopped rocking. "Yes, they're forgotten— forgotten, never to be found."

I thought of Bonnie all those years, in an unmarked grave. She had been all but forgotten until Mother got a gravestone for her after Grandpa died. Now Bonnie can be remembered, which isn't true for those families, nor can it be made right. There's just nowhere to find them.

I thought of Marie. I felt like I had been kicked in my stomach. She had a grave, but—she wasn't there. At this moment, I knew why Miss Virtue had told me this story. She was aware by my expression that I really understood the grief of these people.

CHAPTER 47
VANITY'S GAME

On a Monday evening, Jeanette was burnishing a boyfriend's class pin at the dining room table. By Thursday, it was gone. When Mother inquired, Jeanette seemed very unconcerned and noncommittal about the absence of the pin. Strange, she had shown it off proudly a few days earlier, even though none of us had ever met this young man named Roy.

Friday, as I was coming through the door, I heard Dad on the phone. "No, I had no idea. I'm sorry." There was a pause, as he was obviously concerned and uncomfortable with the speaker on the other end of the line.

"No, we didn't raise her to be like that."

Dad almost stuttered when he replied, "How terrible. I'll have a word with her."

"Again, I'm very sorry." Another pause. "I understand how you feel. What a terrible thing Jeanette did. Goodbye." There was a lingering silence as Dad stood by the phone, until he looked up and saw me standing there in the front doorway.

"Minnie . . . Minnie, I'm—"

Dad told me the story. The girlfriend of Roy had called and wanted to speak to him—Jeanette's father. Between tears and angry outbursts, Jane Pearson described what happened to her this past week. On Monday morning she was wearing Roy's school pin, which she'd worn the past three years. Previously in middle school, they held hands as boyfriend and girlfriend. In the afternoon, her life was shattered. Roy asked for his pin back and pinned it on Jeanette. By Thursday morning, Jeanette returned the pin back to Roy.

According to Jane, Roy and she learned from the grapevine that Jeanette had taken a dare that she could not get Roy's pin. A month earlier, Jeanette had fallen all over Roy. Then she asked him to pin her. He did. Showing off her trophy to her friends and having proven she had been able to get him, Jeanette promptly returned Roy's pin with no explanation. Once Roy knew the story from a friend, he wanted to go back to Jane. She accepted his pin, but she hated Jeanette.

Dad was angry.

As soon as Jeanette walked into the room, Dad lit into her. "I just took a call from Jane."

Jeanette, setting her books down looked up, unconcerned, and said, nonchalantly, "Who?"

"Jane . . . Pearson." Dad stretched out the name. "You know, Roy's girlfriend."

"Oh, her. What did she want?" Jeanette said, dismissively. "I have nothing to say to *her*."

"Maybe you don't, young lady, but you do have something to say to me about your behavior. It's contemptible. I'm ashamed of you. I had to listen to that poor girl—through her tears —tell me what you did. What a cruel, cruel game."

"Daddy," Jeanette started to say, when Dad turned his back on her and began to leave the living room. "Daddy—"

"I'm too angry at you. I don't even want to hear what you have to say. Save it." He went down the hall. There was the sound of his bedroom door as he slammed it shut.

"Minnie, it was just a joke—nothing more."

"Jeanette, don't say that anymore."

"You know how these things are; you're my sister."

I glared at her. "I have no sister!"

"Minnie, I'm your sister."

I growled, "I have no sister."

Jeanette started crying. "I am your sister. I am."

"I have no sister," I hissed repeatedly

Jeanette was now sobbing, and cried out between her tears, "I *am—I am* your sister. Minnie—"

It felt good to see Jeanette crying. I was hurting her and I felt good about it. I didn't leave like Dad but continued to hurt her, saying each time she pleaded with me that she was my sister, "I have no sister." Finally, I yelled, "My sister's dead. Bonnie is dead."

With that, Jeanette ran out of the room, down the hall and up to her room, crying.

I felt no pity for her. So much resentment over the years toward her, toward Mother, toward Dad, and for the years of deprivation, erupted from what felt like a volcano of emotion inside of me. I seethed. Jeanette has everything—she's gorgeous, she can have any boy she wants, and she can throw someone over callously and still get another one.

I sat my purse down, went over to the sofa and picked up the newspaper. I tried to read, but I was still seething. Finally, I put the newspaper down and just sat there, disgusted.

CHAPTER 48
THE APOLOGY

"Minnie, how nice to see you again. I'm so glad you accepted my invitation."

I wasn't comfortable being at Mrs. Trudeau's house since she was Beauregard's aunt, and it was in her house that my future was disastrously changed.

"Minnie," she implored, "this is terribly important. Please, come this way."

We walked down the hall and went back to the sunroom that opened to the garden, which was in full bloom and gorgeous. It almost took my breath away, the variety of flowers Mrs. Trudeau had in her garden. Even the walk up to the house was luxurious since it was lined with a variety of roses. The back, however, seemed to spill over with life and color. The fragrances were overwhelming, having filled the room.

"Why don't we take our lunch under the arbor, where it's a bit cooler? At least we'll get some of the spray from the fountain, which will be refreshing."

As we walked toward the arbor, covered with a climbing rose and honeysuckle, a small round table had been set up. Two white wicker chairs had deep, soft cushions and pale yellow pillows, embroidered with colorful flowers and green vines.

Mrs. Trudeau motioned to me. "Why don't you take the chair on the left? It'll give you the best view of the hollyhocks and delphiniums."

"Oh, Bea," who was standing alert at the door, "please bring us our sweet tea and our sandwiches." Taking her seat, she pointed to me. "Minnie, make yourself comfortable. The days are getting warmer, and the humidity is rising. At least the fountain—"

Mrs. Trudeau could see I was peering at her, my thoughts all but apparent: *Why do you want to see me?*

"Minnie, I see exactly what you must be thinking, but could we put off the discussion until we've had lunch?"

I nodded. For some reason, I felt neither intimidated by Mrs. Trudeau nor rushed by a desire to be done with this visit as soon as possible. Instead I leaned back, and let my gaze wander over the flowers and my senses drink in the fragrances, absorbing the serenity of the moment.

"Wonderful, Bea." We watched as Bea first placed our tea sandwiches before us, then the iced-cold tea in tall crystal goblets. "Minnie, take a sip. It's so refreshing."

Much of lunch was spent chatting about little things: flowers, the weather, and her recent travels abroad— Mrs. Trudeau and her daughter having spent six weeks traveling through France.

I suspected part of the trip was intended to mend their mother-daughter relationship. I couldn't help but think it would take more than a summer trip to France to repair the tension, anger, suspicion and disappointment they held toward one another.

"Minnie, I can see how perceptive you are. Just listening to me speak of the trip, you already know it was probably a lost cause." She waited long enough for me to respond, but when I didn't, she went on. "At least I tried," she said wearily. "Who knows, maybe when—"

I suspected I knew what she was about to say. Instead, she surprised me when she changed course. "If only Mary Jane had been more like you. Unfortunately, parents don't get to choose their children, and *vice versa*." She looked down at her napkin and remained silent, avoiding any embarrassment of having been so honest about her feelings.

Looking up with her all-too-familiar mask, she glanced at me. Then she looked back toward the house. "Ah, Bea—"

Bea was carrying a tray with what looked like dessert on it.

"I hope you like strawberry shortcake, Minnie."

"I love it, ma'am."

Bea placed our empty plates on a small, almost hidden side table outside the arbor. A few moments later, she placed our desserts before us. Effortlessly, she picked up the sandwich plates and began to return to the house when Mrs. Trudeau called out, "Bea, bring a pitcher of iced tea with you. Our glasses are all but empty."

"Yes, ma'am."

We sat there for a moment, waiting, until Bea reappeared with the cold pitcher. After refilling our glasses, the servant turned and went back into the house.

"This certainly has to be one of the best things about a Southern spring—sweet tea, don't you think, Minnie?"

"Oh, yes. I love it. During the summers at the Big House with Grandpa, I must have lived on iced tea."

"Absolutely," Mrs. Trudeau bubbled. "I remember—" Suddenly, she fell quiet, uncomfortable either with her spontaneous outburst or with some part of the unspoken past.

"Minnie, I don't really have anyone I can call a friend. Perhaps the reason for that is disappointment from betrayals, or maybe it's just not in my nature to confide in others. I suspect that's one reason I'm comfortable with you. I know if there were something confidential, you'd never repeat it."

That almost seemed like a question to me. "No, ma'am, I wouldn't."

"Have you ever heard of a psychiatrist?"

"No, ma'am, I haven't."

"He's a doctor the patient goes to talk to—just talk to, nothing more."

"I see—"

"For someone like myself, he is very useful, and, I daresay, somewhat comforting. Part of talking with this kind of doctor has to do with trying to understand ourselves; why we are the way we are, which for the most part has to do with the past.

"For example, Joanna and I had a father who rejected both of us because we were not sons who would inherit his business—a business that survived the War Between the States. Our city, Arlington, which is across the Potomac River from Washington D.C., was occupied by the Union early. Because of that, his father, my grandfather, never converted his money into Confederate dollars. As a result, the plantation wasn't lost, even though carpetbaggers raised the taxes. While my family didn't suffer the deprivations of the War and Reconstruction, my father—and mother to a large extent—never got over the War and remained closed, brooding people. Affection was never shown. Our only approval came when we married into wealth. But I never," Mrs. Trudeau sighed, "stopped trying to get his affection and, to a lesser extent, my mother's. My point, Minnie, is emotional injury comes from rejection."

Mrs. Trudeau hit a nerve. I listened carefully, wanting to know more about her experience and how it affected her.

"Yes, rejection can affect your entire life."

"And your family—your husband and daughter?"

"Exactly. It has explained a lot about the past, which helps me to accept myself and others."

"I see." A part of me did understand but, for the most part, it was impossible for me to accept spending money to tell a doctor such things—especially my secrets.

Mrs. Trudeau looked into the garden wistfully. Taking a deep breath, she mused, "I'd like to have a friend in you, but I'm realistic enough to know that it is impossible because of the circumstances. At least, I want you to know that—that I trust you. You have character, Minnie. Has anyone ever told you that before?"

I shook my head. "No ma'am. No one ever has."

"That's too bad. I'm sorry to hear that, but it doesn't surprise me. That's why you're hearing it from me—someone who rarely gives compliments or acknowledges something like this. Rarely," Mrs. Trudeau lowered her voice, "do I apologize."

"Ma'am?"

"You heard me right." Mrs. Trudeau lifted her napkin and tapped her lips, making sure they weren't wet from the sweet syrup of the strawberries or a bit of the fruit. "I wish what I had to tell you was unconditional, but it has to do with me assuaging my guilt, as well as you not judging me so harshly."

There was a moment of silence while she looked out into the garden, then she brought her gaze back on me with an unwavering stare. "I am apologizing to you, Minnie."

"Me?"

"Yes. I apologize for being a party to your forced marriage. There is nothing I can do or say that really will change it, but at least you'll hear me say I made a terrible mistake, which I deeply regret now."

At first I was angry. I wanted to lash out. Fortunately, she gave me time to sit there and not attack her. I sat there for a long time. When I looked up, Mrs. Trudeau dropped her gaze to her lap and was waiting—just waiting. The more I looked at her the anger faded, and only a dull feeling of loss came. I realized she was genuinely sorry, and it had taken courage to say what she had said to me.

"I appreciate that, ma'am. I don't know why exactly, but it seems to help. You are the only person who has ever apologized to me for anything, so . . . so I have to give this some thought."

"Thank you, Minnie."

"Thank you?"

"Yes, for hearing me out." She reached around herself and picked up a package from a knee-high round table behind us. "This sort of leads me to another reason why I invited you here for lunch." Handing me the package, Mrs. Trudeau said, "This is for you, dear."

I was shocked. I had no idea what she was doing, or why.

"Please, open it."

I unwrapped the package and saw something that looked vaguely familiar. I stopped. I started to hand it back to her when she continued. "Please, open it, dear."

I opened the box. Inside there were the diamond necklace, bracelet, and earrings Beauregard had given me in New Orleans. Old feelings began to resurface. Again I tried to hand the box back to Mrs. Trudeau.

"I thought you'd do that. Hear me out. You're mother-in-law is determined that you have these, not as a present from anyone but her. She wants you to have this present from her and her husband. There are no strings attached. Think of it as a birthday present from them."

I started to say something when Mrs. Trudeau pleaded, "Please, Minnie, do not hurt my sister any more than she's been hurt by her son. It would crush her. Please—"

I nodded my head slowly, neither smiling nor scowling. "Please, tell the Becks how much I appreciate and care about them, that I always have."

"Thank you, Minnie."

"Also, Mrs. Trudeau, I've grown to like and value you, too, though everything you said earlier about us not being able to be friends is true."

"I know. I know you all too well, Minnie. I had hoped, but I really didn't expect that to happen."

The rest of the afternoon was spent chatting as we toured the garden, once the full heat of the sun had gone behind the high hedge. We even joked. Somehow things seemed to have completed themselves and come full circle.

CHAPTER 49
REFLECTIONS

I wanted to walk. It was still a glorious spring day in June. I was reminded of an earlier spring day in June years ago, when I visited the Big House to meet Marie's mother. I was compelled to return to the land where I felt rooted—to the site of my greatest pleasures and security.

Turning off the asphalt road, I began to climb the hill, remembering the many times I climbed it in summer, spring, fall, and once in winter on New Year's Eve. The memories of lugging a pail of fish and Grandpa's fishing pole after many a summer day at the river brought a smile to my face. Ahead, I saw the brick walk and stepped onto it, realizing that was where the stairs had been. Even they had been razed, along with the foundation of the Big House. Only a vine from the honeysuckle crept across my path.

I stood for a moment and looked around, recreating in my imagination the grand house. I knew exactly where everything had been: the columns, the porch with its wicker chairs and table for outdoor sweet tea and Grandpa's mint juleps. I saw the front door, imagining—somehow magically—the house would reappear and I could walk right into it. Voices, sounds, smells, textures, colors all came flooding back to my senses as I waited for the house to reappear. Taking a deep breath, I walked across a small cleared path right through what would have been the house and out into the garden which flourished as well, if not better, than when I was there last.

Looking slightly to my right, I saw the greenhouse. Now before me were the roses, the vegetables, fruit trees, and herbs planted by Marie. Suddenly, I saw an arbor covered by small, pink roses in full bloom. This was new!

I went over and the heady fragrance of the roses overwhelmed my senses. The beautiful little pink roses covered the arbor. Not intending to sit down, I changed my mind, took a chair and made myself comfortable, wrapped in roses and floating on their floral scent. "Cecil Brunners," I murmured, taking a deep breath of the roses.

I saw something move from behind the greenhouse. Moments later, Delia and Lizzie came into view, Delia with a watering hose, Lizzie pulling it from behind. I watched Delia as she sprayed first the vegetables and herbs. Next, she came forward and toward the roses when she caught sight of me, sitting quietly under the arbor. Dropping the hose, she ran as much as her large, heavy frame permitted her to run across the path, smiling and waving at me.

"Hi, Miz Minnie! I never!"

I stood up and we hugged.

Stepping back, she looked at me. "Jus' look at you! You're all growed up—a fine, elegant young lady. I declare, your grandpa would be so—"

She saw the pain cross my face and gently said, "Oh Miz Minnie, I—"

"No, Delia, that was sweet of you to say—just what I needed to hear. How nice it is to see you and Lizzie." Lizzie held back, which seemed quite proper, not having been given the signal to come over by her aunt.

"I knew Mother said she made sure the garden was taken care of. I'm so glad to see how beautiful everything is."

"Oh yes, ma'am. Your mama is very demanding about her garden, especially the roses." Delia thought a moment, "Actually, she cares about everything here. Watches over things like a mother hen with her chicks. Your mama loves her garden."

"Yes, Mother has always said, 'She loves her flowers; she loves her garden'."

"Oh my, how that lady does!" I think she counts every blade of grass, every plant, every flower and tree, making sure nothin' goes wrong. Sometimes she'll come up here and just sit—all by herself, she does—just to be. One time she says she could feel the earth talk to her, and it gives her strength. Isn't that kinda special, ma'am?"

"It is. Most definitely, Delia, it is."

"Oh, Miz Minnie, just look at the fruit trees. Bit early for the peaches, but the apricots are ripe."

When Delia said that, I was reminded of that day when I picked and bit into a sweet apricot, only to see Marie's mother sitting against the back wall of the house, smiling. Minutes later, she told me she loved this time best in the South when everything overflowed with abundance.

I walked over to the tree, reached up and picked three apricots, motioning for Delia and Lizzie, who'd been watching me at a respectable distance, and gave them each an apricot.

Taking a bite, it was just as I remembered—sweet, sweet, sweet. It begged to be made into one of Marie's apricot pies. As delicious as it was, I did feel a heavy sadness creep into the flavor of the moment. Diverting my attention to Delia and Lizzie, I said, "Please, take a bite. They're perfect."

Given permission, each of them bit into their apricot. The pleasure of its sweetness spread across their faces. Encouraged by their enjoyment, I finished my apricot as they did theirs. A slight—almost embarrassing—silence ensued when I said, "I'm going to look around."

As I was still in the greenhouse, Delia appeared and said they would be leaving. "I'll see y'all again," I smiled.

"I hope so, Miz Minnie. Please don't stay away so long. We miss you."

That touched me deeply, and I nodded. "I'll try to come back more often. Y'all have a nice day."

"Goodbye, Miz Minnie."

"Goodbye."

I went back to the arbor and sat there for a long time, reflecting on the beauty and all the wonderful experiences I had at the Big House. Then something extraordinary happened. It was as if I had grown roots. I could feel the earth underneath moving up through my body. I belonged to this place as much as any plant, stone, or creature in the garden. The land, this land, was my home. My very essence was one with everything around me. I understood what Mother meant: She could feel the earth talk to her and it gave her strength."

Thank you, Grandpa, for giving me all of those years. Thank you for the Big House. I have loved you with all my heart. Thank you, Marie, for loving me and . . . loving Grandpa. I love you, too. Rest in peace. It's time for me to go.

CHAPTER 50
WARM SOUTHERN NIGHTS

Jeanette was the queen of the ball. I could see that. Nearly every night was a party, though she hadn't taken her final exams, which would begin next week and the week afterward. Though Jeanette complained about the restrictions of Dad's curfew, he made no allowances for her lateness. When she tested him Tuesday night, breaking the curfew, she lost her privileges for the next three nights. Jeanette was stuck at home, moody, sulking and whining.

The following night, I overheard Jeanette in the kitchen, begging, "Mother, I'm in rags—everybody's got new dresses and shoes. I just don't have a thing to wear."

"You don't. You poor dear." Mother came back into the room, bringing the rest of our dinner to the table.

"Daddy?"

"Jeanette," Dad struck preemptively, "your clothes are not only in your closet, but in our closet and even Minnie's. Your *rags,*" Dad said, exasperated, "haven't kept the boys away. You've been invited to every party and social in town. You're not suffering."

I kept my mouth shut. After my blowup with Jeanette, we were keeping a polite distance from one another. Neither of us wanted to roil the waters. Hence, Jeanette did not turn to me for support, suspecting I might not be sympathetic.

Once Mother started passing the food around, Jeanette couldn't help herself. She tried to re-engage Mother in what obviously would be an extended appeal for what she wanted. Mother avoided the discussion, saying, "We'll talk about it later."

Jeanette couldn't let it go. "Later? By that time, I'll be out of school!"

"Jeanette," Mother's voice was stern, "we'll talk about it later."

Jeanette said no more, but there was no missing her mood. She was sulking—again, hoping to draw someone in. It was only when she realized no one cared that she kept her silence through dinner, that is, other than her 'pitiful' sighs and groans. Picking at her food and hoping to get Mother's attention, she persisted in her sulk. To her continuing dismay, the three of us talked back and forth, ignoring her. Finally, when dessert time came, Jeanette said she wasn't hungry and asked to be excused to go to her bedroom.

"Gladly," Dad responded, "by all means. I assume it's to study."

Jeanette winced, mouthing the words, "Thank you," and left the room.

No one paid any notice and continued with dinner, having dessert—*pie a la mode*, something special. By the time Jeanette returned to the table for dessert, no ice cream was left. This sent her into a funk, which irritated Dad, who said curtly, "Jeanette, take your pie up to your room. You're ruining the mood around the table."

Not expecting that response, she stood up, picked up her plate, and left quietly for her room. Everyone started chuckling and laughing. That was new, something I had never experienced when it came to Jeanette. No one had any time for her tantrum—especially at seventeen years old.

· · · · ·

Over the past few days, I had seen how Jeanette wheedled not one, but two new dresses and a new pair of shoes out of Mother. While I was in the kitchen the night following her tantrum, I heard her assuring Mother her grades were fine and these last tests were just a formality, since she felt assured that she'd accepted by the college of her choice.

The next evening, Friday, Joseph Kimmelstiel stayed for dinner. As one of her best friends, he had a car and drove Jeanette to school. Since they shared French as their last class, he also drove her home, where they often studied together. Afterward, Joseph would join us at the dinner table, bringing his sense of levity and wit to the meal. As well as his humor, we appreciated Joe for his kindness and good manners.

"Thank you," said Joe, accepting a piece of lemon meringue pie. "This is my favorite pie, ma'am."

"I'm glad. I hope it measures up to your mother's."

"Oh, anyone's pie would measure up to hers. Though, to be fair, she does do a good apple strudel."

"Strudel, that's German, isn't it?" questioned Dad.

"As German as it gets, sir."

"Something I don't quite understand about your family," said Dad. "You're Jewish, right?"

"Yes sir," replied Joe, hesitantly.

"Well, why on God's earth would some of your family, according to Jenette, still be in Germany?"

"Mr. Gibson, it's a little complicated."

Joe paused to see if Dad wanted to hear him out.

"Okay, Joseph, I'm listening."

"When my parents came to this country before the last war, there was no problem being German, but once the war came, then Germans had a tough time here, especially if they had an accent like my parents. Incidentally, it didn't help that they spoke and still speak German at home. That's where I learned it. Anyway, because of that fact the rest of the family, that is, my father's parents and his younger sister and husband, along with their three children, didn't want to emigrate when my parents left for America."

"How many are over there now?"

"My grandfather died five years ago, so that leaves my grandmother, my aunt, and her three children, who are younger than me, at home in Berlin."

"That's five, not six, Joseph. I was counting."

"I know. That's why I said at home, Mr. Gibson. My uncle was taken from the house and sent to a labor camp a few months ago. So, we haven't heard from him, which doesn't mean," Joseph said optimistically, "that something bad has happened to him."

"Of course not, son. I understand what you're saying. I'm sure you're right."

Jeanette interjected, "Still, it's awful what the Nazis have done to him."

We all nodded our heads, murmuring similar sentiments, realizing that Joseph, young as he was, felt helpless as well as frustrated.

"Yeah, it is awful, but it's not the German people—at least not most of them, according to the family. It's the rotten Nazis who control everything."

"From the newsreels, it sure looks like a lot of the German people are out there cheering and marching for Hitler, responded Dad."

"Yeah, I've seen them, but most of them are probably not Nazis."

"I see," Dad said, nodding his head.

Joseph slumped back into his chair. "My dad went back in 1934 to try to help them get out. He's an American citizen, so he wasn't worried. When he got there, the family was appreciative, but they told him Hitler would either settle down or the military would get rid of him. Unfortunately, it doesn't seem to be working out that way."

"It must have been a difficult decision for them," I suggested, "when their home and work and friends are there. It would be like us trying to pick up and leave this country. The Depression makes it almost impossible to move around unless you're dead broke or a millionaire."

"They're neither. They do, though, own a small factory and," Joseph smiled, proudly, "have, according to my dad, a nice house right in a good part of the city."

"Which city?"

"Berlin, sir."

"The capital of Germany."

"You know that. I haven't met anybody who knows that."

"I studied German."

"Really, Daddy? I didn't know that."

I thought how little our family talks about things. Here it is over two years since Mother and me heard that Dad had studied German, and Jeanette is just learning about it now.

"Well, at that time, German was the best foreign language if you were going to be an engineer or, for that matter, go into the sciences. Anyway, so your relatives live in Berlin in a nice house."

"Uh huh, and my dad said they didn't want to give up their home and the business. Now, unfortunately, if they could get out, the Nazis would only let them take a few hundred dollars with them. With my uncle in a labor camp, they figure they'll out-wait both the Nazis and the Depression. Things have to get better," said Joseph hopefully.

"I'm sure they will," declared Mother, determined to be positive. "Joseph, how about another piece of pie?"

"Thank you, ma'am. I'd sure would like that." As Joseph was reaching for his dish, he visibly shuddered. "All of these shenanigans in Germany gets me jumpy," he said somewhat under his breath.

Jeanette reached over and put her arm around Joseph's shoulder. "Things have to get better for them, Joseph. They just have to." Jeanette smiled that radiant smile of hers, which got him to smile in return.

Joseph took a deep breath and looked relieved for the moment until he mentioned, "Sometimes I worry about my parents. They don't feel like me or trust what's in the letters from Germany. I guess they feel that the letters are censored.

"I just know your family is going to be okay," assured Jeanette, which seemed to bring Joseph's mood back up.

I was reappraising Jeanette. As a child, I knew she was sensitive and timid, with a fun side, but if she were frightened, she could be brought to tears quickly, or just clam up.

During the conversations tonight, I was reminded of this other side to her nature that I had all but forgotten was there. When Joe spoke of his family in Germany, I saw Jeanette's mood change. She became much more somber. I saw the depth of feeling she was capable of and how much she cared about his suffering. I was glad to see the seriousness and anguish in her caring for others, since I mostly viewed her daily life—other than her studies—as a frivolous existence of gossip and her friends at school. Recently I had seen a soon-to-be eighteen-year-old girl who used her beauty and charm to manipulate anyone to get what she wanted, no matter what the cost. Southern charm oozed from every pore of her body.

I suspected Joseph had been bedazzled by her beauty and charm, which explained why he helped Jeanette with her studies. What else could explain his behavior, since he was a lot more serious student than Jeanette? He had gotten a scholarship to a prestigious school in the East that had a medical school. His plans—and his family's, I surmised—were for him to become a doctor.

Not having the luxury of a home and school at Jeanette's age, I both resented her and didn't understand what life was like for her now. I could relate, though, to the Jeanette who felt deeply and sincerely about something or someone else. She really cared. If I were honest with myself, she really cared about our family too. Maybe because I hid the depth of my feeling, not wanting to get hurt or taken advantage of, I resented the ease with which she showed her emotions. I also was aware that people missed her underlying motives and intentions because her manipulations could be so subtle and seemingly innocent.

I wasn't alone in this awareness of Jeanette's personality. Dad, too, saw this side of her nature. In contrast, Mother, though she had grown stricter with Jeanette, for the most part gave into Jeanette's designs.

. . . . .

Like so many dinners before this one, Joseph was at the dinner table. Something was different. He wasn't gobbling down Mother's meal or complementing her. Rather, he was subdued and introspective. He had retreated into himself.

"Joseph," Dad said, breaking the tension and cutting to the core of whatever was eating at Jeanette's best friend, "what's going on?"

"Beggin' your pardon, sir?"

"You're not your usual self. Something is troubling you."

"Oh, I don't mean to be a party pooper, so it's probably best to keep my thoughts to myself, Mr. Gibson."

"Joseph, you're like a family member. 'C'mon, let's have it."

Dad directly challenged Joseph to come forward and let us know what was troubling him.

Joseph dropped his head, reached into his pocket and pulled out a letter and handed it to Dad, who read aloud, slowly pronouncing each word. "*Konzentrationslager, Dachau, Deutschland.* Looking up at us, Dad translated: *Concentration Camp, Dachau, Germany.*

"Joseph, may I read it?"

"Yes, sir. That's why I brought it over here—for you to see. My family is really upset."

Dad read the one-page document slowly, occasionally asking Joseph the meaning of a word. He looked sadly over the top of the letter. "If I am interpreting this correctly, it says your uncle died unexpectedly of a heart attack, and they disposed of his body. It is written as a very official, matter-of-fact document. The signature is typed."

Joseph's eyes filled with tears. "This really scares me: I worry about the rest of my family. This doesn't feel good."

Dad was trying to find the best way to express his thoughts. Shaking his head, he said flatly, "I could say something positive to keep your spirits up, but I don't think that's best. Joseph, isn't there anything your parents can do to get your family out of that country?"

"No, sir, we can't. I just read a book by Christopher Isherwood, *Goodbye to Berlin.* He mentions being in a restaurant and overhearing a couple of Austrian businessmen talking about a rich Jewish department store owner, Landauer, who was taken to a camp. It was reported in the newspaper that Landauer had died from a heart attack. But," Joseph stammered, "Landauer was only in his thirties."

Dad nodded, looking grave.

Joseph was having trouble continuing. His head drooped and he took a few deep breaths.

"Anyway, the businessman listening to the speaker said, *'A bullet in the heart will stop the heart, too.'*

"The other went on to say, *'This business with the Nazis makes me nervous; it's not good for business.'*"

Dad confesed, "I'd like to be more encouraging, Joseph, but I never had a good feeling about the Nazis. It seems with every passing month, things look more and more sinister." As an afterthought, Dad added, "The Communists aren't any better."

Joseph looked terrified, but he made a half-hearted attempt to be positive: "Maybe like my family over there says, Hitler, too, will pass."

"Think about it, Joseph. Hitler only got one third of the vote, but within months, if not a year, he was in control of the country. All he can talk about is making Germany great again; how the Jews have stabbed the country in the back; taking back what rightfully belongs to Germans. He rouses the people to a fever pitch. The country is on the march."

I saw how miserable Joseph looked and felt. I decided to try to take control of the conversation and redirect it to something like the movies. Everybody likes the movies. "Did you see Mae West in *Belle of the Nineties?*"

I knew I had Jeanette's attention. She competed with me to tell the funniest scenes and the dialogue. It wasn't long before we had everyone laughing, even Joseph.

Next I told of the Hollywood people, including the scriptwriter who was a distant relative, who visited the Big House: Gloria's fabulous jewelry, and the director who thought he was about to get eaten by a snake when we went fishing. Again, everyone was in stitches, laughing hilariously.

. . . . .

Everyone liked Joseph—even Dad who, as Jeanette's father, was protective and cautious about any young man around his daughter. In Joseph's case, Dad had nothing to worry about, though it wasn't for me to tell him what Jeanette had told me in confidence. As good-looking as Joseph was, she said she couldn't see herself romantically involved with a guy who was shorter than she was.

Tonight, six nights before the prom, Joseph brought an older friend, David Schneider, to dinner. His parents owned a department store in Memphis. Going to the door to greet him, I saw he parked in our drive. His car was new and expensive. He was dressed to go out and looked quite dapper. Much taller than Joseph, David had the good looks of a movie star.

During dessert Dad asked, "David, how did you meet Joseph?"

"Sir, we go to the same synagogue, but I haven't seen much of him the last couple of years since I've been away at college."

"What's your major?"

"Engineering, sir."

"I graduated with a degree in engineering and ended up building, then owning riverboats."

David leaned forward. "How interesting. I think I'm going to major in aeronautical engineering. It seems like that's where things are going."

"You may be right," said Dad.

"Actually, I'd like to get involved with rockets."

"Rockets??" questioned Dad, "You mean like in Flash Gordon and stuff?"

"Well, sort of, but the kinds of things I'm interested in are, unfortunately, being done in Germany."

"Yeah, it's not like they're going to be extending an invitation for you to study at Heidelberg anytime soon," retorted Joseph, wryly.

"Anyway, a bright young man like you, you'll do all right in the good ol' U.S. of A. Even if it looks like they've got an edge right now, I'm sure you'll find there's some research going on here," volunteered Dad, positively.

"I appreciate that, sir. I hope you're right."

"So where are you three going tonight?"

"Dancing at the Peabody," chimed in Jeanette, obviously thrilled by the thought of being squired by two young men.

"Jeanette, finish your dinner."

"I really don't have time. I'm just expected—"

"Jeanette, finish your dinner," Dad said, annoyed.

The guests looked at each other and kept their thoughts to themselves, not wanting to get on Dad's bad side. Joseph had a car, but his friend's car was new convertible, which held the magic. Quickly the boys finished their plates, knowing Jeanette was not going to stop until she got her way.

"Dad, I'm expected by just everyone." Glancing first at Mother, then Dad. "Can't you see? Just everyone—"

She was wearing both Dad and Mother down. They were past annoyed and just wanted some peace and quiet. They were tired.

"Jeanette, be home by curfew," said Dad, exasperated.

"Oh yes, of course." Jeanette came around the table and pecked Dad on his cheek. Waltzing around the table in a rose-colored chiffon dress and pearls, she pecked Mother on the cheek. "I'll be home when—"

"By curfew," said Dad.

. . . . .

Three days later, David came to dinner with a corsage. After the meal, he was taking Jeanette dancing at the Peabody. Jeanette was dressed in another new dress—a fine, sheer burgundy-colored silk, with matching shawl and shoes. Dad had not noticed until David commented on how pretty Jeanette looked.

"Is that a new dress, Jeanette?"

"Why, yes, it is."

Dad glared at Jeanette. When she finished primping at the table, she saw Dad's look. He was not happy. He knew he'd been outmaneuvered. I could see he was stewing, but he kept quiet since we had a guest.

By the time dinner was over and Jeanette and David were leaving, Dad said casually, "Jeanette, I want you home an hour earlier."

"Dad!" Jeanette shrieked.

Dad smiled. "Miss your curfew, my lady, and after school you'll be spending your evenings at home until you graduate. Do I make myself clear, Precious?"

He must have been really angry. Seldom did I hear him speak in this fashion. Whether Jeanette fully understood how angry he was remained doubtful. Too full of herself, she started to shrug, which caught Dad's eye.

"Jeanette, I've had just about enough of your—"

She didn't let Dad finish his sentence. I think she saw the flash in his eyes, and knew she had gone too far.

"Yes, sir, I understand." Jeanette said, with a sub-tone to her voice that was anything but friendly, which I detected. Whether Dad did, he didn't respond.

Dad won this round and looked satisfied.

I saw as his spoiled child, who would keep pushing for more.

CHAPTER 51
THE SNAKE

The next day back on the plantation, Tom and I went horseback riding.

We reached the end of the cotton row, not far from the river. On either side of Tom and I were mostly unopened cotton bolls, stretching to the horizon and shimmering in the late spring heat. Nearby, behind the pecan trees was the slope back to the river.

The horses were trotting along when I said to him in the adjacent row, "Tom, I wouldn't go in there. It's not cleared land."

"I like to come down here where the old forests is. There're a couple Indian mounds ahead. Didn't you used to go into the forest where you could feel the Indian spirits?"

"I did, Tom. Those were very special moments for me.

"Well, then, let's ride on in."

Oddly, I felt kinda strange, but the day was nice, and I was with Tom, a friend. It would be a little adventure.

I guided my horse in among the trees that created a magical world hidden in dim light and shadows, the canopy of the trees reaching high above our heads. The girth of the trees was enormous. They must have been hundreds of years old.

"It was the birds," I said, suddenly awestruck. "Ol' man Jones kept the forest because of them." I pulled rein. The horse stopped and snorted. Verdant with their new spring leaves, trees, vines and bushes hid birds and animals. Unseen eyes were keenly watching us.

Tom was close beside me, unspeaking.

I listened to the birdcalls announcing our presence. I was amazed at the variety of birds I had never seen before as they flitted between trees. My eye caught a hawk, gazing down on us from its perch. Somewhere behind the bushes at the base of the tree, there was the sound of a large animal shambling deeper into the safety of the woods.

Just as Tom had said, this was untouched—a forest of hardwoods, giant cypress and undergrowth. This land was no different than when the Indians first settled here. There was even an Indian mound I could make out as a hillock covered by vines. Nothing like that existed anymore. Archeologists had scoured nearly every farm from our northern border with Missouri to our southern border with Louisiana. No Indian mounds had escaped their pillaging, except on this tiny piece of land. Still resting quietly were the native people who had been placed here, surrounded by their most treasured possessions—pottery, shell jewelry, and weapons.

"Tom," I said softly, feeling the sacredness of the world that we had entered, as well as a growing sense of my isolation and vulnerability, "I want to leave."

Suddenly, my horse whinnied. Startled, he reared up. I slid off of his back and hit the leaf-carpeted ground with a soft thud—right on my rear. My horse turned and raced off, out of the forest. Before I could get my bearings, I heard the sound of a shotgun go off near me. Dazed, I watched as Tom pulled reign and got off his horse, his left hand gripping the shotgun. He rushed over to me, kicking a large rattler out of the way.

"Minnie, are you all right?" Tom bent down, gazing at me with a deepening concern.

"I'm fine, Tom." Trying to make light of the moment and my embarrassment, I joked, "It's just my pride that's hurt."

Unexpectedly, Tom whispered, "Beth, the kids, and the rest of the family are away—away for the month visitin' relatives."

I simply nodded, still partly dazed by my fall, trying to understand what he had just said to me. Staring at him, I repeated, "You said the family's gone?"

"Yeah, I get mighty lonesome."

I got his drift.

Tom started to draw closer when I stretched out my arm and slightly pushed against his chest, saying, "Tom help me up." I knew that I had taken command, but partly at the cost of our friendship, reminding him of his place.

Tom reluctantly stood up and reached down to take my hand.

Pulling myself up, I brushed off the dirt. "Well, let's see that varmint." I stepped over to the snake, which was filled with buckshot. Remembering something I'd seen done years ago, I grabbed a dry branch, stuck it through the dead snake, and held up the dangling carcass. "You killed it all right. It's dead as a doornail."

Tom didn't look impressed by his trophy.

"Well, we best get back to the station. When that horse comes in without me, they'll be sending out a posse," I teased.

Tom wasn't amused. Instead, he hopped onto his horse, reached down and pulled me up behind his saddle. I wrapped my arms around him and the horse galloped out of the forest and down the row of cotton.

There was the rhythm of the gallop and me bouncing up and down on the horse's slick white body. I was aware of how broad were Tom's shoulders, how broad his back. I was aware of the heat of the horse's body, pressing against the inside of my thighs as I rode bareback. I was aware of the feel of my arms and hands around Tom's body, his wet shirt pressed against his skin, even more I was aware that underneath his shirt, his stomach was tight and flat. Then came the smell of his sweat—a man's sweat. It was clean and heavy, a workingman's sweat, yet it was personal. It was Tom's own smell that was intoxicating. My breathing was increasingly shallow.

The sensations melded and became heady. I was aware of feelings I hadn't felt since I was with Norton but those were romantic.

Tom must have sensed my feelings and said, "Are you reconsiderin' my invitation?"

I unwrapped my arms, pulled back from his body, and grabbed hold of his hips. I saw him straighten his back, sensing that he knew I had distanced myself.

Tom kicked the horse in the side. Now the animal picked up to a steady trot. We got back to the station where a couple of field hands had already gotten hold of my horse. One of them let go and ran over to us.

"Minnie lost her horse," said Tom, flatly.

"Oh, yeah?"

"Damn snake spooked it and threw her."

The fellow nodded. With hands as tough as leather, the grizzled farm worker reached up to help me off.

Once I was standing upright, Tom started to turn the horse. "Tom! Tom," I stuttered, "thank you."

"You're welcome," Tom said in his laconic style, obviously frustrated. I saw him chewing his lip, which meant he really wanted to say more.

"So—so you know where to find me."

"I do. Thanks for the lift."

Tom tipped his hat. "Giddy up!" With two sharp, violent kicks, he raced the horse down the row and toward the river.

"Wonder what got into him?" said the field hand in his delta drawl and rubbing his chin, thinking.

"I couldn't tell you."

The man looked at me, questioningly. "Yes, ma'am."

There was the sound of the hooves of the horse beating the ground and the sight of Tom kicking the horse to ride faster.

"Reckon that horse needs a good, hard riding, ma'am."

"I think you're right," I said under my breath.

CHAPTER 52
PROM NIGHT

Jeanette really surprised me. She went to her school prom with Joseph, the guy she said she could never get romantic about because, at five-foot-two, he was three inches shorter than her. Joseph was "Out of the question." I was impressed that she'd gone to the prom with a boy whose head she could almost look over at the other couples. She had to have been ribbed by her girlfriends when they learned who was taking her to the most important night of their lives.

She was somewhat sneaky, though. She insisted on them double-dating with another couple. When I watched them leave from the front door, I noticed the girl was short and her prom date was tall. I knew what Jeanette was up to—she'd switch off and dance with him half of the night, convincing her friends it was much more fun that way, and it would confuse everyone.

As they pulled out of the drive, Dad closed the door and enthused, "Ladies, put on your dancing shoes. We're going out to the Peabody for dinner and dancing."

Mother stopped in her tracks and looked over her shoulder, a big smile spreading across her face. "I declare, Daddy, did you really say that?"

"I did, ol' gal, and I expect you to be ready by 6:30. Our reservation is for 7."

"You ol' trickster, you," Mother said, wagging her finger at him.

"Scoot! Or, we'll lose our seating."

Mother rushed out of the room, excited by his surprise.

"Dad, you don't have to take me out. Mother looks so happy to be going on a date with you."

"Minnie, do I have to rough you up? I said, 'we', and 'we' means 'we three.' By the way, there's a little something for you." Dad lifted three boxes from behind the sofa. "Here! Open 'em."

I must have looked like I was in shock because Dad repeated, "I said, 'Open 'em up.'"

I unwrapped the largest box.

"A dress," I squealed. I pulled out a gorgeous emerald green, backless, boatneck silk evening dress. I held it up and could tell it fit me perfectly. "How did you, Dad—?"

"That was your mother's doing."

Before I could say anything, he urged, "Now this one."

Again, I opened the second box and found a golden shawl. Slowly, I took it out of the box to find a beautiful, lightweight, almost diaphanous shawl of the finest quality silk, one I had eyed when Dad suggested we go window-shopping a couple of weeks ago.

"Dad, it is—it is the one I told you was my favorite! I had no idea, you—"

"Well, I needed no help for that. Open the other one."

There was just a silk cord wrapped around the box and tied in a bow on the top. I hesitated.

"Minnie—"

"Yes, sir." I untied the bow and took off the lid. Inside was *the* hat—the very hat I'd pointed out to Dad as my favorite. I lifted it out of the box as if it was the most fragile baby.

I stood up, put it on my head, and walked to the mirror. "My goodness . . . I just never expected . . . I—"

"Now, the shawl."

I gave the shawl to Dad and he draped it over my shoulders. There was the sensation of cool, luxurious silk as it caressed my arms. I walked back to the mirror. I was stunned. I was wearing things I never allowed myself to imagine would be mine. I was speechless. The emerald green summer hat with a small brooch, would complement perfectly the matching emerald green dress I planned to wear.

"Don't you like them?"

"They are so . . . beautiful, Dad." I reached over and kissed him on the cheek. "I just love them! I can't thank you enough. I—"

"Then be sure to thank your mother, too. She wanted you to have them."

"Now, go get yourself all dressed up—wear your best, and don't forget the jewelry. I want to be seen with ladies who are dressed to the nines."

I went to turn when Dad added, "Do me one favor, Minnie?"

"Of course, anything."

"Wear some red nail polish tonight."

Dad knew I didn't like to be flashy like that, preferring clear or pale pink, but tonight I'd doll myself up and do red for him—red nails and bright, red lipstick. Tonight was special. I knew that.

. . . . .

And what a night it was! Both Mother and I made Dad proud. Mother wore emeralds, and I, my pearls and sapphire-and-diamond ring. We were seated at one of the best tables. People we hadn't seen for years greeted us, wanting to know when they could expect to see us at St. Peters.

Mother and Dad were once again 'respectable' people worth knowing, since word had gotten back to some members of the congregation that Dad owned oil wells and Mother had a huge plantation. They played their parts well and looked humble yet proud. It was only when we had gone to the dance floor and I was dancing did I see Beauregard seated alone across the room. He nodded slightly. I showed no recognition.

After the music, Dad took me back to our table. We had taken our seats when I saw both Mother and Dad look up in astonishment. Beauregard was first to speak: "Mr. and Mrs. Gibson, I wanted to come by and wish you well."

Mother and Dad were speechless.

"A few mutual friends came to my table and told me that they'd spoken with you. I needed to come by your table."

I looked at Mother and Dad, who glanced at me, then looked back at Beauregard. They seemed at a loss for words when Beauregard said unexpectedly, "I want to apologize to y'all for all the trouble I caused. I couldn't leave without apologizing."

Dad broke the ice and said simply, "Thank you, Beauregard."

Mother and I said nothing, though Mother did nod her head at him. I refused to look up and sat there stonily.

"This is something I've wanted to say for a long time, especially with my mother on her deathbed."

The expressions on our faces changed.

"I'm flying out tomorrow morning, since my father told me I needed to come home at once if I were going to have a chance to say goodbye to her."

I heard the tone of his voice—the sense of hopelessness and helplessness was in every word. Still, I did not look up.

Mother was first to reply: "I think I can speak for all of us when I say how sorry we are to hear this. Your mother is a very sweet woman, a real comfort. How is your father?"

"Not well at all, Mrs. Gibson. His world is falling apart. He loves . . ." Beauregard stopped, then continued haltingly, "He loves her with all his heart. I just don't know . . ." Beauregard stopped again, either because he couldn't find the right words or because he was overcome with emotion.

"Beau," Dad said, his voice softening, "It will be difficult for him, but I know he's a strong man. He'll pull through this."

"I hope you're right, sir," Beauregard said, unconvinced.

"Minnie, I understand you not wanting to see or hear me, but . . . but there are some things I need to say to you directly. Would you please go to the dance floor with me? Please?"

I refused to look at him or acknowledge him, even under the circumstances. The thought of actually dancing with him and feeling his touch repelled me. I started to turn to say *"NO"* when Mother said in a tone of voice I had never heard her use with me before, "Please, Minnie, please do it. Joanna, his mother, is dying." I saw Dad nod his head at me without saying a word.

I wrapped the shawl around my shoulders, stood up and walked to the dance floor. The music was a sentimental old song, which brought back certain memories of Norton. I almost turned back to leave him standing in the middle of the floor, but I had my pride and my dignity. I let Beauregard reach out and take my hand in his while his other wrapped around my waist. I might dance with him, but I refused to look him in the eyes. I turned my head to the side and stared straight ahead.

"Minnie, thank you. It means a lot to me to tell you I know how badly I treated you. You didn't deserve any of it. I know you have every right to hate me."

Beauregard hesitated, possibly thinking I would say something. I did not. I noticed his eyes were puffy, but I assumed it was from drink, not from crying. I felt no need to try to understand him.

"Minnie, my mother is dying. She has always—both my parents—loved you. I'm asking you to please call her tomorrow before it's too late. It would bring her some peace, and it would mean so much to my father. He's in a real bad way."

Now I turned my head and looked Beauregard in the eye. What I saw were tears staining his cheeks. His hands were trembling.

"Yes, Beauregard, I'll call early tomorrow morning."

"Oh, Minnie—"

"I'm doing it for them, Beauregard."

"I know, and I'm grateful."

I saw he was actually grateful when he said genuinely, "Minnie, I can't tell you how sincerely sorry I am for the pain and grief I caused you. I truly, truly apologize."

A part of me wanted to end the dance that moment, but I did hear deep sorrow and sincerity in his apology. I would not kick him when he was down.

I was glad the music had stopped. "Beauregard, thank you for what you've said. Let's leave the floor."

"Of course, Minnie." He walked me back to the table and said goodbye.

· · · · ·

The first thing in the morning, I called the Becks. I let the phone ring until someone picked up the receiver. I realized it had to be the butler by his accent. I asked to speak to Mr. Beck and was told it was impossible. It was impossible until I told the butler who I was, and that Beauregard had told me last night to call them before his plane left this morning.

There was a long silence. Then I heard Mr. Beck come to the phone. He was emotional.

"Yes, sir, I understand. I understand. Yes, she is a beautiful, kind and loving woman. I will miss her."

Between stifled sobs, he spoke of Beauregard. "Where is he? His younger brother got here yesterday."

"Last night we talked. He said he was catching the earliest plane and expected to be there this morning. Yes, sir." I paused. "I realize that."

Overcome with grief, Mr. Beck, moaned, "Well, he's too late. Joanna died minutes ago without seeing him. Without seeing her son."

"Sir, he really tried. He really did."

Mr. Beck asked me if I was coming to the funeral.

"I wish I could, but that's not possible."

I would let Beauregard handle the details.

"Yes, sir. I love you, too. My and my family's thoughts and prayers are with you. Goodbye."

CHAPTER 53
THE LAST CALIFORNIAN

Sunday night dinner was a happy affair for Jeanette. She'd been formally accepted into a Catholic university not far from Long Beach. Her acceptance letter was passed around the table for the second night. Though the decision of whether Jeanette could stay in the dorms was still controversial and unresolved, Jeanette was on *Cloud Nine,* as they say.

"Mother, Dad, I'm so excited. They accepted me! I—I mean we—just have to decide when I can leave."

Dad looked at Mother. She stared back at him.

Mother stated, "We haven't made a decision about you living at school. So that just leaves your Aunt Ethel."

Jeanette started to say something when Dad scratched his head, saying, "Well, I have to call Ethel to see how she feels about it."

"Ohh," Jeanette thought for a moment, "I'm sure she feels different about everything now. I'm older and more mature, so I won't cause her any worry."

"Like last time," Mother said, somewhat unexpectedly for all of us.

"Well, I'm sorry about that, and I'm sure she knows it."

"Does she?" asked Dad, lifting one eyebrow questioningly, "like that poor boy and girl at school?"

Jeanette, whose eyes filled with tears, was at a loss for words when the telephone suddenly rang.

"Damn," said Mother, "if it's not one thing, it's another." She got up from the table and went into the living room.

I thought about the changes in Mother, since I was a girl to now being in charge of managing the business in Arkansas. The day-to-day in the small Delta town, by and large, with country people certainly had changed Mother's language, which now included the word "damn." She not only had come to tolerate from others what she condemned as "common" not so many years ago, but she had dropped—except for the special occasions—the behavior of the well-bred, genteel Southern woman. Though, to be sure, she hadn't become vulgar, nor would she allow anyone else in her presence to use expletives.

A minute or so had passed when Mother came back to the table. "Daddy, I think you'd better take this call."

"What's the matter?" I asked, concerned by the serious expression on her face.

"We'll let James tell us. He'll have all the facts."

Jeanette and I glanced at one another, each of us shaking our heads, silently in agreement at the seriousness of the situation. Our eyes turned back to Mother, but she averted her gaze, got up and went to the kitchen, saying, "I'll bring out the pie."

At least ten minutes had passed since Mother returned with the pie, plates, and a knife, still not saying anything about the call. "Who wants a piece?"

"Aren't we going to wait for Dad?" asked Jeanette.

"No, I don't know how long this call is going to take."

As Mother was cutting the pie and passing everyone a piece, she saw Dad walk into the room and take his seat at the end of the table with careful deliberation. She stopped what she was doing and waited for Dad to speak.

Dad didn't say anything, but seemed to be collecting his thoughts. Finally, he cleared his throat and said in a soft tone of voice, "Everything's changed. Ethel's dead."

Jeanette broke down in tears. Mother came around and tried to soothe her, wrapping her arms around her and pleading, "Honey, please don't cry. Don't cry, Angel."

I reached across and put my hand on top of Dad's. "I'm sorry, Dad."

Dad genuinely seemed to appreciate my gesture and reached over with his free hand and placed it warmly atop mine. "Thank you, Minnie."

Mother pleaded with Jeanette to stop crying. "Let's hear what Daddy has to say, honey." Mother took Jeanette's napkin and gently wiped away her tears. Looking over at Dad, Mother asked tenderly, "Daddy, what—what happened?"

Ethel was hit by a car, trying to cross the street." He hesitated. "That was her neighbor, Marion Sobel, on the phone. She also said, "Ethel had been battling cancer for some time."

"She never said a word to me," Jeanette began to sob.

It took a while before Dad was able to continue. "I need to make arrangements to leave as soon as possible. I'll see if I can fly out the day after tomorrow—Monday."

"Flying?" questioned Mother, somewhat alarmed. Air travel was still something of a novelty. To fly so far seemed not only expensive, but it is still dangerous.

"Daddy, I want to go. I have to."

"I'm going alone. Should be easier to get one seat on such short notice. Also—" Dad was now preoccupied with planning his trip and was slightly annoyed at Jeanette for diverting his attention, "you've got school." Dad shook his head. "No, I mean you have your graduation."

"Oh, yes, my graduation," Jeanette reconsidered, thinking about the sacrifice she'd have to make.

Jeanette wanted to say something (I suspect to wheedle and plead her case), when Mother put her forefinger to Jeanette's lips. "Ethel would want you to graduate. Do it for Ethel."

While Jeanette nodded her head reluctantly, Dad was planning. He got up and paced back and forth. "Nora, I'll make arrangements for the flight from our neighbor Louise's phone, while you talk to Marion about the details of the funeral. You can get the preliminaries out of the way. Once I know when I'm arriving in Long Beach, I can set the date of the viewing, the funeral, and the internment." As a quick afterthought, Dad added, "See if Marion can make the arrangements for the flowers. She told me to rely on her."

"Of course, James, I'll take care of that first thing tomorrow morning. Then I'll pack your bags."

"Since I'm flying, pack lightly."

"Okay."

Dad was already in motion but he was at loose ends, knowing there were so many other things waiting for him to do regarding the estate, which could only be handled once he got there.

"Dad, I'd like to take a walk. Want to make sure I'm safe?" I said, half-jokingly.

"I'll go, too," chimed in Jeanette, anxiously.

"No, Jeanette. I need you to help me," hastened Mother. Jeanette seemed confused for the moment until Mother went on to say, "You'll feel better this way. We have a lot to discuss. We've got to get you a gown for your graduation, pictures, and all sorts of things. Also, there are parties. We've got to order more graduation announcements and send them out."

Jeanette seemed to brighten after hearing Mother describe all the things that needed to be done and so much to look forward to.

"Also, honey, you're going to college. We're all so proud of you."

Jeanette basked in Mother's words, which soon included, "Now, honey, come help me with the dishes."

Dad and I didn't say anything. I simply got up, and the two of us walked out of the house together into a moonless night. Though summer was technically a few weeks away, it was already muggy. The night air definitely felt better than being indoors, especially with the scent of honeysuckle in bloom. As was our custom, I slipped my arm through his. Tonight, we walked in silence.

. . . . .

Late that evening, I heard my bedroom door open and looked over to see Mother coming into my room. I pulled myself up on my pillow and Mother sat on my bed.

"Minnie, I've had a long talk with James. I've decided to relocate with him to the house in Long Beach."

"I had a sinking feeling. Mother continued, "I want you to understand that it's your decision to either join us or stay here. We are not abandoning you. However, I want you to know that you have a choice."

"What kind of choice?"

"We'd prefer you come to California, but if you choose to stay here, I'd like you to run the plantation."

"That'd mean I'd have to quit my job."

"It would. But if you choose to keep it, I'll get someone else—like Tom—to take charge.

"You'd give up all your hard work on the plantation?"

"Not exactly. I'd come back two months during the planting season and two months at harvest in August. Anyway, I'll check with Tom, Al and Ben by phone most days, less so with Ellen. I'll have her oversee the new assistant bookkeeper at the gin. She'll be a busy little girl."

"I—"

"You don't have to decide now. Think about it."

"Okay."

"It's a long night, so I'm going to bed."

"Goodnight, Mother."

"Goodnight."

. . . . .

Mother had made a relatively light Sunday dinner. Just as we prepared for dessert, there was a knock on the front door.

"I'll get it," I said. Upon opening the door my heart almost stopped. Jeanette's half-brothers, Norton and Gibson stood there. Gibson asked, formally, "May we come in?"

"Of course, of course, you may."

Gibson walked past me, while Norton stopped to say, "How are you, Minnie?"

"Fine, I guess. Please come into the dining room."

Everyone was shocked. First, Dad stood up and rushed over to shake his son's hand, saying, "Come and take a seat."

Jeanette screamed delightedly, running over and embracing Norton warmly and Gibson politely. No one failed to see Jeanette's reception of her two half-brothers. Nothing had changed in her feelings toward them.

Mother, stood up and sputtered, "Sit down, boys, I'll make a plate for you. It'll be kinda skimpy since we ate lightly tonight. I haven't cut the pies, so there's plenty of dessert with ice cream."

Gibson was the first to speak directly while he was taking his seat—as usual—between his father and Jeanette. "No thank you, ma'am. We heard about Aunt Ethel. Got a call from some lady called Sobel, and we rushed right over."

"Dad, we're so sorry," followed Norton in his kind, resonant voice, which carried so much genuine emotion.

"Thank you, boys. I appreciate seeing you. It's very good of you to come over."

"We had to come," answered Norton. "I just happened to be in town and there was no way I wouldn't be here by your side."

Norton had taken his usual seat, which was between Dad and me. I could feel his presence and body heat. I caught the scent of the same aftershave lotion he always had used, mixed with the natural smell of his skin. My emotions began to stir.

Suddenly, Mother asked, "Norton, how are your wife and children?"

I felt my mood darken, knowing that Mother had intentionally asked this question.

"They're fine, ma'am."

"Just how many kids do you have?"

"Only two boys, ma'am. My wife says she can't have any more."

"Oh, that must be hard on her," replied Mother, sympathetically.

"I suppose so."

I knew this must be a real disappointment for Norton, who had promised me that we'd have a house full of children— that he loved kids and wanted a big family.

Strangely, Jeanette had remained quiet, observing everyone around the table. I knew she was aware of the heavy emotions coming from both Norton and me. She also was aware that Norton and I were obviously avoiding looking at and speaking to one another.

Opening her mouth to say something, she was cut off by Norton, who said, suddenly, "Minnie, I'd like to take a walk with you."

Everyone seemed frozen in ice until I answered, "Okay." And I stood up from the table, along with Norton.

We walked out of the house and onto the sidewalk without speaking. The night was dark. There was no moon, only the blinking stars and the occasional defused light of a street lamp.

Breaking his silence, Norton confessed, "Minnie, Dad told me everything a while back, but it never seemed like the right time to come over."

I kept tight rein on my emotions.

"If I hadn't been such a fool, I know we could have talked and worked things out. Nothing was impossible, given how I felt about you."

As we passed a tree, Norton pulled me over and behind it where no one could see us. He leaned his back against the trunk, grabbed me tightly, and pulled me into him. Bending over, he found my lips and kissed me deeply with an unimaginable intensity. I couldn't help myself and returned his hot kisses with the passion I'd kept buried all these years. His lips asked for more. I felt every part of his body pressing against mine. He whispered huskily, "I never stopped thinking of you. Not a single day. I love you. I love you."

Breathily, I whispered, "I love—" Something stopped me from saying *you*. And I regained a faint measure of self-control, asking him, "Are you saying you would leave your wife and *your children . . . for us?*"

Norton hesitated ever so slightly.

At that moment, I knew I was going to California.

"Let's go back to the house."

"Minnie," he pleaded.

"I want to go back to the house now."

CHAPTER 54
A WHIRLWIND

O nce the *pomp and circumstance* was over and Jeanette had graduated and partied, Mother and Jeanette were in a frenzy of packing boxes and trunks during the rest of the week. The more valuable things such as the silver, jewelry, fur coats, and most of the shoes and clothing went into trunks, which would be brought to the train station and loaded into one of their two private compartments for safekeeping under Mother's watchful eye. Of course, a couple of suitcases and train cases would suffice for the day-to-day on the train.

When I got home, I was tired. I was willing to help them pack, but Mother said it wasn't needed or practical. It wasn't necessary she emphasized because they had enough time to do it themselves. It wasn't practical because she might lose track of what went where and how things were labeled. Also, it gave Mother a chance to stop work around 4:00 p.m. and start dinner. This way we could all eat together. Moreover, they wouldn't be too tired for the next day.

Saturday, with only two days more to get everything done, I pitched in and helped them pack.

Mother was taking calls throughout the day from the men in the Delta—Tom, the new manager, Ben having retired, and Al, the manager at the gin, who was grooming Katie's son for his position. Evidently, there was some anxiety from all of them, knowing she was moving out of state and wouldn't be back until August.

Though the family would be living in California, Mother—and when necessary, Dad—would come back and stay at what had been the Parker Barnes' house in the Delta during the spring planting and the harvest seasons in the fall.

"Jeanette," Mother said, having hung up the phone once again, sounded annoyed. I suspected she was annoyed as much by the constant calls from the men, as she was with Jeanette. "I told you already, I'll take care of packing the silver. Do not touch the silver!"

Jeanette, who was just trying to do her part, said plaintively, "I was just trying to help you."

"Well, you're not, so, *please, please,* don't pack the silver. If you see some that I've forgotten, just bring it over to me."

Jeanette nodded.

"Jeanette," I said, trying to keep her from getting into a mood, "why don't you and I box some of these things Mother said she wanted boxed?"

Catching sight of the throw-away pile, Jeanette saw her dolls on the heap.

"Mother," pleaded Jeanette, "you made a mistake. I want to take my dolls, especially these two."

"They're just extra baggage we don't have space for. Leave them here."

"But Mother—"

"No buts. Just help Minnie with the boxing."

Jeanette tried to smile, but she was not happy. She walked over and we got started boxing the linen, then taping and tying up the box tightly. We—at Mother's direction—continued to box more things while Mother took care of the valuables.

I saw Jeanette look longingly and crestfallen at the growing pile of throwaways that included her two most coveted dolls. Going over to the pile, I rummaged around and pulled out the two dolls Jeanette had held up to Mother.

"Come over here," I whispered.

Jeanette almost reluctantly sauntered over, appearing to me to want to avoid the reminder of her dolls. She hadn't forgotten about her dolls by any means. It showed painfully on her face.

"Let's go to my room."

I closed the door behind us and walked over to my clothing trunk. "You really want these?"

"Of course, don't you remember? We used to do tea parties with them. The blonde one's me, Jeannie, and the brunette's you, Minnie."

"I remember." I remembered all too well those days before Dad went bankrupt. The dolls conjured up a mix of emotions, but I could see how sentimental Jeanette was about her dolls. I reached into my trunk and said, "I think I can squeeze them in here." I placed them right next to the box with Marie's cards from Grandpa—the ones I still had not read. I never seemed quite in the right mood, so they remained unread and undisturbed, which meant now they wouldn't be read until I got to California—far enough away that I wouldn't be reminded of the experience surrounding them.

"Oh Sis," Jeanette hesitated. She hadn't called me that since I told her I had no sister. "Sis," she said tentatively, "how sweet of you."

I took her sentiment in the spirit it was meant. Seeing my face change, actually soften, Jeanette reached out and hugged me. (I could have done without the hug to be sure, but I didn't recoil.)

"I really, really appreciate it. I do. Thank you."

"You're welcome. This ought to get them safely out to California."

Jeanette broke into a beautiful, bright smile.

"Oh," Mother reproached us, "there you two are." Standing in the doorway, she motioned for us to follow her.

"Sorry, we got distracted," I said.

"Well, why don't y'all distract yourselves out where I can see you? We've still got some more boxing to do."

"Yes ma'am," cooed Jeanette cheerfully.

Before dinner, we also packed our suitcases and train cases. We would live out of them until Mother and Jeanette left for California, and I went to the Catholic Girls Club to wait for my transfer to the phone company in California.

Dinner was simple.

. . . . .

Sunday, the day before they were to leave, what Mother hadn't given to Louise earlier in the morning was sold off or given away to other neighbors, such as some of the furniture, beds and drawers, and the kitchenware. Of course, Mother's best friend, Louise, had first choice.

"No, no," Mother said to Louise that morning, "you just take it."

"But Nora, you could sell this."

"I said, take it. I want you to have whatever you need. You've been so good to us, especially Jeanette, making a home for her when we've been so busy."

"I did that because I love y'all."

Mother smiled. "And we've appreciated it more than you know, Louise."

"Oh, Nora, you're a dear."

Usually Louise was always good for a laugh, but these last few days with the reality of our moving, came a more serious and, I daresay, sad Louise. Like Mother, Louise was in her mid-forties, and she'd been raised on a farm. Unlike Mother, she had not gone to private school, but what she lacked in years of formal education she made up for by having common sense, sensitivity, and a great sense of humor. Seldom did we have much opportunity to see her husband, George, a big, shambling man, who worked at night.

"It's yours. Matter of fact, take the bed—it's new."

"And that cast iron deep fryer of yours?"

"Louise," Mother grabbed a couple of empty boxes, "do I need to load these up for you?"

"All right, Nora, if you say so."

"I do."

Louise quickly went through the house, picking up and packing a large assortment of things. Finally, she pulled Dad's leather chair away from its place. "George would like this."

"I'd like for George to have that." Mother looked over the dining room table and chairs she had bought a year earlier, "You've got to take that, Louise, before I open up the house to strangers."

"But Nora, you just bought that. It's so expensive. You could get—"

"I could nothing. Nobody has any money. Take it now or, Louise, I swear I'll put everything out on the lawn with a sign that says, 'Take Me—Free'."

"Well, Nora, as my pappy said, 'Don't look a gift horse in the mouth'."

"Good. One less thing to worry about." Mother knew Louise and George's situation. Like most folks, they struggled to meet their bills, let alone be able to afford any luxuries. Mother obviously wanted them to have the things they could never afford to buy. Mother was all but refurnishing their home. At this point, rather little would be left for others. Instead, Louise would be setting out things of her own to sell or to give away.

By twilight, the house was stripped bare. That night, Mother, Jeanette and I stayed at Louise's. Besides a large Southern dinner of fried chicken, yams, snap beans, biscuits, and cherry pie, Louise insisted on us spending the night there. She gave Mother and Jeanette her bed, and a single bed to me in her sewing room. Louise slept on the sofa. This was the way it was with Louise. She was a true friend.

Before I went to bed, I wrote Miss Virtue a letter expressing my appreciation for all she'd done for me, and how lucky I had been to find her after the loss of Marie. I thought of her as a very, very special friend. I also gave her what would be my new address in California.

CHAPTER 55
REVENGE COMES CALLING

Monday morning came early. Tom and his brother arrived in two trucks with a trailer pulled from behind one of them. They loaded up all of the boxes, trunks, and suitcases with barely enough space for everything. We all piled into the cabs and the boys got us to the train station with time to spare.

Later, Tom's brother and the trailer headed back to the Delta, while Tom drove me back to the house. He wanted to take me to the Catholic Girls Club, but I still had things to do. Besides, the ride back with Tom from the station to the house had been plenty of time with him already. He was moody because of Mother and me leaving—especially me. I wanted to keep that door closed. Only heartache and disappointment were behind it.

I spent much of the rest of the day straightening up the house and going through my baggage, making sure I hadn't forgotten anything. Then around 3:00, I closed and locked the door for the last time, placing a note for the mailman with our new address in California. I stopped for one last look at the place I had called home for the past eight years.

Minutes later as the trolley rumbled along with me aboard, I was reminded of that traumatic day almost thirteen years ago, when I'd been sent off by Mother to fend for myself at the Catholic Girls Club. Now my life was changing again. Images of the burlap factory, the flower shop, nursing school, Grandpa, Marie, Norton, the Big House, the plantation, even the river swept by, one after the other, while the trolley rolled across town. I felt the deep well of emotional strength I could always call upon, not just to meet adversity, but to survive the struggle. There were times when I thought the well had gone dry, only to find a few more drops to keep me going until I found a safe place where I could rest and renew myself.

The trolley jolted, and I realized I was nearly there. A minute later, I got off and looked up at the Catholic Girls Club. Unlike my first experience of it, I easily climbed the stairs. I only had a suitcase and a train case—not a trunk with a comforter wrapped around my shoulders. Later, I would buy a trunk for more of my possessions.

Having already made arrangements, I was expected when I walked up to the desk. Miss Jones spoke first: "Minnie?"

"Congratulations, Miss Jones. I see you have been promoted to Manager."

"It's Mrs. Black, Minnie."

"Congratulations twice, then," I said.

Not known either for her personal warmth or her sense of humor, *Mrs.* Black, tall and slender with a hint of rouge on her cheeks and a thin line of lipstick, nodded her head perfunctorily and said, "I see that you're a Mrs. Beck. That's why I didn't recognize who was coming. This must be difficult for you— being alone."

"Is my room available?"

"It is. Unfortunately, because of our overcrowded conditions, we had to book you in your old room. Maybe soon we can move you to something more suitable."

I nodded. I did not want to tell her that I would only be here as long as it took for my transfer from the telephone company to come through. It was best to be discreet. Otherwise, I might not have been given a room at all. Instead, I probably would have been referred to a hotel, which would have been more expensive than the customary fee of half my earnings for room and board.

"The janitor isn't available today, so—"

"I don't mind. I'll carry my things upstairs."

I climbed the stairs and turned left. I knew exactly where to find *my* room. When I opened the door and walked inside, absolutely nothing—nothing at all—had changed, except things looked more worn. The shade was torn, the surface of the small table against the window was riddled with nicks, the hinges on the door to the small closet were rusted. I set my baggage next to the bed and sat down. The mattress sagged. Years earlier, it had been firm.

Vestiges of the emotions I had felt that first night as a thirteen-year-old returned. Depression and isolation enfolded me.

Then, reminding myself that this was temporary and I would soon be leaving for California, my mood shifted. And I began to bounce back. I couldn't help but chuckle that fate brought me back to this very same spot. I'd never given it much thought, but now realized that attitude is key to how I experience my world. My feelings either rose or fell because of my attitude. Without knowing it, I had reached up and was holding onto the phoenix brooch Mrs. McDougall had given me before she died.

"Oh, Dougie, thank you for being there for me," I whispered, running my fingertips across the phoenix. The bird might have come to life at that moment. I'd been so lucky that dear Mrs. McDougall had taken me under her wing all those years ago. I certainly would not be the person I am today had she not been there for me when I needed a friend. She had been a mother and a grandmother rolled into one.

. . . . .

Just three weeks after Mother and Jeanette had left for California, Mrs. Sullivan notified me at work that my transfer had been approved and I was free to leave. After dinner at the Club, I made train arrangements for that Saturday, splurging with a private compartment. Not for the luxury, but to secure my assets.

I would use Wednesday, Thursday, and Friday to take care of business—visit Bonnie's grave, close my personal bank accounts, transfer my trust account to the bank in California, and buy a trunk to store the "loot," as Grandpa referred to the gold and silver cash. I'd put the jewelry, the stock certificate, and other paperwork that seemed important inside the trunk, as well. I also had a letter stating that the company was going public and that my money, per the trust agreement, would be used to purchase founder's shares. I had nearly thrown the certificate away, thinking at the time that all stocks were worthless, having lost 90% of their value.

On Wednesday, my first day free day from work, Mrs. Black waved me over frantically, saying in an excited yet hushed voice, "Both your mother and the sheriff in Arkansas called. You're to call Sheriff Williams at the courthouse immediately." She handed me Mother's phone number and all three for the sheriff—home, work, courthouse.

Mrs. Dell, the woman who answered at the courthouse, didn't wait for me to finish my introductions, saying hurriedly, "I'll get him for you. Just wait. Don't' hang up."

A few minutes passed before Sheriff Williams was on the phone. In a rush, he told me the last three men on Mother's enemy list, who burned down the Big House and murdered Marie, were on trial not for those "accidents," instead these men were being tried for attempting to burn down our gin with our manager inside. He urged me to get on the next train out of Memphis and come to the courthouse immediately—before the verdict.

"I know this is inconvenient for you, Minnie, but your Mother really wants you here."

I had just enough time to buy a ticket and hop on the next train to Arkansas, moments before the whistle blew. My heart beat fast. I didn't know what to expect once I arrived.

One hour later, I walked into the courthouse, packed with townsfolk, and was ushered down the aisle by the sheriff. All eyes were on us, including those of the jury.

"Minnie, sit here behind the prosecutor," whispered Sheriff Williams. "At that table are the defendants, and the court's defense attorney. Unfortunately, none of your family could be here."

I immediately recognized Daryl Small and felt a deep sense of revulsion, and smoldering hatred toward the man. Two other middle-aged men, shabbily dressed, sat to his left. Before I had time to scrutinize them, the bailiff called out, "All rise for Judge Franklin."

I recognized Judge Boyd Franklin, who was noted as the "Second Hanging Judge" after the well-known "Hanging Judge" of the post Civil War Reconstruction Era in Northern Arkansas. After pounding his gavel and announcing the court was in session, he asked, "Has the jury reached its verdicts?"

The lead juror, Mr. Smith of the General Store, said, at first somewhat hesitantly, "We have, Your Honor. In the case of *State of Arkansas v. Daryl Small*, we find the defendant guilty as charged—guilty of attempted arson and attempted murder."

"Duly noted," said the judge.

Small shook his head defiantly.

Smith went on. "In the case of *State of Arkansas v. Cyrus Beal*, we find the defendant guilty of attempted murder and attempted arson."

There was an audible groan. Jumping up, Beal shouted, "No, no, it ain't my fault! It was this snake hyere!" He pointed to Small, who didn't bother to look at him. "Small put us up to it. You gotta listen! You just—"

"Restrain that man," ordered the judge. The bailiff pushed Beal back into his chair as mumbling surged throughout the courtroom.

I restrained myself from smiling, keeping tight control of my emotions.

"Duly noted," said the judge.

"Lastly, in the case of *State of Arkansas v. Jethro Beal*, we find him guilty of aiding and abetting, having driven the truck and remaining to carry said guilty men away once the deed was done."

"Duly noted."

The judge used his gavel and called out sternly, "Mr. Small, stand up!" He pulled himself up from of his chair. "I hereby sentence you to fifteen years of hard labor for attempted murder and attempt to commit arson. You have the right of parole, in no less than ten years for good behavior."

Small stood there, lifted his fisted hand, unrepentant, and scowled at the judge, then slowly turned his gaze on the jury, his lips twisting into a snaggletooth grin. The bailiff handcuffed the defendant as his family became disorderly. The judge had them removed from the courtroom.

The judge spoke harshly, his voice commanding the attention of everyone in the court—most importantly, the defendant, "Mr. Cyrus Beal, stand up."

Seconds later, the judge's voice boomed out, "I sentence you to ten years of hard labor, with the possibility for parole in no less than seven years for good behavior. I'm being more lenient on you, since it is apparent to me that you were easily influenced by Mr. Small, who was able to unduly sway your limited intelligence."

"Oh, my Gawd! What about my family?" he cried out.

I felt no compassion whatsoever, watching Cyrus whimpering. I imagined, if he were allowed, he would have crawled on his knees and begged the judge for mercy. Should he have come to me it would have taken all my willpower not to slap him.

"You should have thought about that sooner," dismissed the judge.

The bailiff handcuffed Cyrus Beal.

"In your case," The judge started, looking directly at the third defendant. "Stand up, man, or I'll double your sentence." The defendant almost jumped out of his seat. "Mr. Jethro Beal, it was your good fortune to have stayed in the car. However, that doesn't excuse your intent in this nefarious plan. You can thank your lucky stars that no one was hurt. You are hereby sentenced to five years of hard labor, with parole for good behavior in three years."

Jethro fell back into his chair, evidently stunned by his sentence and the long separation from his family for years. The bailiff yanked him out of his chair and handcuffed him, too.

Small started to yell his objection when the Judge stood up and used his gavel, pounding the convicted man into silence. "One more word out of you, and I'll change the sentence to no right of parole! Do I make myself clear?

"Bailiff, you may remand the prisoners to the County Jail until such time as they are transferred to the State Prison."

As the prisoners were ushered from the courtroom, it was so quiet in the room you could have heard a pin drop. When the door closed behind them, the judge said promptly, "Court is adjourned and justice is served." He used his gavel one last time, which seemed especially loud in the silent room, and left.

In the silence, I felt the deep satisfaction of revenge. I couldn't have imagined that the hatred that had consumed my soul these past years could and would be released as I watched the men handcuffed and carted off to prison. The sound of the gavel, also, provided a sense of closure rather like what I imagined the blade of the executioner must have been as it came down on the chopping block long ago. I was secretly glad Mother had done everything to get me here to bare witness to justice.

"Minnie, let's go," said the sheriff. "You come on over to the house for dinner."

That evening I felt relieved and emotionally drained by the courtroom proceedings. I was amazed how one man, a tenant farmer named Jones, got cold feet the day before the crime was to take place, and told the sheriff about the men's plan to burn down the gin.

"Minnie," Sheriff Williams said to me at dinner, "I told him, 'Jones, we got all the facts. Boy, you keep your nose clean. Don't go out of town without telling us, and everything's gonna be all right'."

The sheriff explained two other factors were at work in the severity of the sentences: First, Al, the manager of the gin, had been unexpectedly working inside the building; hence, the charge of attempted murder. Secondly, the farmers and the town's overall economic welfare had been threatened by the attempted arson. The sentences were the maximum allowable.

The sheriff had me call Mother, who reversed the charges. She'd been waiting for the call. Once I told her the verdicts and sentences, she said, "Minnie, I knew I could count on you. Thank you. Just a moment."

My God, Mother said she could count on me! I thought she'd known that when I left nursing college to help support the family. But this, I realized, was different. She knew I was *here*. She wanted me to know that she had "evened the score." This way, the pledge she had made to us was fulfilled.

"I got to purge the last of those scoundrels names," she declared.

If anyone asked me at that moment, I would have sworn I could see Mother scratching off the names, folding up the pad and throwing it into the wastepaper basket. As we were finishing up with our conversation, the sheriff said, "Minnie, honey, let me talk to your mama."

Seconds later, smiling, he nodded appreciatively to me as he took the receiver.

"Nora," he chuckled, "didn't I tell you not to worry— everything was in the bag?"

CHAPTER 56
A TIME TO SAY GOODBYE

I was just pinning my phoenix to my dress, thinking to myself that my life seemed less like chapters to a book than a series of books. A knock on the door interrupted my musings.

"Mrs. Beck, your taxi is here."

"Would you tell the men to come up and help me with my baggage, please?"

"They're here with me now."

I had been sitting on my bed, gazing at the room, my trunk, suitcase and my train case, which had my toiletries, some costume jewelry, and various sundry items. The cash was in my purse.

Yesterday, I had removed the contents of my safe deposit box from the bank as discretely as possible. I came back and loaded up the trunk, which I had bought the previous day, along with a few new dresses, hats, and shoes. I was not going to California to be judged as some poor Southerner, seeking Yankee charity.

"Please, come in. The door's unlocked."

When the two young men entered my room, I said politely, "Please, take my baggage to the taxi, but I'll carry this." I reached over and lifted my train case.

"Yes, ma'am."

I watched as the heftier man went for my suitcase. "No, you'd better take the trunk." He hesitated until I said firmly, "Let the other fella take the suitcase. It's not so heavy."

He nodded and initially grabbed the trunk at first with one hand, grunting and groaning as he started to carry it down the hall, then quickly adjusted his grip to use both handles. Even before he got to the staircase, he was straining.

Suddenly, I had a vision of my trunk being dropped, the "loot" spilling out of the canvas bags and boxes, and all of us scrambling to get everything. I could imagine the chaos that would ensue.

Scurrying up behind him just before he descended the staircase, I said hurriedly, "Just a moment. Please, put the trunk down."

He stopped and let it hit the floor with a thump. I could see his annoyance with me, possibly assuming I wanted something from the trunk. Then he'd have to lift it back up.

"Would the two of you take the trunk down together?" Not to offend him I hastened to say, "I think it's not fair for you to carry that ol' thing by yourself." Turning to the other fellow, I said, smiling, "You grab the other end, and I'll carry the suitcase myself."

"Yes, ma'am."

They took the stairs, one step at a time. Traveling through the lobby was easier, but once outside, they met with more stairs. By the time they got to the taxi, the men were panting and sweating.

I followed closely behind them. The door to one side of the taxi was already open. The suitcase was put on the floor, while the trunk was set on the seat. The taxi driver hurried around and opened the other back door.

"Gentlemen, thank you for your assistance. I'm glad y'all are so strong." They liked the compliment, but they especially liked the tip. "Fifty cents for you, and fifty cents for you. I appreciate your help."

"Thank you, ma'am," they said. The younger man grinned. The hefty one took out his handkerchief, wiped his brow and stared at me. I took notice of the suspicious look he gave me as I entered the taxi.

"The train station, please."

"Yes, ma'am. At your service."

I looked out the window, glad to see the Club disappear. I had been thankful at one time for it—to have a roof over my head, a bed to sleep in, and my meals. Most of all, it was there that I had met Mrs. McDougall. However, that was the past. Mother's words came back to me: "Don't look back."

The driver tried to carry on a conversation, but I was in no mood to talk. I was going over for the upteenth time my list— things to pack (all items checked off) and the train schedule (not checked—not yet).

The drive along the streets was strange. When I looked out the windows at the buildings, street names, the park, and people going about their daily business, I wondered when—if ever— I might come back to this city, to the delta, our land and the town that held so many memories for me.

I reached up and ran my forefinger across the pin, recalling Mrs. McDougall's comment about its meaning: transformation. Touching it comforted me. According to Jeanette, I would not miss this high humidity and muggy weather. The snow and ice, she promised was only in the mountains of Southern California.

Most appealing to me was Jeanette's description of the oranges that were falling off the trees at their house. I could have as many as I wanted, since they were not a luxury out there. I wouldn't have to wait for Christmas for a stocking containing a measly two or three. I could eat them 'til I burst! There in California was the good life: ski resorts in the mountains and swimming pools in the desert, where all the Hollywood people went. Summers were for laying on the sandy beaches and gazing at the beautiful blue Pacific Ocean, where wave after wave rolled in. The way she described it, who wouldn't love it?

I was excited, then not. I would be leaving the South, my cousins, Uncle Bob and his wife, Southern ways and manners for a place with people and customs that were foreign. Maybe they wouldn't like my Southern accent. Maybe they wouldn't like me because I was from the South, since California joined the Union and not the Confederacy. Maybe, maybe . . . .

I was aware that I was feeling less and less optimistic. I had already forgotten my insights about the importance of attitude. As the taxi drew closer and closer to my destination, I felt less and less sure about my decision.

. . . . .

As we pulled to a stop, the driver waved over a couple baggage carriers dressed in white jackets. "Take this lady's trunk and suitcase to the train."

"Yes, sir."

The men looked at him, surprised that he wanted both of them for the job. But who's to argue with the customer, especially since they would each get tipped? Their smiles quickly faded as they struggled to lift the trunk out from the cab and onto a dolly.

"Whoeee, ma'am!"

I picked up my cases. The men protested, "But ma'am, it ain't right for a lady—"

"You handle the trunk. I'll carry these."

Maybe it was the tone of my voice or the change in my expression that moments earlier had been so pleasant, that discouraged them from questioning my instructions. I was in no mood to listen to men, or to try to protect or burnish my image of the helpless Southern woman. Images of gold, silver, and jewelry spilling onto the platform, or in the aisle of the train, or in the compartment itself was the very last thing I wanted. I felt so close to being safely ensconced within the safety and security of the compartment, I wasn't about to lose control of the situation now.

We made our way down the aisle of the car—fortunately, not many people were there—and I heard one carrier say, "Whoa there, Sam," which suggested to me he had not only grown up on a farm, but had driven a mule and plow. The two men stopped before a door. "This be it."

Once inside, I stood there, marveling at my accommodations. Red velvet seemed to cover everything. The seats looked plush and comfortable. There was an overhead rack above two adjoining seats, and two sleepers across from me.

"Now, set the trunk on top of the lower sleeper."

"All right, ma'am."

"Please, put it right there."

"Yes, ma'am."

I put my train case on the adjoining seat.

"Now, put my suitcase next to the trunk."

"Yes, yes, ma'am." The carrier dutifully squeezed it next to the trunk on the seat.

"You'll be takin' this whole compartment, ma'am?"

I nodded and smiled. "I will."

"Yes, ma'am."

"Oh, by the way, are either of you married?"

Startled, not knowing what to say, the men stood there for a moment like wooden statues.

"Cat got your tongues?"

"No, ma'am." The older of the two smiled broadly and said, "Why, I am."

The younger man shook his head. "No ma'am, not yet, anyway. Me and my gal plan to real soon."

"Is that so? How soon?"

"I gotta git her a ring first. Otherwise—otherwise, she says there ain't gonna be no weddin'." He shook his head, looking so woebegone. "She done told me, 'I ain't marrin' no poor man who ain't got 'nough money to provide the *basics'*."

"Is that right?"

"Yes, ma'am, it is."

"Hold out your hand."

I pulled my wedding band off my finger and dropped the ring into the middle of his outstretched palm, feeling the weight of the past lifted from my shoulders.

"Oh, no, ma'am. I can't accept that!"

"Oh, yes, you can! I won't need it where I'm going."

"Thank you, ma'am! Oh, thank you for me and . . . my gal."

I handed them their tips—very generous tips at that.

Both of them smiled broadly, thanking me profusely. As they were leaving my compartment, the oldest baggage carrier turned to me and said, "Ma'am, that sure was one heavy load in that trunk of yours!"

"You know how daddies are."

"Beggin' your pardon, ma'am?"

"Daddies always want their tools."

Nodding his head, he still looked confused and closed the door to my compartment.

I stepped over to my trunk, opened it and found my journal, next to Jeanette's dolls. I pulled my pen from my purse and I laid my head back against the plush velvet covering. I wanted to capture a poem I had thought about these last couple of years:

HOME

It is times like these,
sitting and listening
to the sounds of silence
within myself,
that the mood
seeps into my soul,
envelopes me
in a cocoon
of soft remembrance.

The Big House was built
from the timbers
of each day's living,
furnished with mementos
of a thousand experiences.
Our home may be gone,
but it lives forever
within my beating heart.

I heard the whistle of the train, felt the jolt of the car, and listened to the grinding of the wheels against the rails as it pulled out of the station. I watched the people on the platform, one after the other, slip by faster and faster in front of my window as the train gathered speed. Exhilaration hit me: *I am on my way!*

I realized I actually felt happy. With that realization came a fleeting touch of sadness, knowing how long it has been since I've been happy. "No," I whispered. "There is no room for that." I pushed it aside. In this glorious moment, there was only room for the simple, uncomplicated happiness that filled me.

"My God," I gushed, "if only Grandpa and Marie could see me now on my way to California with the loot!"

A NOTE FROM THE AUTHOR

I want to acknowledge all of my readers who have read this latest book in the *Big House* series. It is particularly gratifying for me to know how many readers have found pleasure, comfort and inspiration in the lives of the characters and their stories. It is with sincere gratitude that I express my appreciation to you.

For those of you who would like to hear the spoken word, the audio book for Book One of this series is now available on Amazon.com, Audible.com, and iTunes.com. I commend greatly actor Carrie Barton of Oakley Entertainment, and her ability to capture and bring to life Minnie and the other characters in this book.

My website may hold an interest for you as well: www.jkeck.com. In it are vintage photographs of items and scenes used in the novels, as well as pictures of the real-life characters whose personalities inspired this historical fiction. You will also find a book trailer and my short reading of part of Chapter 1 from Book One on this site.

My very best wishes and many thanks to you all,

J. Keck

Made in the USA
Lexington, KY
28 June 2018